Flowers Of Freethought
Second Series

By

G. W. Foote

Flowers Of Freethought
Second Series
by G. W. Foote

Copyright © 2024

All Rights reserved.

ISBN: 978-93-61423-65-9

Published by

DOUBLE 9 BOOKS

2/13-B, Ansari Road
Daryaganj, New Delhi – 110002
info@double9books.com
www.double9books.com
Tel. 011-40042856

This book is under public domain

ABOUT THE AUTHOR

G. W. Foote became an extremely good parent inside the past due nineteenth and early 20th centuries, recognised for his role as an author, writer, and freethinker. He changed into a prominent propose for secularism, atheism, and rationalism at some stage in a time whilst such views regularly faced robust opposition and censorship. One of Foote's large works is "The Book of God," in which he significantly examined and wondered the spiritual ideals and sacred texts, specially focusing at the Bible. Published in 1896, this e-book changed into a courageous and arguable enterprise, aiming to assignment winning non-secular orthodoxy and encourage critical questioning. In "The Book of God," Foote subjected the Bible to a rational and skeptical evaluation, highlighting inconsistencies, contradictions, and perceived ethical shortcomings. He argued against the divine authorship and infallibility of non-secular scriptures, challenging the traditional expertise of God and spiritual authority. Foote's writings, including "The Book of God," had been instrumental in advancing the purpose of secularism and selling an extra rational and evidence-based totally approach to faith. They stirred debates and discussions approximately the role of faith in society and the need for a more secular, humanist angle.

only remains to say that the articles in this volume are of the same
character as those in its predecessor. They were written at different
s during the past ten or twelve years. I have not attempted to classify
several instances I have appended the date of first publication, as i
necessary, or at least convenient.

FOOTE

1894.

CONTENTS

PREFACE

A little more than a year ago I put forth the title of *Flowers of Freethought*. The little reception, and I now issue a Second Serie only mean that the volume found purch readers; which is, after all, the one thing real importance. Certainly the volume nor even noticed, in the public journ ordinary reviewers to so much as me I charge the said reviewers with be of silence against such productic often very humbly, despite the serve under editors, who serve tastes, the intelligence, and the thus it is, I conceive, that the a popular style and publish a silence, which, in some

I am aware that m "taste." But it is a cu raised by one of two opinions, and there those who, while s anxious to obtain advice of the on

As I said that can be perhaps pa are about a weapo copied for th inve an gh on this p

It genera interva them. In seemed

G. W

June,

LUSCIOUS PIETY

Lord Tennyson's poem, *Locksley Hall: Sixty Years After*, is severe on what he evidently regards as the pornographic tendency of our age.

> *"Feed the budding rose of boyhood with the drainage of your sewer; Send the drain into the fountain, lest the stream should issue pure. Set the maiden fancies wallowing in the troughs of Zolaism, — Forward, forward, ay and backward, downward too into the abysm."*

There is some truth in this, but far more exaggeration. English novels, however they may trifle and sentimentalise with the passion of love, are as a rule exceedingly "proper." For the most part, in fact, they deliberately ignore all the unconventional aspects of that passion, and you might read a thousand of their productions without suspecting, if you did not already know the fact, that it had any connexion with our physical nature. The men and women, youths and maidens, of Thackeray, Dickens, and George Eliot, to say nothing of minor writers, are true enough to nature in other respects, but in all sexual relations they are mere simulacri. George Meredith is our only novelist who triumphs in this region. As Mr. Lowell has noticed, there is a fine natural atmosphere of sex in his books. Without the obtrusion of physiology, which is out of place in art, his human beings are clearly divided into males and females, thinking, feeling and acting according to their sexual characteristics. Other novelists simply shirk the whole problem of sex, and are satisfied with calling their personages John or Mary as the one safe method of indicating to what gender they belong. This is how the English public is pleased to have it; in this manner it feeds the gross hypocrisy which is its constant bane. Hence the shock of surprise, and even of disgust, felt by the ordinary Englishman when he takes up a novel by a great French master of fiction, who thinks that Art, as well as Science, should deal frankly and courageously with every great problem of life. "Shocking!" cry the English when the veil of mystery is lifted. Yet the purism is only on the lips. We are not a whit more virtuous than those plain-spoken foreigners; for, after all, facts exist, however we blink them, and ignorance and innocence are entirely different things.

The great French masters of fiction do not write merely for boys and girls. They believe that other literature is required besides that which is fit for bread-and-butter misses. Yet they are not therefore vicious. They paint nature as it is, idealising without distorting, leaving the moral to convey itself, as it inevitably will. As James Thomson said, "Do you dread that the Satyr will be preferred to Hyperion, when both stand imaged in clear light before us?"

Zolaism, or rather what Lord Tennyson means by the word—for *Nana* is a great and terrible book with all its vice—is not the chief danger to the morals of English youth. Long before the majority of them learn to read French with ease, there is a book put into the hands of all for indiscriminate reading. It is the Bible. In the pages of that book they find the lowest animal functions called by their vulgar names; frequent references, and sometimes very brutal ones, to the generative organs; and stories of lust, adultery, sodomy and incest, that might raise blushes in a brothel; while in the Song of Solomon they will find the most passionate eroticism, decked out with the most voluptuous imagery. The "Zolaism" of the Bible is far more pernicious than the "Zolaism" of French fiction. The one comes seductively, with an air of piety, and authoritatively, with an air of divinity; while the other shows that selfishness and excess lead to demoralisation and death.

There is in fact, and all history attests it, a close connexion between religion and sensuality. No student of human nature need be surprised at Louis XV. falling on his knees in prayer after debauching a young virgin in the *Parc aux Cerfs*. Nor is there anything abnormal in Count Cenci, in Shelley's play, soliciting God's aid in the pollution of his own daughter. It is said that American camp-meetings often wound up in a saturnalia. The Hallelujah lasses sing with especial fervor "Safe in the arms of Jesus." How many Christian maidens are moved by the promptings of their sexual nature when they adore the figure of their nearly naked Savior on a cross! The very nuns, who take vows of perpetual chastity, become spouses of Christ; and the hysterical fervor with which they frequently worship their divine bridegroom, shows that when Nature is thrust out of the door she comes in at the window.

Catholic books of devotion for the use of women and young people are also full of thinly-veiled sensuality, and there are indications that this abomination is spreading in the "higher" religious circles in Protestant England, where the loathsome confessional is being introduced in other than Catholic churches. Paul Bert, in his *Morale des Jesuites*, gave a choice specimen of this class of literature, or rather such extracts as he dared publish in a volume bearing his honored name. It is a prayer in rhyme extending to eleven pages, and occurs in a book by Father Huguet, designed for "the dear daughters of Holy Mary." As Paul Bert says, "every mother would fling it away with horror if Arthur were substituted for Jesus." *Vive Jesus* is the constant refrain of this pious song. We give a sample or two in French with a literal English translation.

> *Vive Jesus, de qui l'amour Me va consumant unit et jour.*
> *Vive Jesus, vive sa force, Vive son agreable amore. Vive Jesus,*
> *quand il m'enivre D'un douceur qui me fait vivre. Vive Jesus,*
> *lorsque sa bouche D'un baiser amoureux me touche. Vive*
> *Jesus, grand il m'appelle Ma soeur, ma colombe, ma belle.*
> *Vive Jesus, quand sa bonte, Me reduit dans la nudite; Vive*
> *Jesns, quand ses blandices Me comblent de chastes delices.*

"Live Jesus, whose love consumes me night and night.—Live Jesus, live his force, live his agreeable attraction.—Live Jesus, when he intoxicates me with a sweetness that gives me life.—Live Jesus, when his mouth touches me with an amorous kiss.—Live Jesus, when he calls me, my sister, my dove, my lovely one.—Live Jesus, when his good pleasure reduces me to nudity; live Jesus, when his blandishments fill me with chaste delight."— And this erotic stuff is for the use of girls!!

THE JEWISH SABBATH

Dr. Edersheim's *Life of Jesus* contains some interesting appendices on Jewish beliefs and ceremonies. One of these deals with the Sabbath laws of the chosen people, and we propose to cull from it a few curious illustrations of Jewish superstitions.

The Mishnic tractate *Sabbath* stands at the head of twelve tractates on festivals. Another tractate treats of "commixtures," which are intended to make the Sabbath laws more bearable. The Jerusalem Talmud devotes 64 folio columns, and the Babylon Talmud 156 double folio pages, to the serious discussion of the most minute and senseless regulations. It would be difficult to understand how any persons but maniacs or idiots could have concocted such elaborate imbecilities, if we did not remember that the priests of every religion have always bestowed their ability and leisure on matters of no earthly interest to anyone but themselves.

Travelling on the Sabbath was strictly forbidden, except for a distance of two thousand cubits (1,000 yards) from one's residence. Yet if a man deposited food for two meals on the Friday at the boundary of that "journey," the spot became his dwelling-place, and he might do another two thousand cubits, without incurring 'God's wrath. If a Jewish traveller arrived at a place just as the Sabbath commenced, he could only remove from his beasts of burden such objects as it was lawful to handle on the Lord's Day. He might also loosen their gear and let them tumble down of themselves, but stabling them was out of all question.

The Rabbis exercised their ingenuity on what was the smallest weight that constituted "a burden." This was fixed at "a dried fig," but it was a moot point whether the law was violated if half a fig were carried at two different times on the same Sabbath. The standard measure for forbidden food was the size of an olive. If a man swallowed forbidden food of the size of half an olive, and vomited it, and then ate another piece of the same size, he would be guilty because his palate had tasted food to the prohibited degree.

Throwing up an object, and catching it with the same hand was an undoubted sin; but it was a nice question whether he was guilty if he caught it with, the other hand. Rain water might be caught and carried away, but if the rain had run down from a wall the act was sinful. Overtaken by the

Sabbath with fruit in his hand, stretched out from one "place" to another, the orthodox Jew would have to drop it, since shifting his full hand from one locality to another was carrying a burden.

Nothing could be killed on the Sabbath, not even insects. Speaking of the Christian monks, Jortin says that "Some of them, out of mortification, would not catch or kill the vermin which devoured them; in which they far surpassed the Jews, who only spared them upon the Sabbath day." This interesting fact is supported by the authority of a Kabbi, who is quoted in Latin to the effect that cracking a flea and killing a camel are equally guilty. Dr. Edersheim evidently refers to the same authority in a footnote. On the whole this regulation against the killing of vermin must have been very irksome, and if the fleas were aware of it, they and the Jews must have had a lively time on the Sabbath. We cannot ascertain whether the prohibition extended to *scratching*. If it did, curses not loud but deep must have ascended to the throne of the Eternal; and if, as Jesus says, every idle word is written down in the great book of heaven, the recording angel must have had anything but a holiday on the day of rest.

No work was allowed on the Sabbath. Even roasting and baking had to be stopped directly the holy period began, unless a crust was already formed, in which case the cooking might be finished. Nothing was to be sent, even by a heathen, unless it would reach its destination before the Sabbath. Kabbi Gamaliel was careful to send his linen to the wash three days before the Sabbath, so as to avoid anything that might lead to Sabbath labor.

The Sabbath lamp was supposed to have been ordained on Mount Sinai. To extinguish it was a breach of the Sabbath law, but it might be put out from fear of Gentiles, robbers, or evil spirits, or in order that a person dangerously ill might go to sleep. Such concessions were obviously made by the Rabbis, as a means of accommodating their religious laws to the absolute necessities of secular life. They compensated themselves, however, by hinting that twofold guilt was incurred if, in blowing out one candle, its flame lit another.

According to the Mosaic law, there was to be no fire on the Sabbath. Food might be kept warm, however, said the Rabbis, by wrapping it in non-conductors. The sin to be avoided was *increasing* the heat. Eggs might not be cooked, even in sand heated by the sun, nor might hot water be poured on cold. It was unlawful to put a vessel to catch the drops of oil that might fall from the lamp, but one might be put there to catch the sparks. Another concession to secular necessity! A father might also take his child in his arms, even if the child held a stone, although it was carrying things on the Sabbath; but this privilege was not yielded without a great deal of discussion.

Care should be taken that no article of apparel was taken off and carried. Fortunately Palestine is not a land of showers and sudden changes of temperature, or the Rabbis would have had to discuss the umbrella and overcoat question. Women were forbidden to wear necklaces, rings, or pins, on the Sabbath. Nose-rings are mentioned in the regulations, and the fact throws light on the social condition of the times. Women were also forbidden to look in the glass on the Sabbath, lest they should spy a white hair, and perform the sinful labor of pulling it out. Shoes might not be scraped with a knife, except perhaps with the back, but they might be touched up with oil or water. If a sandal tie broke on the Sabbath, the question of what should be done was so serious and profound that the Rabbis were never able to settle it. A plaster might be worn to keep a wound from getting worse, but not to make it better. False teeth were absolutely prohibited, for they might fall out, and replacing them involved labor. Elderly persons with a full artificial set must have cut a sorry figure on the Sabbath, plump-faced Mrs. Isaacs resolving herself periodically into a toothless hag.

Plucking a blade of grass was sinful. Spitting in a handkerchief was allowed by one Rabbi, but the whole tribe were at loggerheads about spitting on the ground. Cutting one's hair or nails was a mortal sin. In case of fire on the Sabbath, the utensils needed on that day might be saved, and as much clothes as was absolutely necessary. This severe regulation was modified by a fiction. A man might put on a dress, save it, go back and put on another, and so on *ad infinitum*. Watering the cattle might be done by the Gentile, like lighting a lamp, the fiction being that he did it for himself and not for the Jew.

Assistance might be given to an animal about to have young, or to a woman in childbirth—which are further concessions to property and humanity. All might be done on the Sabbath, too, needful for circumcision. On the other hand, bones might not be set, nor emetics given, nor any medical or surgical operation performed. Wine, oil, and bread might be borrowed, however, and one's upper garment left in pledge for it. No doubt it was found impossible to keep the Jews absolutely from pawnbroking even on the Sabbath, Another concession was made for the dead. Their bodies might be laid out, washed, and anointed. Priests of every creed are obliged to give way on such points, or life would become intolerable, and their victims would revolt in sheer despair.

Nature knew nothing of the Jewish laws, and hens had the perversity to lay eggs on the Sabbath. Such eggs were unlawful eating; yet if the hen had been kept, not for laying but for fattening, the egg might be eaten as a part of her economy that had accidentally fallen off!

Such were the puerilities of the Sabbath Law among the Jews. The Old Testament is directly responsible for all of them. It laid down the basic principle, and the Rabbis simply developed it, with as much natural logic as a tree grows up from its roots. Our Sabbatarians of to-day are slaves to the ignorance and follies of the semi-barbarous inhabitants of ancient Palestine; men who believed that God had posteriors, and exhibited them; men who kept slaves and harems; men who were notorious for their superstition, their bigotry, and their fanaticism; men who believed that the infinite God rested after six days' work, and ordered all his creatures to regard the day on which he recruited his strength as holy. Surely it is time to fling aside their antiquated rubbish, and arrange our periods of rest and recreation according to the dictates of science and common sense.

The origin of a periodical day of rest from labor is simple and natural. It has everywhere been placed under the sanction of religion, but it arose from secular necessity. In the nomadic state, when men had little to do at ordinary times except watching their flocks and herds, the days passed in monotonous succession. Life was never laborious, and as human energies were not taxed there was no need for a period of recuperation, We may therefore rest assured that no Sabbatarian law was ever given by Moses to the Jews in the wilderness. Such a law first appears in a higher stage of civilisation. When nomadic tribes settle down to agriculture and are welded into nations, chiefly by defensive war against predatory barbarians; above all, when slavery is introduced and masses of men are compelled to build and manufacture; the ruling and propertied classes soon perceive that a day of rest is absolutely requisite. Without it the laborer wears out too rapidly—like the horse, the ox, or any other beast of burden. The day is therefore decreed for economic reasons. It is only placed under the sanction of religion because, in a certain stage of human development, there is no other sanction available. Every change in social organisation has then to be enforced as an edict of the gods. This is carried out by the priests, who have unquestioned authority over the multitude, and who, so long as their own privileges and emoluments are secured, are always ready to guard the interest of the temporal powers.

Such was the origin of the day of rest in Egypt, Assyria, and elsewhere. But it was lost sight of in the course of time, even by the ruling classes themselves; and the theological fiction of a divine ordinance became the universally accepted explanation. This fiction is still current in Christendom. We are gravely asked to believe that men would work themselves to death, and civilised nations commit economical suicide, if they were not taught that a day of rest was commanded by Jehovah amidst the lightnings and thunders of Sinai. In the same way, we are asked to believe that theft and murder would be popular pastimes without the restraints of the supernatural decalogue fabled to have been received by Moses. As a matter of fact, the law against theft arose because men object to be robbed, and the law against murder because they object to be assassinated. Superstition does not invent social laws; it merely throws around them the glamor of a supernatural authority.

Priests have a manifest interest in maintaining this glamor. Accordingly we find that Nonconformists as well as Churchmen claim the day of rest as the Lord's Day—although its very name of Sunday betrays its Pagan origin. It is not merely a day of rest, they tell us; it is also a day of devotion. Labor is to be laid aside in order that the people may worship God. The physical benefit of the institution is not denied; on the contrary, now that Democracy is decisively triumphing, the people are assured that Sunday can only be maintained under a religious sanction. In other words, religion and priests are as indispensable as ever to the welfare of mankind.

This theological fiction should be peremptorily dismissed. Whatever service it once rendered has been counterbalanced by its mischiefs. The rude laborer of former times—the slave or the serf—only wanted rest from toil. He had no conception of anything higher. But circumstances have changed. The laborer of to-day aspires to share in the highest blessings of civilisation. His hours of daily work are shortened. The rest he requires he can obtain in bed. What he needs on Sunday is not *rest*, but *change*; true re-creation of his nature; and this is denied him by the laws that are based upon the very theological fiction which is pretended to be his most faithful friend.

The working classes at present are simply humbugged by the Churches. The day of rest is secure enough without lies or fictions. What the masses want is an opportunity to make use of it. Now this cannot be done if all rest on the same day. A minority must work on Sunday, and take their rest on some other day of the week. And really, when the nonsensical solemnity of Sunday is gone, any other day would be equally eligible.

Parsons work on Sunday; so do their servants, and all who are engaged about their gospel-shops. Why should it be so hard then for a railway servant, a museum attendant, an art-gallery curator, or a librarian to work on Sunday? Let them rest some other day of the week as the parson does. They would be happy if they could have his "off days" even at the price of "Sunday labor."

Churches and chapels do not attract so many people as they did. There is every reason why priestly Protective laws should be broken down. It is a poor alternative to offer a working man—the church or the public-house; and they are now trying to shut the public-house and make it church or nothing. Other people should be consulted as well as mystery-men and their followers. Let us have freedom. Let the dwellers in crowded city streets, who work all day in close factories, be taken at cheap rates to the country or the seaside. Let them see the grand sweep of the sky. Let them feel the spring of the turf under their feet. Let them look out over the sea—the highway between continents—-and take something of its power and poetry into their blood and brain. During the winter, or in summer if they feel inclined, let them visit the institutions of culture, behold the beautiful works of dead artists, study the relics of dead generations, feel the links that bind the past to the present, and imagine the links that will bind the present to the future. Let their pulses be stirred with noble music. Let the Sunday be their great day of freedom, culture, and humanity. As "God's Day" it is wasted. We must rescue it from the priests and make it "Man's Day."

PROFESSOR STOKES ON IMMORTALITY

The orthodox world makes much of Sir G. G. Stokes, baronet, M.P., and President of the Royal Society. It is so grateful to find a scientific man who is naively a Christian. Many of the species are avowed, or, at any rate, strongly suspected unbelievers; while others, who make a profession of Christianity, are careful to explain that they hold it with certain reservations, being Christians in general, but not Christians in particular. Sir G. G. Stokes, however, is as orthodox as any conventicle could desire. Perhaps it was for this reason that he was selected to deliver one of the courses of Gilford Lectures. He would be a sort of set-off against the rationalism of Max Muller and the scepticism of Tylor. What other reason, indeed, could have inspired his selection? He has not the slightest reputation as a theologian or philosopher, and one of the leading reviews, in noticing his Clifford Lectures, expresses a mild but decided wonder at his appearing in such a character.

Let the Gifford Lectures, however, pass—for the present. We propose to deal with an earlier effort of Sir G. G. Stokes. Nearly two years ago he delivered a lecture at the Finsbury Polytechnic on the Immortality of the Soul. It was reported in the *Family Churchman*, and reprinted after revision as a twopenny pamphlet, with the first title of "I." This is the only pointed thing about it. The lecture is about "I," or, as Sir G. G. Stokes, might say, "All my I."

Sir G. G. Stokes begins by promising to confine himself to the question, "What is it that personal identity depends upon and consists in?" But he does not fulfil the promise. After some jejune remarks upon this question he drops into theology and winds up with a little sermon.

"I cannot pretend that I am able to answer that question myself," says Sir G. G. Stokes. Why, then, did he not leave it alone? "But I will endeavor," he says, "to place before you some thoughts bearing in that direction which I have found helpful to myself, and which possibly may be of some help to some of you."

Sir G. G. Stokes does not mention David Hume, but that great thinker pointed out, with his habitual force and clearness, that personal identity depends upon memory. Our scientific lecturer, with the theological twist, says it "involves memory," which implies a certain reservation. Yet he abstains from elucidating the point; and as it is the most important one in the discussion, he must be held guilty of short-sightedness or timidity.

Memory involves thought, says Sir G. G. Stokes. This is true; in fact, it is a truism. And what, he asks, does thought depend on? "To a certain extent" he allows that it "depends upon the condition of the brain." But during the present life, at any rate, it depends *absolutely* on the condition of the brain Look at the head of an idiot, and then at the head of Shakespeare; is not the brain difference the obvious cause of the mental difference? Are there not diseases of the brain that affect thought in a definite manner? Is not thought excited by stimulants, and deadened or even annihilated by narcotics? Is it not entirely suspended in healthy sleep? Will not a man of genius become an imbecile if his brain softens? Will not a philosopher rave like a drunken fishfag if he suffers from brain inflammation? Is not thought most vigorous when the brain is mature? And is it not weakest in the first and second childishness of youth and old age?

The dependence of thought on the brain is so obvious, it is so demonstrable by the logical methods of difference and concomitant variations, that whoever disputes it, or only allows it "to a certain extent," is bound to assign another definite cause. A *definite* cause, we say; not a fanciful or speculative one, which is perfectly hypothetical.

Sir G. G. Stokes does not do this. He tries to make good his reservation by a negative criticism of "the materialistic hypothesis." He takes the case of a man who, while going up a ladder and speaking, was knocked on the head by a falling brickbat. For two days he was unconscious, and "when he came to, he completed the sentence that he had been speaking when he was struck." Now, at first sight, this seems a strong confirmation of "the materialistic hypothesis." A shock to the brain stopped its action and suspended consciousness. Automatic animal functions went on, but there was no perception, thought, or feeling.

When the effects of the shock wore off the brain resumed its action, and began at the very point where it left off. But this last circumstance is seized by Sir G. G. Stokes as "a difficulty." *Some* change must have gone on, he says, during the two days the man lay unconscious; there must have been *some* waste of tissues, *some* change in the brain; yet "there is no trace of this change in the joining together of the thought after the interval of unconsciousness with the thought before."

Our reply is a simple one. In the first place, Sir G. G. Stokes is making much of a single fact, which he has not weighed, in despite of a host of other facts, not in the least questionable, and all pointing in one direction. In the second place, he does not tell us *what* change went on in the man's brain. May it not have been, at least with respect to the cerebrum, quite infinitesimal? In the third place, Sir G. G. Stokes should be aware that all brain changes do not affect consciousness, even in the normal state. Lastly, consciousness depends upon perception; and if all the avenues of sensation were closed, and the alteration of brain tissues were exceedingly slight (as it would be if the brain were not working), it is nothing very extraordinary that the man should resume thought and volition at the point where they ceased.

The second "difficulty" raised, rather than discovered, by Sir G. G. Stokes is this. "I am conscious of a power which I call will," he says, "and when I hold up my hand I can choose whether I shall move it to the right or to the left."

"Now, according to the materialistic hypothesis, everything about me is determined simply by the ponderable molecules which constitute my body acting simply and solely according to the very same laws according to which matter destitute of life might act. Well then, if we follow up this supposition to its full extent, we are obliged to suppose that, whether I move at this particular moment of time—4.25, on the 30th of March—my hand to the right or to the left, was determined by something inevitable, something which could not have been otherwise, and must have come down, in fact, from my ancestors."

Now Sir G. G. Stokes "confesses" that this seems to him to "fly completely in the face of common sense." And so it does, if by "determined" he means that *somebody* settled the whole business, down to the minutest details, a thousand, a million, or a thousand million years ago. But if "determined" simply means that every phenomenon is *caused*, in the philosophical—not the theological or metaphysical—meaning of the word, it does not fly in the face of common sense at all. Little as Sir G. G. Stokes may like it, he *does*— body and brain, thought and feeling, volition and taste—come down from his ancestors. That is the reason why he is an Englishman, a Whig, a bit of a Philistine, an orthodox Christian, and a very indifferent reasoner.

After all, does not this objection come with an ill grace from a Christian Theist? Has Sir G. G. Stokes never read St. Paul? Has he never heard of John Calvin and Martin Luther? Has he never read the Thirty-nine Articles of his own Church? All those authorities teach predestination; which, indeed, logically follows the doctrine of an all-wise and all-powerful God. Yet here is Sir G. G. Stokes, a Church of England man, objecting to the "materialistic hypothesis" on the ground that it makes things "determined."

Professor Stokes next refers to "something about us" which we call "will." This he proceeds to treat as an independent force like magnetism or electricity. What he says about it shows him to be a perfect tyro in psychology. At the end of the section he exclaims, "So much for that theory"—the materialistic hypothesis; and we are tempted to exclaim, "So much for Sir G. G. Stokes."

Next comes the "psychic theory," according to which "man consists of body and soul." Here the Professor shows a lucid interval. He points out that if the soul is really hampered by the body, it is strange that a blow on a man's head should "retard the action of his thoughts." He also remarks that, according to this theory, the "blow has only got to be somewhat harder till the head is smashed altogether, and the man is killed, and then the thoughts are rendered more active than ever." Which, as our old friend Euclid observes, is absurd.

Professor Stokes dismisses the "body and soul" theory as "open to very grave objections." He admits that it is held by "many persons belonging to the religious world," nevertheless he does not think it can be "deduced from Scripture," to which he goes on to appeal.

Now we beg our Christian friends to notice this. Here is the great Sir G. Gr. Stokes they make so much of actually throwing up the sponge. Instead of showing *scientifically* that man has a soul, and thus cheering their drooping spirits, he leaves the platform, mounts the pulpit, and plays the part of a theologian. In fact he can tell them no more than the ordinary parson who sticks his nose between the pages of his Bible.

With regard to the Scripture, it will afford very little comfort to the Christians to know that Professor Stokes does not believe that it teaches the immortality of the soul. He supports this view by citing the authority of the present Bishop of Durham and "another bishop," who regard the doctrine of an immortal soul as no part of a Christian faith. Had Sir G. G. Stokes been better read in the literature of his own Church, he might have adduced a number of other divines, including Bishop Courtenay and Archbishop Whately, who took the same position.

"Well, what do we learn from Scripture?" inquires Professor Stokes. And this is his answer. "In scripture," he says, "man is spoken of as consisting of body, soul, and spirit." And in Sir G. G. Stokes's opinion it is the third article which "lies at the very basis of life." It is *spirit*, "the interaction of which with the material organism produced a living being" in the Garden of Eden.

Here we pause to interject a reflection. Ordinary Christians believe in body and soul; Professor Stokes believes in body, soul, and spirit. That is, he says man is made up of three instead of two. But in step our Theosophic friends, who pile on four more, and tell us that man is sevenfold. Now who is right! According to their own account they are *all* right. But this is impossible. In our opinion they are all *wrong*. Their theories are imaginary. All they *know* anything of is the human body.

But to return to Professor Stokes's excursion in the region of Biblical exegesis. Never have we met with anything more puerile and absurd. He finds "soul" and "spirit" in the English Bible, and he supposes them to be different things. He even builds up a fanciful theory on the fact that the expression "living soul" occurs in the New Testament, but he does not remember the expression "living spirit." Hence he concludes that *spirit* is not "living" but "life-making."

Surely a little knowledge is a dangerous thing, and Professor Stokes is a capital illustration of this truth. We get "soul" and "spirit" in the New Testament, as well as in the Old, simply because both words are used indifferently by the English translators. This is owing to the composite character of the English language. One word comes from the Greek, the other from the Latin, and both mean exactly the same thing. The Hebrew *ruach*, the (Greek *pneuma*), and the Latin *spiritus*, all originally meant *the breath*; and as breathing was the most obvious function of life, persisting even in the deepest sleep, it came to signify *life*, when that general conception was reached; and when the idea of soul or spirit was reached, the same word was used to denote it. All this is shown clearly enough by Tylor, and is corroborated by the more orthodox Max Muller; so that Professor Stokes has fallen into a quagmire, made of the dirt of ignorance and a little water of knowledge, and has made himself a laughing-stock to everyone who possesses a decent acquaintance with the subject.

Whatever it is that Professor Stokes thinks a man has apart from his body, he does not believe it to be immortal. The immortality of the soul and a future life, he says, are "two totally different things." The one he thinks "incorrect," the other he regards as guaranteed by Scripture; in other words, by Paul, who begins his exposition by exclaiming "Thou fool!" and ends it by showing his own folly. The apostle's nonsense about the seed that cannot quicken unless it die, was laughed at by the African chief in Sir Samuel Baker's narrative. The unsophisticated negro said that if the seed did die it would never come to anything. And he was right, and Paul was wrong.

There *is* a resurrection, however, for Paul says so, and his teaching is inspired, though his logic is faulty. Men will rise from the dead *somehow*, and with "a body of some kind." Not the body we have now. Oh dear no! Great men have thought so, but it is an "incredible supposition." Being a chemist, Sir G. G. Stokes sees the ineffable absurdity, the physical and logical impossibility, of this orthodox conception, which was taught by Mr.

Spurgeon without the slightest misgiving, and upheld by the teaching of the Church of England.

But what is it that *will* rise from the dead, and get joined with some sort of inconceivable body? We have shown that Professor Stokes's distinction between "soul" and "spirit" is fanciful. It will not do for him, then, to say it is the "spirit" that will rise, for he denies, or does not believe, the renewed life of the "soul." Here he leaves us totally in the dark. Perhaps what will rise is "a sort of a something" that will get joined to "a sort of a body" and live in "a sort of a somewhere."

"What," asks Professor Stokes, "is man's condition between death and the resurrection?" He admits that the teaching of Scripture on this point is "exceedingly meagre." He inclines to think that "the intermediate state is one of unconsciousness," something like when we faint, and thus, as there will be no perceptions in the interval, though it be millions of years, we shall, "when we breathe our last," be brought "immediately face to face with our final account to receive our final destiny." And if our final destiny depends in any way on how we have used our reasoning powers, Professor Stokes will be consigned to a warm corner in an excessively high-temperatured establishment.

After all, Professor Stokes admits that all he has said, or can say, gives no "evidence" of a future life. What *is* the evidence then? "Well," he says, "the great evidence which we as Christians accept is, that there is One Who has passed already before us from the one state of being to the other." The resurrection of Jesus Christ, he tells us, is "an historical event," and is supported by an enormous amount of most weighty evidence. But he does not give us a single ounce of it. The only argument he has for a future state is advanced on the last page, and he retires at the moment he has an opportunity of proving his case.

Professor Stokes says: "I fear I have occupied your time too long. We fear so too." "These are dark subjects," he adds. True, and he has not illuminated them. There is positively no evidence of a future life. The belief is a conjecture, and we must die to prove or disprove it.

PAUL BERT *

Victor Hugo and Gambetta have their places in the Pantheon of history, and Death is beginning his harvest among the second rank of the founders of the present French Republic, Every one of these men was an earnest Freethinker as well as a staunch Republican. Paul Bert, who has just died at Tonquin at the post of duty, was one of the band of patriots who gathered round Gambetta in his Titanic organisation of the National Defence; a band from which has come most of those who have since been distinguished in the public life of France. After the close of the war, Paul Bert became a member of the National Assembly, in which he has held his seat through all political changes. As a man of science he was eminent and far-shining, being not a mere *doctrinaire* but a practical experimentalist whose researches were of the highest interest and importance. His *Manual of Elementary Science*, which has been recently translated into English, is in use in nearly every French school, and there is no other volume of the kind that can be compared with it for a moment. As a friend and promoter of general education, Paul Bert was without a rival. He strove in season and out of season to raise the standard of instruction, to elevate the status of teachers, and to free them from the galling tyranny of priests. It is not too much to say that Paul Bert was the idol of nine-tenths of the schoolmasters and schoolmistresses in the French rural districts, where the evils he helped to remove had been most rampant.

* *November 21, 1886.*

This distinguished Frenchman is now dead at the comparatively early age of fifty-three. Although his illness was so serious, the French premier telegraphed that it would be impolitic for the Resident General to leave Tonquin suddenly. Thereupon Paul Bert replied, "You are right; it is better to die at my post than for me to quit Tonquin at the present moment." That dispatch was the last he was able to send himself. Subsequent dispatches came, from other hands, and at last the news arrived that Paul Bert was dead. The French premier announced the fact from the Tribune in a broken voice and amid profound silence. "The Chamber loses in him," said M. de Freycinet, "one of its eminent members, science an illustrious representative, France one of her most devoted children." The next day the Chamber, by an overwhelming majority, voted a State funeral and a pension of £400 a year to Mdme. Bert, with reversion to her children. The first vote was strenuously opposed by Monseigneur Freppel, Bishop of Angers, on the ground that the deceased was an inveterate enemy of religion, but the bishop was ignominiously defeated by 379 votes against 45. That is probably a fair test of the relative strength of Freethought and Christianity among educated men in France.

Monseigneur Freppel was right Paul Bert was an inveterate enemy of religion. He was a militant Atheist, who believed that the highest service you can render to mankind is to free them from superstition. No wonder the Church hated him. At a famous banquet he proposed the toast, "The eradication of the two phylloxeras—the phylloxera of the vine and the phylloxera of the Church." His handbook on the Morality of the Jesuits was a frightful exposure of the duplicity and rascality of priestcraft. About twelve months before Grambetta's death, that great statesman took the chair at one of Paul Bert's atheistical lectures. It was a bold thing to do, but Gambetta was a bold man. The great statesman did a bolder thing still when he took office. He scandalised the Christian world by appointing his atheistic friend Paul Bert as Minister of Public Instruction and Public Worship. Surely this was a piece of irony worthy the assiduous student of Rabelais and Voltaire. "Clericalism is the enemy," said Gambetta. Paul Bert accepted the battle-cry, but he did not content himself with shouting. He labored to place education on a basis which would make it a citadel of Freethought. The Tory *Standard* allows that he "laid the bases of military education in the schools and *lycees*" that he "first dispensed the pupils in State educational establishments from the obligation of attending any religious service, or belonging to any class in which religious instruction was given," and that he first organised the higher education of girls.

Paul Bert was a typical Frenchman and an illustrious Atheist. What do the clergy make of this phenomenon? Here is a man, trained by his father to hate priests, brought up from his cradle in an atmosphere of Freethought, and owing nothing to the Church; yet he becomes an eminent scientist, a fervid patriot, an educational reformer, a leading statesman, a tender husband and father, and a warm friend of the best men, of his time; and on his decease the State gives him a public funeral and provides for his widow and children. The man, we repeat, was an open, nay a militant Atheist; and again we ask, What do the clergy make of this phenomenon?

During his lifetime Darwin was the *bete noir* of the clergy. They hated him with a perfect and very natural hatred, for his scientific doctrines were revolutionary, and if he was right they and their Bible were certainly wrong. The Black Army denounced his impious teachings from thousands of pulpits. With some of them he was the Great Beast, with others Antichrist himself. And they were all the madder because he never took the slightest notice of them, but treated them with the silent contempt which a master of the hounds bestows on the village curs who bark at his horse's heels. Yet, strange to say, when Darwin died, instead of being buried in some quiet Kentish cemetery or churchyard, he was actually sepulchred in Westminster Abbey. Having fought the living Darwin tooth and nail, the clergy quietly appropriated the dead Darwin. The living, thinking and working man was a damnable heretic, hated of God and his priests, but his corpse was a very good Christian, and it was buried in a temple of the very faith he had undermined. Darwin, with all his gravity, is said to have loved a joke, and really this was so good a joke that he might almost have grinned at it in his coffin.

By and bye, the great naturalist may figure as an ardent devotee of the creed he rejected. The clergy are hypocritical and base enough—as a body we mean—to claim Darwin himself now they have secured his corpse. Who knows that, in another twenty years, the verger or even the Dean of Westminster Abbey, in showing visitors through the place, may not say before a certain tomb, "Here is the last resting-place of that eminent Christian, Charles Darwin. There was a little misunderstanding between him and the clergy while he lived, but it has all passed away like a mist, and he is now accounted one of the chief pillars of the Church"?

What the clergy have done in the concrete with Darwin they have done in the abstract with his predecessors in the great struggle between light and darkness. What are all the lying stories about Infidel Death-Beds but conversions of corpses? Great heretics, whose scepticism was unshaken in their lifetime by all the parson-power of the age, were easily converted in their tombs. What the clergy said about them was true, or why didn't they get up and contradict? All the world over silence gives consent, and if the dead man did not enter a *caveat*, who could complain if the men of God declared that he finished up in their faith?

Recently the clergy have been converting another corpse, but this time it has been able to protest by proxy, and the swindle has been exposed all along the line. Paul Bert, the great French Freethinker, died at Tonquin. The nation voted him a state funeral, and his body was shipped to France. The voyage was a long one, and it gave the pious an opportunity of leisurely converting the corpse, especially as Paul Bert's family were all on board the steamer. Accordingly a report, which we printed and commented on at the time, appeared in all the papers that the atheistic Resident General had sent for a Catholic bishop on his death-bed and taken the sacrament. Thousands of Christians believed the story at once, the wish being father to the thought. They never stopped to inquire whether the report was true. Why indeed should they? They took the whole of their religion on trust, and of course they could easily dispense with proof in so small a matter as an infidel's conversion. Some of them were quite hilarious. "Ha," they exclaimed, "what do you Freethinkers say now?" And with the childish simplicity of their kind, when they were told that the story was in all probability false, they replied, "Why, isn't it in print?"

Now that the fraud is exposed very few of the journals that printed it will publish the contradiction. We may be sure that the story of Paul Bert's conversion will be devoutly believed by thousands of Christians, and will probably be worked up in pious tracts for the spiritual edification of superstitious sheep. Give a lie a day's start, said Cobbett, and it is half round the world before you can overtake it. Give it a week's start, and if it happens to be a lie that suits the popular taste, you may give up all hope of overtaking it at all. First in the way of exposure was a telegram from the Papal Nuncio at Lisbon on December 29, saying that his name had been improperly used. He was not the author of the telegram that had been fathered on him, and he knew nothing of Paul Bert's conversion. A day or two later the ship conveying the heretic's corpse arrived at the Suez Canal. Madame Bert heard of the preposterous story of her husband's conversion, and she immediately telegraphed that it was absolutely and entirely false. Madame Bert, who is a highly accomplished woman, is a Freethinker herself, and she is too proud of her husband's reputation to lose a moment in contradicting a miserable libel on his courage and sincerity.

Before dropping the pen, we take the opportunity of saying a few words on Madame Adam's article on Paul Bert in the *Contemporary Review*. She is an able woman, but not a philosopher, and she labors under the craze of thinking that she is a great force in European politics. She confesses that she hated Paul Bert, and she betrays that her aversion originated in pique and jealousy. We do not wish to be ungallant, but Gambetta had good reasons for preferring Paul Bert to Juliette Lambert, although the lady is ludicrously wrong in saying that "it was to Paul Bert that Gambetta owed all the formulae of his scientific politics." She forgets that Gambetta's speeches before Paul Bert became his friend are in print. She also ignores the fact that Gambetta was a stedfast Freethinker from his college days, and was never infected with that sentimental religiosity from which she assumes that Paul Bert perverted him. Certainly he was incapable of being moved by the hackneyed platitudes about science and religion that form the prelude of Madame Adam's article, and seem borrowed from one of M. Oaro's lectures. Nor did he need Paul Bert to tell him, after the terrible struggle of 1877, that Clericalism was the enemy. Still less, if that were possible, did he require Paul Bert or any other man to tell him that France imperatively needed education free from priestcraft. Madame Adam is so anxious to deal Paul Bert a stab in the dark that she confuses the most obvious facts. Gambetta and he fought against clericalism, and labored for secular education, because they were both Freethinkers as well as Republicans. In venting her spite, and reciting her own witticisms, she fails to see the force of her own admissions. This is what she writes of a very momentous occasion:

"I saw Gambetta at Saint Cloud the Sunday after the mishap at Obaronne. He had just been taking the chair at the Chateau d'Eau, at an anti-clerical meeting of Paul Bert's.

"He came in a little late to dinner. Some dozen of us were already assembled on a flight of steps at the bottom of the garden when he appeared. He spied me at once [a woman speaks!] across the green lawn and a vase of tall fuchsias, and called out in his sonorous voice:

"'Admirable! superb! extraordinary! Never since Voltaire has such an irrefutable indictment been brought against the clergy! And what a style! What consummate art!'

"'And what bad policy!' said a great banker who was with us, in a low voice, to me [note the me].

"Gambetta went on as he approached us:

"'And such an immense success—beyond anything that could be imagined! Ten thousand enthusiastic cheers!'

"'The ten thousand and first would not have come from me,' I said [said I], as we greeted one another.

"'You yourself,' cried Gambetta, 'you yourself, I tell you, would have been carried away; if not by the ideas, by the genius lavished in propounding them.'"

Yes, and notwithstanding Madame Adam's "religion" and the great banker's "policy," Gambetta and Paul Bert were in the right, and miles above their heads.

Following Madame Adam's lively nonsense, the *Echo* says that Paul Bert tried to set up another Inquisition. "In France," says this organ of Christian Radicalism, "they strive to prevent a parent from giving his child a religious education." They do nothing of the kind. They simply insist that the religious education shall not be given in the national school. Every French parent is free to give religious instruction to his children at home, and there are still thousands of State priests who can supply his deficiencies in that respect. Meanwhile national education progresses in good earnest. The Empire left nearly half the population unable to write their names. Now the Republic educates every boy and girl, and Mr. Matthew Arnold assures us that the French schools are among the best in Europe, while the sale of good books is prodigious. Gambetta and Paul Bert worked, fought, and sacrificed for this, and they cannot be robbed of the glory.

BRADLAUGH'S GHOST

Directly after Charles Bradlaugh's death we expressed a belief that the Christians would concoct stories about him as soon as it was safe to do so. It took some time to concoct and circulate the pious narratives of the deathbeds of Voltaire and Thomas Paine, and a proper interval is necessary in the case of the great Iconoclast. Already, however, the more superstitious and fanatical Christians are shaking their heads and muttering that "Bradlaugh must have said something when he was dying, only they wouldn't allow believers in his sick room to hear it." By and bye the more cunning and unscrupulous will come to the aid of their weaker brethren, and a circumstantial story will be circulated in Sunday-schools and Christian meetings.

We are well aware that his daughter took every precaution. She has the signed testimony of the nurses, that her father never spoke on the subject of religion during his last illness. But this may not avail, for similar precautions are admitted to have been taken in the cases of Voltaire and Paine, and, in despite of this, the Christian traducers have forged the testimony of imaginary interlopers, whose word cannot be disproved, as they never existed outside the creative fancy of these liars for the glory of God.

It is quite a superstition that truth is always a match for falsehood. George Eliot remarked that the human mind takes absurdity as asses chew thistles. We add that it swallows falsehood as a cat laps milk. It was humorously said the other day by Colonel Ingersoll that "The truth is the weakest thing in the world. It always comes into the arena naked, and there it meets a healthy young lie in complete armor, and the result is that the truth gets licked. One good, solid lie will knock out a hundred truths." It has done so with respect to the death of Voltaire and Paine, and it will do so with respect to the death of Charles Bradlaugh.

Meanwhile the Spiritualists are having an innings. Charles Bradlaugh was buried by his friends at Woking, but his ghost is said to have turned up at Birmingham. It appears from a report in the *Medium and Daybreak* that Mr. Charles Gray, of 139 Pershore-road, being "sadly sorrow-stricken by the passing away of a son," was "constrained to remain at home" on the evening of May 31. A seance was arranged "with a few friends," and of course a message was received from the dear departed boy. This was conveyed through Mr. Russell, junior, whose age is not stated. Then Mr. Reedman "was controlled to write by C. Bradlaugh." Mr. Reedman wrote "in a perfectly unconscious state, and on the departure of the influence was much surprised on being told of the nature of the communication."

Mr. Reedman's surprise may have been great, but it scarcely equals our own. One would imagine that if Charles Bradlaugh still lived, and were able to communicate with people in this world, he would speak to his beloved daughter, and to the friends who loved him with a deathless affection. Why should he go all the way to Birmingham instead of doing his first business in London? Why should he turn up at the house of Mr. Gray? Why should he control the obscure Mr. Reedman? This behavior is absolutely foreign to the character of Charles Bradlaugh. It was not one of his weaknesses to beat about the bush. He went straight to his mark, and found a way or made one, Death seems to change a man, if we may believe the Spiritualists; but if it has altered Charles Bradlaugh's character, it has effected a still more startling change in his intellect and expression.

Here is a "correct copy" of Charles Bradlaugh's message to mankind, and most of our readers will regard it as a very Brummagen communication:—

"As I am not to speak (so says the 'Warrior Chief'), I am to say in writing, I have found a life beyond the grave that I did not wish for nor believe in; but it is even so. My voice shall yet declare it. I have to undo all, or nearly all, I have done, but I will not complain. My mind is subdued, but I will be a man. It is a most glorious truth that has now more clearly dawned upon my mind, that there is a grand and noble purpose before all men, worth living for! May this be the dawn of a new and glorious era of the spiritual life of your humble friend Charles Bradlaugh!

"There is a God! There is a Divine principle. There is more in life than we wot of, but vastly more in death! Oh! for a thousand tongues to declare the truths which are now fast dawning upon my bewildered mind! Death, the great leveller, need have no more terrors for us, for it has been conquered by the Great Spirit, in giving us a never-ending life in the glorious spheres of immortal bliss. O my friends! may I be permitted to declare, more fully and fervently, the joys which fill my mind. Language fails, no tongue can describe."

Our own impression is that Professor Huxley was justified in saying that Spiritualism adds a new terror to death. Fancy the awful depth of flaccid imbecility into which Charles Bradlaugh must have fallen, to indulge in "ohs," and gasp out "glorious," "glorious," and talk of his "subdued" and "bewildered" mind, and bid himself be "a man." It was not thus that he spoke in the flesh. His language was manly, firm, and restrained; his attitude was bold and self-reliant. After four months in the "spirit world" he is positively trembling and drivelling! It is enough to make the rugged Iconoclast turn in his grave. Messrs. Gray and Reedman may rely upon it that Charles Bradlaugh is *not* able to enter No. 139 Pershore-road, Birmingham; if he were, he would descend in swift wrath upon his silly traducers, who have put their own inanity into his mouth, making the great, virile Atheist talk like a little, flabby Spiritualist after an orgie of ginger-beer.

Anyone may see at a glance that the style of this message, from beginning to end, is not Charles Brad-laugh's. *Whose* style it is we cannot say. We do not pretend to fathom the arcana of Spiritualism. It may be Mr. Reedmam's, it may be another's. If it be Mr. Reedman's, he must have been guilty of fraud or the victim of deception. Three distinct hypotheses are possible. Either someone else produced or concocted the message while he was in a foolish trance, or he wrote it himself consciously, or he had been thinking of Charles Bradlaugh before falling into the foolish trance and the message was due to unconscious cerebration.

We forbear to analyse this wretched stuff, though we might show its intrinsic absurdity and self-contradiction. One monstrous piece of folly bestrides the rest like a colossus—"Your humble friend Charles Bradlaugh." Shade of Uriah Heep! Charles Bradlaugh the *"humble* friend" of the illustrious Gray and Reedman! Think of it, Lord Halsbury; think of it, Lord Randolph Churchill. The giant who fought you, and beat you, in the law courts and in Parliament; the man whose face was a challenge; the man who had the pride, without the malignity, of Lucifer; this very man crawls into a Birmingham house, uninvited and unexpected, and announces himself as the *"humble* friend" of some pudding-headed people, engaged in a fatuous occupation that makes one blush for one's species.

Surely if Charles Bradlaugh's ghost is knocking about this planet, having a mission to undo the work of his lifetime in the flesh, it should begin the task in London. It was at the Hall of Science that Charles Bradlaugh achieved his greatest triumphs as a public teacher, and it is there that he should first attempt to undo his work, to unteach his teaching, to disabuse the minds of his dupes. Of course we shall be told that he must communicate through "mediums," and that the medium must be "controlled" by Charles Bradlaugh's spirit; but to this we reply that Charles Bradlaugh controlled men easily while he was "in the flesh," and it is inconceivable that he has lost that old power if he still survives.

On the whole, we think the Spiritist trick is worse than the malignity of orthodox Christians. A lie about a man's death-bed ends there, and consigning him to hell for his infidelity is only a pious wish that cannot affect his fate. But getting hold of a man's ghost ("spirit" they call it) after his death; making it turn up at public and private sittings of obscure fools; setting it jabbering all the flatulent nonsense of its manipulators; and using it in this manner until it has to be dismissed for a newer, more fashionable, and more profitable shadow; all this is so hideous and revolting that the ordinary Christian lies about infidels seem almost a compliment in comparison.

This Gray-Reedman story is probably the beginning of a long and wretched business. The Philistines are upon thee, Charles Bradlaugh! They will harness thee in their mill, and make thee grind their grist; and fools that were not worth a moment of thy time while thou livedst will command thee by the hour; and Sludge the Medium will use thy great name to puff his obscene vanity and swell his obscener gains. This is the worst of all thy trials, for thou canst not defend thyself; and, in thy helplessness, fools and pigmies cut capers over thy grave.

CHRIST AND BROTHERHOOD

Clergymen are supposed to be educated; that is, they go to college before taking holy orders, and study what are called "the classics"—the masterpieces of Greek and Roman literature. Theology is not enough to fit them for the pulpit. They must also be steeped in "the humanities," It is felt that they would never find all they require in the Bible. They find a great deal of it in Pagan writings, and as these are unknown to the people, it is safe for the clergy to work the best "heathen" ideas into their interpretation of the Christian Scriptures. There was a time, indeed, when Christian preachers were fond of references to Pagan poets and philosophers. The people were so ignorant, and such implicit believers, that it could be done with security. But now the case is altered. The people are beginning to "smell a rat." It dawns upon them that if so many fine things were said by those old Pagans—not to mention the still more ancient teaching of India and Egypt— Christianity can hardly merit such epithets as "unique" and "wonderful." Accordingly it is becoming the fashion in clerical circles to avoid those old Pagans, or else to damn them all in a sweeping condemnation. Some indeed go to the length of declaring—or at least of insinuating—that all the real truth and goodness there is in the world began with the Christian era. This extreme is affected by the Evangelical school, and is carried to its highest pitch of exaggeration by such shallow and reckless preachers as the Rev. Hugh Price Hughes. Soon after the *Daily Chronicle* correspondence on "Is Christianity Played Out?" this reverend gentleman, and most accomplished "perverter of the truth," screamed from the platform of St. James's Hall that women and children were regarded as slaves and nuisances before the time of Christ; which is either a deliberate falsehood, or a gross misreading both of history and of human nature. Mr. Hughes has since been gathering his energies for a bolder effort in the same direction. He now publishes in the *Methodist Times* his latest piece of recklessness or fatuity. It is a sermon on "The Solidarity of Mankind," and is really an exhibition of the solidity of Mr. Hughes's impudence. It required nothing but "face," as Corbett used to call it, to utter such monstrous nonsense in a sermon; it would need a great deal more courage than Mr. Hughes possesses to utter it on any platform where he could be answered and exposed.

Mr. Hughes believes in our "common humanity," and he traces it from "the grand old gardener" (Tennyson). "We are all descended from Adam," he says, "and related to one another." Now this is not true, even according to the Bible; for when Cain fled into the land of Nod he took a wife there, which clearly implies the existence of other people than the descendants of Adam. But this is not the worst. Fancy a man at this time of day—a burnin' an' a shinin' light to a' this place—gravely standing up and solemnly telling three thousand people, most of whom we suppose have been to school, that the legendary Adam of the book of Genesis was really the father of the whole human race!

This common humanity is claimed by Mr. Hughes as "a purely Christian conception." Yet he foolishly admits that "the Positivists in our own day have strongly insisted on this great crowning truth which we Christians have neglected." Nay, he states that when Kossuth appealed in England on behalf of Hungary, he spoke in the name of the "solidarity" of the human race. And why *solidarity*? Because the word had to be taken from the French. And why from *the French*? "Because the French," Mr. Hughes says, "have risen to a loftier level of human brotherhood than we." Indeed! Then what becomes of your "purely *Christian* conception," when "infidel France" outshines "Christian England"? How is it, too, you have to make the "shameful" confession that "we"—that is, the Christians—took "nineteen centuries to find out the negro was a man and therefore a brother"? You did not find it out, in fact, until the eighteenth century—the century of Voltaire and Thomas Paine—the century in which Freethought had spread so much, even in England, that Bishop Butler in the Advertisement to his *Analogy*, dated May, 1736, could say that "many persons" regarded Christianity as proved to be "fictitious" to "all people of discernment," and thought that "nothing remained but to set it up as a principal subject of mirth and ridicule." How is it your "Christian conceptions" took such a surprising time to be understood? How is it they had to wait for realisation until the advent of an age permeated with the spirit of scepticism and secular humanity?

Mr. Hughes is brave enough—in the absence of a critic—to start with Jesus Christ as the first cosmopolitan. "He came of the Jewish stock," we are told, "and yet he had no trace of the Jew in him." Of course not—in Christian sermons and Christian pictures, preached and painted for non-Jewish, and indeed Jew-hating nations. But there is a very decided "trace of the Jew in him" in the New Testament. To the Canaanite woman he said, "I am not sent but unto the lost sheep of the house of Israel." To the twelve he said, "Go not into the way of the Gentiles, and into any city of the Samaritans enter ye not: But go rather to the lost sheep of the house of Israel." It was Paul who, finding he could not make headway against the apostles who had known Jesus personally, exclaimed, "Lo, we turn to the Gentiles." That exclamation was a turning point. It was the first real step to such universalism as Christianity has attained. No wonder, therefore, that Comte puts Paul instead of Jesus into the Positivist calendar, as the real founder of Christianity.

Even in the case of St. Paul, it is perfectly idle to suppose that his cosmopolitanism extended beyond the Roman empire. A little study and reflection would show Mr. Hughes that the very fact of the Roman empire was the secret of the cosmopolitanism. Moral conceptions follow in the wake of political expansion. The morality of a tribe is tribal; that of a nation is national; and national morality only develops into international morality with the growth of international interests and international communication. Now the Roman empire had broken up the old nationalities, and with them their local religions. The human mind broadened with its political and social horizon. And the result was that a cosmopolitan sentiment in morals, and a universal conception in religion, naturally spread throughout the territory which was dominated by the Roman eagles. Christianity itself was at first a Jewish sect, which developed into a cosmopolitan system precisely because the national independence of the Jews had been broken up, and all the roads of a great empire were open to the missionaries of a new faith.

But let us return to Mr. Hughes's statements. He tells us that the solidarity of mankind was "revealed to the human race through St. Paul" — which is a great slur upon Jesus Christ, and quite inconsistent with what Mr. Hughes affirms of the Nazarene. It is also inconsistent with the very language of St. Paul in that sermon of his to the Athenians; for the great apostle, in enforcing his argument that all men are God's children, actually reminds the Athenians that "certain also of your own poets have said, For we are also his offspring."

Mr. Hughes goes on to say that "our common humanity" is "a perfectly new idea." "Max Muller," he tells us, "says that there was no trace of it until Christ came. It is a purely Christian conception." Professor Max Muller, however, is not infallible. He sometimes panders to Christian prejudices, and this is a case in point. What he says about "humanity" is an etymological quibble. Certainly the Greeks knew nothing about it, simply because they did not speak Latin. But they had an equivalent word in *philanthropia*, which was in use in the time of Plato, four hundred years before the birth of Christ.*

> * *Mr. Hughes talks so much that he must have little time for*
> *reading. Every educated man, however, is supposed to be*
> *acquainted with Bacon's Essays, the thirteenth of which*
> *opens as follows: — "I take goodness in this sense, the*

affecting of the weal of men, which is that the Grecians
called Philanthropia; and the word humanity (as it is used)
is a little too light to express it." Bacon not only knew
the antiquity of Philanthropia, but preferred it to the
later and less weighty term so ignorantly celebrated by Mr.
Hughes.

Max Muller or no Max Muller, we tell Mr. Hughes that he is either reckless or ignorant in declaring that the idea of human brotherhood owes its origin to Christ, Paul, or Christianity. To say nothing of Buddha, whose ethics are wider than the ethics of Christ, and confining ourselves to Greece and Rome, with the teaching of whose thinkers Christianity comes into more direct comparison—it is easy enough to prove that Mr. Hughes is in error, or worse. Four centuries before Christ, when Socrates was asked on one occasion as to his country, he replied, "I am a citizen of the world." Cicero, the great Roman writer, in the century before Christ, uses the very word *caritas*, which St. Paul borrowed in his fine and famous chapter in the first of Corinthians. Cicero, and not St. Paul, was the first to pronounce "charity" as the tie which unites the human race. And after picturing a soul full of virtue, living in charity with its friends, and taking as such all who are allied by nature, Cicero rose to a still loftier level. "Moreover," he said, "let it not consider itself hedged in by the walls of a single town, but acknowledge itself a citizen of the whole world, as though one city." In another treatise he speaks of "fellowship with the human race, charity, friendship, justice."

We defy Mr. Hughes to indicate a single cosmopolitan text in the New Testament as strong, clear, and pointed as these sayings of Socrates and Cicero—the one Greek, the other Roman, and both before Christ. Let him ransack gospels, epistles, acts, and revelations, and produce the text we call for.

From the time of Cicero—that is, from the time of Julius Caesar, and the establishment of the Empire—the sentiment of brotherhood, the idea of a common humanity, spread with certainty and rapidity, and is reflected in the writings of the philosophers. The exclamation of the Roman poet, "As a man, I regard nothing human as alien to me," which was so heartily applauded by the auditory in the theatre, expressed a growing and almost popular sentiment. The works of Seneca abound in fine humanitarian passages, and it must be remembered that if the Christians were tortured by Nero at Rome, it was by the same hand that Seneca's life was cut short. "Wherever there is a man," said this thinker, "there is an opportunity for a deed of kindness." He believed in the natural equality of all men. Slaves were such through political and social causes, and their masters were bidden to refrain from ill-using them, not only because of the cruelty of such conduct, but because of "the natural law common to all men," and because "he is of the same nature as thyself." Seneca denounced the gladiatorial shows as human butcheries. So mild, tolerant, humane, and equitable was his teaching that the Christians of a later age were anxious to appropriate him. Tertullian calls him "Our Seneca," and the facile scribes of the new faith forged a correspondence between him and their own St. Paul. One of Seneca's passages is a clear and beautiful statement of rational altruism. "Nor can anyone live happily," he says, "who has regard to himself alone, and uses everything for his own interests; thou must live for thy neighbor, if thou wouldest live for thyself." Eighteen hundred years afterwards Auguste Comte sublimated this principle into a motto of his Religion of Humanity — *Vivre pour Autrui*, Live for Others. It is also expressed more didactically by Ingersoll — "The way to be happy is to make others so" — making duty and enjoyment go hand in hand.

Pliny, who corresponded with the emperor Trajan, and whose name is familiar to the student of Christian Evidences, exhorted parents to take a deep interest in the education of their children. He largely endowed an institution in his native town of Como, for the assistance of the children of the poor. His humanity was extended to slaves. He treated his own with great kindness, allowing them to dispose of their own earnings, and even to make wills. Of masters who had no regard for their slaves, he said, "I do not know if they are great and wise; but one thing I do know, they are not men." Dion Chrysostom, another Stoic, plainly declared that slavery was an infringement of the natural rights of men, who were all born for liberty; a dictum which cannot be paralleled in any part of the New Testament. It must be admitted, indeed, that Paul, in sending the slave Onesimus back to his master Philemon, did bespeak humane and even brotherly treatment for the runaway; but he bespoke it for him as a Christian, not simply as a man, and uttered no single word in rebuke of the institution of slavery.

Plutarch's humanity was noble and tender. "The proper end of man," he said, "is to love and to be loved." He regarded his slaves as inferior members of his own family. How strong, yet how dignified, is his condemnation of masters who sold their slaves when disabled by old age. He protests that the fountain of goodness and humanity should never dry up in a man. "For myself," he said, "I should never have the heart to sell the ox which had long labored on my ground, and could no longer work on account of old age, still less could I chase a slave from his country, from the place where he has been nourished for so long, and from the way of life to which he has been so long accustomed." Sentiments like these were the natural precursors of the abolition of slavery, as far as it could be abolished by moral considerations.

Epictetus, the great Stoic philosopher, who had himself been a slave, taught the loftiest morality. Pascal admits that he was "one of the philosophers of the world who have best understood the duty of man." He disdained slavery from the point of view of the masters, as he abhorred it from the point of view of the slaves. "As a healthy man," he said, "does not wish to be waited upon by the infirm, or desire that those who live with him should be invalids, the freeman should not allow himself to be waited upon by slaves, or leave those who live with him in servitude." It is idle to pretend, as Professor Schmidt of Strasburg does, that the ideas of Epictetus are "colored with a reflection of Christianity." The philosopher's one reference to the Galileans, by whom he is thought to have meant the Christians, is somewhat contemptuous. Professor Schmidt says he "misunderstood" the Galileans; but George Long, the translator of Epictetus, is probably truer in saying that he "knew little about the Christians, and only knew some examples of their obstinate adherence to the new faith and the fanatical behavior of some of the converts." It should be remembered that Epictetus was almost a contemporary of St. Paul, and the accurate students of early Christianity will be able to estimate how far it was likely, at that time, to have influenced the philosophers of Rome.

Marcus Aurelius was one of the wisest and best of men. Emperor of the civilised world, he lived a life of great simplicity, bearing all the burdens of his high office, and drawing philosophy from the depths of his own contemplation. His *Meditations* were only written for his own eyes; they were a kind of philosophical diary; and they have the charm of perfect sincerity. He was born a.d. 121, he became Emperor a.d. 161, and died a.d. 180, after nineteen years of a government which illustrated Plato's words about the good that would ensue when kings were philosophers and philosophers were kings. Cardinal Barberini, who translated the Emperor's *Meditations* into Italian, in 1675, dedicated the translation to his own soul, to make it "redder than his purple at the sight of the virtues of this Gentile."

Marcus Aurelius combines reason with beautiful sentiment. His emotion is always accompanied by thought. Here, for instance, is a noble passage on the social commonwealth—"For we are made for co-operation, like feet, like hands, like eyelids, like the rows of the upper and lower teeth. To act against one another then is contrary to nature; and it is acting against one another to be vexed and to turn away." In a still loftier passage he says—and let us remember he says it to himself, not to an applauding audience, but quietly, and with absolute truth, and no taint of theatricality—"My nature is rational and social; and my city and country, so far as I am Antoninus, is Rome; but so far as I am a man, it is the world." In his brief, pregnant way, he states the law of human solidarity—"That which is not good for the swarm, neither is it good for the bee." And who could fail to appreciate this sentiment, coming as it did from the ruler of a great empire?—"One thing here is worth a great deal, to pass thy life in truth and justice, with a benevolent disposition even to liars and unjust men."

Here again, it is the fashion in some circles, to pretend that Marcus Aurelius was influenced by the spread of Christian ideas. George Long, however, speaks the language of truth and sobriety in saying, "It is quite certain that Antoninus did not derive any of his Ethical principles from a religion of which he knew nothing." To say as Dr. Schmidt does that "Christian ideas filled the air" is easy enough, but where is the proof? No doubt the Christian writers made great pretensions as to the spread of their religion, but they were notoriously sanguine and inaccurate, and we know what value to attach to such pretensions in the second century when we reflect that even in the fourth century, up to the point of Constantine's conversion, Christianity had only succeeded in drawing into its fold about a twentieth of the inhabitants of the empire. Enough has been said in this article to show that the idea of our common humanity is not "a purely Christian conception," that it arose in the natural course of human development, and that in this, as in other cases, the apologists of Christianity have simply appropriated to their own creed the fruits of the political, social, and moral growth of Western civilisation.

THE SONS OF GOD

"The sons of God saw the daughters of men that they were fair."

—*Genesis vi. 8.*

According to the first book of the Bible, the earth fell into a very wicked condition in the days of the patriarchs. God made everything good, but the Devil turned everything bad; and in the end the Lord put the whole concern into liquidation. It was a case of universal bankruptcy. All that was saved out of the catastrophe was a consignment of eight human beings and an unknown number of elephants, crocodiles, horses, pigs, dogs, cats, and fleas.

Among other enormities of the antediluvian world was the fondness shown by the sons of God for the daughters of men. That fondness has continued ever since. The deluge itself could not wash out the amatory feelings with which the pious males regard those fair creatures who were once supposed to be the Devil's chief agents on earth. Even to this day it is a fact that courtship goes on with remarkable briskness in religious circles. Churches and chapels are places of harmless assignation, and how many matches are made in Sunday-schools, where Alfred and Angelina meet to teach the scripture and flirt. As for the clergy, who are peculiarly the sons of God, they are notorious for their partiality to the sex. They purr about the ladies like black tom-cats. Some of them are adepts in the art of rolling one eye heavenwards and letting the other languish on the fair faces of the daughters of men. It is also noticeable that the Protestant clericals marry early and often, and generally beget a numerous progeny; while the Catholic priest who, being strictly celibate, *never* adds to the population, "mashes" the ladies through the confessional, worming out all their secrets, and making them as pliable as wax in his holy hands. Too often the professional son of God is a chartered libertine, whose amors are carried on under a veil of sanctity. What else, indeed, could be expected when a lot of lusty young fellows, in the prime of life, foreswear marriage, take vows of chastity, and undertake to stem the current of their natures by such feeble dams as prayers and hymns?

Who the original "sons of God" were is a moot point. God only knows, and he has not told us. But Jewish and Christian divines have advanced many theories. According to some the sons of Gods were the offspring of Seth, who was born holy in succession to righteous Abel, while the daughters of men were the offspring of wicked Cain. Among the oriental Christians it is said that the children of Seth tried to regain Paradise by living in great austerity on Mount Hermon, but they soon tired of their laborious days and cheerless nights, and cast sheep's-eyes on the daughters of Cain, who beauty was equal to their father's wickedness. Marriages followed, and the Devil triumphed again.

According to the Cabbalists, two angels, Aza and Azael, complained to God at the creation of man. God answered, "You, O angels, if you were in the lower world, you too would sin." They descended on earth, and directly they saw the ladies they forgot heaven. They married and exchanged the hallelujahs of the celestial chorus for the tender tones of loving women and the sweet prattle of little children. Having sinned, or, to use the vile language of religion, "polluted themselves with women," they became clothed with flesh. On trying to regain Paradise they failed, and were cast back on the mountains, where they continued to beget giants and devils.

"There were giants in the earth in those days" says Scripture. Of course there were. Every barbarous people has similar legends of primitive ages. The translators of our Revised Version are ashamed of these mythical personages as being too suggestive of Jack and the Beanstalk, so they have substituted Anakim for giants. In other words, they have shirked the duty of translators, and left the nonsense veiled under the original word.

The Mohammedans say that not only giants, but also Jins, were born of the sons of God, who married the daughters of men. The Jins soon had the world in their power. They ruled everywhere, and built colossal works, including the pyramids.

Of the giants, the most remarkable was Og. He was taller than the last Yankee story, for at the Deluge he stopped the windows of heaven with his hands, or the water would have risen over his head. The Talmud says that he saved himself by swimming close to the ark in company with the rhinoceros. The water there happened to be cold, while all the rest was boiling hot; and thus Og was saved while all the other giants perished. According to another story, Og climbed on the roof of the ark, and when Noah tried to dislodge him, he swore that he would become the patriarch's slave. Noah at once clinched the bargain, and food was passed through a hole for the giant every day.

When we look into them we find the myths of the Bible wonderfully like the myths of other systems. The Giants are similar to the Titans, and the union of divine males with human females is similar to the amors of Jupiter,

Apollo, Neptune, and Mars with the women of old. In this matter there is nothing new under the sun. Every fresh myth is only the recasting of an ancient fable, born of ignorance and imagination.

Let it finally be noted that this old Genesaic story of the angelic husbands of earthly women gives us a poor idea of the felicity of heaven. In that unknown region, as Jesus Christ informed his disciples, there is neither marrying nor giving in marriage; that is, no males, no females, no courting, no loving, no children, and no homes. Men cease to be men and women cease to be women. Everybody is of the neuter gender.

Or else all the angels are gentlemen, without a lady amongst them. Perhaps the latter view is preferable, as it harmonises with the Bible, in which the angels are always *he's*. In that case heaven would be, to say the least, rather a dull place. No whispering in the moonlight, no clasped hands under the throbbing stars. Not even a kiss under the misletoe. Oh, what must it be to be there! No wonder the sons of God wandered from their cheerless Paradise, visited this lower world, and saw the daughters of men that they were fair.

MELCHIZEDEK

Melchizedek is the most extraordinary person of whom we have any record. Christ was born and Adam was made, but Melchizedek never began to be and will never cease to exist. If the Bible were not such an intensely serious book without a gleam of humor, except of the unconscious Hibernian kind, we might conclude that Melchizedek was *nobody*, for the description admirably suits that character. But the Bible does not play and must not be played with. All its personages are *bona fide* realities, from the Ancient of Days with white woolly hair on the throne of heaven to the prophet Jonah who took three days' lodging in the belly of a whale.

The name Melchizedek means *king* of justice, being derived from *melec*, a king, and *tzedec*, justice. When the gentleman bearing this name is introduced to us in the fourteenth of Genesis, he is king of Salem, which means peace. Salem was a city on the site of Zion.

Originally it was called Jebus, then Zadek, then Salem, and finally Jerusalem. So says Rabbi Joseph Ben-Gorion. But other writers, no doubt just as well informed, differ from him; and while the doctors disagree, simple laymen may well hold their judgment in suspense; or, better still, dismiss Jebus, Zadek, Salem, and Jerusalem, to the limbo of learned trivialities. Counting the spots on a leopard, the quills on a porcupine, or the hairs in a cat's whiskers, is just as amusing and quite as edifying as most of the problems of divines and commentators.

When Abraham returned from a successful campaign, in which he defeated five kings and their armies with three hundred and eighteen raw recruits, Melchizedek came out to meet him with victuals and drink. These two friends joined in the friendly office of *scratching* each other. They were, in fact, a small mutual admiration society. Abraham, although at other times a rank coward, was on this occasion a bold warrior laden with spoil; and Melchizedek besides being King of Salem, was "the priest of the most high God." "Bully for you, Abraham," said Melchizedek. "Bully for you, Melchizedek," said Abraham. As usual, however, the priest got the best of it, for the patriarch paid him tithes, which were a capital return for his compliments. Genesis is a little confused, indeed; and what scripture is not? "And he gave him tithes of all" is not very clear. It reminds one of the West of England yokel, who gave his evidence on a case of homicide in this way:

"He had a stick, and he had a stick; and he hit he, and he hit he. And if he'd only hit he as hard as he hit he, he'd a' killed he, and not he he."

But we must not be too hard on Bibles and yokels. So long as we can get a scintillation of their meaning we must be satisfied. Scripture, we may take it, means that the *he* who paid tithes was Abraham, and the *him* who received them was Melchizedek.

Now the book of Genesis is not an early, but a very late portion of the Jewish scriptures, dating only a few centuries before Christ. And we may depend on it that this little sentence about *tithes*, and perhaps the whole story that leads up to it, was got up by the priests, to give the authority of Abraham's name and the sanction of antiquity to an institution which kept them in luxury at the expense of their neighbors.

Our view of the case is supported by the fact that Melchizedek's name does not appear again in the whole of the Old Testament, except in the hundred and tenth Psalm, where somebody or other (the parsons of course say Christ) is called "a priest for ever after the order of Melchizedek." Paul, or whoever wrote the Epistle to the Hebrews, works up this hint in fine style. It would puzzle a lunatic, or a fortune-teller, or the Archbishop of Canterbury, or God Almighty himself, to say what the Seventh of Hebrews means. We give it up as an insoluble conundrum, and we observe that every commentator with a grain of sense and honesty does the same. But there is one luminous flash in the jumble of metaphysical darkness. Melchizedek is described as "without father, without mother, without descent, having neither beginning of days nor end of life." It will be easy to recognise a gentleman of that description when you meet him. When we *do* meet him we shall readily acknowledge him as our king and priest, and pay him an income tax of two shillings in the pound; but until then we warn all kings and priests off our doorsteps.

Jewish traditions say that Melchizedek was the son of Shem, and set apart for the purpose of watching and burying Adam's carcase when it was unshipped from the Ark. Some, however, maintain that he was of a celestial race; while other (Christian) speculators have held that he was no less than Jesus Christ himself, who put in an early appearance in Abraham's days to keep the Jewish pot boiling. St. Athanasius tells a long-winded story of Melchizedek and Abraham, which shows what stuff the early Christians believed. According to the Talmud, Melchizedek composed the hundred and tenth Psalm himself; and although he is without end of days, his tomb was shown at Jerusalem in the time of Gemelli Oarrere the traveller.

There was an heretical sect called the *Melchizedekiana* in the third century. They held that Jesus Christ was, according to Hebrews, only of the order of Melchizedek, and therefore that Melchizedek himself was the more venerable. This heresy revived in Egypt after its suppression elsewhere, and its adherents claimed that Melchizedek was the Holy Ghost. The last time Melchizedek was heard of he was a London coster-monger's donkey, but whether this was a real incarnation of the original Melchizedek no one is able to decide, unless the Lord should again, as in the case of Balaam's companion, "open the mouth of the ass" and inform the world of the things that belong unto its peace.

S'W'ELP ME GOD

Whoever has seen a Hebrew money-lender in a County Court take up a copy of the Old Testament, present the greasy cover to his greasy lips, and, like honest Moses in the *School for Scandal*, "take his oath on that," must have had a lively impression as to the value of swearing as a religious ceremony. And this impression must have been heightened when he has seen an ingenuous Christian, on the other side of the suit, present a copy of the New Testament to *his* pious lips, and quietly swear to the very opposite of all that the God-fearing Jew had solemnly declared to be the truth, the whole truth, and nothing but the truth. One's appreciation of the oath is still further increased by watching the various litigants and witnesses as they caress the sacred volume: Here a gentleman wears an expression of countenance which seems to imply "I guess they'll get a good deal of truth out of me"; and there anothers face seems to promise as great a regard for truth as is consistent with his understanding with the solicitor who subpoenaed him as an independent witness in the interest of justice and a sound client. Hard swearing is the order of the day. So conflicting is the evidence on simple matters of fact that it is perfectly obvious that the very atmosphere is charged with duplicity. The thing is taken as a matter of course. Judges are used to it, and act accordingly, deciding in most cases by a keen observation of the witnesses and an extensive knowlege of the seamy side of nature. But sometimes the very judges are nonplussed, so brazen are the faces of the gentlemen who "have kissed the book" Very often, no doubt, their honors feel inclined to say, like the American judge in directing his jury, "Well, gentlemen, if you believe what these witnesses swear, you will give a verdict for the plaintiff; and if you believe what the other witnesses swear, you will give a verdict for the defendant; but if, like me, you don't believe what either side swears, I'm hanged if I know what you will do."

The fact is, the oath is absolutely useless if its object is to prevent false witness. Should there be any likelihood of a persecution for perjury, a two-faced Testament-kisser will be on his guard, and be very careful to tell only such lies as cannot be clearly proved against him. He dreads the prospect of daily exercise on the treadmill, he loathes the idea of picking oakum, and his gorge rises at the thought of brown bread and skilly. But so long as that danger is avoided, there are hosts of witnesses, most of them very good Christians, who have been suckled on the Gospel in Sunday Schools, and fed afterwards on the strong meat of the Word in churches and chapels, who will swear fast and loose after calling God to witness to their veracity. They ask the Almighty to deal with them according as they tell the truth, yet for all that they proceed to tell the most unblushing lies. What is the reason of this strange inconsistency? Simply this. Hell is a long way off, and many things may happen before the Day of Judgment. Besides, God is merciful; he is always ready to forgive sins; a man has only to repent in time, that is a few minutes before death, and all his sins will be washed out in the cleansing blood of Christ. Notwithstanding all his lies in earthly courts, the repentant sinner will not lose his right of walking about for ever and ever in the court of heaven, although some poor devil whose liberty or property he swore away may be frizzling for ever and ever in hell.

We are strongly of opinion that if the oath were abolished altogether there would be fewer falsehoods told in our public courts. No doubt the law of perjury has some effect, but it is less than is generally imagined, partly because the law is difficult to apply, and partly because there is a wide disinclination to apply it, owing to a sort of freemasonry in false witness, which is apt to be regarded as an essential part of the game of litigation. Here and there, too, there may be a person of sincere piety, who fears to tell a lie in what he considers the direct presence of God. But for the most part the fear of punishment, in this world or in the next, will not make men veracious. The fact is proved by universal experience; nay, there are judges, as well as philosophers, who openly declare that the oath has a direct tendency to create perjury. Anyone, with a true sense of morality will understand the reason of this. Fear is not a moral motive; and when the threatened punishment is very remote or very uncertain, it has next to no deterrent effect. Cupidity is matched against fear, and the odds of the game being in its favor, it wins. But if a moral motive is appealed to, the case is different. Many a man will tell a lie in the witness-box who would scruple to do so "on his honor"; many a man will lie before God who would scruple to deceive a friend. Let a man feel that he is trusted, let his self-respect be appealed to, and he is more likely to be veracious than he would be if he were threatened with imprisonment in this life and hell-fire in the next.

Why Christians should cling to this relic of barbarity it is difficult to conceive. Their Savior plainly commanded them to "Swear not at all," and the early Church obeyed this injunction until it rose to power under

Constantine. It is also a striking fact that the apostle Peter, when he disobeyed his Master, and took an oath, used it to confirm a palpable lie. When the damsel charged him in court with having been a follower of Jesus, he "Denied it with an oath." "You were one of them," said the damsel. "I wasn't," said Peter. "You *were* with him," she rejoined. Whereupon Peter exclaimed "S'w'elp me God, I never knew him." Surely if self-interest made Peter commit flat perjury in the bodily presence of his Savior, it is idle to assert that the oath in any way promotes veracity.

INFIDEL HOMES *

* *The Influence of Scepticism on Character. Being the sixteenth Fernley Lecture. By the Rev. William L. Watkinson. London: T. Woolmer.*

John Wesley was a man of considerable force of mind and singular strength of character. But he was very unfortunate, to say the least of it, in his relations with women. His marriage was a deplorable misunion, and his latest biographer, who aims at presenting a faithful picture of the founder of Wesleyanism, has to dwell very largely on his domestic miseries. Wesley held patriarchal views on household matters, the proper subordination of the wife being a prime article of his faith. Mrs. Wesley, however, entertained different views. She is therefore described as a frightful shrew, and rated for her inordinate jealousy, although her husband's attentions to other ladies certainly gave her many provocations.

In face of these facts, it might naturally be thought that Wesleyans would say as little as possible about the domestic infelicities of Freethinkers. But Mr. Watkinson is not to be restrained by any such consideration. Although a Wesleyan (as we understand) he challenges comparisons on this point. He has read the biographies and autobiographies of several "leading Freethinkers," and he invites the world to witness how selfish and sensual they were in their domestic relations. He is a pulpit rhetorician, so he goes boldly and recklessly to work. Subtlety and discrimination he abhors as pedantic vices, savoring too much of "culture." His judgments are of the robustious order. Like Jesus Christ, he fancies that all men can be divided into sheep and goats. The good are good, and the bad are bad. And naturally the good are Christians and bad are Freethinkers.

The first half of Mr. Watkinson's book of 162 pages (it must have been a pretty long lecture!) is a preface to the second half, which contains his fling at Goethe, Mill, George Eliot, Harriet Martineau, Carlyle, and other offenders against the Watkinsonian code. We think it advisable, therefore, to follow him through his preface first, and through his "charges" afterwards.

Embedded in a lot of obscure or questionable matter in Mr. Watkinson's exordium is this sentence—"What we believe with our whole heart is of the highest consequence to us." True, but whether it is of the highest consequence to other people depends on what it is. Conviction is a good thing, but it cannot dispense with the criterion of truth. On the other hand, what passes for conviction may often be mere acquiescence. That term, we believe, would accurately describe the creed of ninety-nine out of every hundred, in every part of the world, whose particular faith is merely the result of the geographical accident of their birth. Assuredly we do not agree with Mr. Watkinson that "all reasonable people will acknowledge that the faith of Christian believers is to a considerable extent most real; nay, in tens of thousand of cases it is the most real thing in their life." Mr. Cotter Morison laboriously refutes this position in his fine volume on *The Service of Man*. Mill denied and derided it in a famous passage of his great essay *On Liberty*. Mr. Justice Stephen denies it in the *Nineteenth Century*. Carlyle also, according to Mr. Fronde, said that "religion as it existed in England had ceased to operate all over the conduct of men in their ordinary business, it was a hollow appearance, a word without force in it." These men may not be "reasonable" in Mr. Watkinson's judgment, but with most people their word carries a greater weight than his.

Mr. Watkinson contends—and what will not a preacher contend?—that "the denial of the great truths of the Evangelical faith can exert only a baneful influence on character." We quite agree with him. But evangelicalism, and the great truths of evangelicalism, are very different things. It is dangerous to deny any "great truth," but how many does evangelicalism possess? Mr. Watkinson would say "many." We should say "none." Still less, if that were possible, should we assent to his statement that "morals in all spheres and manifestations must suffer deeply by the prevalence of scepticism." Mr. Morison, asserts and proves that this sceptical age is the most moral the world has seen, and that as we go back into the Ages of Faith, vice and crime grow denser and darker.

If the appeal is to history, of which Mr. Watkinson's references do not betray a profound knowledge, the verdict will be dead against him.

Mr. Justice Stephen thinks morality can look after itself, but he doubts whether "Christian charity" will survive "Christian theology." This furnishes Mr. Watkinson with a sufficient theme for an impressive sermon. But his notion of "Christian charity" and Mr. Justice Stephen's are very different. The hard-headed judge means the sentimentalism and "pathetic exaggerations" of the Sermon on the Mount, which he has since distinctly said would destroy society if they were fully practised. "Morality," says Mr. Watkinson, "would suffer on the mystical side." Perhaps so. It might be no longer possible for a Louis the Fifteenth to ask God's blessing when he went to debauch a young girl in the *Parc aux Cerfs*, or for a grave philosopher like Mr. Tylor to write in his *Anthropology* that "in Europe brigands are notoriously church-goers." Yet morality might gain as much on the practical side as it lost on the mystical, and we fancy mankind would profit by the change.

Now for Mr. Watkinson's history, which he prints in small capitals, probably to show it is the real, unadulterated article. He tell us that "the experiment of a nation living practically a purely secular life has been tried more than once" with disastrous results. He is, however, very careful not to mention these nations, and we defy him to do so. What he does is this. He rushes off to Pompeii, whose inhabitants he thinks were Secularists! He also reminds us in a casual way that "they had crucified Christ a few years before," which again is news. Equally accurate is the statement that Pompeii was an "infamous" city, "full" of drunkenness, cruelty, etc. Probably Mr. Watkinson, like most good Christians who go to Pompeii, visited an establishment, such as we have thousands of in Christendom, devoted to the practical worship of Venus without neglecting Priapus. He has forgotten the immortal letter of Pliny, and the dead Roman sentinel at the post of duty. He acts like a foreigner who should describe London from his experience at a brothel.

Philosophy comes next. Mr. Watkinson puts in a superior way the clap-trap of Christian Evidence lecturers. If man is purely material, and the law of causation is universal, where, he asks, "is the place for virtue, for praise, for blame?" Has Mr. Watkinson never read the answer to these questions? If he has not, he has much to learn; if he has, he should refute them. Merely positing and repositing an old question is a very stale trick in religious controversy. It imposes on some people, but they belong to the "mostly fools."

"Morality is in as much peril as faith," cries Mr. Watkinson. Well, the clergy have been crying that for two centuries, yet our criminal statistics lessen, society improves, and literature grows cleaner. As for the "nasty nude figures" that offend Mr. Watkinson's eyes in the French Salon, we would remind him that God Almighty makes everybody naked, clothes being a human invention. With respect to the Shelley Society "representing the *Cenci* and other monstrous themes," we conclude that Mr. Watkinson does not know what he is talking about. There is incest in the *Cenci*, but it is treated in a high dramatic spirit as a frightful crime, ending in bloodshed and desolation. There is also incest in the Bible, commonplace, vulgar, bestial incest, recorded without a word of disapprobation. Surely when a Christian minister, who says the Bible is God's Word, knowing it contains the beastly story of Lot and his daughters, cries out against Shelley's *Cenci* as "monstrous," he invites inextinguishable Rabelaisian laughter. No other reply is fitting for such a "monstrous" absurdity, and we leave our readers to shake their sides at Mr. Watkinson's expense.

Mr. Watkinson asks whether infidelity has "produced new and higher types of character." Naturally he answers the question in the negative. "The lives of infidel teachers," he exclaims, "are in saddest contrast to their pretentious philosophies and bland assumptions." He then passes in review a picked number of these upstarts, dealing with each of them in a Watkinsonian manner. His rough-and-ready method is this. Carefully leaving out of sight all the good they did, and the high example of honest thought they set to the world, he dilates upon their failings without the least regard to the general moral atmosphere of their age, or the proportion of their defects to the entirety of their natures. Mr. Smith, the greengrocer, whose horizon is limited to his shop and his chapel, may lead a very exemplary life, according to orthodox standards; but his virtues, as well as his vices, are rather of a negative character, and the world at large is not much the better for his having lived in it. On the other hand a man like Mirabeau may be shockingly incontinent, but if in the crisis of a nation's history he places his genius, his eloquence, and his heroic courage at the service of liberty, and helps to mark a new epoch of progress, humanity can afford to pardon his sexual looseness in consideration of his splendid service to the race. Judgment, in short, must be pronounced on the sum-total of a man's life, and not on a selected aspect. Further, the faults that might be overwhelming in the character of Mr. Smith, the Methodist greengrocer, may sink into comparative insignificance in the character of a great man, whose intellect and emotions are on a mightier scale. This truth is admirably expressed in Carlyle's *Essay on Burns*.

"Not the few inches of deflection from the mathematical orbit, which are so easily measured, but the *ratio* of these to the whole diameter, constitutes the real aberration. This orbit may be a planet's, its diameter the breadth of the solar system; or it may be a city hippodrome; nay the circle of a ginhorse, its diameter a score of feet or paces. But the inches of deflection only are measured: and it is assumed that the diameter of the ginhorse, and that of the planet, will yield the same ratio when compared with them! Here lies the root of many a blind, cruel condemnation of Burnses, Swifts, Rousseaus, which one never listens to with approval. Granted, the ship comes into harbor with shrouds and tackle damaged; the pilot is blameworthy; he has not been all-wise and all-powerful: but to know *how* blameworthy, tell us first whether his voyage has been round the Globe, or only to Ramsgate and the Isle of Dogs."

We commend this fine passage to Mr. Watkinson's attention. It may make him a little more modest when he next applies his orthodox tape and callipers to the character of his betters.

Goethe is Mr. Watkinson's first infidel hero, and we are glad to see that he makes this great poet a present to Freethought. Some Christians claim Goethe as really one of themselves, but Mr. Watkinson will have none of him. "The actual life of Goethe," he tells us, "was seriously defective." Perhaps so, and the same might have been said of hundreds of Christian teachers who lived when he did, had they been big enough to have their lives written for posterity. Goethe's fault was a too inflammable heart, and with the license of his age, which was on the whole remarkably pious, he courted more than one pretty woman; or, if the truth must be told, he did not repel the pretty women who threw themselves at him. But there were thousands of orthodox men who acted in the same way. The distinctive fact about Goethe is that he kept a high artistic ideal always before him, and cultivated his poetic gifts with tireless assiduity. His sensual indulgences were never allowed to interfere with his great aim in life, and surely that is something. The result is that the whole world is the richer for his labors, and only the Watkinsons can find any delight in dwelling on the failings he possessed in common with meaner mortals. To say that Goethe should be "an object of horror to the whole self-respecting world" is simply to indulge in the twang of the tabernacle.

Carlyle is the next sinner; but, curiously, the *Rock*, while praising Mr. Watkinson's lecture, says that "Carlyle ought not to be classed with the sceptics." We dissent from the *Rock* however; and we venture to think that Carlyle's greatest fault was a paltering with himself on religious subjects. His intellect rejected more than his tongue disowned. Mr. Watkinson passes a very different criticism. Taking Carlyle as a complete sceptic, he proceeds to libel him by a process which always commends itself to the preachers of the gospel of charity. He picks from Mr. Froude's four volumes a number of tid-bits, setting forth Carlyle's querulousness, arrogance, and domestic storms with Mrs. Carlyle. Behold the man! exclaims Mr. Watkinson. Begging his pardon, it is not the man at all. Carlyle was morbidly sensitive by nature, he suffered horribly from dyspepsia, and intense literary labor, still further deranging his nerves, made him terribly irritable. But he had a fine side to his nature, and even a sunny side. Friends like Professor Tyndall, Professor Norton, Sir James Stephen, and Mrs. Gilchrist, saw Carlyle in a very different light from Mr. Froude's. Besides, Mrs. Carlyle made her own choice. She deliberately married a man of genius, whom she recognised as destined to make a heavy mark on his age. She had her man of genius, and he put his life into his books. And what a life! And what books! The sufficient answer to all the Watkinson tribe is to point to Carlyle's thirty volumes. This is the man. Such work implies a certain martyrdom, and those who stood beside him should not have complained so lustily that they were scorched by the fire. Carlyle did a giant's work, and he had a right to some failings. Freethinkers see them as well as Mr. Watkinson, but they are aware that no man is perfect, and they do not hold up Carlyle, or any other sceptic, as a model for universal imitation.

Mr. Watkinson's remarks on George Eliot are simply brutal. She was a "wanton." She "lived in free-love with George Henry Lewes." She had no excuse for her "license." She was "full of insincerity, cant, and hypocrisy." And so on *ad nauseam*. To call Mr. Watkinson a liar would be to descend to his level. Let us simply look at the facts. George Eliot lived with George Henry Lewes as his wife. She had no vagrant attachments. Her connection with Lewes only terminated with his death. Why then did they not marry? Because Lewes's wife was still living, and the pious English law would not allow a divorce unless all the household secrets were dragged before a gaping public. George Eliot consulted her own heart instead of social conventions. She became a mother to Lewes's children, and a true wife to him, though neither a priest nor a registrar blessed their union. She chose between the law of custom and the higher law, facing the world's frown, and relying on her own strength to bear the consequences of her act. To call such a woman a wanton and a kept mistress is to confess one's self devoid of sense and sensibility. Nor does it show much insight to assert that "infidelity betrayed and wrecked her life," and to speculate how glorious it might have been if she had "found Jesus." It will be time enough to listen to this strain when Mr. Watkinson can show us a more "glorious" female writer in the Christian camp.

William Godwin is the next Freethinker whom Mr. Watkinson calls up for judgment. All the brave efforts of the author of *Political Justice* in behalf of freedom and progress are quietly ignored. Mr. Watkinson comments, in a true vein of Christian charity, on the failings of his old age, censures his theoretical disrespect for the marriage laws, and inconsistently blames him for his inconsistency in marrying Mary Woolstonecraft. Of that remarkable woman he observes that scepticism "destroyed in her all that fine, pure feeling which is the glory of the sex." But the only proof he vouchsafes of this startling statement is a single sentence from one of her letters, which Mr. Watkinson misunderstands, as he misunderstands so many passages in Carlyle's letters, through sheer inability to comprehend the existence of such a thing as humor. He takes every jocular expression as perfectly serious, being one of those uncomfortable persons in whose society, as Charles Lamb said, you must always speak on oath. Mr. Watkinson's readers might almost exclaim with Hamlet, "How absolute the knave is! We must speak by the card, or equivocation will undo us."

The next culprit is Shelley, who, we are told, "deserted his young wife and children in the most shameful and heartless fashion." It does not matter to Mr. Watkinson that Shelley's relations with Harriet are still a perplexing problem, or that when they parted she and the children were well provided for, Nor does he condescend to notice the universal consensus of opinion among those who were in a position to be informed on the subject, that Harriet's suicide, more than two years afterwards, had nothing to do with Shelley's "desertion." Instead of referring to proper authorities, Mr. Watkinson advises his readers to consult "Mr. Jeafferson's painstaking volumes on the *Real Shelley*." Mr. Jeafferson's work is truly painstaking, but it is the work of an advocate who plays the part of counsel for the prosecution. Hunt, Peacock, Hogg, Medwin, Lady Shelley, Rossetti, and Professor Dowden—these are the writers who should be consulted. Shelley was but a boy when Harriet Westbrook proposed to run away with him. Had he acted like the golden youth of his age, and kept her for a while as his mistress, there would have been no scandal. His father, in fact, declared that he would hear nothing of marriage, but he would keep as many illegitimate children as Shelley chose to get. It was the intense chivalry of Shelley's nature that turned a very simple affair into a pathetic tragedy. Mr. Watkinson's brutal methods of criticism are out of place in such a problem. He lacks insight, subtlety, delicacy of feeling, discrimination, charity, and even an ordinary sense of justice.

James Mill is another flagrant sinner. Mr. Watkinson goes to the length of blaming him because "his temper was constitutionally irritable," as though he constructed himself. Here, again, Mr. Watkinson's is a purely debit account. He ignores James Mill's early sacrifices for principle, his strenuous labor for what he considered the truth, and his intense devotion to the education of his children. His temper was undoubtedly austere, but it is more than possible that this characteristic was derived from his forefathers, who had been steeped in the hardest Calvinism.

John Stuart Mill was infatuated with Mrs. Taylor, whom he married when she became a widow. But Mr. Watkinson conceals an important fact. He talks of "selfish pleasure" and "indulgence," but he forgets to tell his readers that Mrs. Taylor was *a confirmed invalid*. It is perfectly obvious, therefore, that Mill was attracted by her mental qualities; and it is easy to believe Mill when he disclaims any other relation than that of affectionate friendship. No one but a Watkinson could be so foolish as to imagine that men seek sensual gratification in the society of invalid ladies.

Harriet Martineau is "one of the unloveliest female portraits ever traced." Mr. Watkinson is the opposite of a ladies' man. Gallantry was never his foible. He hates female Freethinkers with a perfect hatred. He pours out on Harriet Martineau his whole vocabulary of abuse. But it is, after all, difficult to see what he is in such a passion about. Harriet Martineau had no sexual sins, no dubious relations, no skeleton in the domestic cupboard. But, says Mr. Watkinson, she was arrogant and censorious. Oh, Watkinson, Watkinson! have you not one man's share of those qualities yourself? Is there not "a sort of a smack, a smell to" of them in your godly constitution?

We need not follow Mr. Watkinson's nonsense about "the domestic shrine of Schopenhauer," who was a gay and festive bachelor to the day of his death. As for Mr. Watkinson's treatment of Comte, it is pure Christian; in other words, it contains the quintessence of uncharitableness. Comte had a taint of insanity, which at one time necessitated his confinement. That he was troublesome to wife and friends is not surprising, but surely a man grievously afflicted with a cerebral malady is not to be judged by ordinary standards. Comte's genius has left its mark on the nineteenth century; he was true to *that* in adversity and poverty. This is the fact posterity will care to remember when the troubles of his life are buried in oblivion.

Mr. Watkinson turns his attention next to the French Revolution, which he considers "as much a revolt against morals as it was against despotism." If that is his honest opinion, he must be singularly ignorant. The moral tone of the Revolutionists was purity itself compared with the flagrant profligacy of the court, the aristocracy, and the clergy, while Freethinkers were imprisoned, and heretics were broken on the wheel. We have really no time to give Mr. Watkinson lessons in French history, so we leave him to study it at his leisure.

It was natural that Voltaire should come in for his share of slander. All Mr. Watkinson can see in him is that he wrote "an unseemly poem," by which we presume he means *La Pucelle*. But he ought to know that the grosser parts of that poem were added by later hands, as may be seen at a glance in any variorum edition. In any case, to estimate Voltaire's *Pucelle* by the moral standard of a century later is to show an absolute want of judgment. Let it be compared with similar works of *his* age, and it will not appear very heinous. But Voltaire did a great deal besides the composition of that poem. He fought despotism like a hero, he stabbed superstition to the heart, he protected the victims of ecclesiastical and political tyranny at the risk of his own life, he sheltered with exquisite generosity a multitude of orphans and widows, he assisted every genius who was trodden down by the age. These things, and the great mass of his brilliant writings, will live in the memory of mankind. Voltaire was not perfect; he shared some of the failings of his generation. But he fought the battle of freedom and justice for sixty years. Other men indulged in gallantry, other men wrote free verses. But when Calas was murdered by the priests, and his family desolated, it was Voltaire, and Voltaire alone, who faced the tyrants and denounced them in the name of humanity. His superb attitude on that critical occasion inspired the splendid eulogium of Carlyle, who was no friendly witness: "The whole man kindled into one divine blaze of righteous indignation, and resolution to bring help against the world."

ARE ATHEISTS CRUEL? *

* April 26,1891.

There seems to be an ineradicable malignancy in the heart of professional Christianity. St. Paul, indeed in a fine passage of his first epistle to the Corinthians, speaks with glowing eloquence of the "charity" which "thinketh no evil." But the hireling advocates and champions of Christianity have ever treated the apostle's counsel with contempt in their dealings with sceptics and heretics. Public discussion is avoided by these professors of the gospel of love and practisers of the gospel of hatred. They find it "unprofitable." Consequently they neglect argument and resort to personalities. They frequently insinuate, and when it is safe they openly allege, that all who do not share their opinions are bad husbands, bad fathers, bad citizens, and bad men. Thus they cast libellous dust in the eyes of their dupes, and incapacitate them from seeing the real facts of the case for themselves. A notable illustration of this evil principle may be found in a recent speech by the Bishop of Chester. Dr. Jayne presided at a Town Hall meeting of the local branch of the National Society for the Prevention of Cruelty to Children, and took advantage of the occasion to slander a considerable section of his fellow citizens. With a pious arrogance which is peculiar to his boastful faith, he turned what should have been a humanitarian assembly into a receptacle for his discharge of insolent fanaticism. Parentage is a natural fact, and the love of offspring is a well-nigh universal law of animal life. It would seem, therefore, that a Society for preventing cruelty to children by parents of perverted instincts, might live aloof from sectarian squabbles. But the Bishop of Chester is of a different opinion. He is a professional advocate of one form of faith, and his eye is strictly bent on business. He appears to be unable to talk anything but "shop." Even while pressing the claims of poor, neglected, ill-used children on the sympathy and assistance of a generous public, he could not refrain from insulting all those who have no love for his special line of business. And the insult was not only gratuitous; it was groundless, brutal, and malignant; so much so, indeed, that we cherish a hope that the Bishop has overreached himself, and that his repulsive slander will excite a re-action in favor of the objects of his malice.

Dr. Jayne told the meeting that "the persons who were most liable to be guilty of cruelty to their children were those artisans who had taken up Secularist opinions, and who looked upon their children as a nuisance, and were glad to get them out of the way."

Now, on the face of it, the statement is positively grotesque in its absurdity. If Secular principles tend to make parents hate their own children, why should their evil influence be confined to artisans? And if Secular principles do not produce parental hatred in the wealthier classes, why does Dr. Jayne hurl this disgraceful accusation at the poorer class of unbelievers? It cannot be simply because they are poorer, for he was delighted to know that "poverty by no means necessarily meant cruelty." What, then, is the explanation? It seems to us very obvious. Dr. Jayne was bent on libelling sceptics, and, deeming it *safer* to libel the *poorer* ones, he tempered his valor with a convenient amount of discretion. He is not even a brave fanatic. His bigotry is crawling, cowardly, abject, and contemptible.

Dr. Jayne relied upon the authority of Mr. Waugh, who happened to be present at the meeting. This gentleman jumped up in the middle of the Bishop's speech, and said "it was the case, that the class most guilty of cruelty to children were those who took materialistic, atheistic, selfish and wicked views of their own existence." Surely this is a "fine derangement of epitaphs." It suggests that Mr. Waugh is less malignant than foolish. What connection does he discover between Secularism and selfishness? Is it in our principles, in our objects, or in our policy? Does he really imagine that the true character of any body of men and women is likely to be written out by a hostile partisan? Such a person might be a judge of our *public* actions, and we are far from denying his right to criticise them; but when he speaks of our *private* lives, before men of his own faith, and without being under the necessity of adducing a single scrap of evidence, it is plain to the most obtuse intelligence that his utterances are perfectly worthless.

We have as much right as Mr. Waugh to ask the world to accept our view of the private life of Secularists. That is, we have no right at all. Nevertheless we have a right to state our experience and leave the reader to form his own opinion. Having entered the homes of many Secularists, we have been struck with their fondness for children The danger lies, if it lies anywhere, in their tendency to "spoil" them. It is a curious fact—and we commend it to the attention of Dr. Jayne and Mr. Waugh—that the most sceptical country in Europe is the one where children are the best treated, and where there is no need for a Society to save them from the clutches of cruelty. There is positively a child-cultus in the great French cities, and especially in Freethinking Paris. In this Bible-and-beer-loving land the workman, like his social "superior," stands or sits drinking in a public-house with male cronies; but the French workman usually sits at the *cafe* table with his wife, and on Sundays with his children, and takes his drink, whatever it may be, under the restraining eyes of those before whom a man is least ready to debase himself.

One Secular home, at least, is known to us intimately. It is the home of the present writer, who for the moment drops the editorial "we" and speaks in the first person My children are the children of an Atheist, yet if they do not love me as heartily as Dr. Jayne's or Mr. Waugh's children love their father, "there's witchcraft in it." There is no rod, and no punishment in my home. We work with the law of love. Striking a child is to me a loathsome idea. I shrink from it as I would from a physical pollution. Strike a child once, be brutal to it once, and there is gone forever that look of perfect trust in the child's eyes, which is a parent's dearest possession, and which I would not forfeit for all the prizes in the world.

I know Christians who are less kind to their children than I am to mine. They are not my natural inferiors. Humanity forbid that I should play the Pharisee! But they are degraded below their natural level by the ghastly notion of parental "authority" I do not say there are no rights in a family. There *are*; and there are also duties. But all the rights belong to the children, and all the duties belong to the parents.

Personally I am not fond of talking about myself. Still less am I anxious to make a public exhibition of my home. But if the Dr. Jaynes and the Mr. Waughs of the Christian world provoke comparisons, I have no fear of standing with my little ones opposite them with theirs, and letting the world judge between us.

Dropping again into the editorial style, we have a question to ask of the Bishop of Chester, or rather of Mr. Waugh. It is this. Where are the statistics to justify your assertion? Men who are sent to gaol, for whatever reason, have their religions registered. Give us, then, the total number of convictions your Society has obtained, and the precise proportion of Secularists among the offenders. And be careful to give us their names and the date and place of their conviction.

We have a further word to all sorts and conditions of libellous Christians. Where are the evidences of Atheistic cruelty? The humanest of the Roman emperors were those who were least under the sway of religion. Julius Caesar himself, the "foremost man of all this world," who was a professed Atheist, was also the most magnanimous victor that ever wore the purple. Akbar, the Freethinker, was the noblest ruler of India. Frederick the Great was kind and just to his subjects. But, on the other hand, who invented and who applied such instruments of cruelty as racks, wheels, and thumbscrews? Who invented separate tortures for every part of the sensitive frame of man? Who burnt heretics? Who roasted or drowned millions of "witches"? Who built dungeons and filled them? Who brought forth cries of agony from honest men and women that rang to the tingling stars? Who burnt Bruno? Who spat filth over the graves of Paine and Voltaire? The answer is one word—Christians. Yet with all this blood on their hands, and all this crime on their consciences, they turn round and fling the epithet of "cruel" at the perennial victims of their malice.

ARE ATHEISTS WICKED?

One of the most effective arts of priestcraft has been the misrepresentation and slander of heretics. To give the unbeliever a bad name is to prejudice believers against all communication with him. By this means a twofold object is achieved; first, the faithful are protected from the contagion of scepticism; secondly, the notion is propagated that there is something essentially immoral involved in, or attendant upon, unorthodox opinions; and thus the prevalent religious ideas of the age become associated with the very preservation and stability of the moral order of human society.

This piece of trickery cannot, of course, be played upon the students of civilisation, who, as Mill remarked, are aware that many of the most valuable contributions to human improvement have been the work of men who knew, and rejected, the Christian faith. But it easily imposes on the multitude, and it will never be abandoned until it ceases to be profitable.

Sometimes it takes the form of idle stories about the death-beds of Freethinkers, who are represented as deploring their ill-spent life, and bewailing the impossibility of recalling the wicked opinions they have put into circulation. At other times it takes the form of exhibiting their failings, without the slightest reference to their virtues, as the sum and substance of their character. When these methods are not sufficient, recourse is had to insinuation. Particular sceptics are spared perhaps, but Freethinkers are depicted—like the poor in Tennyson's "Northern Farmer"—as bad in the lump. It is broadly hinted that it is a moral defect which prevents them from embracing the popular creed; that they reject what they do not wish to believe; that they hate the restraints of religion, and therefore reject its principles; that their unbelief, in short, is only a cloak for sensual indulgence or an excuse for evading irksome obligations.

We are so accustomed to this monstrous theory of scepticism in religious circles, that it did not astonish us, or give us the least surprise, to read the following paragraph in the *Christian Commonwealth*—

"Free Life, and No Compulsory Virtue, was the title of a placard borne by a pamphlet seller of the public highway a few days ago. What the contents of the pamphlets were we do not know, but the title is a suggestive sign of the times, and a rather more than usually plain statement of what a good deal of modern doubt amounts to. Lord Tennyson was severely taken to task a few years ago for making the Atheist a villain in his 'Promise of May,' but he was about right. Much of the doubt of the day is only an outcome of the desire to discredit and throw off the restraints of religion and moral law in the name of freedom, wrongly used. Free love, free life, free divorce, free Sundays, in the majority of cases, are but synonyms for license. Those who hold the Darwinian doctrine of descent from a kind of ape may yet see it proved by a reversion to the beast, if men succeed in getting all the false and pernicious freedom they want."

Now, in reply to this paragraph, we have first to observe that our contemporary takes Lord Tennyson's name in vain. The villain of the "Promise of May" is certainly an Agnostic, but are not the villains of many other plays Christians? Lord Tennyson does not make the rascal's wickedness the logical result of his principles; indeed, although our contemporary seems ignorant of the fact, he disclaimed any such intention, A press announcement was circulated by his eldest son, on his behalf, that the rascal was meant to be a sentimentalist and ne'er-do-well, who, whatever his opinions, would have come to a bad end. When the *Commonwealth*, therefore, talks of Lord Tennyson as "about right," it shows, in a rather vulgar way, the danger of incomplete information. Were we to copy its manners we might use a swifter phrase.

That Atheists, in the name of freedom, throw off the restraints of moral law, is a statement which we defy the *Commonwealth* to prove, or in the slightest degree to support, and we will even go to the length of suggesting how it might undertake the task.

Turpitude of character must betray itself. Moral corruption can no more be hidden than physical corruption. Wickedness "will out," like murder or smallpox. A man's wife discovers it; his children shun him instead of clinging about his knees; his neighbors and acquaintances eye him with suspicion or dislike; his evil nature pulsates through an ever-widening circle of detection, and in time nis bad passions are written upon his features in the infallible lines of mouth and eyes and face. How easy, then, it should be to pick out these Atheists. The most evil-looking men should belong to that persuasion. But do they? We invite our contemporary to a trial. Let it inquire the religious opinions of a dozen or two, and see if there is an Atheist among them.

Again, a certain amount of evil disposition *must* produce a certain percentage of criminal conduct. Accordingly the gaols should contain a large proportion of Atheists. But *do* they? Statistics prove they do *not*. When the present writer was imprisoned for "blasphemy," and was asked his religion, he answered "None," to the wide-eyed astonishment of the official who put the question. Atheists were scarce in the establishment. Catholics were there, and red tickets were on their cell-doors; Protestants were there, and white tickets marked their apartments; Jews were there, and provision was made for their special observances; but the Atheist was the *rara avis*, the very phoenix of Holloway Gaol.

Let us turn to another method of investigation. During the last ten years four members have been expelled from the House of Commons. One of them was not expelled in the full sense of the word; he was, however, thrust by brute force from the precincts of the House. His name was Charles Bradlaugh, and he was an Atheist. But what was his crime? Simply this: he differed from his fellow members as to his competence to take the parliamentary oath, and the ultimate event proved that he was right and they were wrong. Now what were the crimes of the three other members, who were completely and absolutely expelled? Captain Verney was found guilty of procuration for seduction, Mr. Hastings was found guilty of embezzlement, and Mr. De Cobain was pronounced guilty of evading justice, while charged with unnatural offences. Mr. Jabez Spencer Balfour might also have been expelled, if he had not accepted the Chiltern Hundreds. Now all these *real* delinquents were Christians, and even ostentatious Christians. Compare them with Charles Bradlaugh, the Atheist, and say which side has the greatest cause for shame and humiliation.

Are Atheists conspicuous in the Divorce Court? Is it not Christian reputations that are smirched in that Inquisition? Do Atheists, or any species of unbelievers, appear frequently before the public as promoters of bubble companies, and systematic robbers of orphans and widows? Is it not generally found, in the case of great business collapses, that the responsible persons are Christians? Is it not a fact that their profession of Christianity is usually in proportion to the depth of their rascality?

Not long since the Bishop of Chester, backed up by Mr. Waugh, of the Society for the Prevention of Cruelty to Children, publicly declared that the worst ill-users of little ones were artisan Secularists. He was challenged to give evidence of the assertion, but he preferred to maintain what is called "a dignified silence." Mr. Waugh was challenged to produce proofs from the Society's archives, and he also declined. It is enough to affirm infamy against Freethinkers; proof is unnecessary; or, rather, it is unobtainable. Singularly, there have been several striking cases of brutal treatment of children since Mr. Waugh and Bishop Jayne committed themselves to this indefensible assertion, and in no instance was the culprit a Secularist, though some of them, including Mrs. Montagu, were devout Christians.

There are other methods of inquiry into the wickedness of Atheists, but we have indicated enough to set the *Commonwealth* at work, and we invite it to begin forthwith. And while it is getting ready we beg to observe that theologians have always described "free-dem" as "license," whereas it is nothing of the kind. Freedom is the golden mean between license and slavery. The breaking of arbitrary fetters, forged by ignorance and intolerance, does not mean a fall into loose living. The heretic in religion, while resenting outside control, by his very perception of the vast and far-reaching consequences of human action, is often chained to "the most timid sanctities of life."

With respect to "the Darwinian theory of descent from a kind of ape," we have a word for our contemporary. The annual meeting of the British Association was held at Oxford in 1860. Darwin's *Descent of Man* had recently been published, and the air was full of controversy. Bishop Wilberforce, in the course of a derisive speech, turned to Professor Huxley and asked whether it was on the mother's or father's side that his grandfather had been an ape. Huxley replied that man had no reason to be ashamed of having an ape for a grandfather. "If there is an ancestor," he continued, "whom I should feel shame in recalling it would be a *man*" —one who meddled with scientific questions he did not understand, only to obscure them by aimless rhetoric, and indulgence in "eloquent digressions and appeals to religious prejudice." This rebuke was administered thirty-three years ago, but it is still worth remembering, and perhaps the *Commonwealth* may find in it something applicable to itself.

RAIN DOCTORS

The prolonged drought has already inflicted serious injury on the farmers. They are, as a rule, a loyal class of men, but their loyalty will probably be shaken when they realise that the Lord has spoiled their crops to provide Queen's weather for the Jubilee. An occasional shower might wet the Queen's parasol or ruffle the plumage of the princes and princelings in her train. Occasional showers, however, are just what the farmers want. The Lord was therefore in a fix. Though the Bible says that with him nothing is impossible, he was unable to please both sides; so he favored the one he loved best, gave royalty unlimited sunshine, and played the deuce with the agricultural interest.

Possibly the Lord knows better than we do, but we venture to suggest that a slight exercise of intelligence, though we admit it may have been a strain upon his slumbrous brain, would have surmounted the difficulty. The windows of heaven might have been opened from two till four in the morning. That would have been sufficient for a proper supply of rain, and the whole of the day could have been devoted to "blazing" without injuring anyone. Or, if the early morning rain would have damaged the decorations, the celestial turnkey might have kept us a week without water giving us an extra supply beforehand. On the whole, if we may hazard so profane an observation, the powers above are singularly behind the age. Their affairs are frightfully mixed, and the result is that capital and labor are both in a state of uncertainty. The celestial dynasty will have to improve, or its imperial power will be questioned, and there will be a demand for Home Rule with regard to the weather. It is a perfect nuisance, with respect to a matter which vitally affects us, not to be able to know what a day will bring forth.

Meanwhile we turn to the clergy, and inquire why they do not perform their professional duties in this emergency. There is a form of prayer for such cases in the Prayer-book. Why has it not been used? Do the clergy think the Lord is growing deaf with old age? Have they a secret suspicion that praying for a change of weather is as useful as whistling for the wind? Or has the spirit of this sceptical age invaded the clerical ranks so thoroughly as to make them ashamed of their printed doctrines? When a parish clerk was told by the parson one morning that the prayer for rain would be read, he replied, "Why, sir, what's the use of praying for rain with the wind in that quarter?" We fancy that parish clerk must have a good many sympathisers in the pulpit.

Still the clergy should do what they are paid for, or resign the business. They are our rain doctors, and they should procure us the precious fluid. If they cannot, why should we pay them a heavenly water-rate? The rain doctors of savages are kept to their contract. They are expected to bring rain when it is required, and if they do not, the consequences are unpleasant. They are sometimes disgraced, and occasionally killed. But the rain doctors in civilised countries retain all the advantages of their savage prototypes without any of their risks and dangers. Modern Christians allow the clergy to play on the principle of "heads I win, tails you lose." If the black regiments pray and there is no answer, Christians resign themselves to the will of God. If there *is* an answer, they put it to the credit of the priests, or the priests put it to their own credit, which is much the same thing.

We should be sorry to charge such a holy body of men with duplicity, but is there not "a sort of a smack, a smell to?" They are reluctant to pray for rain, on the alleged ground that Omnipotence should not be interfered with rashly. But the sincerity of this plea is questionable when we reflect that it obviously favors the clergy. Our climate is variable, long spells of particular weather are infrequent, and if when one occurs the clergy hold back till the very last, their supplication for a change cannot long remain unanswered. But perhaps this is only an illustration of the wisdom of the serpent which Jesus recommended to his apostles.

If the clergy are anxious to exhibit their powers they should pray for rain in the desert of Sahara. Missionaries might be sent out to establish praying stations, and in the course of time the desert might bloom as a garden, and the wilderness as a rose. We make the suggestion in all sincerity. We are anxious to be convinced, if conviction is possible. Praying for rain in a watery climate is one thing, praying for rain where none ever falls is another. If the clergy can bring down a fruitful shower on the African sands, we shall cry, "A miracle," and send them a quarter's pew-rent.

Seriously—for we can be serious—we ask the clergy to do their level best. The farmers are swearing wholesale, and by taking the name of the Lord their God in vain they incur the peril of eternal damnation. The fruit crop is injured, and children suffer unusually from the stomach-ache. Worst of all, infidel France is flooding our markets with cherries and other fruits, and we are supporting the accursed sceptical brood because the Lord has not nourished our own growths. Surely then it is time to act. If the parsons lose this fine opportunity they may rely on it that the anti-tithe agitation will develop into alarming proportions. Their livings are at stake, and we ask them to consider the interests of their wives and families. If our generous warning is unheeded the clergy may find the nation carrying out the principle of free trade in religion, and importing some rain doctors from Africa. Many of these magical blackmen would be glad to exchange their present pickings for a vicarage and five hundred a year. If they thought there was a chance of obtaining a bishopric, with a palace and six or ten thousand a year, they would start for England at once. Many of them are of excellent reputation, and would come to us with the best of testimonials. Would it not be well to give them a trial? We should find out who was best at the business. He might be constituted our national rain doctor at a liberal salary, and the rest discharged; for surely the Lord does not require thirty thousand praying to him at once, unless on the principle that he must be surrounded to prevent the prayer from going into one ear and out at the other.

PIOUS PUERILITIES

Faith and credulity are the same thing with different names. When a man has plenty of faith he is ready to believe anything. However fantastic it may be, however childish, however infantile, he accepts it with gaping wonder. His imagination is not necessarily strong, but it is easily excited. Macaulay held that savages have stronger imaginations than civilised men, and that as the reason developes the imagination decays. But, in our opinion, he was mistaken. The imagination does not wither under the growth of reason; on the contrary, it flourishes more strongly. It is, however, disciplined by reason, and guided by knowledge; and it only appears to be weaker because the relation between it and other faculties has changed. The imagination of the savage seems powerful because his other faculties are weak. In the absence of knowledge it cuts the most astonishing capers, just as a bird would if it were suddenly deprived of sight. Now the savage is a mental child, and the ignorant and thoughtless are mental savages. They credit the absurdest stories, and indulge in the most ridiculous speculations. When religion ministers to their weakness, as it always does, they gravely discuss the most astonishing puerilities. Indeed, the history of religious thought—that is, of the infantile vagaries of the human mind—is full of puerilites. There is hardly an absurdity which learned divines have not debated as seriously as scientists discuss the nebular hypothesis or the evolution theory. They have argued how many angels could dance on the point of a needle; whether Adam had a navel; whether ghosts and demons could cohabit with women; whether animals could sin; and what was to be done with a rat that devoured a holy wafer. We believe the decision of the last weighty problem, after long debate, was that the rat, having the body of Christ in its body, was sanctified, and that it had to be eaten by the priest, by which means the second person of the Trinity was saved from desecration.

But of all the pious puerilities on record, probably the worst are ascribed to the rabbis. The faith of those gentlemen was unbounded, and they were so fond of trivialities, that where they found none they manufactured them. The rabbis belonged to the most credulous race of antiquity. "Tell that to the Jews," as we see from Juvenal, was as common as our saying, "Tell that to the marines." The chosen people were infinitely superstitious. They had no head for science, nor have they to this day; but they were past-masters in every magical art, and connoisseurs in amulets and charms. Their rabbis were the hierophants of their fanatical folly. They devoted amazing industry, and sometimes remarkable ingenuity, to its development; frequently glossing the very scriptures of their religion with dexterious imbecilities that raise a sinister admiration in the midst of our laughter. This propensity is most noticeable in connection with Bible stories. When the chroniclers and prophets record a good solemn wonder, which reads as though it ought to be true if it is not, they allege or suggest little additions that give it an air of ostentatious silliness. Hundreds of such instances have come under my eyes in foraging for extra-Biblical matter for my *Bible Heroes*, but I have only room for one or two specimens.

King Nimrod was jealous of young Abraham, as Herod was jealous of young Jesus. He tried various methods to get rid of the boy, but all in vain. At last he resolved to burn Abraham alive. This would have made a striking scene, but the pious puerility of the sequel spoils it all. The king issued a decree, ordering every man in his kingdom to bring wood to heat the kiln. What a laughable picture! Behold every adult subject wending his way to the crematorium with a bundle of sticks on his back—"For Abraham." The The Mussulman tradition (Mohammedans and Jews are much alike, and both their religions are Semitic) informs us that Nimrod himself died in the most extraordinary manner. A paltry little gnat, with a game leg and one eye, flew up his nostril, and lodged in his brain, where it tormented him for five hundred years. During the whole of that period, in which the gnat displayed a longevity that casts Methuselah's into the shade, the agonising king could only obtain repose by being struck on the head; and relays of men were kept at the palace to pound his royal skull with a blacksmith's hammer. The absurdity of the story is transcendent. One is charitably tempted to believe, for the credit of human nature, that it was the work of a subtle, solemn wag, who thought it a safe way of satirising the proverbial thick-headedness of kings.

What reader of the Bible does not remember the pathetic picture of Esau falling on Jacob's neck and weeping, in a paroxysm of brotherly love and forgiveness? But the rabbis daub it over with their pious puerilities. They solemnly inform us that Esau was a trickster, as though Jacob's qualities were catching? and that he tried to bite his brother's neck, but God turned it into marble, and he only broke his teeth. Esau wept for the pain in his grinders. But why did Jacob weep? This looks like a poser, yet later rabbis surmounted the difficulty. Jacob's neck was not turned into marble, but toughened. It was hard enough to-hurt Esau's teeth, and still tender enough to make Jacob suffer, so they cried in concert, though for different reasons.

Satyrs are mentioned in the Bible, although they never existed outside the superstitious imagination. The rabbis undertook to explain the peculiar structure of these fabulous creatures, as well as of fauns, who somewhat resemble them. The theory was started, therefore, that God was overtaken by the Sabbath, while he was creating them, and was obliged to postpone finishing them till the next day. Hence they are misshapen! The rabbis also say that God cut off Adam's tail to make Eve of. The Bible origin of woman is low, but this is lower still. However, if Adam exchanged his tail for a wife he made a very good bargain, despite the apple and the Devil.

Captain Noah, says the Talmud, could not take the rhinoceros into the ark because it was too big. Rabbi Jannai solemnly asserts that he saw a young rhinoceros, only a day old, as big as Mount Tabor. Its neck was three miles long, its head half a mile, and the river Jordan was choked by its excrement. Let us pause at this stretcher, which "stands well for high."

Perhaps the Christian will join us in laughing at such pious puerilities. But he should remember that the Bible is loaded with absurdities that are little inferior. Ravens bring a prophet sandwiches, another prophet besieges a tile, an axe swims on the water, a man slays a thousand men in battle with the jawbone of a donkey, an ass speaks, and a whale swallows and vomits a man. Had these pious puerilities occurred in any other book, they would have been laughed to scorn; but being in the Bible, they must be credited on pain of eternal damnation.

"THUS SAITH THE LORD"

Dogmatism, said Douglas Jerrold, is only puppyism grown to maturity. This sarcastic wit never said a truer thing. We call a young fellow a puppy when he is conceited and impudent, and we call a man dogmatic when he betrays the same qualities in controversy. Yet every Church prides itself on being dogmatic. Rome is dogmatic and Canterbury is dogmatic. Without dogma there is no theology. And what is dogma? An opinion, or a set of opinions, promulgated by somebody for the blind acceptance of somebody else. Arrogance, therefore, is of its very essence. What right has one man to say to another, "This is the truth; I have taken the trouble to decide that point, and all you have to do is to accept what I present you "? And if one man has no such right to impose his belief on another, how can twenty thousand men have such a right to impose their belief on twenty millions? This, however, is precisely what they do without the least shame or compunction. Before we are able to judge for ourselves, the priests thrust certain dogmas upon us, and compel us to embrace them. Authority takes the place of judgment, dogmatism supplants thought. The young mind is rendered slavish, and as it grows up it goes through life cringeing to the instruments of its own abasement.

When a superior mind rises from this subjection and demands reasons for believing, he is knocked down with the Bible. A text is quoted to silence him. But who wrote the text? Moses, Isaiah, Ezekiel, Matthew, John, Peter, or Paul. Well, and who made them lords over us? Have we not as much right to our own thoughts as they had to theirs? When they state an opinion in the pompous language of revelation, are they less fallible than the rest of us? Obviously not. Yet prophets and evangelists have a trick of writing, which still clings to their modern representatives, as though they could not be mistaken. "I am Sir Oracle," they seem to say, "and when I ope my lips let no dog bark." No doubt this self-conceit is very natural, but self-conceited people are not usually taken at their own estimate. Nowadays we laugh at them and try to take the conceit out of them. But what is absurd to-day is treated as venerable because it happened thousands of years ago, and prophets are regarded as inspired who, if they existed now, would be treated with ridicule and contempt.

The style of downright God-Almighty-men is very simple. They need not argue, they have only to assert, and they preface every statement with "Thus saith the Lord." Now suppose such a declaration were made today. A man with no greater reputation for sense than his neighbors stands up and shouts "Thus saith the Lord." Should we not look at him with curiosity and amusement? Would he not strike us as a silly fanatic? Might we not even reflect that he was graduating for a strait-waistcoat? The fellow is simply an ignorant dogmatist. What he believes you must believe. Reasons for his belief he has none, and he cannot conceive that you want any either. Yet it would never do to exclaim, "I am your lord and master," so the grown-up puppy shouts "Thus saith the Lord," in order to assure you that in rejecting him you reject God.

Suppose we heckle this loud-mouthed preacher for a minute. "You tell us, Thus saith the Lord. Did he say so to you, and where and when? And are you quite sure you did not dream the whole business?" Probably he answers, "No, the Lord did not say it to me, but he said it to the blessed prophets and apostles, and I am only repeating their words." "Very well then," a sensible man would reply, "you are in the second-hand business, and I want new goods. You had better send on the original traders—Moses, Isaiah, Paul and Co.—and I'll see what I can do with them." If, however, the preacher says, "Yes, the Lord did say it to me," a sensible man replies, "Well, now, I should have thought the Lord would have told somebody with more reputation and influence. Still, what you assert may be true. I don't deny it, but at the same time your word is no proof. On the whole, I think I'll go my way and let you go yours. The Lord has told you something, and you believe it; when he tells me, I'll believe it too. I suppose the Lord told you because he wanted you to know, and when he wants me to know I suppose he'll give me a call. What you got from him is first-hand, what I get from you is second-hand; and, with all due respect, I fancy your authority is hardly equal to the Almighty's." "Thus saith the Lord" is no argument. It is simply

> *The dark lanthorn of the spirit*
>
> *Which none can see by but those who bear it.*

Nay more, it dispenses with reason, and makes every man's faith depend on somebody else's authority. Discussion becomes impertinence, criticism is high treason. Hence it is but a step from "Thus saith the Lord." Very impolite language, truly, yet it is the logical sequence of dogmatism, Fortunately the time is nearly past for such impudent nonsense. This is an age of debate. And although there are many windy platitudes abroad, and much indulgence in empty mouthing, the very fact of debate being considered necessary to the settlement of all questions makes the public mind less hasty and more cautious. "Thus saith the Lord" men can only succeed at present among the intellectual riff-raff of the populace.

Looking over the past, we see what an immense part dogmatism has played in history. "Thus saith the Lord" cried the Jewish prophets, and they not only terrified their contemporaries, but overawed a hundred generations. "Thus saith the Lord" cried the Christian apostles, and they converted thousands of open-mouthed slaves to a "maleficent superstition." "Thus saith the Lord" cried Mohammed, and the scimitars of Islam flashed from India to Spain. "Thus saith the Lord" cried Joe Smith, and Mormonism springs up in the practical West, with its buried gold tablets of revelation and its retrogressive polygamy. "Thus saith Reason" has been a still small voice, sometimes nearly inaudible, though never quite drowned; but now it is swelling into a mighty volume of sound, overwhelming the din of sects and the anathemas of priests.

BELIEVE OR BE DAMNED

Christian ministers are showing a disposition to fight shy of the second half of the last chapter of Mark, where Jesus is represented as saying to his apostles, "Go ye into all the world, and preach the gospel to every creature. He that believeth and is baptised shall be saved; but he that believeth not shall be damned." Some of them tell us to look at the Revised Version, where we shall see in the margin that this portion of the chapter does not exist in the earliest manuscripts; and they innocently expect that Freethinkers will therefore quietly drop the offensive passage. Oh dear no! Before they have any right to claim such indulgence they must put forth a new edition of the whole Bible, showing us what they desire excised, and what they wish to retain and are ready to defend as the infallible word of God. We should then discuss whether their selection is justifiable, and after that we should discuss whether the amended Bible is any diviner than the original one. But we cannot allow them to keep the Bible as it is, to call it God's Word, to revile people who doubt it, and to persecute people who oppose it; and yet, at the same time, to evade responsibility for every awkward text. This will never do. The clergy cannot have the authority of inspiration in their pulpits and the ease of eclecticism on the platform and in the press.

Besides, although the text in Mark is the most striking piece of impudent bigotry, there are many passages of Holy Writ that display the same spirit. The Jews were expressly ordered to kill heretics in this world, and the victims only escaped eternal damnation because the chosen people knew nothing at that time of future rewards and punishments. A glance at the first few pages of *Crimes of Christianity* will also show that the earliest apostles of Christianity were thoroughly imbued with the spirit of persecution. Paul smote Elymas with blindness for opposing him, and even "the beloved disciple" said "If there come any unto you, and bring not this doctrine, receive him not into your house, neither bid him God speed." Paul tells the Galatians, "If any man preach any other gospel unto you than that ye have received, let him be accursed." These passages plainly imply that the unbeliever is to be shunned like poison, and that the teacher of unbelief is a devil. What difference is there between this and the passage in Mark? As a matter of fact, all the Christian Churches, from the beginning till now, have taught that faith is necessary to salvation; and this historic consensus of opinion justifies the Freethinker in regarding bigotry as of the essence of the Bible.

Now what is belief? It is an automatic act of the mind, over which the will has absolutely no power. The will might, indeed, turn the eyes from regarding evidence in a particular direction, or the entire mind from attending to the subject at all. But given the evidence before you, and your own powers of thought, and your judgment is a logical necessity. You cannot help believing what your intellect certifies as true; you cannot help disbelieving what your intellect certifies as false. If you were threatened with everlasting torment for believing that twice two are four, you could not, by the most tremendous effort of volition, alter your conviction in the slightest degree. You might be induced to *assert* that twice two are five, but whatever your tongue might utter, your belief would remain unchanged.

The effect of threats, therefore, is not to change belief, but to produce hypocrisy. Yet this much must be allowed. The threats may succeed *if they are carried out*. Fear will make multitudes *profess* without *investigating*, and as liars often come to believe their own lies, habitual profession produces a state of mind that has a superficial resemblance to real belief; and, on the other hand, if the threats of future punishment are supplemented by penal laws against heresy, there is a process of artificial selection by which independent minds are eliminated, while the slavish survive. Even when penal laws are relaxed, social ostracism will have a similar, though perhaps a weaker effect. Prizes offered to one form of opinion, and losses inflicted on others, will necessarily make a difference in their relative success. How slowly Christianity advanced during the first three centuries, when it was under a cloud! How swiftly it progressed when Constantine gave it wealth and privileges, and used the temporal sword to repress or extinguish its enemies!

Nothing is truer than that the religious belief of more than ninety-nine hundredths of mankind is determined by the geographical accident of birth. Born in Spain they are Catholics; born in England they are Protestants; born in Turkey they are Mohammedans; born in India they are Brahmanists; born in Ceylon they are Buddhists; born in the shadow of a synagogue they are Jews. Their own minds have not the smallest share in deciding their faith. They take it at secondhand, as they do their language and their fashion of dressing. To call their "faith" belief is absurd. It is simply a prejudice. Belief, in the proper sense of the word, follows evidence and reflection. What evidence has the ordinary Christian, and has he ever reflected on his creed for five minutes in the whole course of his life?

Philosophically speaking, men think as they *can*, and believe as they *must*; and as belief is independent of the will, and cannot be affected by motives, it is not a subject for praise or blame, reward or punishment. Religions, therefore, which promise heaven for belief and hell for unbelief, are utterly unphilosophical. They are self-condemned. Truth invites free study. Falsehood shuns investigation, and denounces that liberty of thought which is fatal to its pretensions.

There is a not too refined, but a very true piece of verse, which was first published more than a generation ago in a pungent Freethought journal, and we venture to quote its conclusion. After relating the chief "flams" of the Bible, it says:

> *And when with this nonsense you're crammed,*
>
> *To make you believe it all true,*
>
> *They say if you don't you'll be damned;*
>
> *But you ought to be damned if you do.*

CHRISTIAN CHARITY

Jesus Christ told his disciples that, in bestowing alms, they were not even to let their left hand know what their right hand did. But this self-sacrificing method has not been generally approved, and comparatively few Christians "do good by stealth and blush to find it fame." They more often "do good for fame and publish it by stealth." Nay more, their "charity" is actually their boast in their controversies with "infidels." Look at our hospitals, they say; look at our orphanages, look at our almshouses, look at our soup-kitchens. It is a wonder they do not boast of their asylums, but perhaps they think it would invite the retort that they not only build them but fill them. Such boasting, however, is utterly absurd from every point of view. Since the world was in any degree civilised it has never lacked some kind of benevolent institutions. It is absolutely certain that hospitals are not of Christian origin; and there is hardly a country in the world, with any pretension to rank above barbarians, in which some species of provision is not made by the rich for the necessities of the poor. Every Mohammedan, for instance, is required by his religion to devote a tenth of his income to charity; whereas the Christian system of tithes is entirely for the profit and aggrandisement of the clergy.

Still more ridiculous, if possible, is the Christian cry, "Where are your Freethought hospitals, almshouses, and orphanages?" Freethought is a poor, struggling cause; its adherents are comparatively few and scattered; it has no endowments to lessen the current cost of its propaganda; and it is unable to exact subscriptions by the orthodox method of boycotting, or to acquire them in return for a good advertisement. Still, the Freethought party does manage to relieve its necessitous members; and the Freethinkers' Benevolent Fund is not only well supported, in excess of all demands, but is probably the *only* Fund which is administered without a single farthing of expense. Besides this, Freethinkers support ordinary local charities, when deserving, just like other people; although frequently, as in the case of almost every hospital, religion is forced on the recipients of such charity, whether they wish it or not, and religious tests are maintained in the administration.

As a rule, however, Freethinkers are not inclined to attach so much importance as Christians to organised almsgiving. At the best it is but a clumsy way of alleviating the worst effects of social disease. The Freethinker attaches more importance to the study of causes. He is like the true health reformer who believes a great deal more in exercise, fresh air, and wholesome diet, than in physic. For this reason Freethinkers are generally students of social and political questions. They are Radicals in the philosophical sense of the word; that is, they recognise that real, lasting improvement can only be achieved by dealing with the causes of poverty and degradation. Many Christians, on the other hand, thoroughly believe that the poor will never cease out of the land; and they seem to regard these unfortunates as whetstones, provided by a beneficent providence, on which the wealthy may sharpen their benevolence.

Christian charity, even in its highest form, is infinitely less merciful than science; a truth which Mr. Cotter Morison enforces in the seventh chapter of his *Service of Man*. Sanitation, medical science, free trade, popular education, co-operation, and such agencies, have done tremendously more than religion to diminish evil and mitigate suffering. On the other hand, it is indisputable that much of our boasted charity is worse than wasted, as it tends to produce the very helplessness and pauperism that furnish it with objects of compassion.

Charity is very good in its way, but what we really want is justice. Let us go in for justice first, and when we have got that we shall see what remains for charity to do. Probably it will be found that unjust laws inflict a hundred times more misery than charity could ever alleviate. If that be the case, the most charitable man, after all, is he who devotes some of his time, thought, and energy to political and social reform. Good health for the next generation is more valuable than medicine for the diseases of the present generation.

Charity, also, in its largest sense, is far wider than almsgiving. It is a questionable charity which gives you a shilling if you are hard-up, and persecutes you if you think for yourself. Most of us do not require soup-tickets, but we do require civil treatment, respect for our independence, and smiling rather than frowning faces. The man who lifts me up from the road when I stumble, deserves my thanks; but I doubt the sincerity of his kindness if, when he learns that I honestly differ from him on the Atonement, he knocks me down again. Assisting people who agree with you, and wilfully injuring those who differ, savors less of charity than of zeal. You may be a very good Christian, but I venture to say you are a very bad man.

When Saladin died he ordered charities to be distributed to the poor, without distinction of Jew, Christian, or Mohammedan. Yet this brilliant ruler had to repel Christian attacks on his dominions, and to witness the most abominable cruelty wrought by the soldiers of the Cross. Where, in the annals of Christendom, shall we find such a noble example of true charity; of charity which overflows the petty barriers of creeds, and loses itself in the great ocean of humanity?

RELIGION AND MONEY

"Every religion is a getting religion; for though I myself get nothing, I am subordinate to those that do. So you may find a lawyer in the Temple that gets little for the present; but he is fitting himself to be in time one of those great ones that do get." —Selden's Table Talk.

"The Divine stands wrapt up in his cloud of mysteries, and the amused Laity must pay Tithes and Veneration to be kept in obscurity, grounding their hope of future knowledge on a competent stock of present ignorance." — George Farquhar.

Religion and priestcraft may not be the same thing in *essence*. That is a point on which we do not intend to dogmatise, and this is not the opportunity to argue it. But *practically* religion and priestcraft *are* the same thing. They are inextricably bound up together,. and they will suffer a common fate. In saying this, however, we must be understood to use the word "religion" in its ordinary sense, as synonymous with *theology*. Religion as non-supernatural, as the idealism of morality, the sovereign bond of collective society, is a matter with which we are not at present concerned.

Priestcraft did not *invent* religion. To believe that it did is the error of an impulsive and uninformed scepticism. But priestcraft developed it, systematised it, enforced it, and perpetuated it. This could not be effected, however, except in alliance with the temporal power; and accordingly, in every country—savage, barbaric, or civilised—the priests and the privileged classes are found in harmony. They have occasional differences, but these are ultimately adjusted. Sometimes the priesthood overrules the temporal power, but more frequently the former gives way to the latter; indeed, it is instructive to watch how the course of religion has been so largely determined by political influences. The development of Judaism was almost entirely controlled by the political vicissitudes of the Hebrews. The political power really decided the great controversy between Arianism and Athanasianism. Politics again, twelve hundred years later, settled the bounds of the Reformation, not only for the moment, but for subsequent centuries. Where the prince's sword was thrown into the scale, it determined the balance. England, for instance, was non-papal Catholic under Henry VIII., Protestant under Edward VI., papal-Catholic under Mary, and Protestant again under

Elizabeth; although every one of these changes, according to the clergy, was dictated by the Holy Ghost.

Priests and the privileged classes *must* settle their differences in some way, otherwise the people would become too knowing, and too independent. The co-operation of impostor and robber is necessary to the bamboozlement and exploitation of the masses. This co-operation, indeed, is the great secret of the permanence of religion; and its policy is twofold—education and the power of money.

The value of *education* may be inferred from the frantic efforts of the clergy to build and maintain schools of their own, and to force their doctrines into the schools built and maintained by the State. In this respect there is nothing to choose between Church and Dissent. The reading of the Bible in Board schools is a compromise between themselves, lest a worse thing should befall them both. If one section were strong enough to upset the compromise it would do so; in fact, the Church party is now attempting this stroke of policy on the London School Board, with the avowed object of giving a Church color to the religious teaching of the children. The very same principle was at work in former days, when none but Churchmen were admitted to the universities or public positions. It was a splendid means of maintaining the form of religion which was bound up with the monarchy and the aristocracy. Learning and influence were, as far as possible, kept on the side of the established faith, which thus became the master of the masters of the people. This is perfectly obvious to the student of history, and Freethinkers should lay its lesson to heart. It is only by driving religion entirely out of education, from the humblest school to the proudest college, that we shall ever succeed in breaking the power of priestcraft and freeing the people from the bondage of superstition.

We could write a volume on this theme—the power of education in maintaining religion; but we must be satisfied with the foregoing at present, and turn our attention to the power of *money*. It is a wise adage that money is the sinews of war. Fighting is very largely, often wholly, a question of resources. Troops may be ever so brave, generals ever so skilful, but they will be beaten unless they have good rifles and artillery, plenty of ammunition, and an ample commissariat. Now the same thing obtains in *all* warfare. It would be foolish, no less than base, to deny the inspiring efficacy of ideas, the electric force of enthusiasm; but, however highly men may be energised, they cannot act without instruments; and money buys them, whether the instruments be rifles and artillery, or schools, or churches, or any kind of organisation.

Given churches with great wealth, as well as control over public education, and it is easy to see that they will be able to perpetuate themselves. Endowments are specially valuable. They are rooted, so to speak, in the past, and hold firm. They bear golden fruit to be plucked by the skilful and adventurous. Besides, the very age of an endowed institution gives it a venerable ora; and its freedom from the full necessity of "cadging" lends it a certain "respectability" —like that of a man who lives on his means, instead of earning his living.

It is not an extravagant calculation that, in England alone, twenty millions a year are spent on religion. The figures fall glibly from the tongue, but just try to realise them! Think first of a thousand, then of a thousand thousand, then of twenty times that. Take a single million, and think what its expenditure might do in the shaping of public opinion. A practical friend of ours, a good Radical and Freethinker, said that he would undertake to create a majority for Home Rule in England with a million of money; and if he spent it judiciously, we think he might succeed. Well then, just imagine, not one million, but twenty millions, spent *every year* in maintaining and propagating a certain religion. Is it not enough, and more than enough, to perpetuate a system which is firmly founded, to begin with, on the education of little children?

Here lies the strength of Christianity. It is not true, it is not useful. Its teachings and pretensions are both seen through by tens of thousands, but the wealth supports it. "Without money and without price," is the fraudulent language of the pious prospectus. It would never last on those terms. The money keeps it up. Withdraw the money, and the Black Army would disband, leaving the people free to work out their secular salvation, without the fear and trembling of a foolish faith.

CLOTTED BOSH

"A heterogeneous mass of clotted bosh."
—*Thomas Carlyle.*

The death of Tennyson has called forth a vast deal of nonsense. Much of it is even insincere. The pulpits have spouted cataracts of sentimentality. Some of them have emitted quantities of sheer drivel. A stranger would think we had lost our only poet, and well-nigh our only teacher; whereas, if the truth must be told, we have lost one who was occasionally a great poet, but for the most part a miraculous artist in words. No man in his senses—certainly no man with a spark of judgment—could call Tennyson a profound thinker. Mainly he gave exquisite expression to ideas that floated around him. Nor did he possess a high degree of the creative faculty, such as Shakespeare possessed in inexhaustible abundance. Surely it is possible to admire our dead poet's genius without telling lies over his grave.

Among the pulpit utterances on Tennyson we note the Rev. Hugh Price Hughes's as perhaps the very perfection of slobbery incapacity. He appears to be delivering a course of addresses on the poet. The first of these escaped our attention; the second is before us in the supplement to last week's *Methodist Times*. We have read it with great attention and without the slightest profit. Not a sentence or a phrase in it rises above commonplace. That a crowd of people should listen to such stuff on a Sunday afternoon, when they might be taking a walk or enjoying a snooze, is a striking evidence of the degeneration of the human mind, at least in the circles of Methodism.

Mr. Hughes praises Tennyson for "conscientiousness in the use and choice of words." He should have said "the choice and use of words," for *choice* must precede *use* to be of any service. Mr. Hughes says it is of great importance that we should all be as conscientious as Tennyson. He might as well say it is of great importance that we should all be as strong as Sandow.

Let us take a few examples of *Mr. Hughes's* "conscientiousness." He talks of "shining features" which "lie upon the very surface" of Tennyson's poems. Now features seldom shine, they do not lie, and they must be (not *upon*, but) *at* the surface. Six lines further the shining features change into "shining qualities," as though *features* and *qualities* were synonyms. Mr. Hughes speaks, in the style of a penny-a-liner, of Tennyson's "amazing and unparalleled popular influence." Will he tell us if anything could amaze us *without* being unparalleled? He remarks that Tennyson was "not merely and mainly a poet of the educated classes." He should have said "merely *or* mainly." He enjoins upon us to "define our terms" and "know the exact meanings of the terms we use"—which is absolute tautology. He says of flirtation—on which he seems an authority—that "I greatly fear, and am morally certain" it is as much perpetrated by men as by women. But if he fears he cannot be certain, and if he is certain he cannot fear. He calls duelling a form of "insanity and barbarism." But while it may be one or the other, it cannot be both at once. The disjunctive, therefore, not the copulative, is the proper conjunction. Mr. Hughes misspells the name of Spenser, translates *mariage de convenance* as a marriage of convenience, and inserts one of his own inventions in a line of *Locksley Hall*, which runs thus in the Hughes edition of Tennyson—

Puppet to a father's threat and servile to a mother's shrewish tongue.

"Mother's" spoils the line. It is not Tennyson's. Mr. Hughes may claim it—"an ill-favored thing, sir, but mine own." It does equal credit to his "conscientiousness" and his ears.

Mr. Hughes's style as a critic does not rise to the level of an active contempt. Let us look at his matter and see if it shows any superiority.

"Yet although," Mr. Hughes says, with characteristic elegance—"yet although he wrote so much, Tennyson never wrote a single line that would bring a painful or anxious blush to the cheek of the most innocent or sensitive maiden." What a curious antithesis! Why should a man write impurely for writing much? And is *this* the supreme virtue of a great poet? It might be predicated of Martin Tupper. Milton, on the other hand, must have made many a maiden rosy by his description of Eve's naked loveliness—to say nothing of the scene after the Fall; while Shakespeare must have turned many a maiden cheek scarlet, though we do not believe he ever did the maiden any harm. Tennyson was not as free-spoken as some poets—greater poets than himself. But what does Mr. Hughes mean by his "Christ-like purity"? Is there a reference here to the twelfth verse of the nineteenth chapter of Matthew?

Purity, if properly understood, is undoubtedly a virtue. Mr. Hughes forgets, however, that his eulogy on Tennyson in this respect is a slur upon the Bible. There are things in the Old Testament—not to mention the New Testament—calculated to make "the most innocent or sensitive maiden" vomit; things that might abash a prostitute and make a satyr squeamish. We suggest, therefore, that Mr. Hughes should cease canting about "purity" while he helps to thrust the Bible into the hands of little children.

"In all superstition," he says, "wise men follow fools." This is a bold, [signi]ficant utterance. Fools are always in the majority, wise men are few, they are obliged to bow to the power of the multitude. Kings respect, priests organise, the popular folly; and the wise men have to sit aloft [and] nod to each other across the centuries. There is a freemasonry amongst [them?], and they have their shibboleths and dark sayings, to protect them [again]st priests and mobs.

[P]erhaps the story of Balaam is a subtle anticipation of Lord Bacon's [philosophy?]. It was the ass that first saw the angel. Baalam only saw it afterwards, [when h]is wits were disordered by the wonder of a talking donkey. Thus the [prophe]t followed the ass, as wise men follow fools.

[Sup]erstition is worse than Atheism, in Lord Bacon's judgment; the one [is unbe]lief, he says, but the other is contumely; and "it were better to have [no opini]on of God at all, than such an opinion as is unworthy of him." He [quote]s the saying of Plutarch, that he "had rather a great deal men should [say there] was no such man as Plutarch, than that they should say there was [a Plutar]ch that would eat his children as soon as they were born" —which, [as par]t of Lord Bacon, looks like a thrust at the doctrine of original sin [and] damnation.

[With h]is keen eye for "the good of man's estate," Lord Bacon remarks of [superstitio]n, that "as the contumely is greater towards God, so the danger [is greater to]wards men."

[Atheis]m leaves a man to sense, to philosophy, to natural piety, to [repu]tation; all which may be guides to an outward moral virtue, [thoug]h religion were not; but superstition dismounts all these, and erecteth [an absolute m]onarchy in the minds of men; therefore Atheism did never [perturb states;] for it makes men wary of themselves, as looking no farther, [and we see th]e times inclined to Atheism (as the time of Augustus Caesar) [were civil tim]es; but superstition hath been the confusion of many states, [and bringeth i]n a new *primum mobile* that ravisheth all the spheres of [government.]

[By "settled tim]es" Lord Bacon means settled, quiet, orderly, progressive [civilisation. And it is rather singular that he should pick [out the period imm]ediately preceding the advent of Christianity. Whateve[r] [Christianis]m, it is no danger to human society. This is Lord Bacon['s view]. [W]e commend it to the attention of the fanatics of faith, wh[o] [paint Atheism a]s a horrid monster, fraught with cruelty, bloodshed, an[d]

The reward of Tennyson's purity, according to Mr. Hughes, was that "he was able to understand women." "The English race," exclaims the eulogist, "has never contemplated a nobler or more inspiring womanhood than that which glows on every page of Tennyson." This is the hectic exaggeration in which Mr. Hughes habitually indulges. Tennyson never drew a live woman. Maud is a lay figure, and the heroine of "The Princess" is purely fantastic. George Meredith beats the late Laureate hollow in this respect. He is second only to Shakespeare, who here, as elsewhere, maintains his supremacy.

Mr. Hughes's remarks on *Locksley Hall* are, to use his own expression, amazing. "How terribly," he says, "does he [Tennyson] paint the swift degeneration of the faithless Amy." Mr. Hughes forgets—or *does* he forget?— that in the sequel to this poem, entitled *Sixty Years After*, Tennyson unsays all the high-pitched dispraise of Amy and her squire. *Locksley Hall* is a piece of splendid versification, but the hero is a prig, which is a shade worse than a Philistine. Young fellows mouth the poem rapturously; their elders smile at the disguises of egotism.

Loveless marriage was reprobated by Tennyson, and Mr. Hughes goes into ecstacies over the tremendous fact. Like the Psalmist, he is in haste; he cannot point to a poet who ever hinted the dethronement of love.

A choice Hughesean sentence occurs in this connexion. "I very much regret," the preacher says, "that Maud's lover was such a conventional idiot that he should have been guilty of the supreme folly of challenging her brother to a duel." Shade of Lindley Murrey, what a sentence! A boy who wrote thus would deserve whipping. And what right, we ask, has a Christian minister to rail at duelling? It was unknown to Greek or Roman society. Indeed, it is merely a form of the Ordeal, which was upheld by Christianity. The duel was originally a direct and solemn appeal to Providence. Only a sceptic has the right to call it a folly.

Enough of Mr. Hughes as a stylist, a critic, and teacher. What he really shines in is invention.

His story of the converted Atheist shoemaker displays a faculty which has no scope in a sermon on Tennyson.

LORD BACON ON ATHEISM

The pedants will be down upon us for speaking of Lord Bacon. It is true there never was such a personage. Francis Bacon was Baron of Verulam, Viscount St. Alban, and Lord High Chancellor of England. But this is a case in which it is impossible to resist the popular usage. After all, we write to be understood. The pedants, the heralds, and all the rest of the tribe of technical fanatics, rejoice to mouth "Lord Verulam." But the ordinary man of letters, like the common run of readers, will continue to speak of Lord Bacon; for Bacon was his name, and the "Lord" was but a pretty feather in his hat. And when his lordship took that splendid pen of his, to jot down some of his profoundest thoughts for posterity, did he not say in his grand style, "I, Francis Bacon, thought on this wise"? You cannot get the "Bacon" out of it, and as the "Lord" will slip in, we must let it stand as Lord Bacon.

Lord Bacon was was a very great man. Who does not remember Pope's lines?—

If parts allure thee, think how Bacon shined,

The wisest, brightest, meanest of mankind.

But his hardship was fond of wielding the satiric lash, and that spirit leads to exaggeration. Bacon was not the meanest of mankind, Pope himself did things that Bacon would never have stooped to. Nor was Bacon the wisest and brightest of mankind. A wiser and brighter spirit was contemporary with him in the person of "a poor player." The dullards who fancy that Lord Bacon wrote the plays of Shakespeare have no discrimination. His lordship's mind might have been cut out of the poet's without leaving an incurable wound. Some will dissent from this, but be it as it may, the *styles* of the two men are vastly different, like their ways of thinking. Bacon's essay on Love is cynical. The man of the world, the well-bred statesman, looked on Love as "the child of folly," a necessary nuisance, a tragi-comical perturbation. Shakespeare saw in Love the mainspring of life. Love speaks "in a perpetual hyperbole," said Bacon. Shakespeare also said that the lover "sees Helen's beauty in a brow of Egypt," The poet knew all the philosopher knew, and more. What Bacon laughed or sneered at, Shakespeare recognised as the magic of the great enchanter, who touches our imaginations and kindles in us the power of the ideal. Exaggeration there must be in passion and imagination; it is the defect of their quality; but what are we without them?

Dead driftwood on the tide; dismantled hulls rotting in har' that awaits destruction, to give its imprisoned forces a chan themselves in new forms of being.

Bacon was not a Shakespeare; still, he was a very great n are a text-book of worldly wisdom. His philosophical proverbial. Nor was he wanting in a certain "dry" poetry writer, not even Plato, equals him in the command of illum and the fine dignity of his style is beyond all praise. Th his pen with exquisite ease and felicity. He is never in a He writes like a Lord Chancellor, though with someth office; and if he is now and then familiar, it is only a like the joke of a judge, which does not bring him d litigants.

The opinions of such a man are worth study is often quoted in condemnation of Atheism, we actually says about it, what his judgment on this worth, and what allowance, if any, should be n which he expressed himself. This last point, inc importance. Lord Bacon lived at a time wher Raleigh and other great men of that age we ventilated in private conversation. In writir suggested; and, in this respect, a writer's *sile* that is, we must judge by what he does *not* say.

Some writers, like Letourneau, the Fr' length of arguing that Lord Bacon was ; utterances were all perfunctory: as it w philosopher was obliged to burn on the is certain—Lord Bacon rarely speaks c a statesman. He is apt to sneer at the There is no piety, no unction, in his religion as a social bond, an agency to say that he took a Christian view thought upon Death, and I find it "Men fear death as children fear t in children is increased with tale'

Lord Bacon has an essay o by another on Superstition. T' apologists, but we shall deal v

Flowers Of F

sig and and and then again

P dictu when prophe

Su is unbel no opin approve say there one Pluta on the pa and infant

With h superstitio is greater to

"Atheis laws, to rep though relig an absolute perturb state and we see th were civil tim and bringeth government."

By "civil ti times—times of out the age imn fault is in Atheis judgment, and w point to Atheism social disruption.

Coming now to Lord Bacon's essay on Atheism itself, we find him opening it with a very pointed utterance of Theism. "I had rather," he says, "believe all the fables in the legend, and the Talmud, and the Alcoran, than that this universal frame is without a mind." The expression is admirable, but the philosophy is doubtful. When a man says he would *rather* believe one thing than another, he is merely exhibiting a personal preference. Real belief is not a matter of taste; it is determined by evidence — if not absolutely, at least as far as our power of judgment carries us.

"A little philosophy," his lordship says, "inclineth man's mind to Atheism, but depth in philosophy bringeth men's minds about to religion." The reason he assigns is, that when we no longer rest in second causes, but behold "the chain of them confederate, and linked together," we must needs "fly to providence and Deity." The necessity, however, is far from obvious. All the laws, as we call them, of all the sciences together, do not contain any new principle in their addition. Universal order is as consistent with Materialism as with Theism. It is easy to say that "God never wrought miracles to convince Atheism, because his ordinary works convince it"; but, as a matter of fact, it is the God of Miracles in whom the multitude have always believed. A special providence, rather than a study of the universe, has been the secret of their devotion to "the unseen."

Lord Bacon drops below the proper level of his genius in affirming that "none deny there is a God, but those for whom it maketh that there were no God." This is but a milder expression of the incivility of the Psalmist. It is finely rebuked by the atheist Monk in the play of "Sir William Crichton," the work of a man of great though little recognised genius — William Smith.

For ye who deem that one who lacks of faith Is therefore conscience-free, ye little know How doubt and sad denial may enthral him To the most timid sanctity of life.

Lord Bacon, indeed, rather doubts the existence of the positive Atheist.

"It appeareth in nothing more, that Atheism is rather in the lip than in the heart of man, than by this, that Atheists will ever be talking of that their opinion, as if they fainted in it within themselves, and would be glad to be strengthened by the opinion of others: nay more, you shall have Atheists strive to get disciples, as it fareth with other sects; and, which is most of all, you shall have of them that will suffer for Atheism, and not recant; whereas, if they truly think that there is no such thing as God, Why should they trouble themselves?"

Although Lord Bacon was not the "meanest of mankind," there was certainly a lack of the heroic in his disposition; and this passage emanated from the most prosaic part of his mind and character. "Great thoughts," said Vauvenargues, "spring from the heart." Now the heart of Lord Bacon was not as high as his intellect; no one could for a moment imagine his facing martyrdom. He had none of the splendid audacity, the undaunted courage, the unshakable fortitude, of his loftier contemporary, Giordano Bruno. So much truth is there in Pope's epigram, that his lordship was capable at times of grovelling; witness his fulsome, though magnificent, dedication of the *Advancement of Learning* to King James—the British Solomon, as his flatterers called him, to the amusement of the great Henry of France, who sneered, "Yes, Solomon the son of David," in allusion to his mother's familiarity with David Rizzio. And in this very passage of the essay on Atheism we also see the grovelling side of Lord Bacon, with a corresponding perversion of intelligence. Being incapable of understanding martyrdom, except under the expectation of a reward in heaven, his lordship cannot appreciate the act of an Atheist in suffering for his convictions. His concluding words are positively *mean*. Surely the Atheist might trouble himself about truth, justice, and dignity; all of which are involved in the maintenance and propagation of his principles. But, if the closing observation is mean, the opening observation is fatuous. This is a strong word to use of any sentence of Lord Bacon's, but in this instance it is justifiable. If an Atheist mistrusts his own opinion, because he talks about it, what is to be said of the Christians, who pay thousands of ministers to talk about their opinions, and even subscribe for Missionary Societies to talk about them to the "heathen"? Are we to conclude that an Atheist's talking shows mistrust, and a Christian's talking shows confidence? What real weakness is there in the Atheist's seeking for sympathy and concurrence? It is hard for any man to stand alone; certainly it was not in Lord Bacon's line to do so; and why should not the Atheist be "glad to be strengthened by the opinion of others"! Novalis said that his opinion gained infinitely when it was shared by another. The participation does not prove the truth of the opinion, but redeems it from the suspicion of being a mere maggot of an individual brain.

Lord Bacon then turns to the barbaric races, who worship particular gods, though they have not the general name; a fact which he did not understand. More than two hundred years later it was explained by David Hume. It is simply a proof that monotheism grows out of polytheism; or, if you like, that Theism is a development of Idolatry. This is a truth that takes all the sting out of Lord Bacon's observation that "against Atheists the very savages take part with the very subtilest philosophers." We may just remark that the philosophers must be very hard pressed when they call up their savage allies.

Contemplative Atheists are rare, says Lord Bacon—"a Diagoras, a Bion, a Lucian perhaps, and some others." They seem more than they are, for all sorts of heretics are branded as Atheists; which leads his lordship to the declaration that "the great Atheists indeed are hypocrites, which are ever handling holy things, but without feeling; so as they must needs be cauterised in the end." This is a pungent observation, and it springs from the better side of his lordship's nature. We also have no respect for hypocrites, and for that very reason we object to them as a present to Atheism. Religion must consume in its own smoke, and dispose of its own refuse.

The causes of Atheism next occupy Lord Bacon's attention. He finds they are four; divisions in religion, the scandal of priests, profane scoffing in holy matters, and "learned times, especially with peace and prosperity." "Troubles and adversities," his lordship says, "do more bow men's minds to religion." Which is true enough, though it only illustrates the line of the Roman poet that religion always has its root in fear.

It will be observed that, up to the present, Lord Bacon has not considered one of the reasons *for* Atheism. What he calls "causes" are only *occasions*. He does not discuss, or even refer to, the objections to Theism that are derived from the tentative operations of nature, so different from what might be expected from a settled plan; from ugly, venomous and monstrous things; from the great imperfection of nature's very highest productions; from the ignorance, misery, and degradation of such a vast part of mankind; from the utter absence of anything like a moral government of the universe. Only towards the end of his essay does Lord Bacon begin business with the Atheists. "They that deny a God," he says, "destroy a man's nobility; for certainly man is of kin to the beasts by his body; and, if he be not of kin to God by his spirit, he is a base and ignoble creature." This is pointed and vigorous, but after all it is a matter of sentiment. Some prefer the fallen angel, others the risen ape.

Lord Bacon, like Earl Beaconsfield, is on the side of the angels. We are on the other side. A being who has done something, and will do more, however humble his origin, is preferable to one who can only boast of his fine descent.

Finally, his lordship takes the illustration of the dog, to whom man is "instead of a God." What generosity and courage he will put on, in the "confidence of a better nature than his own." So man gathereth force and faith from divine protection and favor. Atheism therefore "depriveth human nature of the means to exalt itself above human frailty." But this is to forget that there may be more than one means to the same end. Human nature may be exalted above its frailty without becoming the dog of a superior intelligence. Science, self-examination, culture, public opinion, and the growth of humanity, are more than substitutes for devotion to a deity. They are capable of exalting man continuously and indefinitely. They do not appeal to the spaniel element in his nature; they make him free, erect, noble, and self-dependent.

On the whole we are bound to say that Lord Bacon's essay on Atheism is unworthy of his genius. If it were the only piece of his writing extant, we should say it was the work of one who had great powers of expression but no remarkable powers of thought. He writes very finely as a strong advocate, putting a case in a way that commands attention, and perhaps admiration for its force and skill. But something more than this is to be expected when a really great man addresses himself to a question of such depth and importance. What then are we to conclude? Why this, that Lord Bacon dared not give the rein to his mind in an essay on Atheism. He was bound to be circumspect in a composition level to the intelligence of every educated reader. We prefer to take him where he enjoys greater freedom. Under the veil of a story, for instance, he aims a dart at the superstition of a special providence, which is an ineradicable part of the Christian faith.

Bion, the Atheist, being shown the votive tablets in the temple of Neptune, presented by those who prayed to the god in a storm and were saved, asked where were the tablets of those who were drowned. Bacon tells the story with evident gusto, and it is in such things that we seem to get at his real thoughts. In a set essay on Atheism, a man of his worldly wisdom, and un-heroic temper, was sure to kneel at the regular altars. The single query "Why should they trouble themselves?" explains it all.

CHRISTIANITY AND SLAVERY *

* *Christianity and Slavery. No. 18 of Oxford House Papers.*
By H. Henley Henson, B.A., Head of the Oxford House in
Bethnal Green. London: Rivingtons.

Some time ago I delivered a lecture in the London Hall of Science on "Christianity and Slavery." Among my critics there was one gentleman, and the circumstance was so noteworthy that my friend the chairman expressed a wish, which I cordially echoed, that we might have the pleasure of hearing him again. A few days ago a pamphlet reached me on the subject of that lecture, written by my friendly opponent, who turns out to be the head of the Oxford House in Bethnal Green. Mr. Henson sends me the pamphlet himself "with his compliments," and I have read it carefully. Indeed, I have marked it in dozens of places where his statements strike me as inaccurate and his arguments as fallacious; and, on the whole, I think it best to give him a set answer in this journal. Mr. Henson's paper is not, in my opinion, a very forcible one on the intellectual side. But perhaps that is, in a certain sense, one of its merits; for the Christian case in this dispute is so bad that sentiment does it more service than logic. I must, however, allow that Mr. Henson is a courteous disputant, and I hope I shall reciprocate his good feeling. When he opposed me at the Hall of Science, he admits that I treated him "with a courtesy which relieves controversy of its worst aspects." I trust he will be equally satisfied with my rejoinder. Whenever I may have occasion to express myself strongly, I shall simply be in earnest about the theme, without the least intention of being discourteous. I mean no offence, and I hope I shall give none.

Mr. Henson says he is dealing in a brief compass with a big subject, but "the outlines are clear, and may be perceived very readily by any honest man of moderate intelligence." Well, whether it is that I am not an honest man, or that I possess immoderate intelligence, I certainly do not see the outlines of the subject as Mr. Henson sees them. The relation of Christianity to slavery is an historical question, and Mr. Henson treats it as though it were one of dialectics. However, I suppose I had better follow him, and show that he is wrong even on his own ground.

Mr. Henson undertakes to prove three things. (1) That slavery is flatly opposed to the teaching of the New Testament. (2) That the abolition of slavery in Europe was mainly owing to Christianity. (3) That at this present time Christianity is steadily working against slavery all over the world.

Before I discuss the first proposition I must ask why the *Old* Testament is left out of account. Mr. Henson relegates it to a footnote, and there he declares "once for all, that the Mosaic Law has nothing to do with the question." But Mr. Henson's "once for all" has not the force of a Papal decree. It is simply a bit of rhetorical emphasis, like a flourish to a signature. Does he mean to say that the author of the Mosaic Law was not the same God who speaks to us in the New Testament? If it was the same God, "the same, yesterday, to-day, and for ever," the Mosaic Law has very much to do with the question; unless—and this is a vital point—Jesus distinctly abrogates it in any respect. He *did* distinctly abrogate the *lex talionis*, an eye for an eye and a tooth for a tooth; but he left the laws of slavery exactly as he found them, and in this he was followed by Peter and Paul, and by all the Fathers of the Church.

Mr. Henson tells us that "the Jews were a barbarous race, and slavery was necessary to that stage of development," and that "the Law of Moses moderated the worst features of slavery." The second statement cannot be discussed, for we do not know what was the condition of slavery among the Jews before the so-called Mosaic Law (centuries after Moses) came into vogue. The first statement, however, is perfectly true; the Jews *were* barbarous, and slavery among them was inevitable. But that is speaking *humanly*. What is the use of God's interference if he does not make people wiser and better? Why did he lay down slavery laws without hinting that they were provisional? Why did he so express himself as to enable Christian divines and whole Churches to justify slavery from the Bible long after it had died out of the internal polity of civilised states? Surely God might have given less time to Aaron's vestments and the paraphernalia of his own Tabernacle, and devoted some of his infinite leisure to teaching the Jews that property in human flesh and blood is immoral. Instead of that he actually told them, not only how to buy foreigners (Leviticus xxv. 45, 46), but how to enslave their own brethren (Exodus xxi. 2-11).

When Jesus Christ came from heaven to give mankind a new revelation he had a fine opportunity to correct the brutalities of the Mosaic Law. Yet Mr. Henson allows that he "did not actually forbid Slavery in express terms," and that he "never said in so many words, Slavery is wrong." But why not? It will not do to say the time was not ripe, for Mr. Henson admits that in Rome "the fashionable philosophies, especially that of the Stoics, branded Slavery as an outrage against the natural Equality of Men." Surely Jesus Christ might have kept abreast of the Stoics. Surely, too, as he did not mean to say anything more for at least two thousand years, he might have gone *in advance* of the best teaching of the age, so as to provide for the progress of future generations.

But, says Mr. Henson, Jesus Christ "laid down broad principles which took from Slavery its bad features, and tended, by an unerring law to its abolition." Well, the tendency was a remarkably slow one. Men still living can remember when Slavery was abolished in the British dominions. I can remember when it was abolished in the United States. Eighteen centuries of Christian *tendency* were necessary to kill Slavery! Surely the natural growth of civilisation might have done as much in that time, though Jesus Christ had never lived and taught. How civilisation *did* mitigate the horrors of Slavery, and was gradually but surely working towards its abolition, may be seen in Gibbon's second chapter. This was under the great Pagan emperors, some of whom knew Christianity and despised it.

"Slavery is cruel," says Mr. Henson, while "Christianity teaches men to be kind and to love one another." But *teaching* men to love one another, even if Christianity taught nothing else—which is far from the truth—is a very questionable expenditure of time and energy; for how is love to be *taught*? Besides, a master and a slave might be attached to each other—as was often the case—without either seeing that Slavery was a violation of the law of love. What was needed was the sentiment of *Justice*. That has broken the chains of the slave. The Stoics were on the right track after all, while Christianity lost itself in idle sentimentalism.

"Slavery denies the Equality of Men," says Mr. Henson, while "Christianity asserts it strongly." I regret I cannot agree with him. Certain amiable texts which he cites might easily be confronted with others of a very different character. What did Christ mean by promising that when he came into his kingdom his disciples should sit on twelve thrones judging the twelve tribes of Israel? How is this consistent with his saying, "call no man master"? What did Paul mean by ordering unlimited obedience to "the powers that be"? What did he and Peter mean by telling slaves to obey their owners? Is all this consistent with the doctrine of human equality? Mr. Henson simply reads into certain New Testament utterances what was never in the speakers' minds. His abstract argument is indeed perilous in regard to such composite writings as the Gospels and the Epistles. Let it be assumed, for argument's sake, that Christianity does somewhere assert the Equality of Men. Then it condemns Royalty as well as Slavery; yet

Peter says, "Fear God and honor the King." I leave Mr. Henson to extricate himself from this dilemma.

I repeat that all this dialectic is a kind of subterfuge; at least it is an evasion. The great fact remains that Jesus Christ never breathed a whisper against slavery when he had the opportunity. Yet he could denounce what he disapproved in the most vigorous fashion. His objurgation of the Scribes and Pharisees is almost without a parallel. Surely he might have reserved a little of his boisterous abuse for an institution which was infinitely more harmful than the whole crowd of his rivals. Those who opposed *him* were overwhelmed with vituperation, but not once did he censure those who held millions in cruel bondage, turning men into mere beasts of burden, and women, if they happened to be beautiful, into the most wretched victims of lust.

Let us now turn to Paul, the great apostle whose teaching has had more influence on the faith and practice of Christendom than that of Jesus himself. Mr. Henson says that "the Apostle does not say one word for or against slavery as such." Again I regret to differ. Paul never said a word *against* slavery, but he said many words that sanctioned it by implication. He tells slaves (*servants* in the Authorised Version) to count their owners worthy of all honor (1 Tim. vi. 1); to be obedient unto them, with fear and trembling, as unto Christ (Ephesians vi. 5); and to please them in all things (Titus ii. 9). I need not discuss whether servants means *slaves* and masters *owners*, for Mr. Henson admits that such is their meaning. Here then Paul is, if Jesus was not, brought face to face with slavery, and he does not even suggest that the institution is wrong. He tells slaves to obey their owners as they obey Christ; and, on the other hand, he bids owners to "forbear threatening" their slaves. But so much might have been said by Cicero and Pliny; the former of whom, as Lecky says, wrote many letters to his slave Tiro "in terms of sincere and delicate friendship"; while the latter "poured out his deep sorrow for the death of some of his slaves, and endeavored to console himself with the thought that as he had emancipated them before their death, they had at least died free men."

Paul does indeed say that both bond and free are "all one in Christ." But Louis the Fourteenth would have admitted *that* kinship between himself and the meanest serf in France, "One in Christ" is a spiritual idea, and has relation to a future life, in which earthly distinctions would naturally cease.

Mr. Henson is obliged to face the story of Onesimus, the runaway slave, whom Paul deliberately sent back to his master, Philemon. "The Apostle's position," he says, "is practically this"; whereupon he puts into Paul's mouth words of his own invention. I do not deny his right to use this literary artifice, but I decline to let it impose on my own understanding. There is a certain pathetic tenderness in Paul's letter to Philemon if we suppose that he took the institution of Slavery for granted, but it vanishes if we suppose that he felt the institution to be wrong. Professor Newman justly remarks that "Onesimus, in the very act of taking to flight, showed that he had been submitting to servitude against his will, and that the house of his owner had previously been a prison to him." Nor do I see any escape from the same writer's conclusion that, although Paul besought Philemon to treat Onesimus as a brother, "this very recommendation, full of affection as it is, virtually recognises the moral rights of Philemon to the services of his slave." Mr. Benson apparently feels this himself. "Christian tradition," he says, "declares that Philemon at once set Onesimus free." But "tradition" can hardly be cited as a fact. Mr. Henson says "it is more than probable," or, in other words, *certain*; yet he cannot expect me to follow him in his illogical leap. Nor, indeed, is the "traditional" liberation of Onesimus of much importance to the argument. Not Philemon's but Paul's views are in dispute; and if Philemon did liberate Onesimus—which is a pure assumption—Paul certainly did not advise him to do anything of the kind.

Paul's epistle to Philemon does not, from its very-nature, seem intended for publication. Why then, in the ease of private correspondence, did he not hint that Slavery was only tolerated for the time and would eventually cease? Instead of that he sent back Onesimus to a servitude from which he had fled. How unlike Theodore Parker writing his discourse, with a runaway slave in the back room, and a revolver on his desk! How unlike Walt Whitman watching the slumber of another fugitive, with one hand on his trusty rifle!

Mr. Henson lives after the abolition of Slavery, and as he clings to his Bible as God's Word he reads into it the morality of a later age. Let him consult the writings of Christian divines on the subject, and he will see that they have almost invariably justified Slavery from scripture. Ignatius (who is said to have seen Jesus), St. Cyprian, Pope Gregory the Great, St. Basil, Tertullian, St. Isidore, St. Augustine, St. Bernard, St. Thomas Aquinas, and Bossuet, all taught that Slavery is a divine institution. During all the centuries from Ignatius to Bossuet, what eminent Christian ever denounced Slavery as wicked? Even the Christian jurisprudists of the eighteenth century defended negro slavery, which it was reserved for the sceptical Montesquieu and the arch-heretic Voltaire to condemn. Montesquieu's ironical chapter on the subject is worthy of Molliere, and Voltaire's is an honor to humanity. He called Slavery "the degrada of the species"; and, in answer to Puffendorff, who claimed that slavery had been established by the free consent of the opposing parties, he exclaimed, "I will believe Puffendorff, when he shows me the original contract."

Negro slavery was defended in America by direct appeal to the Bible. Mr. Henson seeks to lessen the force of this damning fact by referring to these defenders of slavery as "certain clergymen and other Christians," and as "ignorant and unworthy members of the Church." *Certain* clergymen! Why, the clergy defended slavery almost to a man, and in the Northern States they were even more bigoted than in the South. Mrs. Beecher Stowe said that the Church was so familiarly quoted as being on the side of Slavery, that "Statesmen on both sides of the question have laid that down as a settled fact." Theodore Parker said that if the whole American Church had "dropped through the continent and disappeared altogether, the anti-Slavery cause would have been further on." He pointed out that no Church ever issued a single tract, among all its thousands, against property in human flesh and blood; and that 80,000 slaves were owned by Presbyterians, 225,000 by Baptists, and 250,000 by Methodists. Wilberforce himself declared that the American Episcopal Church "raises no voice against the predominant evil; she palliates it in theory, and in practice she shares in it. The mildest and most conscientious of the bishops of the South are slaveholders themselves." The Harmony Presbytery of South Carolina deliberately resolved that Slavery was justified by Holy Writ. The Methodist Episcopal Church decided in 1840 against allowing any "colored persons" to give testimony against "white persons." The College Church of the Union Theological Seminary, Prince Edward County, was endowed with slaves, who were hired out to the highest bidder for the pastor's salary. Lastly, Professor Moses Stuart, of Andover, who is accounted the greatest American theologian since Jonathan Edwards, declared that "The precepts of the New Testament respecting the demeanor of slaves and their masters beyond all question recognise the existence of Slavery." So much for Mr. Henson's "certain clergymen."

Mr. Henson also argues that the Northern States were "the most distinctly Christian," and that they were opposed to Slavery. History belies this statement Harriet Martineau, when she visited America and stood on the anti-slavery platform, says she was in danger of her life in the North while scarcely molested in the South. When William Lloyd Garrison delivered his first anti-slavery lecture in Boston, the classic home of American orthodoxy, every Catholic and Protestant church was closed against him, and he was obliged to accept the use of Julian Hall from Abner Kneeland, an infidel who had been prosecuted for blasphemy. It was not "the true spirit of Christianity" which abolished Slavery in the United States, but "the true spirit of Humanity," which inspired some Christians and more Freethinkers to vindicate the natural rights of men of all colors. Even in the end, Slavery was not terminated by the vote of the Churches; it was abolished by Lincoln as a strategic act in the midst of a civil war, precisely as was predicted by Thomas Paine, who not only hated Slavery while his Christian defamers lived by it, but was more sagacious in his political forecast than all the orthodox statesmen of his age.

"A movement headed by Clarkson and Wilberforce," says Mr. Henson, "could be no other than Christian," But why? Were not the slave-owners also Christians? Was not the strength of Freethinkers, from Jeremy Bentham downwards, given to the abolition movement? Were not the Freethinkers all on one side, while the Christians were divided? And why did the abolition movement in England wait until new ideas had leavened the public mind? Had it been purely Christian, would it not have triumphed long before? The fact is there was plenty of Christianity during the preceding thousand years, but the sceptical and humanitarian work of the eighteenth century was necessary before there could be any general revolt against injustice and oppression. No perversion of history can alter the fact that, in the words of Professor Newman, "the first public act against Slavery came from republican France, in the madness of atheistic enthusiasm." Mr. Henson sees this clearly himself, and therefore he pretends that all the best ideas of the French Revolution were borrowed from Christianity. Shades of Voltaire and Diderot, of Mirabeau and Danton, listen to this apologist of the faith you despised! Voltaire's face is wreathed with ineffable irony, Diderot contemplates the speaker as a new species for a psychological monograph, Mirabeau flings back his leonine head with a swirl of the black mane and a glare of the great eyes, and Danton roars a titanic laugh that shakes the very roof of Hades.

Now let us turn to the old indigenous Slavery of Europe. Mr. Henson appeals to "the witness of history," and he shall have it. He undertakes to prove "That among the various causes which tended to assuage the hardship and threaten the permanence of Slavery, the most powerful, the most active, and most successful was Christianity"; also "That when the barbarian conquests re-established slavery in a new form, the Church exerted all her energies on the side of freedom."

That Christianity "threatened" the permanence of Slavery is, of course, purely a matter of opinion. Mr. Henson takes one view, I have given reasons for another, and the reader must judge between us. That it softened the rigors of Slavery is a very questionable statement. When Mr. Henson says that "Roman Slavery was, perhaps, the most cruel and revolting kind of Slavery," he is guilty of historical confusion. Roman Slavery lasted for very many centuries. In the early ages it was brutal enough, but under the great emperors, and especially the Antonines, it was far more merciful than negro Slavery was in Christian America. Slaves were protected by law; the power of putting them to death was taken from the masters and entrusted to the magistrates; and, as Gibbon says, "Upon a just complaint of intolerable treatment, the injured slave either obtained his deliverance or a less cruel master." Compare this with the condition of serfs under the Christian feudal system, when, in Mr. Henson's own language, "the serf was tied to the soil, bought and sold with it, the chattel of his master, who could overwork, beat, and even kill him at will."

The phrase "re-established Slavery in a new form," seems to imply that Christianity had abolished Slavery before the barbaric conquests. But it had done nothing of the kind. Nay, as a matter of fact, Constantine and his successors drew a sharper line than ever between slaves and freemen. Constantine (the first Christian emperor) actually decreed death against any freewoman who should marry a slave, while the slave himself was to be burnt alive!

Much of what Mr. Henson says about the manumission of slaves by some of the mediaeval clergy is unquestionably true. But who doubts that, during a thousand years, a humane and even a noble heart often beat under a priest's cassock? These manumissions, however, were of Christian slaves. The Pagan slaves—such as the Sclavonians, from whom the word *slave* is derived—were considered to have no claims at all. Surely the liberation of fellow Christians might spring from proselyte zeal. "Mohammedans also," as Professor Newman says, "have a conscience against enslaving Mohammedans, and generally bestow freedom on a slave as soon as he adopts their religion." Manumission of slaves was common among humane owners under the Roman Empire; indeed Gibbon observes that the law had to guard against the swamping of free citizens by the sudden inrush of "a mean and promiscuous multitude." Clerical manumission of slaves in mediaeval times was therefore no novelty. On the other hand, bishops held slaves like kings and nobles. The Abbey of St. Germain de Pres, for instance, owned 80,000 slaves, and the Abbey of St. Martin de Tours 20,000. The monks, who according to Mr. Henson, did so much to extinguish slavery, owned multitudes of these servile creatures.

The acts of a few humane and noble spirits are no test of the effects of a system. The decisions of Church Councils are a much better criterion. They show the influence of *principles*, when personal equation is eliminated. Turning to these Councils, then, what do we find? Why that from the Council of Laodicea to the Lateran Council (1215)—that is, for eight hundred years—the Church sanctioned Slavery again and again. Slaves and their owners might be "one in Christ," but the Church taught them to keep their distance on earth.

Civilisation, not Christianity, gradually extinguished Slavery in Europe. Foreign slavery, such as that in our West Indian possessions, is an artificial thing, and may be abolished by the stroke of a pen. But domestic slavery has to die a natural death. The progress of education and refinement, and the growth of the sentiment of justice, help to extinguish it; but behind these there is an economical law which is no less potent. Slave labor is only consistent with a low industrial life; and thus, as civilisation expands, slavery fades into serfdom, and serfdom into wage-service, as naturally as the darkness of night melts into the morning twilight, and the twilight into day.

Mr. Henson throws in some not ineloquent remarks about the abolition by Christianity of the gladiatorial shows at Rome. He himself has stood within the ruined Colosseum and re-echoed Byron's heroics. Mr. Henson even outdid Byron, for he looked up to the dome of St. Peter's, where gleamed the Cross of Christ, and rejoiced that "He had triumphed at last." "If only Mr. Foote had been there!" Mr. Henson exclaims. Well, Gibbon was there before Mr. Henson and before Byron. What he thought in the Colosseum I know not, but I know that the great project of *The Decline and Fall of the Roman Empire* took shape in his mind one eventful evening as he "sat musing amidst the ruins of the Capitol, while the barefooted friars were singing vespers in the temple of Jupiter." Yet I suppose Gibbon's fifteenth chapter is scarcely to Mr. Henson's taste. Had I "been there" with Mr. Henson, I too might have had my reflections, and I might have thrown this Freethought *douche* on his Christian ardor. "Yes, the Cross *has* triumphed. There it gleams over the dome of St. Peter's, the mightiest church in the world. Below it, until the recent subversion of the Pope's temporal power, walked the most ignorant, beggarly and criminal population in Europe. What are these to the men who built up the glory of ancient Rome? What is their city to the magnificent city of old, among whose ruins they walk like pigmies amid the relics of giants? This time-eaten, weather-beaten Colosseum saw many a gladiator 'butchered to make a Roman holiday.' But has not Christian Rome witnessed many a viler spectacle? Has it not seen hundreds of noble men burnt alive in the name of Christ? When Rome was Pagan, thought was free. Gladiatorial shows satisfied the bestial craving in vulgar breasts, but the philosophers and poets were unfettered, and the intellect of the few was gradually achieving the redemption of the many. When Rome was Christian, she introduced a new slavery. Thought was scourged and chained, while the cruel instincts of the multitude were gratified with exhibitions of suffering, compared with which the bloodiest arena was tame and insipid. Your Christian Rome, in the superb metaphor of Hobbes, was but the ghost of Pagan Rome, sitting throned and crowned on the grave thereof; nay, a ghoul, feeding not on the dead limbs of men, but on their living hearts and brains. Look at your Cross! Before Christ appeared it was the symbol of life; since it has been the symbol of misery and humiliation; and in the name of your Crucified One the people have been crucified between the spiritual and temporal thieves. But happily your Cross has had its day. St. Peter's may yet crumble before the Colosseum, and the statue of a Bruno may outlast the walls of the Vatican."

CHRIST UP TO DATE

This is an age of weak conviction and strong pretence. Christianity is perishing of intellectual atrophy. Its scriptures and its dogmas are falling into more and more discredit. Mr. Gladstone may defend the Bible with passionate devotion and lofty ignorance, but better informed Christians see that the Old Testament is doomed. They say it must be read in a new light. Its science and history must be regarded as merely human; nay, its very morality savors of the barbarism of the Jews. Only its best ethical teaching, and its upward aspirations, are to be regarded as the workings or God in the Jewish mind. Nor is this all. There is a revolt against the supernaturalism of the New Testament. Christians like Dr. Abbott explain away the Resurrection as no physical fact, but a spiritual conception. The creed of Christendom is gradually melting away like a northern iceberg floating into southern seas. Pinnacle after pinnacle of glittering dogma, loosens, falls, and sinks for ever. Only the central block remains intact, and we are assured it will never change. The storms of controversy will never rend it; the rays of the sun of science will never make an impression on its marble firmness. But Freethinkers smile at this cheap boast. They know the thaw will continue until the last fragment has melted into the infinite ocean.

The central, indissoluble part of Christianity is Jesus Christ. He will never fade, we are told. He is not for an age, but for all time. When all the dogmas of the Churches have perished, the divine figure of Christ will survive, and flourish in immortal beauty. All the world will yet worship him. "Christ" will be the universal passport in the depths of China, in the wilds of Africa, on the Tartar steppes, and among the haunted ruins of old Asia, as well as in the present Christendom of Europe and America.

This prophecy is very pretty, but it lacks precision. The prophets forget to tell us whether the divine figure of Christ is to be human or supernatural; the grandest of men or the smallest of gods. If he be indeed a god, they are playing strange tricks with his works and sayings; while, if he be indeed a mere man, they forget to explain how it is likely that the human race will ever look back to a single dead Jew as the moral microcosm, the consummate spiritual flower of humanity, the beacon of ideal life to every generation of voyagers on the sea of time.

Logic, however, must not be expected of Christians, at least in an age of dissolving views like the present. They will go on quoting Kenan's prize-essay panegyric on Christ, without any reference to the rest of his Vie de Jesus. *They will persist in quoting Mill's farfetched eulogy, without referring to other passages in the essay* On Liberty. But this is not all, nor even the worst. The sentimentalism of "popular" and "advanced" Christianity is turning Jesus Christ into a hero of romance. He is taking the place of King Arthur, of blameless memory; and we shall soon see the Apostles take the place of the Knights of the Round Table. Rancid orators and flatulent poets are gathering to the festival Jesus Christ will make a fine speech for the one set, and fine copy for the other. The professional biographers will cut in for a share in the spoil, and the brains of impudence will be ransacked to eke out the stories of Matthew, Mark, Luke, and John.

Lives of Christ are becoming quite fashionable. Fleetwood's honest but prosaic book had fallen into-neglect. The very maulers of old bookstalls thrust out their tongues at at. The still older book of Jeremy Taylor—a work of real genius and golden eloquence—was too stiff reading for an idle generation. Just in the nick of time the English translation of Kenan appeared. The first edition was less scientific than the thirteenth. Kenan had only just broken away from the Catholic Church; he was also under the influence of his visit to Palestine; his *Vie de Jesus* was therefore a sentimental Parisian romance; the smell of patchouli was on every page. Yet here and there the quick reader caught the laugh of Voltaire.

Kenan's book set a new vogue. The severe, critical Strauss was laid aside in England, and "the Savior's" life was "cultivated on new principles." By and bye the writers and publishers found there was "money in it." Jesus Christ could be made to pay. Dr. Farrar made thousands out of his trashy volumes, and his publishers netted a fortune. Mr. Haweis has done the same trick with four volumes. Ward Beecher spent his last days on a Life of Christ. Talmage is occupied on the same labor of love—and profit. Even the Catholic Church is not behindhand. Pere Didon has put forth *his* Life of Christ in two fat volumes as an antidote to the poison of Kenan. And the end is not yet. Nevertheless we see the beginning of the end. It was bound to come. After the prose writers prance the versifiers, and Sir Edward Arnold is first in the motley procession.

Sir Edward Arnold's *Light of Asia* was a fairly good piece of work. He had caught the trick of Tennysonian blank-verse, and he put some of the best features of Buddhism before the English public in a manner that commanded attention. Standing aloof from Buddhism himself, though sympathising with it, he was able to keep an impartial attitude. Further, he stuck to the Buddhist stories as he found them. All the license he took was that of selection and versification. But his recent *Light of the World* is another matter. He dishes up Jesus Christ in it, and Pontius Pilate and Mary Magdalene and the Wise Men of the East, as freely as Tennyson dishes up Arthur and Launcelot and Guinevere and the rest of that famous company. His style, too, is Tennysonian, to a certain degree. It is something like the Master's on its general level, but we miss the flashing felicities, the exquisite sentence or image that makes us breathless with sudden pleasure. Sir Edward's style has always a smack of the *Daily Telegraph*. He is high-flown in expressing even small ideas, or in describing trivialities.

Like a true Christian and courtier, Sir Edwin Arnold dedicates his book to "the Queen's Most Excellent Majesty." Those who fear God must also honor the king; and did not Jesus himself tell us to render unto Caesar the things that be Caesar's, as well as unto God the things that be God's? We presume Sir Edwin's dedication is "with permission." We also presume it will help the sale and promote his chance of the poet-laureateship.

After the dedication comes the "Proeme" of eight couplets, occupying a separate page, faced and backed with virgin paper.

The sovereign voice spake, once more, in mine ear: "Write, now, a song unstained by any tear!"

"What shall I write?" I said: the voice replied: "Write what we tell thee of the crucified!"

"How shall I write," I said, "who am not meet One word of that sweet speaking to repeat?"

"It shall be given unto thee! Do this thing!" Answered the voice: "Wash thy lips clean, and sing!"

This "proeme" is, to say the least of it, peculiar. The "sovereign voice" can hardly be the Queen's. It must be God Almighty's. Sir Edwin Arnold is therefore inspired. He writes as it is "given unto" him. And before he begins, by divine direction, he washes his lips clean; though he omits to tell us how he did it, whether with a flannel or a pocket-handkerchief.

It is well to know that Sir Edwin is inspired. Carnal criticism is thus disarmed and questions become blasphemous. But if Sir Edwin had *not* been inspired we should have offered certain remarks and put certain queries. For instance, how does he know that the star of the Nativity was "a strange white star"? May it not have been red, yellow, blue, or green—especially green? How did he discover that the Magi, or priests of the Zoroastrian religion, were really Buddhists and came from India? Had Sir Edwin less communication with the "sovereign voice," we should have imagined that the Magi were transformed into Buddhists for the sake of convenience; Sir Edwin knowing comparatively little of the Persic faith, but a good deal of the Indian, and possessing a natural itch to display his own learning. Further we should have asked him how he discovered that by three years after the Crucifixion the Christian faith had spread to Athens and Rome. According to all previous records the statement is simply preposterous. But the "sovereign voice" has spoken through Sir Edwin Arnold, and thrown quite a fresh light on the earliest history of Christianity. Then, again, we should have been curious to know why Sir Edwin accepted the legend of Mary Magdalene being the tenant of Magdal Tower, a place that never existed (as we thought) but in the geography of faith. Humanly speaking, it seemed probable that the lady's name had relation to head-dressing. But we live and learn, and in the course of time the "sovereign voice" settles all these things.

There is no clear record in the gospels of Jesus Christ's visit to Tyre, but Sir Edwin assures us he spent a few hours there—perhaps on an excursion—and we bow to the "sovereign voice." Nor is there a scholar in Christendom who regards the pretended letter from Publius Lentulus to the Roman Senate as anything but a puerile forgery. Yet Sir Edwin mentions it in a footnote, apparently with respect; indeed, he founds upon it his personal description of Jesus. Once again, scholarship must bow to the "sovereign voice." By the way, however, the Lentulus epistle describes the hair of Jesus as "wine-color." This is adopted by Sir Edwin, who construes is as "hazel," though—barring inspiration and the "sovereign voice"—it might have meant the color which is sometimes politely, if not accurately, called auburn. Anyhow, the ancients were acquainted with various colored wines, and it is satisfactory to know the precise hue intended by the gentleman who wrote the epistle of Lentulus.

Sir Edwin represents Jesus as a Nazarite. Now, the Nazarites eschewed scissors and razors, but Sir Edwin says they parted their hair in the middle, which is another tip from the "sovereign voice." Sir Edwin flashes his inspiration on another point. Critics are satisfied that the Emperor Julian, the last of the Pagans, did *not* cry, *Vicisti Galilae*! Mr. Swinburne, however, as a merely carnal poet, employed the legend in his splendid "Proserpina," using it with superb effect in the young Pagan's retort, "Thou hast conquered, O pale Galilean!—thy dead shall go down to thee dead." But now the "sovereign voice" speaks through Sir Edwin Arnold, and the legend must stand as history.

Under the guidance of the "sovereign voice" Sir Edwin is able to enlighten us on the physiology of angels. These creatures are usually painted with wings. But this is a mistake. They are wingless; for where these live there blows no wind, Nor aught spreads, gross as air, nor any kind Of substance, whereby spirits' march is stopped.

Sir Edwin knows all about them. Angels do not need wings, and have none, moving apparently *in vacuo*. But what havoc this truth would make in the picture galleries of Europe. Raphael himself was mistaken. He took angels to be a species of fowl, whereas they are—well, Sir Edwin does not tell us. He tells us what they are *not*. What they are is, as usual, left to the fancy of the reader, who pays his money and takes his choice. Only he must beware of *wings*.

Positively the most gratifying thing in Sir Edwin's book is this. Under the influence of the "sovereign voice" he is able to tell us how God Almighty likes to be designated. Perhaps it is better not to name him at all, but if we *must* name him—and it seems hard to refrain from some term or other—we should call him *Eloi*. That is what Jesus called him, and we see no reason why it should not become fashionable.

Sir Edwin Arnold's method of dishing up Jesus Christ is certainly artful. It does credit to his *Daily Telegraph* training. Everybody knows that one of the chief difficulties of novelists is to make their wonderful heroes act and talk. Sir Edwin does not jump this difficulty. He shirks it. He takes up the story of Jesus after his death, resurrection, and ascension. Three years are allowed to elapse, to give the risen Nazarene time to get clean away, and then Sir Edwin begins business. After a preliminary section, in, which the three Magi are brought upon the scene, the body of the poem opens with Mary Magdalene, who does nearly all the talking to the very end. Indeed the poem should have been called after her, for it is really "Mary Magdalene on Jesus Christ." The lady gives her reminiscences—that is, Sir Edwin gives them for her. By this method he is able to omit all mention of the cruder features of the Gospel story. When Jesus played the devil with the pigs, for instance, Mary Magdalene was absent, and the incident forms no part of her narrative. Apparently, too, she was absent, or deaf, or thinking of something else, when he preached hell-fire and "believe or be damned." And as this pretty method of Mary-Arnold selection is pursued throughout, it will easily be seen that the poem is an arbitrary piece of highly-colored fiction, in which Jesus Christ is made to serve the author's purposes. In short it is "Christ Up to Date."

Sir Edwin's second piece of strategy is still more transparent. Mary Magdalene is represented as several ladies rolled into one, and her house is a perfect museum of relics. She is Mary Magdalene, Mary of Bethany, the woman who anointed Christ's feet, and the Mary who helped to embalm him. She keeps the famous alabaster box in her cabinet; she boards and lodges the young woman that Jesus raised from the dead; and her brother Lazarus is also on show when required. Lazarus, too, is many single gentlemen rolled into one. He is the resurrected man, the young man who was told to sell his property and give the proceeds to the poor, and the young man who fled stark naked at the arrest of Jesus, leaving his clothes in the hands of his pursuers. This is a very convenient plan. It is history made easy, or the art of poetical bam-boozling.

Mary Magdalene has a long talk with Pontius Pilate, who is haunted by the memory of the pale Galilean. Afterwards she has several days' talk with an old Indian, who turns out to be the sole survivor of those three wise men from the East, come to find out all about the King of the Jews. His two colleagues had died without satisfying their curiosity. He himself did without news for thirty-six years, and only went back to Palestine after the King of the Jews had ended his career; the visit, of course, being timed to suit Sir Edwin Arnold's convenience.

Throughout the poem Mary Magdalene talks. Arnoldese. Here is a typical passage.

"It may be there shall come in after days—When this Good Spell is spread—some later scribes, Some far-off Pharisees, will take His law,—Written with Love's light fingers on the heart, Not stamped on stone 'mid glare of lightning-fork—Will take, and make its code incorporate; And from its grace write grim phylacteries To deck the head of dressed Authority; And from its golden mysteries forge keys To jingle in the belt of pious pride."

Can anyone imagine the seven-devilled Mary Magdalene conversing in this way?

Considered in the light of its title this poem is a mistake and a monstrous failure. It is also labored and full of "fine writing." Not only are the Gospel story and the teachings of Jesus played fast and loose with, but the simplest things are narrated in grandiose language, with a perfect glut of fanciful imagery, fetched in not to illustrate but to adorn. Here and there, however, the language of Jesus is paraphrased and damnably spoiled. What reader of the Gospes does not remember the exquisite English in which our translators have rendered the lament over Jerusalem? Sir Edwin parodies it as follows:—

How oft I would have gathered all thy children in As a hen clucks her chickens to her wings.

Surely this is perfectly ridiculous. The collecting and sheltering are put into the background by that dreadful "cluck," and the reader is forced to imagine Jesus as a clucking hen. On the whole, the Gospel writers were better artists than Sir Edwin Arnold.

To conclude. The poem contains plenty of "fine writing" and some good lines. But as a whole it is "neither fish, flesh, fowl, nor good red herring." As a picture of Jesus Christ it is a laborious absurdity; as a marketable volume it may be successful; and as a sample of Sir Edwin Arnold's powers and accomplishments it will perhaps impose on half-educated sentimentalists.

SECULARISM AND CHRISTIANITY

A Letter to the "Suffolk Chronicle," January 8, 1893.

Sir,—A friend has favored me with a copy of your last issue, containing a long report of the Rev. W. E. Blomfield's sermon at Turret Green Chapel, apparently in reply to my lecture on "Secularism superior to Christianity." Mr. Blomfield declines to meet me in set debate, on the ground that I am not "a *reverent* Freethinker," which is indeed true; but I observe that he does not really mind arguing with me, only he prefers to do it where I cannot answer him.

Mr. Blomfield finds the pulpit a safe place for what can hardly be called the courtesies of discussion. He refers to certain remarks of mine (I presume) as "petty jokes and witticisms fit only for the tap-room of a fourth-rate tavern." I will not dispute the description. I defer to Mr. Blomfield's superior knowledge of taverns and tap-rooms.

I notice Mr. Blomfield's great parade of "reverence." I notice also that he speaks of Freethought arguments or objections as "short-sighted folly" and "sheer nonsense." I judge, therefore, that "reverence" is not intended by Mr. Blomfield to be reciprocal. He claims a monopoly of it for his own opinions.

If he would only take the trouble to think about the matter, it might occur to him that "reverence" is not, properly speaking, a preliminary but a result. Let us have inquiry and discussion first and "reverence" afterwards. If I find anything to revere I shall not need Mr. Blomfield's admonitions. I revere truth, goodness, and heroism, though I cannot revere what I regard as false or absurd. "Reverence" is often the demand that imposture makes on honesty and superstition on intelligence. Long faces are highly valued by the professors of mystery.

Mr. Blomfield did not hear my lecture. Had he done so he would have found an answer to many of his questions. It is all very well to bid the Ipswich people to "Beware of false prophets," but it is better to hear before condemning.

How much attention, Mr. Blomfield asks, am I to give to this world and how much to another? Just as much as they deserve. We know a great deal about this world, and may learn more. There are plenty of guesses about another world, but no knowledge. It is easy to ask "Is there a future life?" but we must die to find out. Meanwhile this life confronts us, with its hard duties and legitimate pleasures. It is our wisdom to make the best of it, on the rational belief that, if there should be a future life—which no one is in a position to affirm or deny—this must be the best preparation for it, whether our future be decided by evolution or divine justice.

Mr. Blomfield's arguments against Utility as the test of conduct were answered in my lecture. He says the principle is of difficult application. So are all principles in intricate cases; why else have Christian divines written so many tons of casuistry? In any case the Utilitarian principle is the only one which is honored in practice. Other principles do very well on Sunday, but they are cast aside on Monday. The only question asked by statesmen, county councillors, School Board members, or other public representatives, is "Will the proposal tend to benefit the people?" This can be debated and settled. "Is it according to the will of God?" is a question to set people by the ears and raise an endless quarrel.

Mr. Blomfield says the fear of God saved poor Joseph, yet I dare say Potiphar's wife was a religious woman. The will of God sanctions many crimes. It tells the Thug to kill travellers; it told the Inquisition to torture and burn heretics; it told the Catholics and Protestants to rack and slaughter witches; it told Christians and Mohammedans to fight each other on hundreds of bloody battle-fields; it tells Christians now to keep up laws against liberty of thought. There never was a time when these things would not have been denounced by Secularism as crimes against humanity.

Motives to morality do not come from religion. They come from our social sympathies. Preach to a tiger and he will eat you. Differ from a Torquemada and he will burn you. When one man wants another to help him, he does not judge by the name of his sect, but by the glance of his eye and the lines of his mouth. Some men are born philanthropists, others are born criminals; between these are multitudes in whom good and bad tendencies are variously mixed, and who may be made better or worse by education and environment. The late Professor Clifford was an Atheist, and one of the gentlest, kindest, and tenderest men that ever lived. Jay Gould was a member of a Christian church and sometimes went round with the plate. He left twenty millions of money, and not a penny to any charity or good cause. Lick, the Freethinker, built and endowed the great observatory which is one of the glories of America.

I do not propose to follow Mr. Blomfield in his excursion into ancient history. I will only remark that if he thinks there was any lack of "religion" in the worst days of the Pagan world he is very much mistaken. Coming to more modern times, I decline to accept his present of priests and popes who were "atheistic." Whatever they were is a domestic question for the Christian Church. Nor need I discuss Luther's "fresh vision of God." He was a great man, but a savage controversialist, who called his opponents asses, swine, foxes, geese, and fools; which, I suppose, is worthy of the tap-room of a *first-rate* tavern. As to the "awful collapse" of "unbelieving France" I do not know when it occurred. It was certainly not France that collapsed in the Revolution. The monarchy, the aristocracy, and the Church collapsed; but France inaugurated a new epoch of modern history.

With respect to prayer, on which Mr. Blomfield is very hazy, I would like to discriminate between its "objective value" and its "subjective benefits." Prayer as a means of inducing patience when you do not get what you ask for, is outside my province. I leave it to the clergy. Prayer as a means of obtaining what you require is my concern, and I defy Mr. Blomfield to prove a single case. Yet if prayer is not answered objectively, the Secular principle holds the field that science is man's only providence. I am aware that Christians employ doctors, insure their houses, and put lightning-conductors over their church steeples. They leave as little to God as possible. Mr. Blomfield says this is quite right, and I agree with him; but I will give him, if he cannot find them, twenty texts in support of the honest old doctrine of prayer from the New Testament.

Mr. Blomfield tells me I do not understand the Bible. Well, as I am not exactly a fool, the fault may be in the book. Why was it not made plainer? Why did God write it so that thousands of gentlemen get a fine living by explaining it—in all sorts of different ways? I am reminded that the Bible is not a handbook of physical science. But did the Church think so when it imprisoned Galileo and made him swear that the earth did *not* go round the sun? Mr. Blomfield says that "Genesis gives an account of the origin of matter, and of life, and, finally, of man, which science has not disproved, on the admission of her most eminent sons." The Bible is a handbook of science after all then! But what has science to do with the origin of matter? The origin of life is still an open question. The origin of man is *not* an open question. Genesis gives us a piece of mythology; Darwin gave us the truth. Among the eminent sons of science who is greater than he? Yet he has utterly exploded the Adam and Eve story. Darwin has left it on record that he rejected all revelation, and that for nearly forty years of his life he was a disbeliever in Christianity. He did subscribe to a Missionary Society that was attempting to reform South American savages, but he never subscribed a penny for the propagation of Christianity in England. I myself might think Christianity good for savages.

If I understand Mr. Blomfield rightly, God was unable to teach the Jews any faster than he did, although he is both omnipotent and omniscient. Were I to imitate Mr. Blomfield I should call this "sheer nonsense."

In my lecture I stated that the Old Testament sanctioned slavery, and that there was not a word against it in the New Testament. Mr. Blomfield replies that "the principles of the New Testament sapped the foundations of that system." But let us deal with one question at a time. Let the reverend gentleman indicate the text which I say does not exist. As for the "generous spirit" of the Old Testament laws about slavery, am I to find it in the texts allowing the Jews to buy and sell the heathen, to enslave their own countrymen, to appropriate their children born in slavery, and to beat them to death providing they did not expire within forty-eight hours?

My point is not that the Jews held slaves. That was common in ancient times. I merely take objection to the doctrine that God laid down the slavery laws of the Old Testament.

With regard to Jesus Christ, I am not aware that I have spoken of him as a "trickster." Kenan, however, whom Mr. Blomfield appears to admire, suggests that the raising of Lazarus was a performance arranged between him and Jesus. This is a line of criticism I have never attempted. I do not regard the New Testament miracles as actual occurrences, but as the products of Christian imagination.

Mr. Blomfield is angry with me for saying that the books of the Bible are mostly anonymous, yet he declares that "their anonymity is little against them." I leave Mr. Blomfield to settle the point of fact with Christian writers like Canon Driver and Professor Bruce. With respect to the New Testament, I am told that my statement is "palpably incorrect." But what are the facts? With the exception of four of Paul's epistles, and perhaps the first of Peter, the whole of the New Testament books are anonymous, in the sense that they were not written—as we have them—by the men whose names they bear, and that no one knows who *did* write them. This is practically admitted by Christian scholars, and I am ready to maintain it in discussion with Mr. Blomfield.

Mr. Blomfield talks very freely, in conclusion, about the "fruits" of Christianity and Secularism. He even condescends to personal comparisons, which I warn him are dangerous. He compares Spurgeon with Bradlaugh. Well, the one swam with the stream, and the other against it; the one lived in the world's smile, the other in the world's frown; the one enjoyed every comfort and many luxuries, the other was poor, worried, and harassed into his grave. Spurgeon was no doubt a good man, but Bradlaugh was the more heroic figure.

Jesus Christ said some good things. Among them was the injunction not to let one hand know the other's charity. Mr. Blomfield disregards this. He challenges Secularists to a comparison. He asks where are our Secularist hospitals. We do not believe in such things. Sectarianism in charity is a Christian vice. On the other hand, our party is comparatively small and poor, and Christian laws prevent our holding any trusts for Secularism. Still, we do attend to our own poor as well as we can. Our Benevolent Fund is sufficient for the relief of those who apply in distress. We cannot build "almshouses," but "Atheist widows" are not neglected. On the whole, however, we are not so loud as the Christians in praise of "charity," Much of it is very degrading. If we had justice in society there would be less for "charity" to do.

It is obvious that Mr. Blomfield picks his fruits of Christianity with great discrimination. Is it logical to select all you admire in Christian countries and attribute it to Christianity? The same process would prove the excellence of Buddhism, Brahminism, and Mohammedanism. There are almshouses and hospitals in Chrisendom, but there are also workhouses, gin-palaces, brothels, and prisons. Drunkenness, prostitution, and gambling, are the special vices of Christian nations. It is Christian countries that build ironclads and make cannon, gatling guns, deadly rifles, and terrible explosives. It is Christians who do most of the fighting on this planet.

Mr. Blomfield may or may not consider these things. I scarcely expect him to reply. He prefers the "humble, obedient heart" to the "curious intellect." At any rate he preaches the preference to the young men of Ipswich. For my part, I hope they will reject the counsel. I trust they will read, inquire, and think for themselves. Their "intellect" should have enough "curiosity" to be satisfied as to the truth of what they are asked to believe.

ALTAR AND THRONE *

* *June 11, 1893.*

Myriads of honest, industrious women in England are laboring excessively for a bare pittance; day after day they go through the same monotonous and exhausting round of toil; and the end of it all is a bit of bread for some who are dear to them, and a squalid, cheerless existence for themselves. Sometimes, when work is scarce, and sheer starvation confronts them, they are driven to the last resource of selling their bodies, and enter the unspeakable inferno of prostitution.

England has thousands of other women who are lapped in an enervating and degrading luxury—without occupation, with none but frivolous cares—who fancy themselves infinitely superior to their poor, slaving, ill-dressed, and toilworn sisters.

These disparities are as great as any that existed in the "infamous" days of pagan Rome. The world has had eighteen hundred years of Christianity, and its "salvation" is still in the dim and distant future.

While the clergy have preached a hell after death, the people have been left simmering in a real hell in this life—the hell of ignorance, poverty, oppression, and misery.

Christianity is now boasting of what it is *going* to do. It says it begins to understand Jesus Christ; it means to follows in its Master's footsteps; it will strain every nerve to raise the downtrodden, to better the condition of the poor, and to give true comfort to the afflicted. There are some individual Christians who mean this and try to practise it. But for the most part these fine new promises of Christianity are nothing but sermon decorations, words for deeds, sawdust for bread, flash notes for good coin of the realm.

We have but to look around us at this moment to see the true fruits of Christianity. It is the same fruit that *all* religion bears. Under the pretence of being the best friend of the people, Christianity (like other religions) has been the real friend of the privileged classes. It has also fostered a public sentiment in this direction. To prove this let us take a case in point.

Some time ago an English princess lost her lover by death. She was said to be inconsolable. But before long it was whispered that she was to marry her lover's brother. At length it was announced in the papers, only to be contradicted as a false rumor which very much hurt the feelings of all the parties it concerned. Those who understood the nature of such contradictions smiled. By and bye the contradicted rumor was announced authoritatively. Princess May *was* to marry the gentleman in question. "Now is the winter of our discontent made glorious summer by this sun of York."

All England was soon astir with loyal enthusiasm, and people were everywhere set subscribing for presents to the dear Princess. Soldiers and sailors are sweated. Pressure is put upon theatrical people. "You *must* give *something,*" is the cry. The City of London is to spend £2,500 on a necklace. One lady gives the royal couple a splendid country house with magnificent grounds. Committees are formed right and left, and tens of thousands of pounds will be raised, on the ground that "unto him that hath shall be given"—in some cases, also, without neglecting the rest of the text, that "from him that hath not shall be taken away even that which he hath."

Who is the Princess May? Very likely a pleasant young lady. Happily there are myriads of them in England. What has she ever done? She took the trouble to be born. Her husband that is to be has an income from "the service." His father has £36,000 a year, voted by Parliament, for the express purpose of providing for his children—in addition to his big income from other sources. All things considered, it does not seem that Princess May and the Duke of York are in want of anything. But how many other women—to say nothing of men—*are* in want! Is not this lavish generosity to a pair of royal and well-provided lovers an insult to the working people of England? Is it not a special insult to the multitude of poor, struggling women, whose earnings are taxed to support the classes who lord it over them? It may, of course, be replied that poor women like the idea of all these presents to the Princess. Perhaps they do. But that only makes it worse. It shows their training has corrupted them. The last vice of a slave is to admire his oppressor.

Christianity is satisfied with this state of things. Christian ministers will wink at it, when they do not bless it and approve it with a text. The Archbishop of Canterbury will officiate at the royal wedding, and deliver one of those courtier-like homilies which may be expected from one who takes £15,000 a year to preach the blessings of poverty and the damnable nature of wealth. This is what comes of eighteen hundred years of the "poor Carpenter's" religion. His texts of renunciation are idle verbiage. His name is used to bamboozle the people, to despoil them, and to make them patient asses under their burdens.

Religion and privilege go together. What does the New Testament say? "Fear God and honor the king." Fearing God means supporting the clergy. Honoring the king means keeping one family in foolish luxury, as a symbol of the whole system of privilege which is maintained by the systematic exploitation of the people. We are crucified between two thieves who mock us, but do not share our cross; the spiritual thief, who robs us of our birthright of mental freedom, and the temporal thief, who robs us of the fruit of our labor. *Arcades ambo.*

Some people will think we have written too plainly. We beg to tell them that we have had to practise self-restraint. The fat would be in the fire with a vengeance if we gave free expression to our disgust. The only hope for the future of society lies in the absolute extermination of Christianity. That is the superstition which fools and degrades Europe, and we must fight it to the death.

MARTIN LUTHER

Reformation Day, as it is called, was celebrated on October 31 throughout the Protestant part of Germany. Three hundred and seventy-five years have rolled by since Martin Luther broke from the Roman Catholic Church. Emperor William went to Wittenberg, with a great array of Evangelical personages; and, as usual, the Emperor made a speech, which for him was excellent. "There is no coercion," he said, "in matters of religion. Here only free conviction of the heart is decisive, and the perception of this fact is the blissful fruit of the Reformation."

This is a fine-sounding declaration, but it has the misfortune to be untrue. Liberty of conscience is not the fruit of the Reformation, but an indirect and unintended result. Nor is liberty of conscience a reality in any part of the German empire. Christians are allowed to differ among themselves, but Freethinkers are prosecuted for dissenting alike from Catholic and Protestant. Since the present Emperor's accession there have been many blasphemy prosecutions, sometimes for what would be regarded in other countries as very mild expressions of disbelief. Several men and women have been sentenced to severe penalties for exercising the right of free speech, which, in the land of Goethe, Heine, Strauss, and Schopenhauer, is still confined to professed Christians.

The Reformation, in fact, was a superficial movement. Except for its moral revolt against the sale of indulgences, it touched no deep and durable principle. It merely substituted an infallible Bible for an infallible Church. Differences of opinion crept into the Protestant fold, but that was an accident, arising from the varied and discordant nature of the Bible itself. Every new Protestant sect had to fight as strenuously for its right to exist as ever Martin Luther fought against the Catholic Church. Protestantism, in short, was one priesthood saying to another priesthood "We are right and you are wrong." The Catholic Church had an immense advantage in its central organisation; the Protestant Church could only operate from different points; hence it was unable to bring about the same uniformity.

The movement that was not superficial was the scientific and humanist movement, of which the Reformation was in a certain sense an episode. Italy and France did more for the world than Germany. Martin Luther was a great fighter, but not a more heroic one than Giordano Bruno. Melancthon was not so important a man as Galileo. Rabelais even, with all his dirt and jesting, was more in the stream of progress than Luther, and far more than Calvin. In the long run, it is knowledge and idea? that rule the world. Luther was not great in knowledge, and certainly not great in ideas. He was a born fighter and a strong character. His proper place is among the heroic figures of history. He was a man of leading, but scarcely a man of light.

Luther was violently opposed to the scientific movement. He called Copernicus an old fool. He would hear nothing against the accepted Biblical theory of the universe. Genesis was to him, as well as to the Pope, the beginning and the end of sound science. Nor was he more friendly to philosophy. Draper truly asserts that the leaders of the Reformation "were determined to banish philosophy from the Church." Aristotle was villified by Luther as "truly a devil, a horrid calumniator, a wicked sycophant, a prince of darkness, a real Apollyon, a beast, a most horrid impostor on mankind, a public and professed liar, a goat, a complete epicure, this twice execrable Aristotle." Such was Luther's style in controversy. We commend it to the attention of Protestants who rail at the *Freethinker*.

Liberty of conscience is a principle of which Luther had no conception. He claimed the right to think against the Pope; he denied the right of others to think against himself. His attitude towards the Anabaptists was fiendish. During the Peasants War he urged the authorities to exterminate the rebels, to "stab, kill, and strangle them without mercy." Melancthon taught that heretics "ought to be restrained by the sword." Luther likewise declared that whoever denied even one article of the Protestant faith should be punished severely. Referring to a false teacher, he exclaimed, "Drive him away as an apostle of hell; and if he does not flee, deliver him up as a seditious man to the executioner."

Hallam, Buckle, Lecky, and all reputable historians, agree that the Protestant party held the same principle of persecution as the Catholics. It was not disputed that death was the proper punishment of obstinate heresy. The only dispute was—which were the heretics, and who should die?

Luther's influence was very great in England, as Calvin's was in Scotland, and the leaders of the Reformation in our own country had no doubt as to the justice of killing men for a difference of opinion. Cranmer taught that heretics were first to be excommunicated; if that made no impression on them they were to suffer death. It satisfies one sense of the fitness of things that Cranmer himself perished at the stake. Becon taught that the duty of magistrates with regard to heretics was to punish them— "yea, and also to take them out of this life." This same Becon called upon the temporal rulers to "be no longer the pope's hangmen." He preferred their being the hangmen of Protestantism. Latimer himself said of the Anabaptists who were executed, "Well, let them go!" Bishop Jewel, the great apologist of the Protestant Church of England, in answering Harding the Jesuit, replies in this way to the charge of being of the brotherhood of Servetus, David George, and Joan of Kent: "We detected their heresies, and not you. We arraigned them; we condemned them. We put them to the execution of the laws. It seemeth very much to call them our brothers, because we burnt them."

Calvin held the same persecuting doctrine. All who opposed him were dealt with ruthlessly. He was a veritable Pope of Geneva. His treatment of Servetus was infamous. But so universal was the principle on which Calvin acted, that even the mild Melancthon called the cruel roasting of Servetus at a slow fire "a pious and memorable example for all posterity."

Protestantism boasts of having asserted the right of private judgment. It never did anything of the kind. Not a single leader of the Reformation ever asserted such a principle. Erasmus did, though not in decisive language; but Erasmus never belonged to the Protestant Church, and his humanity, no less than his philosophy, brought upon him the vituperation of Luther. The hero of Protestantism did not intend the consequences of his revolt against Rome. He would have been appalled at the thought of them. He made a breach, for his own purposes, in the great wall of faith. He did not anticipate that others would widen it, or that the forces of reason would march through and occupy post after post. He simply did his own stroke of work, and we do not judge him by later standards. We only object to the extravagance of Protestant laudation.

THE PRAISE OF FOLLY

What is the greatest novel in the English language? This is a hard question, which we shall not attempt to answer. We leave every one of our readers to enjoy his own selection. But the question has been answered, in his own way, by a living novelist. Mr. Walter Besant declares that the greatest novel in the English language is Charles Reade's *The Cloister and the Hearth*. That it is a *great* book no one fit to judge will deny, or hesitate to affirm. It is full of adventure and hairbreadth escapes; it exhibits a large variety of life and character; its wit, insight, and pathos show the mind and hand of a master; and a certain vivid actuality is derived from the fact that its pictures and portraits are to a large extent historical. Gerard and Margaret, the hero and heroine of the story, are the father and mother of the great Erasmus; respecting whom Charles Reade closes his book with a noble and pregnant piece of writing.

"First scholar and divine of his epoch, he was also the heaven-born dramatist of his century. Some of the best scenes in this new book are from his mediaeval pen, and illumine the pages whence they come; for the words of a genius, so high as his, are not born to die; their immediate work upon mankind fulfilled, they may seem to lie torpid; but, at each fresh shower of intelligence Time pours upon their students, they prove their immortal .race; they revive, they spring from the dust of great libraries; they bud, they flower, they fruit, they seed, from generation to generation, and from age to age."

Erasmus was born at Rotterdam, probably on October 28, 1467. He was a "love child." His father, Gerard of Tergou, being engaged to Margaret, daughter of a physician of Sevenbergen, anticipated the nuptial rites. Gerard's relations drove him from his country by ill usage; when he went to Rome, to earn a living by copying ancient authors, they falsely sent him word that his Margaret had died; upon which he took holy orders, and became a sworn son of the Church. Finding his Margaret alive on his return, he of course lived apart from her, and she did not marry another. They had a common interest in their boy, whose education they superintended. Margaret died of the plague, when Erasmus was thirteen; and Gerard, inconsolable for her loss, soon followed her to the grave. Their boy was left to the guardianship of relatives, who cheated him of his little patrimony, and compelled him to adopt a religious life. Erasmus was thus a priest, though a very uncommon one. How curious that so many great wits and humorists should have worn the clerical garb! To mention only four, there were Rabelais, Erasmus, Swift and Sterne; each of whom has added to the world's gaiety, and also helped to free it from superstition. Christians who prate about the "ridicule" of holy things in which Freethinkers indulge, should be reminded that these four priests of the Christian religion could easily, between them, carry off the palm for profanity; while for downright plain speech, not always avoiding the nastiest of subjects, there is hardly a professed sceptic who could hold a candle to them.

Erasmus divorced himself from religious duties as early as possible. He detested the monks, regarding them for the most part as illiterate, bigoted, persecuting, and parasitical vermin. His life was devoted to literature, and in the course of his travels he contracted a friendship with the most eminent and able men of the age, including our own Sir Thomas More, the author of the famous *Utopia*. Erasmus died on July 12,1536. The money he had accumulated by the exercise of his pen, after deducting some handsome legacies to personal friends, he left to relieve the sick and poor, to marry young women, and to assist young men of good character. This was in keeping with his professed principles. He always regarded *charity* as the chief part of *useful* religion, and thought that men should help each other like brothers, instead of fighting like wild beasts over theology.

Erasmus was a contemporary of Luther, and there is an excellent Essay by Mr. Froude on both these great men. He gives the palm to Luther on account of his courage, and thinks that Erasmus should have joined the Reformation party. But the truth is that Erasmus had far more *intellect* than Luther; he knew too much to be a fanatic; and while he lashed the vices and follies of the Catholic Church, he never left her fold, partly because he perceived that Luther and the Reformers were as much the slaves of exclusive dogmas as the very Schoolmen themselves. Erasmus believed in freedom of thought, but Luther never did. To sum up the difference between them in a sentence: Luther was a Theologian, and Erasmus a Humanist. "He was brilliantly gifted," says Mr. Froude, "his industry never tired, his intellect was true to itself, and no worldly motives ever tempted him into insincerity."

The great mass of the writings of Erasmus are only of interest to scholars. His two popular books are the *Colloquies* and the *Praise of Folly*, both written in Latin, but translated into most of the European tongues. The *Colloquies* were rendered into fine, nervous English by N. Bailey, the old lexicographer. The *Praise of Folly*, illustrated with Holbein's drawings, is also to be read in English, in the translation of Sir Roger L'Estrange; a writer who, if he was sometimes coarse and slangy, had a first-rate command of our language, and was never lacking in racy vigor.

Erasmus wrote the *Praise of Folly* in the house of Sir Thomas More, with whom he lodged on his arrival in England in 1510. It was completed in a week, and written to divert himself and his friend. A copy being sent to France, it was printed there, and in a few months it went through seven editions. Its contents were such, that it is no wonder, in the words of Jortin, that "he was never after this looked upon as a true son of the Church." In the orthodox sense of the term, it would be difficult to look upon the writer of this book as a true Christian.

Folly is made to speak throughout. She pronounces her own panegyric She represents herself as the mainspring of all the business and pleasure of this world, yes, and also of its worship and devotion. Mixed up with capital fooling, there is an abundance of wisdom, and shrewd thrusts are delivered at every species of imposture; nay, religion itself is treated with derision, under the pretence of buffoonery.

Long before Luther began his campaign against the sale of Pardons and Indulgences, they were satirically denounced by Erasmus. He calls them "cheats," for the advantage of the clergy, who promise their dupes in return for their cash a lot of happiness in the next life; though, as to their own share of this happiness, the clergy "care not how long it be deferred." Erasmus anticipated Luther in another point. Speaking of the subtle interpreters of the Bible in his day, who proved from it anything and everything, he says that, "They can deal with any text of scripture as with a nose of wax, and knead it into what shape best suits their interest." Quite as decisively as Luther, though with less passion and scurrility, he condemns the adoration of saints, which he calls a "downright folly." Amidst a comical account of the prayers offered up to their saintships, he mentions the tokens of gratitude to them hung upon the walls and ceilings of churches; and adds, very shrewdly, that he could find "no relics presented as a memorandum of any that were ever cured of Folly, or had been made one dram the wiser." Even the worship of the Virgin Mary is glanced at—her blind devotees being said "to think it manners now to place the mother before the Son."

Erasmus calls the monks "a sort of brainsick fools," who "seem confident of becoming greater proficients in divine mysteries the less they are poisoned with any human learning." Monks, as the name denotes, should live solitary; but they swarm in streets and alleys, and make a profitable trade of beggary, to the detriment of the roadside mendicants. They are full of vice and religious punctilios. Some of them will not touch a piece of money, but they "make no scruple of the sin of drunkenness and the lust of the flesh."

Preachers are satirised likewise. They are little else than stage-players. "Good Lord! how mimical are their gestures! What heights and falls in their voice! What teeming, what bawling, what singing, what squeaking, what grimaces, making of mouths, apes' faces, and distorting of their countenance; and this art of oratory, as a choice mystery, they convey down by tradition to one another." Yes, and the trick of it still lives in our Christian pulpits.

"Good old tun-bellied divines," and others of the species, come in for their share of raillery. They know that ignorance is the mother of devotion. They are great disputants, and all the logic in the world will never drive them into a corner from which they cannot escape by some "easy distinction." They discuss the absurdest and most far-fetched questions, have cats' eyes that see best in the dark, and possess "such a piercing faculty as to see through an inch-board, and spy out what really never had any being." The apostles would not be able to understand their disputes without a special illumination. In a happy phrase, they are said to spend their time in striking "the fire of subtlety out of the flint of obscurity." But woe to the man who meddles with them; for they are generally very hot and passionate. If you differ from them ever so little, they call upon you to recant; it you refuse to do so, they will brand you as a heretic and "thunder out an excommunication."

Popes fare as badly as preachers, monks, and divines. They "pretend themselves vicars of Christ." Reference is made to their "grooms, ostlers, serving men, pimps, and somewhat else which for modesty's sake I shall not mention." They fight with a holy zeal to defend their possessions, and issue their bulls and excommunications most frequently against "those who, at the instigation of the Devil, and not having the fear of God before their eyes, do feloniously and maliciously attempt to lessen and impair St. Peter's patrimony."

Speaking through the mouth of Folly, the biting wit of Erasmus does not spare Christianity itself. "Fools," he says, "for their plainness and sincerity of heart, have always been most acceptable to God Almighty." Princes have ever been jealous of subjects who were too observant and thoughtful; and Jesus Christ, in like manner, condemns the wise and crafty. He solemnly thanks his Father for hiding the mysteries of salvation from the wise, and revealing them to babes; that is, says Erasmus, *to fools*. "Woe unto you scribes and pharisees" means "Woe unto you wise men."

Jesus seemed "chiefly delighted with women, children, and illiterate fishermen." The blessed souls that in the day of judgment are to be placed on the Savior's right hand "are called sheep, which are the most senseless and stupid of all cattle."

"Nor would he heal those breaches our sins had made by any other method than by the 'foolishness of the cross,' published by the ignorant and unlearned apostles, to whom he frequently recommends the excellence of Folly, cautioning them against the infectiousness of wisdom, by the several examples he proposes them to imitate, such as children, lilies, sparrows, mustard, and such like beings, which are either wholly inanimate, or at least devoid of reason and ingenuity, guided by no other conduct than that of instinct, without care, trouble, or contrivance."

"The Christian religion," Erasmus says, "seems to have some relations to Folly, and no alliance at all to wisdom." In proof of which we are to observe; *first*, that "children, women, old men, and fools, led as it were by a secret impulse of nature, are always most constant in repairing to church, and most zealous, devout and attentive in the performance of the several parts of divine service "; *secondly*, that true Christians invite affronts by an easy forgiveness of injuries, suffer themselves like doves to be easily cheated and imposed upon, love their enemies as much as their friends, banish pleasure and court sorrow, and wish themselves out of this world altogether. Nay, the very happiness they look forward to hereafter is "no better than a sort of madness or folly." For those who macerate the body, and long to put on immortality, are only in a kind of dream.

"They speak many things at an abrupt and incoherent rate, as if they were actuated by some possessing demon; they make an inarticulate noise, without any distinguishable sense or meaning. They sometimes screw and distort their faces to uncouth and antic looks; at one time beyond measure cheerful, then as immoderately sullen; now sobbing, then laughing, and soon after sighing, as if they were perfectly distracted, and out of their senses."

But perhaps the worst stroke of all against Christianity is the following sly one. Folly is said to be acceptable, or at least excusable, to the gods, who "easily pass by the heedless failures of fools, while the miscarriages of such as are known to have more wit shall very hardly obtain a pardon."

Did space permit we might give several extracts from the *Praise of Folly*, showing that Erasmus could speed the shafts of his satire at the very essentials of religion, such as prayer and providence. Were he living now, we may be sure that he would be in the van of the Army of Liberation. Living when he did, he performed a high and useful task. His keen, bright sword played havoc with much superstition and imposture. He made it more difficult for the pious wranglers over what Carlyle would call "inconceivable incredibilities" to practise their holy profession. Certainly he earned, and more than earned, the praise of Pope.

> At length Erasmus, that great injur'd name
>
> (The glory of the priesthood and the shame!)
>
> Stemm'd the wild torrent of a barbarous age,
>
> And drove those holy Vandals off the stage.

Erasmus was, in fact, the precursor of Voltaire. Physically, as well as intellectually, these two great men bore a certain resemblance. A glance at the strong, shrewd face of Erasmus is enough to show that he was not a man to be easily imposed upon; and the square chin, and firm mouth, bespeak a determination, which, if it did not run to martyrdom, was sufficient to carry its possessor through hardship and difficulty in the advocacy of his ideals.

Rome, says, the proverb, was not built in a day; and Christianity was not built in a century. It took hundreds of years to complete, as it is taking hundreds of years to dissolve. For this reason it is a very complicated structure. There is something in it for all sorts of taste. Those who like metaphysics will find it in Paul's epistles, and in such dogmas as that of the Trinity. Those who like a stern creed will find it in the texts that formed the basis of Calvinism. And those who like something milder will find it in such texts as "Love one another" and "Father forgive them, they know not what they do."

It must be confessed, however, that the terrible aspects of Christianity have been most in evidence. Religion had its first roots in ignorance and terror, and it must continue to derive sustenance from them or perish. People were never allured by the simple prospect of heaven; they were frightened by the awful prospect of hell. Of course the two things were always more or less mixed. The recipe was brimstone and treacle, but the brimstone predominated, and was the more operative ingredient.

Present-day sermons tell us chiefly of God's goodness; older sermons tell us chiefly of what is called his justice. Puritan discourses, of the seventeenth century, were largely occupied in telling people that most of them *would* be damned, and explaining to them how just and logical it was that they *should* be damned. It was a sort of treatment they should really be thankful for; and, instead of protesting against it, they should take it with folded hands and grateful submission.

How many preachers have depicted the torments of the damned! How many have described the fate of lost souls! They positively delighted in the task, as corrupted organs of smell will sometimes delight in abominable stenches. Even the average Christian has regarded damnation—especially the damnation of other people—with remarkable complacency, as a part of the established economy of the universe. But now and then a superior spirit revolted against it instinctively. Thus we hear of Gregory the Great, in an age when it was devoutly believed that the noblest Pagans were all in hell, being deeply impressed with the splendid virtues of the emperor Trajan, and begging for his release; a prayer which (the legend says) was granted, with a caveat that it should never be repeated. Thus, also, we hear of the great Aquinas kneeling all night on the stone floor of his cell, passionately beseeching God to save the Devil.

This revolt against eternal damnation has mightily increased. Civilised men and women will not—positively *will* not—be damned at the old rate. The clergy are obliged to accommodate their preaching to the altered circumstances; hence we hear of "Eternal Hope," and "Ultimate Salvation," and similar brands on the new bottles in which they seek to pour the diluted old wine of theology.

Archdeacon Farrar is the type of this new school—at least in the Church of England. He is a wealthy pluralist; in addition to which he earns a large income as a writer of sentimental books, that immensely tickle the flabby souls of "respectable" Christians. Not quite illiterate, yet nowise thoughtful, these people are semi-orthodox and temporising. They take the old creed with a faint dash of heresy. Hell, at any rate, they like to see cooled a bit, or at least shortened; and Archdeacon Farrar satisfies them with a Hell which is not everlasting, but only eternal. We believe that Dr. Farrar expressed a faint hope that Charles Bradlaugh had not gone to hell. It was just possible that he might get a gallery seat in the place where the Archdeacon is booked for a stall. Dr. Farrar is not sure that all the people who were thought to go to hell really go there. He entertains a mild doubt upon the subject. Nor does he believe that hell is simply punitive. He thinks it is purgative. After a billion years or so the ladies and gentlemen in the pit may hope to be promoted to the upper circles. Some of them, however, who are desperate and impenitent, and perfectly impervious to the sulphur treatment, will have to remain in hell forever. The door will be closed upon them as incorrigible and irredeemable; and the saints in heaven will go on singing, and harping, and jigging, regardlesss of these obstinate wretches, these ultimate failures, these lost souls, these everlasting inheritors of perdition.

Humanity is growing day by day. So is common sense. Every decently educated person will soon insist on the abolition of hell. The idea of a lost soul will not be tolerated.

A theologian of painful genius (in its way) imagined a lost soul in hell. He had been agonising for ages. At last he asked a gaoler "What hour is it?" and the answer came "Eternity!"

Thoughtful, sensitive men and women, in ever increasing number, loathe such teaching, and turn with disgust from those who offer it to their fellows.

We are not aware that men have souls, but if they have, why should any soul be *lost*? We are not aware that there is a God, but if there is, why should he *let* any soul be lost? Sending souls to hell at all is only punishing his own failures. If he is omnipotent he could have made them as he pleased, and if they do not please him it is not their fault, but his own. Let it be distinctly understood that a creator has no right over his creatures; it is the creatures who have a right to the best assistance of their creator. The contrary doctrine comes down to us from the "good old times" when children had no rights, and parents had absolute power of life and death over them.

In the same way, God had absolute power over his creatures; he was the potter and they were the clay; one vessel was made for honor, and one for dishonor; one for heaven, and one for hell. But civilisation has changed our conceptions. We regard the parent as responsible for the child, and God is responsible for the welfare of his creatures. A single "lost soul" would prove the malignity or imbecility of "our father which art in heaven."

HAPPY IN HELL

Professor St. George Mivart is a very useful man to the Jesuits. He plays the jackal to their lion; or, it might be said, the cat to their monkey. Some time ago he argued that Catholicism and Darwinism were in the happiest agreement; that the Catholic Church was not committed, like the Protestant Church, to a cast-iron theory of Inspiration; and that he was quite prepared to find that all the real Word of God in the Bible might be printed in a very small book and easily carried in a waistcoat pocket. That article appeared in the *Nineteenth Century*. In the current number of the same review Mr. Mivart has another theological article on "Happiness in Hell." He says he took advice before writing it, so he speaks with permission, if not with authority. Such an article, being a kind of feeler, was better as the work of a layman. If it did not answer, the Church was not committed; if it did answer, the Church's professional penmen could follow it up with something more decisive.

Professor Mivart perceives, like the Bishop of Chester, that Christianity *must* alter its teaching with respect to Hell, or lose its hold on the educated, the thoughtful, and the humane. "Not a few persons," he says, "have abandoned Christianity on account of this dogma." The "more highly evolved moral perceptions" of to-day are "shocked beyond expression at the doctrine that countless multitudes of mankind will burn for ever in hell fire, out of which there is no possible redemption." Father Pinamonti's *Hell Open to Christians* is stigmatised as "repulsive," and its pictures as "revolting." Yet it is issued "with authority," and Mr. Mivart falls short of the truth in admitting it has never "incurred any condemnation." This little fact seems a barrier to his attempt at proving that the Catholic Church is not committed to the doctrine of a hell of real fire and everlasting agony.

"Abandon all hope, ye who enter here" wrote Dante over his Inferno, and Mr. Mivart allows that "the words truly express what was the almost universal belief of Christians for many centuries." That belief flourished under the wing of an infallible Church; and now Mr. Mivart, a member of this same infallible Church, comes forward to declare that the belief was a mistake. Nevertheless, he argues, the clergy of former times did right to preach hell hot and strong, stuff it with fire, and keep it burning for ever. They had coarse and ignorant people to deal with, and were obliged to use realistic language. Besides, it was necessary to exaggerate, in order to bring out the infinite contrast between heaven and hell, the elect and the reprobates, the saved and the damned. Mr. Mivart maintains, therefore, that the old representation of hell "has not caused the least practical error or misled anyone by one jot or tittle"—which is as bold, or, as some would say, as impudent a statement as could be well conceived.

Briefly stated, Mr. Mivart's contention is that the fire of hell is figurative. The pains of damnation, even in the case of the worst of sinners, have not been liberally described by Popes and Councils. "What is meant by the expression 'hell fire' has never been defined," says Mr. Mivart. Perhaps not. There are some things which, for practical purposes, do not need definition, and *fire* is one of them. Nor is it greatly to the purpose to say that "Saint Augustine distinctly declares our ignorance about it." Saint Augustine was not God Almighty. Ample set-offs to this Father may be found in the pages of Dr. Pusey's *What is of Faith as to Everlasting Punishment?* Besides, if fire does not mean fire, if torment does not mean torment, and everlasting does not mean everlasting, perhaps hell does not mean hell; in which case, it is a waste of time to argue about details, when the whole establishment, to use a Shakespearian epithet, is simply "tropical."

"Some positive suffering," thinks Mr. Mivart, "will never cease for those who have voluntarily and deliberately cast away from them their supreme beatitude." Do you want to know what this positive suffering is? Well, wait till you get there. All in good time. Whatever it is, the "unbelievers" will get *their* share of it. The editor of the *Freethinker* may look out for a double dose. Professor Huxley will not escape. He is an aggressive Agnostic; one of those persons who, in the graceful language of Mivartian civility, do not "possess even a rudiment of humility or aspiration after goodness." "Surely," exclaims our new Guide to Hell, "surely if there is a sin which, on merely Theistic principles, merits the severest pains of hell, it is the authorship of an irreligious book." Which leads *us* in turn to exclaim, "Surely, yea thrice surely, will hell never be wholly abolished or deprived of its last torture-chamber, while Christians require a painful place for those who boldly differ from them." Mr. Mivart, it is true, confesses that "those who are disturbed and distressed by difficulties about hell include many among the best of mankind." But they must not write irreligious books on the subject. They must wait, in patience and meekness, until Mr. Mivart gives them satisfaction.

Let us now summarise Mr. Mivart's position. Uni-versalism, or the final restitution of all men, he rejects as "utterly irreconcilable with Catholic doctrine." Those who are saved go to heaven—after various delays in purgatory—and enjoy the Beatific Vision for ever. Those who are lost go to hell and remain there for all eternity. They lose the Beatific Vision, and that is their chief punishment. But hell is not a really dreadful place—except, of course, for the writers of irreligious books. It may have its equator, and perhaps its poles; but between them are vast regions of temperate clime and grateful soil. The inhabitants are in a kind of harmony with their environment. They are even under a law of evolution, and "the existence of the damned is one of progress and gradual amelioration." We suppose it may be said, in the words of Napoleon, that the road is open to talent; and enterprising "damned ones" may cry with truth—"Better to reign in hell than serve in heaven."

Hell must be regarded as a most desirable place. Mr. Mivart knows all about it, and we have his authority for saying it is "an abode of happiness transcending all our most vivid anticipations, so that man's natural capacity for happiness is there gratified to the very utmost." And this is hell! Well, as the old lady said, who would have thought it? Verily the brimstone has all turned to treacle.

Curious! is it not? While the Protestants are discussing whether hell-fire is actual fire, and whether sinners are roasted for everlasting, or only for eternity, in steps a Catholic and declares that hell is a first-class sanitarium, far superior to the east-end of London, better than Bournemouth, and ahead of Naples and Mentone. "Be happy in heaven," he cries, "and if you won't, why, damn you, be happy in hell."

But before we leave Mr. Mivart we have a parting word to say. He admits the comparative novelty of his view of hell. "Our age," he says, "has developed not only a great regard for human life, but also for the sufferings of the brute creation." This has led to a moral revolt against the old doctrine of eternal torment, and the Church is under the necessity of presenting the idea of hell in a fresh and less revolting fashion. Precisely so. It is not theology which purifies humanity, but humanity which purifies theology. Man civilises himself first, and his gods afterwards, and the priest walks at the tail of the procession.*

> * *Professor Mivart is a man to be pitied. First of all, his views on Hell were opposed by Father Clarke, against whom the hell-reformer defended himself. Last of all, however, Professor Mivart's articles on this subject were placed upon the Index of Prohibited Books, which no good Catholic is*

allowed to read, except by special permission. Rome had spoken, and the Professor submitted himself to Holy Mother Church. In doing so, he destroyed the value of his judgment on any question whatever, since he submits not to argument, but to authority.

THE ACT OF GOD

A CURIOUS litigation has just been decided at the Spalding County Court. The Great Northern Railway was sued for damages by a farmer, who had sent a quantity of potatoes to London shortly before Christmas, which were not delivered for nearly ten days, and were then found to be spoiled by the frost. The Company's defence was that a dense fog prevailed during the Christmas week, and disorganised the traffic; that everything was done to facilitate the transit of goods; and that, as the fog was the act of God, there was no liability for damage by delay. After an hour's deliberation, the jury returned a verdict for the defendants, and judgment was given them with costs.

We sincerely pity that Lincolnshire farmer. It is very hard lines to receive only thirteen and fourpence for four tons of potatoes; and harder still to pay the whole of that sum, and a good deal more, for attempting to obtain compensation. The poor man is absolutely without a remedy. The person who delayed and rotted his potatoes is called God, but no one knows where he resides, and it is impossible to serve a summons upon him, even if a court of justice would grant one. God appears to be the chartered libertine of this planet. He destroys what he pleases, and no one is able to make him pay damages.

Christians may call this "blasphemous." But calling names is no argument. Certainly it will not pay for that farmer's potatoes. We fail to see where the blasphemy comes in. An English judge and jury have accepted the Great Northern Railway Company's plea that the fog was the act of God. We simply take our stand upon their verdict and judgment. And we tell the Christians that if God sent the fog—as the judge and jury allow—he has a great deal more to answer for than four tons of rotted potatoes. That terrible fog cost London a gas bill amounting to twenty or thirty thousand pounds. It is impossible to estimate the cost to the community of delayed traffic and suspended business. Hundreds of people were suffocated or otherwise slaughtered. Millions of people were made peevish or brutally ill-tempered, and there was a frightful increase of reckless profanity.

Many persons, doubtless, will say that God did *not* send the fog. They will assert that it came in the ordinary course of nature. But does nature act independently of God? Is he only responsible for *some* of the things that happen? And who is responsible for the rest?

Those who still believe in the Devil may conveniently introduce him, it is curious, however, that they never do, except in cases of *moral* evil. Criminal indictments charge prisoners with acting wickedly under the instigation of the Devil. But *physical* evil is ascribed to Jehovah. Bills of lading exonerate shipowners from liability if anything happens to the cargo through "the act of God or the Queen's enemies." Old Nick does not raise storms, stir up volcanoes, stimulate earthquakes, blight crops, or spread pestilence. All those destructive pastimes are affected by his rival. Even cases of sudden death, or death from lightning are brought in by jurors as "died by the visitation of God." Which seems to show that a visit from God is a certain calamity.

The time will come, of course, when all this nonsense about "the act of God" will disappear. But it will only dissappear because real belief in God is dying. While men are sincere Theists they cannot help seeing God in the unexpected and the calamitous. That is how theology began, and that is how it must continue while it has a spark of vitality. But theology declines as knowledge increases. Our dread of the unknown diminishes as we gain command over the forces of nature; that is, our dread of the unknown diminishes as we turn it into the *known*.

"The act of God" is to be frustrated by Science. We cannot prevent storms, but we are growing more able to foresee them. We cannot prevent the angry waves from rising, but we can build ships to defy their fiercest wrath. We cannot prevent mist from ascending in certain conditions of sky and soil, but we can drain low-lying ground, and prevent the mist from being fatally charged with smoke. We cannot abolish the microbes with which our planet swarms, and if we could we should be surrounded with intolerable putrifaction; but we can observe the laws of public and private sanitation, maintain a high state of vitality, and make ourselves practically invulnerable.

Science is the instrument for achieving the triumph of man. Ultimately it will subdue the planet for us, and we shall be able to exclaim with Mr. Swinburne, "Glory to man in the highest, for man is the master of things." The paradise the theologians dream of will be realised on earth. We shall not abolish death, but we shall make life strong, rich, and glorious, and when death comes it will bring no terror, but rest and peace in the shadow of its wings.

Meanwhile "the act of God" will to some extent survive in the mental life of the multitude. All prayer is based upon this superstition. Those who pray for relief or exemption from storm, famine, or disease; those who pray to be preserved from "battle, murder, and sudden death"; those who pray to be saved from any evil, are, all praying against "the act of God." It is God who is sending the mischief, and therefore he is begged to take it away or pass it on to other persons. Hamburg would be grateful to God even if he transferred the cholera to Berlin. Thus do ignorance and selfishness go hand in hand; thus does superstition cloud the intellect and degrade the character.

KEIR HARDIE ON CHRIST

For some time the Labor leaders have been assiduously courted by the Churches. It is reckoned good business to have one on exhibition at Congresses and Conferences. Ben Tillett is in frequent request as a preacher. Tom Mann, who was once heterodox, is now declared by the *Christian Commonwealth* to be a member of a Christian Church. "We are not aware," our contemporary says, "that John Burns is opposed to the religion of Jesus Christ."

This appropriation of the Labor leaders is an excellent piece of strategy. Churches have seldom had the harmlessness of doves, but they have generally had the cunning of serpents. They often stoop, but always to conquer. And this is precisely what they are doing in the present case.

A year or two ago a leading Socialist, who is also an Atheist, remarked to us how the clericals were creeping into the Socialist movement. "Yes," we observed, "and they will appropriate and stifle it. They will talk about the Socialism of Jesus Christ, bamboozle your followers, and get them out of your control. Then the Socialism will gradually disappear, and Jesus Christ will be left in sole possession of the field. The clericals, in fact, will trump your best cards, if you let them take part in the game."

We warn the Labor leaders, whether they listen to us or not, that they are coquetting with the historic enemy of the people. All religion is a consecration of the past, and every minister is at heart a priest. The social and political object of Churches is to keep things as they are; or, if they *must* be altered, to control the alteration in the interest of wealth and privilege. Fine words may be uttered and popular sentiments may be echoed; but history teaches us that when the leaders of religion talk in this way, they are serving their one great purpose as surely as when they curse and damn the rebellious multitude.

The course of events will show whether we are right or wrong. Meanwhile let us "return to our sheep." Not that Mr. Keir Hardie is a sheep. We don't mean that, though he is certainly being attended to by the wolves.

Mr. Keir Hardie has been interviewed by the *Christian Commonwealth*. "His father," we are informed, "is a very vigorous and militant Atheist, so that the son was brought up without any religious belief." To some extent we believe this is true. Mr. Hardie's brother, and another member of the family, attended our last lectures at Glasgow. But we do not understand that Mr. Keir Hardie was ever a professed Atheist, or a member of any Freethought society. The scepticism he was "weaned from" by the Evangelical Union Church could hardly have been of a very robust order. He seems to have imbibed a sentimental form of Christianity as easily and comfortably as a cat laps milk.

During his last election contest the statement was circulated that Mr. Keir Hardie was an Atheist. "Whereupon," we are told, "Dr. James Morison, the venerable founder of the Evangelical Union, and Dr. Fergus Ferguson, of Glasgow, both wrote in the most eulogistic terms to a local clergyman as to Mr. Hardie's moral character and religious work in Scotland." This is extremely affecting. It is good to see parliamentary candidates walking about with certificates of moral character—written out by a local minister. It is also reassuring to find that such a certificate is an absolute answer to the charge of Atheism, No doubt Mr. Keir Hardie will print the testimonial as a postscript to his next election address at West Ham.

Mr. Keir Hardie calls himself a Christian. He does not say, however, if he believes in the supernatural part of the Gospels. Does he accept the New Testament miracles? Does he embrace the Incarnation and Resurrection? If he does, he is a Christian. If he does not, he has no more right to call himself a Christian than we have to be designated a Buddhist or a Mohammedan.

The Christianity of the schools, Mr. Keir Hardie says, is dead or dying. By this he means "the old theological sects." But here we should like him to be more explicit. Does he think there can be a Christianity *without* "theology"? Or does he mean that the "sects" comprise all persons who have more theology than himself?

But if the Christianity of the schools is dead or dying, the "humanitarian Christianity of Christ is again coming to the front." Now what *is* this humanitarian Christianity of Christ? Upon this point Mr. Keir Hardie throws but a single ray of light. "The whole of Christ's teachings and conduct," he says, "proves that he was intensely interested in the bodily welfare of those with whom he came in contact as a preparative to their spiritual well-being." This is a clear statement; all we now want is the clear proof. Mr. Keir Hardie should give it. We believe he cannot; nay, we defy him to do so. It is idle to cite the so-called "miracles of healing." They were occasional and special; they had as much effect on the "bodily welfare" of the Jewish people as tickling has on the gait of an elephant; and as for their being a "preparative to spiritual well-being," we may ask the "humanitarian Christians of Christ" to tell us, if they can, how much of this quality was afterwards displayed by the ladies and gentlemen who were the lucky subjects (or objects) of Christ's miracles. Mr. Keir Hardie might also recollect that the said miracles, if they ever happened, are of no "bodily" importance to the present generation. Humanitarians of to-day are unable to work miracles; they have to sow the seed of progress, and await its natural harvest.

Mr. Keir Hardie is undoubtedly an earnest social reformer. We wish him all success in his efforts to raise the workers and procure for them a just share of the produce of their industry. Some of his methods may be questionable without affecting his sincerity. If we all saw eye to eye there would be no problems to settle. What we object to is the fond imagination that any light upon the labor question, or any actual social problem, can be found in the teachings of Christ. Jesus of Nazareth never taught industry, or forethought, or any of the robuster virtues of civilisation. On one occasion he said that his kingdom was not of this world. He might certainly have said so of his teaching. It is all very well for Mr. Keir Hardie to assert that our "industrial system is foreign to the spirit of Christianity." What *is* the spirit of Christianity? Twenty different things in as many different minds. *Some* industrial system is a necessity, and whatever it is you will never find its real principles in the Gospels. Christ's one social panacea was "giving to the poor," and this is the worst of all "reformations." It only disguises social evils. The world could do very well without "charity" if it only had justice and common sense.

Charles Bradlaugh, the Atheist, was laughed at for advocating the compulsory cultivation of waste lands. He wanted to see labor and capital employed upon them, even if they yielded no rent to landlords. Mr. Keir Hardie, the Christian, also desires to bring the people into "contact with nature and mother earth," though his recipe, of "open spaces laid down in grass" seems ludicrously inadequate. The loss of this contact, he told his interviewer, is "accountable for much of the Atheism which is a natural product of city life." This "tender thought" was spoken in a voice "which sank almost to a whisper." Very naturally it struck the interviewer as "the finest and most beautiful of Mr. Hardie's utterances."

Both the interviewer and Mr. Keir Hardie forgot a fact of Christian history. Christianity spread in the towns of the Roman Empire. The pagans were the villagers—*paganus* meaning a countryman or rustic. Possibly some of the pagans said to themselves, "Ah, this Christianity is a natural product of the towns."

The diagnosis is in both cases empirical. In a certain sense, however, Mr. Keir Hardie has touched a truth. Progressive ideas must always originate in the keen life of cities. But in another sense Mr. Keir Hardie is mistaken. He seems to regard Atheism as a city malady, like rickets and anemia. Now this is untrue. It is also absurd. Mr. Keir Hardie would find a good many of these "afflicted" Atheists able to make mincemeat of his "humanitarian Christianity of Christ." He would also find, if he cared to look, a great many of them in the Socialist camp. It would be rare sport to see Mr. Keir Hardie defending his "new school" Christianity against the young bloods of the Fabian Society, though it might necessitate the interference of the Society for the Prevention of Cruelty.

But we do not wish to part from Mr. Keir Hardie in a spirit of sarcasm. If he is a hopeless sentimentalist there is no more to be said; but, if he is capable of reason in matters of religion, we appeal to him, in all sincerity, not to press the new wine of Humanitarianism into the old bottles of Christianity. He will only break the bottles and lose the wine. We also implore him to cease talking nonsense about Christianity being "a life, and not a doctrine." It never can be the one without the other. Finally, we beg him to consider what is the real value of Christianity if, after all these centuries, it is necessary to put "humanitarian" in front of it, in order to give it a chance in decent society.

BLESSED BE YE POOR

A leading London newspaper, the *Daily Chronicle*, has recently opened it columns to a discussion of the question, "Is Christianity Played Out?" Mr. Robert Buchanan thinks that it is, and we are of the same opinion. But in a certain sense Christianity is *not* played out. To use a common expression, "there's money in it." That is incontestable. Despite the "poverty" of the "lower clergy," for whom so many appeals are made, the clerical business beats all others, if we compare the amount of investment with the size of the dividend. Relatively speaking, the profits are magnificent. There are curates with only a workman's wages, and of course they merit our deepest sympathy. It is quite shocking to think that a disciple of the *"poor Carpenter of Nazareth"* has to subsist, and support his ten children, on such a miserable pittance. It is a calamity which calls for tears of blood. But, on the other hand, there are Archbishops with princely incomes, Bishops with lordly revenues, Deans and Canons with fine salaries and snug quarters; and between the two extremes of the fat bishop and the lean curate is a long line of gradations, in which, if we strike an average, the result is very far from despicable. It may be added that while the leading Nonconformist ministers, at least in England, do not rival the great Church dignitaries in the matter of income, they often run up to a thousand a year and sometimes over it. Taking the average of their incomes, we have no hesitation in saying it is beyond what they would earn in the ordinary labor market. Still, so far as they are not paid by the State, as the Church clergy *are*, we have no personal reason for complaint. This is a free country—especially for Christians; and if the lay disciples of the poor Carpenter like to pay his professional apostles a fancy price for their work, it is no concern of ours from a business point of view. Nevertheless, as the said apostles are *public* men, who set up as other people's *teachers*, we have a right to express an opinion as to the consistency between their preaching and their practice.

Our gallant colleague, Joseph Symes, who is nobly upholding the Freethought banner in Australia, once asked, "Who's to be Damned if Christianity is True?" Certainly, he said, the clergy stand a fine chance. They are more likely to go to Hades than the congregations they preach to. On on average they are better off. They preach, or *should* preach, the blessings of poverty, and the curse, nay, the damnableness, of wealth. According to the teaching of Jesus, as we read it in the Sermon on the Mount, and as we find it illustrated in the parable of Dives and Lazarus, every pauper is pretty sure of a front seat in heaven; and every man of property or good income is equally sure of warm quarters in hell. But you do not meet parsons in workhouses, though some of them get a good deal of outdoor relief. Go into a country parish and look for the clergyman's house; you will not find it difficult to discover. The best residence is the squire's, the next best is the parson's. Everywhere the clericals appropriate as much as they can of the good things of this world. They find it quite easy to worship God and Mammon together. The curate has his eye on a vicarage; the vicar has his on a deanery; the dean has his on a bishopric. The Dissenting minister is open to improve his position. Sometimes he is invited to another church. He wrestles with the Lord, and makes inquiries. If they prove satisfactory, he recognises "a call." Other people, in ordinary business, would honestly say they were accepting a better situation; but the man of God is above all that, so he obeys the Lord's voice and goes to a position of "greater service," though it would puzzle him to show an extra soul saved by the exchange. Yes, the poor Carpenter's apostles strive to make the best of this world, and take their chance of the next. They are wise in their generation; they resemble the serpent in the text, however they neglect the dove. And for all these things God shall bring them into account—that is, if the gospel be true; for nothing is more certain, according to the gospel, than that the poor will be saved, and those who are not poor will be damned.

Benjamin Disraeli called the Conservative government of Sir Robert Peel "an organised hypocrisy." Modern Christianity appears to us to merit the same description. The note of modern apologetics is the phrase of "Christ-like." In one respect the gentlemen who strike this note *are* Christ-like. They live on the gifts of the faithful, including those of "rich women." But the likeness ends there. In other respects they are dissimilar to their Master. He *died* upon the cross, and they *live* upon the cross. Yes, and many of them get far more on the cross than they would ever get on the square.

Doubtless we shall be censured in vigorous biblical language for speaking so plainly. But we mean every word we say, and are prepared to make it good in discussion. Men should practise what they preach. Those who teach that poverty is a blessing should themselves be poor. Those who teach that God Almighty cried "Woe unto you rich!" should avoid the curse of wealth. If they do not, they are hypocrites. It is no use mincing the matter. Plain speech is best on such occasions. When the great Dr. Abernethy told a gouty, dyspeptic, rich patient to "live on sixpence a day and earn it," his advice was more wholesome than the most dexterous rigmarole.

Nothing could better show than the conduct of the clergy that Christianity *is* played out, if it means the teaching of the Sermon on the Mount. Those who preach it cannot practise it; what is more, they do not mean to. The late Archbishop of York, while Bishop of Peterborough, wrote a magazine article on this Sermon on the Mount, in which he urged that any Society that was based upon it would go to ruin in a week. He was paid at that time £4,500 a year to-preach this Sermon on the Mount, and he did so—in the pulpit; then he mounted another rostrum, and cried, "For God's sake don't practise it."

"Blessed be ye poor" and "Woe unto you rich" are texts with which the Church has bamboozled the multitude in the interest of the privileged classes. The disinherited sons of earth were promised all sorts of fine compensations in Kingdom-Come; meanwhile kings, aristocrats, priests, and all the rest of the juggling and appropriating tribe, battened on the fruits of other men's labor. The poor were like the dog crossing the stream, and seeing the big shadow of his piece of meat in the water. "Seize the shadow!" the priests cried. The poor did so. But the substance-was not lost. It was snapped up and shared by priestcraft and privilege.

The people have been told that the gospel is a cheap thing—without money and without price. That is the prospectus. But the gospel is frightfully dear in reality. Religion costs more than education. England spends more in preparing her sons and daughters for the next world than in training them for this world. Yet the next world may be nothing but a dream, and certainly we *know* nothing about it; while this world is a solid and often a solemn fact, with its business as well as its pleasures, its work as well as its enjoyments, its duties as well as its privileges. To keep people out of hell, and guide them to heaven (places that only exist in the map of faith), we spend over twenty millions a year. This is a sum which, if wisely devoted, would remedy the worst evils of human society in a single generation. It would found countless institutions of culture and innocent recreation; and, by means of experiments, it would solve a host of social problems. Instead of doing this, we keep up a huge army of black-coats to fight an imaginary Devil; yet we call ourselves a *practical* people. Christianity has it roots-deep down in the *wealth* of England, and this is the secret of its power, allied of course with its usurped authority over the minds of little children. The-churches and chapels are mostly social institutions, Sunday resorts of the "respectable" classes. For any purpose connected with the real welfare of the people Christianity might just as well be dead and buried—as it will be when the people see the truth.

CONVERTED INFIDELS

Christian logic is a curious thing. There is nothing like it, we should imagine, in the heavens above or the waters under the earth. Certainly there is nothing like it on the earth itself, unless we make an exception in the case of Christian veracity, which is as much like Christian logic as one cherry is like another.

It is a long time since Christians began arguing—it would be an outrage on the dictionary to call it reasoning. They have been at it for nearly two thousand years. Their founder, Jesus Christ, seldom argued. He uttered himself dogmatically at most times; occasionally he spoke in parables; and whenever he was cornered he escaped on a palpable evasion. His great disciple, Paul, however, was particularly fond of arguing. His writings abound in "for" and "whereas." The argument he most affected was the circular one. He could run round a horseshoe, skip over from point to point, and run round again as nimbly as any man on record. In a famous chapter in Corinthians, for instance, he first proves the resurrection of the dead by the resurrection of Jesus Christ, and then proves the resurrection of Jesus Christ by the resurrection of the dead. It is in the same chapter that he enunciates the botanical truth (a truth of Bible botany, observe) that a seed does not bear anything unless it dies. Altogether the great Apostle is a first-rate type of the Christian logician, and there are some who declare him to be a first-rate type of the Christian truth-teller.

Speeding down the stream of time to the present age, we see that Christian logic (yes, and Christian veracity) has undergone little if any alteration. It is as infantile and as impudent as ever. Arguments that would look fallacious in the nursery are used in the pulpit, generation after generation, with an air of solemn profundity, as though they were as wise as the oracles of omniscience. To select from such a plethora is almost impossible; the difficulty is where to begin. But happily we are under no necessity of selection. A case is before us, and we take it as it comes. It is a "converted infidel" case, in the report of a recent sermon—the last of a series on "Is Christianity Played Out?"—by the Rev. Dr. Hiles Hitchens; the gentleman referred to in one of our last week's paragraphs as wishing for an old three-legged stool or something made by Jesus Christ. Dr. Hitchens, alas! cannot find the stool, and has to put up with the creed instead; though, perhaps, he gets as much out of the creed as he would make by selling the stool to the British Museum.

Dr. Hitchens preached from the text, "The earth shall be full of the knowledge of the Lord"—a statement which, after the lapse of so many centuries, has still to be couched in the future tense. The delay has been excessive, but Dr. Hitchens is hopeful. He believes in the ultimate and speedy fulfilment of the prophecy. One of his grounds for so believing is this (we quote from the *Christian Commonwealth*), that "Out of 20 leading lecturers, authors, editors, and debaters on the side of Infidelity 17 have been brought to Christ within the last 30 years, have left their infidel associations, openly professed the religion of Jesus, and engaged in Christian work." The last he named, we are told, was "the case of a National Secular lecturer, of whom the sceptics were greatly proud, who has recently been received by, and now lectures for, the Christian Evidence Society."

We leave the consideration of these "facts" for a moment, and deal in the first place with Dr. Hitchens's peculiar logic. It is truly Christian. The species is unmistakable. Seventeen Freethinkers have been converted to Christianity! Wonderful! But how many Christians have been converted to Freethought? Ay, there's the rub. For every specimen Dr. Hitchens produces we will produce a thousand. Not only were the rank and file of the Freethought party very largely brought up as Christians, but its leaders are of the same category. Charles Bradlaugh was brought up as a Christian, so was Colonel Ingersoll. Can Dr. Hitchens produce two names among his "converts" of the same weight, or a half, a quarter, or a tithe of it? Every leader of Freethought in England, we believe, is a convert from Christianity. As to the "leading" men Dr. Hitchens refers to, we presume they are the persons initialed in the late Mr. Whitmore's tract, and those among them who were leaders were not converted, and those who were converted were not leaders. The real leaders of the Freethought party, those who were long in its service, and were entrusted with power and responsibility, were never converted. And the cases on Mr. Whitmore's list are old. They have an ancient and fish-like smell. Dr. Hitchens will perhaps be good enough to tell us the name of any man of real distinction in the Freethought party who has been "converted" during the last twenty years. We defy him to do so. If he goes back far enough he will find a few men who were not trusted in our party, and a few weaklings who could not fight an uphill battle, who went over to the enemy. Real leaders of our party fought, suffered, and starved, but they never deserted the flag. Christianity could not convert a Bradlaugh or a Holyoake; it could only bribe or allure a Sexton or a Gordon, or others of the "illustrious obscure" in Mr. Whitmore's fraudulent catalogue. In short, the "conversions" to Christianity so trumpeted are mostly dubious, generally insignificant, and all ancient. If the prophecy which Dr. Hitchens preached from is to be accomplished, it will have to quicken its rate of fulfilment during the past twenty years. We convert tremendously more Christians than you do Freethinkers; the balance is terribly to your disadvantage; you can only make out a promising account by setting down your infinitesimal gains and making no entry of your tremendous losses.

The only recent case that Dr. Hitchens refers to is that of "a National Secular lecturer, of whom the sceptics were greatly proud." Dr. Hitchens evidently takes this gentleman at his own estimate. That *he* thinks the sceptics were greatly proud of him is intelligible; it is quite in keeping with his shallow, vulgar, And egotistical nature. But the truth is "the sceptics," in any general sense, were *not* proud of him. He was a very young man, with a great deal to learn, who had a very brief career as a Secularist in East London. In a thoughtless moment a local Secular Society gave him office, and that fact is his entire stock-in-trade as a "converted Freethinker." He was never one of the National Secular Society's appointed lecturers; he was neither "author, editor, or debater"; and he was utterly unknown to the party in general. Dr. Hitchens has, in fact, discovered a mare's nest. We are in a position to speak with some authority, and we defy him to name any Freethinker "of whom the sceptics were greatly proud" who has of late years been converted to Christianity. It is easy enough to impose on an ignorant congregation, and Dr. Hitchens is probably aware of the lengths to which a reckless pulpiteer may carry his mendacity. But candid investigators will conclude that "converted infidels" cannot be very plentiful, when the majority of them are so ancient; nor very important, when an obscure youth has to be advertised as "a leader" of whom the sceptics (nine out of ten of them never having heard of him) were "greatly proud."

We should imagine that Dr. Hitchens is rather new to this line of advocacy. In the course of time he will learn—if indeed he has not already learnt, and is concealing the fact—that the "converted infidels" will not stand a minute's scrutiny. The only safe method is to drop questionable cases and resort to sheer invention. Even that method, however, is not devoid of peril, as one of its practitioners has recently discovered. The Rev. Hugh Price Hughes must by this time be extremely sorry he circulated that false and foolish story of the converted Atheist shoemaker. The exposure of it follows him wherever he goes, and illustrates the truth of at least one Bible text—"Be sure your sin will find you out."

MRS. BOOTH'S GHOST

The Booth family have all keen eyes for business. If they shut their eyes you can see it by their noses. It is not surprising, therefore, to find Mrs. Booth-Tucker capping Mr. Stead's ghost stories with a fine romance about her dead mother. While the "Mother of the Salvation Army" was dying, the Booth family made all the capital they could out of her sufferings; and when she expired, her corpse was shunted about in the financial interest of their show. Perhaps they would be exhibiting her still if there were no law as to the disposition of corpses. But as that avenue to profit is closed, the only alternative is to make use of Mrs. Booth's ghost, and this has just been done by one of her daughters.

Mrs. Booth-Tucker contributes her ghost story to the Easter number of *All the World*. No doubt Easter was thought a seasonable time for its publication. Christians are just then dreaming about the great Jerusalem ghost, and another "creeper" comes in appropriately.

Mr. Stead catches up Mrs. Booth-Tucker's ghost story and prints it in the *Review of Reviews*. He admits the want of evidence "as to its objectivity," which is a euphemism for "no evidence at all," and then observes most sapiently that if it was only a dream, "the coincidence of its occurrence at the crisis in her illness is remarkable"—which is precisely what it is not.

Mrs. Booth-Tucker was very ill on board a steamer when she saw her mother, fresh from "the beautiful land above." "Those with me," she says, "thought I was dying, and I thought so too." When a person is in that state, after a wasting illness, the brain is necessarily weak. But this was not all. "I had not slept," the lady says, "for some days, at any rate not for many minutes together." Her brain, therefore, was not only weak, but overwrought; and in ingenuously stating this at the outset the lady gives herself away. Given a wasted body, weakness "unto death," a brain ill supplied with blood and ravaged with sleeplessness; does it, we ask, require a "rank materialist" to explain the presence of "visions" without the aid of supernaturalism?

"Suddenly," Mrs. Booth-Tucker says, "I saw her coming to me." But how "coming"? The lady tells us she was lying in "a small sea cabin." This does not leave much room for the "coming" of the ghost. We should also like to know why a lady thought to be dying was *left alone*. It is certainly a very unusual circumstance.

Mrs. Booth's ghost, after as much "coming" as could be accomplished in "a small cabin," at last "sat beside" her sick daughter "on the narrow bunk." No doubt the seat was rather incommodious, but why should a ghost sit at all? It really seems to have been a mixed sort of ghost. Apparently it came through the ship's side, or the deck, or the cabin-door, or the key-hole; yet it was solid enough to touch Mrs. Booth-Tucker's hand and kiss her? Nay, it was solid enough to carry on a long conversation, which does not seem possible without lungs and larynx.

Mrs. Booth's ghost said a great deal. "*Wonderful words* they were," says Mrs. Booth-Tucker. This whets our curiosity. We are always listening for "wonderful words." But, alas, we are doomed to disappointment. The lady knows her mother's words were "wonderful," but she cannot reproduce them. Here memory is defective. "I can remember so few of the actual words," she says. Nevertheless, she gives us a few samples, and they do not seem *very* "wonderful." Here are two of the said samples: "Live, live, live, remembering that night comes always *quickly*, and all is nothingness that dies with death!" "Fight the fight, darling; the sympathy of Christ is always with you, and every effort you make is heaping up treasure for you in Heaven."

We fancy we have heard those "wonderful words" before. For all their wonderfulness, ghosts are seldom original. Mrs. Booth-Tucker reminds us of the gushing lady novelist, who describes her hero as divinely handsome and miraculously clever, but when she opens his mouth, makes him talk like a jackass.

"General" Booth's daughter does not see that she found words for her mother's ghost. She is not so sharp as Dr. Johnson, who carried on a discussion with an adversary in a dream, and got the worst of it. For a time he felt humiliated, but he recovered his pride on reflecting that he had provided the other fellow with arguments.

When Mrs. Booth-Tucker tells that "the radiance of her face spoke to me," we can easily understand the subjective nature of her "vision," and as readily dispense with a budget of those "wonderful words."

Nor are we singular in incredulity. Mr. Stead cannot put his tongue in his cheek at a member of the Booth family, but the *Christian Commonwealth* says "the story is both improbable and absurd," and adds, "it is just such fanaticism as this that brings religion into contempt with many educated people." Our pious contemporary, like any wretched materialist, declares that many persons have seen ghosts "when under the influence of fever or in a low state of health."

All this is sensible enough, and in a Christian journal very edifying. But if our pious contemporary only applied this criticism backwards, what havoc it would make with the records of early Christianity! Mrs. Booth-Tucker is not in all points like Mary Magdalene, but she resembles her in fervor of disposition. Out of Mary Magdalene we are told that Jesus cast "seven devils," which implies, rationalistically, that she was strongly hysterical. She was more likely to be a victim of "fanaticism" than Mrs. Booth-Tucker. Yet the ghost story of Mrs. Booth's daughter is discredited, and even stigmatised as discreditable, while the brain-sick fancies of Mary Magdalene are treated as accurate history. She was at the bottom of the Jerusalem ghost story, and her evidence is regarded as unimpeachable. So much do circumstances alter cases!

Our pious contemporary regards all modern ghosts as "fever dreams." So do we, and we regard all ancient ghosts in the same light The difference between ancient and modern superstition is only a question of environment. Superstition itself is always the same; it no more changes than the leopard's spots or the Ethiopian's skin. But the environment changes. From the days when there was no scientific knowledge or rigorous criticism we have advanced to an age when the electric search-light of science sweeps every corner and criticism is remorseless. Hence the modern ghosts are served up in Christmas "shockers," while the ancient ghosts are worshipped as gods. But this will not last for ever. The rule of "what is, has been," will eventually be applied to the whole of human history, and the greatest ghost of the creeds will "melt into the infinite azure of the past."

TALMAGE ON THE BIBLE

Talmage is the Spurgeon of America. He has all the English preacher's vogue as well as his orthodoxy. But he resembles Spurgeon with a difference. He is distinctly American. No one equals the Yankee at "tall talk," and what Yankee equals Talmage in this species of composition? The oracle of the Brooklyn Tabernacle licks creation in that line. Here is a specimen of his spread-eagle eloquence, taken from the sermon we are about to criticise:— "The black and deep-toned bell of doom hangs over their heads, and I take the hammer of that bell, and I strike it three times with all my might, and it sounds Woe! Woe! Woe!" Perhaps it does, but Talmage is wrong in his spelling. What the bell of doom, so impudently struck by this mannikin, really sounds is doubtless "Woh! Woh! Woh!" It wants the presumptuous spouter to leave off playing the part of God Almighty.

Over in America, as well as here in England, the Bible is meeting with misfortune. Christian ministers are showing up its blunders and inconsistencies. Its foes are now of its own household. Talmage is not frightened, however; he keeps a stiff upper-lip; and it must be admitted, he has a good deal of upper-lip to keep stiff. Since he visited the Holy Land his faith is strong enough to swallow whales. Now he knows that what the Bible says is true.. He has seen the place where it happened.

But faith is a tender plant. Talmage says it is easily destroyed. "I can give you a recipe for its obliteration," he cries; and it is this—"Read infidel books; have long and frequent conversations with sceptics; attend the lectures of those antagonistic to religion." Yes, faith *is* a tender plant. The believer is a hot-house production. He dies in the open-air. The Bible can be read by Freethinkers, and it confirms them in their scepticism; but if a Christian reads infidel books he is lost. Hearing the other side is fatal to his faith. It is Talmage who states so, and, as old Omar Khayyam says, he knows, he knows.

Somewhat paradoxically—but who expects logic from the pulpit?— the great Talmage declares, "I do not believe there is an infidel now alive who has read the Bible through." He offers a hundred dollars reward to any infidel "who has read the Bible through twice"—which discounts his certainty that no infidel had read it through *once*. A good many infidels might apply for that hundred dollars, but Talmage will never hand it over.

An infidel's word is not good enough—not for Talmage. "I must have the testimony," he exclaims, "of someone who has seen him read it all through twice." A very safe condition! for who has ever *seen* any man read the Bible through? And if the witness happened to be an infidel—as is likely— Talmage would want the testimony of someone else who had seen him see the other man reading it; Talmage is not very wise, but he is not exactly a fool, and he and *his* money are *not* soon parted.

There is an "infidel" in America who *has* read the Bible through. His name is Robert G. Ingersoll. Talmage should discuss the Bible with him. But he won't. He knows what his fate would be in such an encounter. "And they gathered up of the fragments that remained twelve baskets full."

There is also an "infidel" in England who has read the Bible through. *More* than one, of course, but we know this one so intimately. He was shut up in Holloway Gaol for knowing too much about the Bible. During the first eight weeks of his sojourn there the "blessed book" was his only companion. It was the Bible, the whole Bible, and nothing but the Bible. That prisoner read it through from the first mistake in Genesis to the last curse in Revelation; read it through as Talmage *never* did, for there were no distractions, no letters to answer, no morning and evening newspapers, no visitors dropping in. It was a continuous, undisturbed reading, and the man who did it would be happy to let the public decide whether he does not know the Bible as well as Talmage.

Talmage has a very poor opinion of infidels. He thinks that "bad habits" have much to do with scepticism. His narrow little mind cannot understand how anyone can differ from him without being wicked. Still, for decency sake, he makes exceptions. "Mind you," he cries, "I do not say that all infidels are immoral." How kind! How generous! No doubt the infidels will shed tears of gratitude. They are not *all* immoral. Some of them may be nearly as good as Talmage. Certainly some of them are not so avaricious. Infidels speakers don't insist on having fifty pounds paid in the ante-room before they mount the platform to deliver a lecture.

It appears that Talmage once knew a "pronounced infidel." He was the father of one of the Presidents of the United States. Talmage accepted an invitation to spend a night in his house. "Just before retiring at night, he said, in a jocose way: 'I suppose you are accustomed to read the Bible before going to bed, and here is my Bible from which to read. He then told me what portions he would like to have me read, and he only asked for those portions on which he could easily be facetious."

Talmage gives himself away in this observation. He contends that God wrote the Bible. Why, then, did God write it so that you could *easily* be facetious about it? It is not so *easy* to be facetious about Homer, or Plato, or Aristotle, or Dante, or Spinoza, or Shakespeare, or Bacon. There is no humor in the Bible, no wit, and only a little sarcasm. We do not laugh *with* it, but *at* it, which is the most fatal form of laughter. It is awfully solemn, but dreadfully absurd. There are things in it to tickle an elephant. Surely it is strange that God should write a book that lends itself so easily to ridicule.

The Spurgeon of Yankeeland goes on to speak about the "internal evidence" of the Bible. This he says is "paramount," though he takes care to skip off as quickly as possible to outside testimony. He cites a number of persons trained up as Christians in favor of the "supernatural" character of the Bible. The first is Chief Justice Chase, of the Supreme Court of the United States—against whom we put a great jurisprudist like Bentham, and a great judge like Sir James Stephen. The second is President Adams—against whom we put President Lincoln. The third is Sir Isaac Newton—against whom we put Charles Darwin. The fourth is Sir Walter Scott—against whom we put Byron and Shelley. The fifth is Hugh Miller—against whom we put Sir Charles Lyell. The sixth is Edmund Burke—against whom we put Thomas Paine, or, if that will not do, Lord Bolingbroke. The seventh is Mr. Gladstone—against whom we put John Morley. "Enough! Enough!" says Talmage. We say so too. Our names quite balance his names collectively. The game of "authorities" can be played on both sides. But is it worth playing at all? Is a great name a substitute for argument? Is authority as good as evidence? Should the jury decide according to the eminence of the pleader's friends, or according to his facts and the force of his reasoning?

Taking advantage of his congregation's ignorance, or exposing his own, Talmage declares that "The discovered monuments of Egypt have chiselled on them the story of the sufferings of the Israelites in Egyptian bondage, as we find it in the Bible." Now, to put it mildly, this is not true. We are also told that "the sulphurous graves of Sodom and Gomorrah have been identified." To put it mildly again, *this* is not true. We are told next that "the remains of the Tower of Babel have been found." This is not true. Assyrian documents are also said to "echo and re-echo the truth of Bible history," This is not true, according to Professor Sayce, who knows more about Assyrian history than Talmage knows about all things whatsoever. The witness of Assyria repeatedly contradicts the Bible story, not merely in small matters, but in important features. The fact is, Talmage does not know what he is talking about; or, he *does* know what he is talking about, in which case he is playing a very dirty trick on his hearers' credulity.

With respect to the Pentateuch, it does not trouble Talmage whether it was written by "Moses or Hilkiah or Ezra or Samuel or Jeremiah, or another group of ancients." He declares that "none of them wrote it," for "God wrote the Pentateuch"—that is to say, they "put down only what God dictated; he signed it afterward." But where is the signature? And what a paltry way is this of evading the question at issue! It is all very well to say that the writers of the Pentateuch were "Jehovah's stenographers or typewriters." What we want to know first of all is, who they were, and when they lived.

It is useless to follow Talmage any farther. Suffice it to say that he winds up by warning young Christians against a "Voltaire cyclone" on the one side, and a "Tom Paine cyclone" on the other side. There is something worse than either—a Talmage puddle. The young man who sports in that is only fit for—well, Exeter Hall, or Colney Hatch.

MRS. BESANT ON DEATH AND AFTER

When we first criticised Mrs. Besant's newly-found Theosophy, and thereby incurred her severe displeasure, we predicted that her enthusiastic nature would carry her far on the road, which she thought of true philosophy, but which we thought of gross superstition. Our prediction has been realised; and, unless for some accident, or some sudden turn in Mrs. Besant's mind or life, it will be realised still further. In this, as in other matters (as the French say) it is the first step which costs, because it involves all the following steps. Mrs. Besant placed her feet upon the high road of credulity when she succumbed to the Theosophical high priestess, whose life is a highly interesting and instructive chapter in the history of imposture. Madame Blavatsky had seen much of the world, and was up to most things. She had a surprising power of bamboozling people of some intelligence and culture. The broad-set eyes, and the great tiger-bar between and over them, indicated the species to which she belonged. Mrs. Besant, with her innocences and enthusiasms, was a baby in the hands of this female Cagliostro. She actually gave the Blavatsky credit for what she obviously did not possess. Her manners, for instance, were not such as might be expected from one who had tasted of spiritual wisdom at its secret sources; while her pretentious ignorance was enough to alarm any student not under the glamor of her audacity. She made the most grotesque mistakes in science, while pompously setting right in their own province such colossal authorities as Darwin and Haeckel. She had certainly read very widely (or got others to read very widely for her) in "occult" literature; but wherever one's own knowledge enabled one to test, she was a poor smatterer; and the same judgment is delivered upon her by specialists in most of the fields she invaded. It was not her learning or her intellectual power that captivated Mrs. Besant; it was her strong personality, her masculine dominance, her crafty self-possession. From the first minute of her enchantment, Mrs. Besant lost all sense of logic in relation to Theosophy. For instance, it was asserted, and the assertion was supported by positive, detailed-evidence, that the Blavatsky had practised the grossest imposture in India. And how did Mrs. Besant dispose of these charges? She says she read them, and immediately joined the Theosophical Society—as though that were any *answer*. It is like saying, "I don't rebut the evidence against the prisoner in the dock, but I shall shake hands with him." What possible effect could that have on the sensible part of the jury? But this sort of logic has been displayed by Mrs. Besant ever since; indeed, she seems to have a dim perception of her weakness, for she dares not discuss Theosophy, or any part of it, with an out-and-out Freethinker—one who would subject it to the critical tests with which she herself was familiar when she stood upon the Secular platform.

There is one aspect of Mrs. Besant's advocacy of Theosophy which we censured at first, and which we now think is something short of honest. Mrs. Besant used to present Secularism in its naked truth, to be embraced or rejected; but she follows a different course in regard to Theosophy; she puts its plausible features forward and conceals the rest, so that people who have heard her are positively astonished when they are told of some of her printed teachings. This seems especially the case when she addresses meetings, somewhat too chivalrously organised by Freethinkers. Now this is not fair, it is not really honest; though it may be in accord with the ethics of those who divide truth into "exoteric" and "esoteric." To our mind, it is rather suggestive of the spider and the fly. "Will you walk into my parlor?" "Oh yes," says the giddy fly, "it looks so nice, positively inviting?" But what of the other rooms in your house; your garret near the sky, where you do star-gazing, and your basement, where crawl the foul things of savage superstition?

Many of our readers have heard Mrs. Besant in the sweet persuasive vein, and felt pleased if rather muddled. For their sakes, and not for our own satisfaction, we shall criticise her little volume on *Death—and After?* just issued as No. III. of a series of Theosophical Manuals. When we have done they will know more about Theosophy than if they had listened to Mrs. Besant (especially from Freethought platforms) for ten thousand years.

First, let us notice Mrs. Besant's attitude. Her devotion to the Blavatsky is complete; she mentions the great woman with profound veneration, swears to all she taught, and, in fact, just stews down the Blavatsky's voluminous nonsense. Mrs. Besant is also a patient disciple of the Masters—to wit, the Mahatmas. These Masters of Wisdom never appear for inspection. They lurk in the secret fastnesses of Tibet, which is a very unexplored part of the world, large enough to hide a good many things, even things that do not exist. They know a lot, but what dribbles out of them is very commonplace when it is not pompously silly. They inhabit higher planes of life than our greatest saints and sages, but somehow they have done nothing for Tibet, which is one of the poorest, dirtiest, and most degraded countries on earth. Still, they are going to give a tremendous lift to the civilisation of Europe; and if we live long enough we shall see what we *do* see. Mahatmas are really the distinctive feature of Theosophy; it is absolutely nothing without them;

and, in our opinion, they are a most farcical swindle Madame Blavatsky created *these* out of her own fertile imagination, she put them where they could not be found, and she said, "If you want to know anything about them come to me; I am the chosen vehicle of their sublime revelations." And if you laughed at her Mahatmas, she was capable of indulging in expletives that would strike envy into the soul of a trooper. How curious it is, if these Mahatmas are real personages, that they do not communicate with *our* Masters of Wisdom. Why do they neglect our Spencers and Huxleys? Why do they choose to speak through a woman like Madame Blavatsky, or a popular lecturess like Mrs. Besant? Why are they so fond of the ladies? Cannot they have some dealings with *a man*, a man of great eminence as a philosopher, of high and undisputed character, and of vast influence with the educated and thoughtful classes? Why, in short, do the Mahatmas confine their attention to smaller persons *with fish to fry*?

Relying upon these Mahatmas, and upon Madame Blavatsky, her great guide, philosopher, and friend, Mrs. Besant has an extremely easy task. She makes no attempt to prove, she simply asserts, and it seems to be a kind of blasphemy to ask for evidence. She dishes everything up in Hindu terminology, on the ground that "the English language has as yet no equivalents." But will it ever have them? Never, we suspect, by the assistance of Theosophists. The oriental lingo is part of the fascination to those who like to look profound on a small stock of learning. Besides, it imposes on the open-mouthed; and, if the Hindu terminology were translated into vernacular English, they would probably exclaim, "Good God! there's nothing in it." It is all very well for Mrs. Besant to pour out second-hand praise of "technical terms." We all know their value. But how is it we have not got them already? Because—and this is the only answer—because we are ignorant of the *things*. Western experience does not coincide with oriental dreams.

Mrs. Besant opens her little volume with the famous story of the conversion to Christianity of Edwin, but she tells it very loosely, and in fact wrongly; which is a proof that the infallibility of the Mahatmas has not fallen upon their disciple. She states that while Paulinus, the Christian missionary, was speaking to-Edwin of life, death, and immortality, a bird flew in through a window, circled the hall, and flew out again into the darkness; whereupon the Christian priest "bade the king see in the flight of the bird within the-hall the transitory life of man, and claimed for his faith that it showed the soul, in passing from the' hall of life, winging its way, not in the darkness of night, but in the sunlit radiance of a more glorious world." Now the bird did not fly into the hall as Paulinus was speaking, nor did he preach this sermon upon its movements. It was one of Edwin's suite who introduced the bird's flight as a metaphor, reminding the king that sometimes at supper, in the winter, a sparrow would fly in out of the storm, entering at one door and passing out at another, staying but a minute, and after that minute returning to winter as from winter it came. "Such is the life of man," said the Saxon speaker, "and of what follows it, or what has preceded it, we are altogether ignorant; wherefore, if this new doctrine should bring anything more certain, it well deserves to be followed." This is how the incident is related by Bede, though it is probably apocryphal; nevertheless it ought not to be hashed up by fresh cooks; and if the matter is in itself of trifling importance, it is as well to be accurate, especially when you pretend a close acquaintance with the Masters of Wisdom.

Many hundred years have elapsed since Paulinus talked with Edwin, and to-day, says Mrs. Besant, there are "more people in Christendom who question whether a man has a spirit to come anywhere or to go any-whither, than, perhaps, in the world's history could ever before have been found at one time." We are also reminded that man has always been asking whence the soul comes, and whither it goes, and "the answers have varied with the faiths." *This* is true, at any rate; but it does not suggest to Mrs. Besant any lesson of modesty or hesitation. Despite the discord of so many ages, she is most coolly dogmatic. It does not, apparently, occur to her to ask *why* the discord has perpetually prevailed. In matters of science, after investigation and discussion, the world comes to an agreement; in matters of theology (or, if you like, Theosophy) the world grows more and more at variance. *Why* is this? There must be an explanation. And to our mind the explanation is very simple. In matters of science men deal with *facts*, while in those other matters they deal with *fancies*, and the more freedom you give them the greater will be the variety of their preferences.

Mrs. Besant's new superstition of Theosophy is, in our judgment, more foolish and less dignified than Christianity. We are therefore moved to say that she does injustice to Christianity in representing it as responsible for all the black paraphernalia and lugubrious ceremonies of death. There was, indeed, nothing of all this among the primitive Christians. Such things belong to the world's common customs and superstitions. Black was not merely a sign of sorrow, or at least of depression; it was also thought to be protective against ghosts; so that these trappings and suits of woe belong to the very "spookology" which is an integral part of Theosophy. Of course I freely admit that the ordinary gloom of death has been deepened by the Christian doctrine of hell, though Mrs. Besant seems to think otherwise. She inclines to the belief that the Western fear of death is ethnological, being the antithesis of its vigorous life. But it may be objected that the old Romans were comparatively free from this terror. On the other hand, it must be allowed that Mrs. Besant is right in her observation that "the more mystical dreamy East" has little dread of the "shadow cloaked from head to foot," since it is ever ever seeking to escape from "from the thraldom of the senses," and is apt to look upon "the disembodied state as eminently desirable and as most conducive to unfettered thought." In other words, that "when the brains are out," as Macbeth says, man's intellect undergoes a wonderful improvement; an opinion, by the way, which is quite in harmony with Theosophical teaching.

After giving the Theosophical view of the "body," Mrs. Besant says that when once we *thus* come to regard it, death loses all its terrors. But this is not the sole achievement of Theosophy. What terror had death to Charles Bradlaugh? What terror had death to Mrs. Besant while she was an Atheist? There are thousands of sceptics who do not want Theosophy to redeem them from a terror which they have long cast behind them, with the superstition by which it was bred and cherished.

Let us pause to remark that Mrs. Besant quotes from *Paradise Lost* its magnificent description of Death. She appreciates at least the splendor of the diction, but she does not notice how poor in comparison are the words she quotes from her "Masters." How is it that Milton beats the Mahatmas? What objects they look when the great English poet rises "with his singing robes about him"! How thin their music when he strikes upon his thrilling lyre, or blows his rousing trumpet, or rolls from his mighty organ the floods of entrancing harmony!

But to return to the main subject. It is absurd, as Mrs. Besant points out, to claim for Christianity that it "brought life and immortality to light." The belief in a future life was an intense conviction—or, perhaps we should say, a perfect truism—among the people of ancient India and Egypt. Yet here again, with her taste for dogmatic rhetoric, Mrs. Besant gratuitously exaggerates. "The whole ancient world," she says, "basked in the full sunshine of belief in the immortality of man, lived in it daily, voiced it in their literature, and went with it in calm serenity through the gate of Death." Now "calm serenity" is bad tautology, and the general assertion of this passage is equally open to censure. "The whole ancient world," as the Americans would say, is a large order. Greece and Rome (to say nothing of the pre-Maccabean Jews) were very important parts of "the whole ancient world," and whoever asserts that *their* citizens "basked in the sunshine of belief in immortality" is simply making a confession of ignorance. Greek and Roman poets and philosophers in many cases doubted, or even denied, a life beyond the grave. Even when the doctrine was entertained it does not appear to have been productive of much "sunshine." Does not the poet make the shade of the great Achilles say that he would rather be the veriest day-drudge on earth than command all the armies of the ghosts in the cold pale realm of the dead? We do not ignore, on the other hand, the Islands of the Blest; we are only objecting to Mrs. Besant's loose and sweeping assertions, which prove very clearly that her new "faith" is not remarkable in the cultivation of accuracy.

With regard to man—the *entire* human being, mortal and immortal— Mrs. Besant remarks that "un-instructed Christians" chop him into two, the body-that perishes at death, and the "something that survives death." She omits to notice that a good many Christians chop him into three, to say nothing of others, like the Christadelphians, who leave him one and indivisible. Mrs. Besant, for her part, as a true Theo-sophist, goes farther than the sharpest Christian dissectors. She chops man into *seven*. When she was a Materialist she never suspected that her nature was so composite, and we are still in the same benighted condition. One begins to feel that the injunction, "Man, know thyself," is a terrible burden. It is hard enough to get a fair knowledge of our organism, its physical constitution, its intellectual faculties, and its moral tendencies; but the task is absolutely appalling when, we have to get a satisfactory knowledge of our Atma, our Buddhi, our Manas, our Kama, our Prana, our Linga Sharira, and our Sthula Sharira. Anyone who can master all that may as well go on unto seventy times seven.

The immortal soul consists of the upper three, which are a trinity in everlasting unity. The heavens may wax old as a garment, but they "go on for ever," and flourish in immortal youth. Death is the first step in the process of their separation from the lower and perishable four. One after another of these is shed, as the serpent sloughs its skin, or the butterfly its chrysalis; or, to use a more familiar and pungent illustration, which we make a present of to Mrs. Besant, as you peel an onion, fold after fold, until you get to the tender core. Sthula Sharira goes first, and the organism becomes a corpse, which is buried, or cremated, or eaten by cannibals. Linga Sharira, the Astral Double, had been attached to it by a "delicate cord," which is our old friend "the thread of life"—a convenient metaphor turned into a positive proposition. This delicate cord is snapped, not immediately, "but some hours" (as many as thirty-six occasionally) after "apparent death." It is necessary, therefore, to be very quiet in the death-chamber, while the Linga Sharira is eloping. One shudders to think of what might happen, of the indecent haste to which Number Six might be compelled, if a corpse were cremated a few hours after death; the corpse, for instance, of a man who died from cholera or the plague.

This "delicate cord" which attaches Number Seven to Number Six is perceptible if your eyes are constructed that way; that is, if you are a clairvoyant, one who is able to see beyond the real. Mrs. Besant does not say she has seen it herself; indeed, she is always relying on someone else. She refers us to Andrew Jackson Davis, the "Poughkeepsie Seer" (and a Spiritist, though she does not say so), who "watched this escape of the ethereal body" and states that "the magnetic cord did not break for some thirty-six hours." "Others," says Mrs. Besant, "have described, in similar terms, how they saw a faint violet mist rise from the dying body, gradually condensing into a figure which was the counterpart of the expiring person, and attached to that person by a glittering thread." Thus the attachment is "delicate," "magnetic," and "glittering." In the course of time, we dare say, it will be decorated with a much larger variety of adjectives. Meanwhile we may observe that if Mrs. Besant were to preach this sort of "higher wisdom" to savages she would find an attentive and sympathetic audience. The violet mist, the Astral Double, and the delicate, magnetic, glittering cord, are things that they are to some extent already familiar with; and if she could only get them to accept her terminology, and talk of Sthula Sharira and Linga Sharira, they would be extremely promising candidates for the Theosophical kingdom of heaven.

Mrs. Besant tells us that the Linga Sharira, or Astral Double, rots away (disintegrates) in time. It is "the ethereal counterpart of the gross body of man," and takes a longer time in dropping into nothingness.

"Sometimes this Double is seen by persons in the house, or in the neighborhood... the Double may be seen or heard; when seen it shows the dreamy hazy consciousness alluded to, is silent, vague in its aspect, and unresponsive.... This astral corpse remains near the physical one, and they disintegrate together; clairvoyants see these astral wraiths in churchyards, sometimes showing likeness of the dead body, sometimes as violet mists or lights. Such an astral corpse has been seen by a friend of my own."

At this point we think it well to part company with Mrs. Besant. Who would have imagined, ten years ago, that the colleague of Charles Bradlaugh would ever descend so far into superstition as to write and talk seriously about churchyard spooks? What she may have to say about Theosophy after this can hardly be of interest to any thoroughly sane person. We therefore close with an expression of profound regret that an earnest, eloquent lady who once did such service in the cause of progress, should thus fall a victim to some of the most childish superstitions of the human race.

THE POETS AND LIBERAL THEOLOGY *

* The Development of Theology as Illustrated in English Poetry from 1780 to 1830. By Stopf ord A. Brooke. London: Green, Essex-street.

Unitarianism has had wealth and learning on its side for several generations, it has also enjoyed the services of some men of singular ability, yet it has signally failed to make an impression upon the general public. In all probability it ever *will* fail. Those who like theology at all, for the most part like it hot and strong. To purge it of its "grosser" features is to rob it of its chief attraction. The ignorant and thoughtless multitude want plenty of supernaturalism. Those who think for themselves, on the other hand, are apt to grow dissatisfied with theology altogether, and to advance beyond the somewhat arbitrary and fantastic limits of the Unitarian faith. For this reason Unitarianism was called by Erasmus Darwin, the grandfather of the great Charles Darwin, a feather bed to catch a falling Christian. Others regard it as a halfway house between Christianity and Atheism, or even as a bathing machine for those who would wade, and fear to plunge, in the waters of Freethought.

Let us not, however, deny the distinction of such advocates of the Unitarian faith as Dr. Martineau and Dr. Stopf ord Brooke. The latter was once a clergyman of the Church of England, which he left because he no longer held her tenets, and in this he was more honest and courageous than some others who eat the Church's bread and undermine her faith. Mr. Brooke regards himself as a teacher of positive religion, but in our judgment his service to liberalism is really negative. His writings and sermons are a protest, however decorous, against the orthodox theology; and the protest may be all the more effective, with a certain order of minds, because it does not show them the ultimate consequences of freethinking. When they see the preacher aglow with the ardor of his "purified" faith in God and Immortality, they are encouraged to advance as far as he has gone, and thus to leave behind them the worst portions of the creed of their childhood.

Mr. Brooke is well known in the field of literature, and is held to shine as a critic of poetry. Hence it was that the British and Foreign Unitarian Association appointed him to deliver the first lecture of a course "dealing with some aspect of the history and development of Christianity as viewed from a liberal and progressive standpoint." The special subject selected was the development of theology as illustrated in English poetry, and the lecture is now published in a neat little volume for the general reader.

We notice the frequent recurrence of the phrase "liberal theology." Naturally we like everybody to be liberal, but we cannot see the appropriateness of the epithet in this instance. It would sound strange to talk of "liberal geology" or "liberal chemistry." Why then should we talk of "liberal theology"? If theology is anything but an effort of imagination—as *we* conceive it—it must be a system of ascertained truth. Its propositions are therefore true or false, but they cannot be good or bad, liberal or illiberal. Introduce these epithets, and you make it a matter of taste and preference, or of conformity or non-conformity to the spirit of advancing civilisation. This is indeed what Mr. Brooke appears to mean. He seems to regard theology as liberal or otherwise as it adapts itself to the growth of knowledge and morality. He goes to the length of admitting that secular progress precedes religious progress. "The Church," he says, "has always followed society." The change in theology, which has made it "liberal," or produced that variety of it, could not have appeared "in early Christian times, nor in the middle ages; not as long, that is, as the imperialistic or feudal theory of humanity and its rulers existed." Still more decisively, if possible, he repeats this statement:—"There was no chance then of theology changing until the existing views of human society changed. If theology was to be enlarged, they must first be enlarged." Now this is a truth which we have always insisted on, and the reason of it is destructive to "liberal" and all other kinds of theology. We are told that God made man, but the fact is that man made God, and what he made he is able to keep in repair. The growing idea of God's "love" is not forced upon theologians by a study of nature, nor by a study of scripture. It is forced upon them by the advancing spirit of humanity. God was once a being who loved and hated, and all the "liberal" theologians have done is to minimise his hatred and maximise his love. God has not made any fresh disclosures of himself, as Mr. Brooke teaches; the theologians have simply brought him up to date, and they have done so under the compulsion of secular progress.

Mr. Brooke's conception of the Fatherhood of God is creditable to his feelings. The deity he worships is one who will "effectually call to himself and effectually keep, at last, all his children to whose free-will only one thing is impossible—final division from the sovereignty of his love." But how far is this creditable to Mr. Brooke's intelligence? It is certainly inconsistent with the teaching of Christ, and Mr. Brooke calls himself a Christian. It is no less inconsistent with all we know of Nature, who is supremely indifferent to the fate of individuals. To talk so consumedly of God's love in this age of Darwinism, with its law of natural selection based on a universal struggle for existence, is to fly in the face of common sense. But here, alas, as in so many other cases, the voice of reason is drowned in the chorus of sentimentalism.

With respect to democracy, which is a kind of John the Baptist to Mr. Brooke's form of Christianity, there can be little doubt, we think, that it has been chiefly indebted to science, which has in three centuries, since the days of Copernicus and Galileo, done more to advance the brotherhood of man than has been done by religion from the "first syllable of recorded time." Mr. Brooke does not concern himself with science, however; but he nearly agrees with us in the matter of chronology. A vast alteration in thought, due to whatever causes, had been going on for centuries. It was a change "from exclusiveness to universality," and it "took a literary and philosophical form in the eighteenth century writers in France, and finally emerged a giant in the French Revolution." In that mighty upheaval "the whole of the ideas of the old society perished for ever and ever," and what seems to be left of them is "but their ghosts, a host of pale-eyed, weary phantoms."

This is true and well expressed, but it should be added that most of the eighteenth century writers in France, particularly those who may be called philosophical, were vehemently opposed to Christianity, as were most of the eminent actors in the Revolution. Several of them were downright Atheists, who would have regarded the "liberal theology" of Mr. Brooke as a sign of mental feebleness.

Out of the Revolution sprang the vivid conception of the Brotherhood of Man, and it was this, Mr. Brooke says, that made possible "the conception of God's universal Fatherhood." In other words, a change in human ideas rendered necessary a change in theology. Still, we have Mr. Brooke's word for it, the Churches and sects were the last to move. "In England," he declares, "the resistance offered to these ideas by the religious bodies has been always steady and often rancorous." It was another class of men who seized upon them. These were the Poets, the "most emotional, the most imaginative, the most prophetic, and the most clear-sighted of men." Sometimes they kept the name of Christians, but more often they were called "heretics or infidels, blasphemers or atheists." Occasionally they *were* Atheists, as in the case of Shelley, though it could hardly be expected that Mr. Brooke would emphasise the fact.

After some pithy criticism on William Blake, who was a forceful protestor against the old theology, Mr. Brooke passes on to Burns and Cowper. Of the exquisite satire of *Holy Willie's Prayer*, despite its "irreverence and immorality," which are after all but matters of opinion, Mr. Brooke says that it "weakened the worst doctrines of Calvinism far more than ten thousand liberal sermons have done." Cowper weakened Calvinism too, though he did so unintentionally. The pathos and horror of some of his poems, written under the heavy shadow of this awful creed, did a great deal to discredit it amongst thoughtful and sensitive readers. The poet was asked how he felt when dying. His answer was, "I feel unutterable despair." These terrible words prompt Mr. Brooke to write as follows:—

"They are words which all the good deeds of the professors of Calvinism will never get over. 'He was mad,' they say; but what drove him mad? Did Jesus teach in order that men might become insane? for Cowper is one among millions whom this doctrine of God has ruined morally, intellectually, or physically. But they have perished, unknown, unheard. This man was a poet, and his words have told. His personal acceptance of the horror revealed, as the mockery of Burns did not, the idolatrous foulness of this doctrine concerning God."

Coleridge's one specific contribution as a poet to a wider theology, in the opinion of Mr. Brooke, was the closing verse of the *Ancient Mariner*— which, by the way, is not the closing verse, but the antepenultimate.

> *He prayeth best who loveth best*
>
> *All things both great and small;*
>
> *For the dear God who loveth us*
>
> *He made and loveth all.*

Mr. Brooke holds that Wordsworth did a far ampler work by his doctrine of immanence, which is perilously near Pantheism. Understood, however, in the spirit of "liberal theology," it will not only finally govern, but also "bring about at last the complete reconcilement of science and religion." But we must remind Mr. Brooke that this is sheer prophecy. It is simple enough to utter the counter prophecy that Wordsworth's doctrine will do nothing of the kind.

It is in relation to Byron and Shelley that Mr. Brooke really comes to the point of his essay. Wordsworth and Coleridge turned their backs upon the Revolution. They were disenchanted. They failed to see that the throes of birth were not the end of the progressive process. One sought refuge in Toryism, modified by benevolence; the other in metaphysical moonshine and esoteric theology. Byron, on the other hand, while not in the least constructive, or enamored of the more advanced ideas in religion, politics, and sociology, was filled with a bitter hatred and satiric contempt for the old order of things, with its lies, hypocrisies, and oppressions. He embodied what Mr. Brooke calls "the destroying element of the Revolution," which in him was "directed by great mental force and a reckless daring." Among other things, he struck at "the ancient, accredited doctrines of theology, and he struck savagely." Mr. Brooke is of opinion that the poet "brought free inquiry on theology to the surface of society." But we think the critic is mistaken. Free inquiry on theology had been going on in England for more than a century, and it culminated, on the popular side, in Paine's *Age of Reason.* How far Byron aided the movement is easy of estimation. To tell the truth, he hinted disbelief, and scattered doubt over his pages; but he did no more, he never faced any question manfully; on the problems of religion his mind was chaotic to the very end. It is this phenomena which leads Mr. Brooke to infer that Byron believed in the arbitrary, vengeful God whom he depicted in Cain. "He believes," Mr. Brooke says, "hates what he believes, stamps with fury on his belief, and yet clings to it." Such a conclusion, however, is one we cannot accept. Byron did *not* believe; his prose, and his letters, prove that conclusively. But he had not the courage to disbelieve and to proclaim his disbelief boldly like Shelley, who had a hundred times more real courage than his attitudinising friend, *Manfred* is terrible posing; Mr. Meredith calls it "an after dinner's indigest"; and *Cain* is rather skimble-skamble stuff, though Mr. Brooke calls it "the most powerful, the most human, the most serious thing he ever wrote, and the most effective" — which is surely a most inept criticism. Byron rarely succeeded as a serious poet; when he did so it was only in short flights. He found the proper field for his genius in *Don Juan.* His province was satire, and the *Vision of Judgment* is at the top of English achievement in this direction, A creative imagination he did not possess, any more than a profound intellect; and it was the perception of this fact which prompted his impertinent sneers at Shakespeare. But he had imagination enough to give wings to his satire, and an inexhaustible wit which played like lightning around the objects of his indignation or contempt. Never did he reason like Shelley, and it is clear that he was afraid to; he attacked in his own way what he *felt* to be false and despicable, and the sword he wielded was ravishingly (or terribly) brilliant, though it *never cut deep enough.* One loves to think of him at last, however, laying down his life, as he gave his substance, for the freedom of Greece. With all his faults, no pious or cowardly fear of death ever haunted his mighty spirit. How gloriously he would have died on the battle-field, fighting desperately for the cause of the people! The last verses he ever wrote showed the troubled stream of his life running pure at its close. Noble and sincere in its language, it was a fitting farewell to the world; and although the poet did not find his "soldier's grave," he died none the less for the cause to which he had pledged his fortune and the remnant of his strength.

"Shelley did also a work of destruction," says Mr. Brooke, "though in a very different way from Byron." We should think so indeed! The "also" is singularly weak in this instance, for Shelley attacked the Christian superstition directly, and *Queen Mab* had far more readers than *Cain*, the cheap, pirated editions being circulated extensively among the working classes.

"He began," says Mr. Brooke, "by being an Atheist, he ended by being what we call an Agnostic." But is this any more than a verbal distinction? It appears to us that Shelley's principles are the same in *Prometheus Unbound* as in *Queen Mab*. The change is in their presentation; the passionate vehemence of youth is succeeded by the restrained power of manhood. It is true that Shelley sang the praises of Love—"immortal" Love if you choose to call it so; but Mr. Brooke has to admit that he did not "give it a personal life." Shelley also "thinks Immortality improbable," yet, Mr. Brooke says, he "glides into words in his poems which continually imply it." But this we deny. Allowing for personification and emphasis, without which there can be no poetry, we venture to affirm that there is not a single passage, line, or phrase in Shelley's later poems which is not in essential harmony with his belief in the mortality of man and the practical immortality of the race. It is one of the offences of theologians ("liberal" or otherwise) in relation to Shelley, that they try to turn metaphors into logical propositions, in order to make the poet give evidence against himself.

In one respect, however, we quite agree with Mr. Brooke. "Liberal theology" has *not* yet "reached the level of Shelley's thought," nor can it ever do so until it ceases to be Theology and becomes simple Humanity. Mr. Brooke may flatter himself that he has "a higher faith than Shelley had," but we think he is mistaken. Substitute "blinder" for "higher" and the expression would be more accurate. Shelley did believe that Love—not alone, but co-operating with Knowledge—would achieve the salvation of mankind; but he resolutely refused to talk about man's "destiny in God the Father," which seems to afford such comfort to the devotees of "liberal theology." For this he deserves the gratitude of all scientific Humanitarians, who should protest with all their might against the attempt to emasculate him into a prophet, or even an advance agent, of some new form of Godism. "Liberal theology" should beget its own poet, if it can; it should not try to steal the poet of Humanity.

CHRISTIANITY AND LABOR*

*Sept. 24,1893.

Whatever else may be thought about the present coal-strike, or lock-out, as it might be more accurately described, it will be admitted by many persons who do not rail at Political Economy that the miners are following a sound instinct in demanding that a decent wage shall be a fixed element in price. To dig coal out of the earth is worth a minimum of (say) thirty shillings a week, and if it will not yield that modest remuneration to the worker let it stay where it is, and let the community do without coal altogether. Morally speaking, society has no right to demand that an important industry shall be carried on under conditions involving the misery, and still less the degradation, of those employed in it. Nor is this a wild, revolutionary doctrine; it is eminently conservative, in the best sense of the word; and it will have to be admitted, and acted upon, in the interest of social order. Of course it means an inroad on rent and speculative profit, but that is not an immeasurable calamity.

So much, by way of introduction, on the moral and economic aspects of the matter. Our special object is rather theological. We desire to notice the part which religion plays in the struggle between capital and labor; or, more properly perhaps, between the "haves" and the "have-nots."

Everyone with an elementary knowledge of the social and political history of the last hundred years must be aware that the working classes, as such, have had no help whatever from Christian Churches. Here and there an individual clergyman has spoken a word on their behalf, but the great mass of the men of God have been on the side of "the powers that be," and have insulted and derided the advocates and leaders of Trade Unionism, whom they are still fond of calling "pestilent agitators." Yet the Gospel, and especially the Sermon on the Mount, is stuffed with platitudes about the blessings and virtues of poverty, and the curse and wickedness of wealth. Logically, therefore, judging by the letter of scripture, the clergy should have been on the side of the poor, the wretched, and the oppressed. But this is a case in which "the letter killeth," and with an eye to their own interests and privileges, to say nothing of their ease and comfort, the clergy found that "the spirit" of the Gospel meant the preservation of the existing conditions of society. It would be bad for the rich, and well for the poor, in the next life; but, in this life, they were to keep their relative places, and remain content in the positions which Providence had assigned them.

It is not surprising, then, that the Christian Churches—with all their wealth, power, and at least pretended influence—should be idle or unctuously hypocritical spectators of the struggles of labor to obtain a fair share of the blessings of civilisation. They extend just sufficient verbal patronage to labor to save themselves from being howled at, and throw all their real weight in the scale against it. And it is folly to expect any better of them. The religion and the training of the clergy make them what they are, and they can no more alter than the Ethiopian can change his skin or the leopard his spots. Religion is always the consecration of the past; never the spirit of the future working in the present; and the clergy, who, as Sidney Smith said, are a third sex—neither male nor female, but effeminate—are instinctively conservative, thoroughly enamored of what is, and obstinately averse to all radical changes. Their timidity would be quite phenomenal, if they were *not* the third sex; and, like all timid people, they can shriek and yell and curse and foam at the mouth when they are well frightened.

Were it otherwise, were Christianity a real agency for social improvement, and the clergy the moral leaders of the people, we should have seen by this time a tremendous alteration in the condition, and the relations, of all classes of society. There might still be differences, but they would be on a higher plane, and less grievous and exasperating. As the case stands, all the best of the clergy can do is to preach harmless platitudes once a week. One Bishop has been actually harangueing the miners, and only provoking contemptuous remarks about his salary. The truth is, that Christian ministers are, in the main, only fit to preach kingdom-come. That is their proper work, ana they are exactly cut out for it.

We are not in love with all the details of the elaborate ecclesiasticism of Comte's Religion of Humanity, but we are bound to say that a philosophical priesthood, such as he planned, would be better fitted than a Christian priesthood for the work of moral control and social diplomacy. There is an ethical as well as an economical element in most of these disputes between labor and capital; and a philosophical priesthood, vowed to study and simplicity of life, would be able to intervene with some effect. It would be something, indeed, to have the deliberate judgment of a dispassionate though sympathetic tribunal, even though it had—and could and should have—no authority to enforce its decisions. At present, however, all this is Utopian, and perhaps it always will be so. We will return, therefore, to our immediate object, which is to point out the utter uselessness of Christianity in the midst of class antagonisms. It cannot control the rich, it cannot assist the poor. Its chief idea is to stand between the two, not as an ambassador of justice, but as a dispenser of charity. And *this* charity, instead of really helping the people, only serves to obscure the problems to be solved, and to perpetuate the evils it affects to relieve.

AN EASTER EGG FOR CHRISTIANS *

* April, 1893.

Christian Fellow Citizens,—

We are living together in this world, but I do not know whether we shall live together in the next world. You probably consider yourself as booked for heaven, and me as booked for the other establishment. But that is a question I will not discuss at present. I will only remark that you may be mistaken. Existence, you know, is full of surprises; and, as the French say, it is always the unexpected that happens.

Well, my fellow citizens of this world, it is now the time when you celebrate the death and resurrection of your "Savior." Not being of your faith, I cannot join in the commemoration. I shall, however, regard the season after a more primitive fashion. Your Church adopted an old Pagan festival, the rejoicing at the renewal of the earth in the genial springtide. At the vernal equinox the sun is increasing in power, the world is astir with new life, and begins to reassume its mantle of green. Such a time inspired jollity in the human breast. It was commemorated with feast and dance and song. Perhaps it will be so again, even in sombre England, when the gloom of your ascetic creed has lifted and disappeared. Meanwhile I, as a "heathen man and a sinner," will imitate as far as I may the example of the Pagans of old. I will not sing, for I am no adept in that line; and my joints are getting too stiff for dancing. But I will feast, within the bounds of reason; I will leave this million-peopled Babylon and put myself in touch with Mother Nature; I will feel, if only for a brief while, the spring of the turf under my feet; I will breathe air purified by "the moving waters at their priest-like task Of pure ablution round earth's human shores"; I will watch the seahorses, with their white crests, in endless rank, charging the shore; I will listen to the sound which Homer heard so long before your Christ was born—the sound so monotonous, so melancholy, yet so soothing and sustaining, which stirs a pulse of poetry in the very dullest and most prosaic brain. But before I go I send you this Easter egg, to show that I do not forget you. Keep it, I pray you; study well its inscriptions; and perhaps, after all, you will not pelt me with it at the finish.

I have said, my Christian fellow citizens, that your Church appropriated an ancient Pagan festival—the festival of spring. I may be told by scholars amongst you that the time of Christ's crucifixion and resurrection was fixed by the Jewish Passover. I reply that the Passover was itself a spring festival, whose original and natural meaning was obscured by priestly arts and legendary stories. That it happened at this time of the year, that it depended on astronomical signs, that its commemoration included the sacrifice of the firstlings of the flock—shows clearly enough that it was a Jewish counterpart of the common Gentile celebration. Has it ever occurred to you that if Christ died, he died on a particular day; and that if he rose from the dead, he rose on a particular morning? That day, that morning, should have been observed in the proper fashion of anniversaries. But it never was, and it is not now. Good Friday—as you curiously, and almost facetiously call the day on which the founder of your faith suffered a painful and ignominious death—and Easter Sunday, when he left his sepulchre, never fall on the same date in successive years. They are determined by calculations of the position of the sun and the phases of the moon—a planet sacred to lovers and lunatics, and naturally dear therefore to devotion and superstition. You decorate your churches with evergreens and flowers as the Pagans decorated their temples and altars. You use Easter eggs like the pre-Christian religionists. You show, and your creed shows, in everything that Easter is really a spring festival. The year springs from the tomb of winter, and Christ springs at the same time from the tomb of death.

I am disposed to regard your "Savior" as a purely mythical personage, like all other Saviors and sun-gods of antiquity, who were generally, if not always, born miraculously of virgin mothers, mysteriously impregnated by celestial visitors; and whose careers, like that of your Christ, were marked by portents and prodigies, ending in tribulation and defeat, which were followed by vindication and triumph. Whether there was a man called Jesus, or Joshua (the Jewish form of the name), who lived and taught in Galilee and died at Jerusalem, is more than I will undertake to determine, and it seems to me a question of microscopic importance. But I am convinced that the Christ of the Gospels is the product of religious imagination; an ideal figure, constructed out of materials that were common in the East for hundreds and perhaps for thousands of years.

To confine ourselves, however, to the Easter aspect of the matter, I think you will find—if you read the Gospel story with unprejudiced eyes—that the closing scenes of Christ's career are quite imaginary. The story of his Trial and Crucifixion is utterly at variance with Roman law and Jewish custom. It also includes astonishing incidents—such as the earthquake which rent the veil of the temple, the three hours' eclipse of the sun, and the wholesale resurrection of dead "saints"—of which the Romans and the Jews were in a still more astonishing ignorance. What must have startled the whole or the then known world, if it happened, made absolutely no impression on the Hebrew and Gentile nations, and not a trace of it remains in the pages of their historians. Can you believe that the most remarkable occurrences on record escaped the attention of all who were living at the time, with the exception of a handful of men and women, who never took the trouble to write an account of their experiences, but left them to be chronicled by unknown writers long after they themselves were dead?

All the documentary evidence we possess is Christian. It is the witness of an interested party, uncorroborated by a particle of testimony from independent sources. I do not forget that the literature of your early Church includes a letter from Pontius Pilate to the emperor Tiberius, giving a detailed account of the trial, sentence, crucifixion, and resurrection of Christ; but this is one of the many forgeries of your early Church, and is now universally rejected as such alike by Protestant and by Catholic scholars. To my mind, indeed, this forgery itself proves the falsehood of the Gospel narrative; it shows that the early Christians felt the necessity of some corroborative evidence, and they manufactured it to give their own statements an air of greater plausibility.

Taking the Gospels as they stand, I will ask you to read the story in Matthew (not that I believe *he* wrote it) of the watch at Christ's sepulchre. The Jewish priests come to Pilate, and ask him to let the sepulchre be sealed and guarded; for the dead impostor had declared he would rise again on the third day, and his disciples might steal his body and say he had risen. The guard is set, but an angel descends from heaven, terrifies the soldiers, rolls away the stone, and allows Jesus to escape. Whereupon the Jewish priests give the soldiers money to tell Pilate that they slept at their posts.

How, I ask, did those Jewish priests know that Jesus had said "After three days I will rise again"? According to John (xx. 9), his very disciples were ignorant of this fact—"For as yet they knew not the scripture, that he must rise again from the dead." Could it be unknown to his intimates, who had been with him day and night for three years, in all parts of Palestine; yet well known to the priests, who had only seen him occasionally during a few days at Jerusalem?

There was an "earthquake" before the angels descended. Would not this have attracted general attention? And is it conceivable that the soldiers would take money to say they had slept at their posts? The punishment for that offence was death. Of what use then was the bribe? Do men sell their honor for what they can never enjoy, and count their lives as a mere trifle in the bargain? Is it conceivable that the priests were so foolish as the story depicts them? Would bribing the soldiers protect them against Christ? If he had risen he was lord of life and death. Would they not have abandoned their projects against him, and sought his forgiveness? He who had the power to revive himself had the power to destroy them.

The appearances of Jesus, after his resurrection, are grotesque in their self-contradiction. Now he is a pure ghost, suddenly appearing and suddenly vanishing, and entering a room with shut doors. Then he appears as solid flesh and blood, to be felt and handled. He even eats broiled fish and honeycomb.

Such conditions are quite irreconcilable. We may imagine a ghost going through a keyhole, but is it possible to imagine broiled fish and honeycomb going through the same aperture? Or is the stomach of a ghost capable of digesting such victuals?

Has it never struck you as strange, also, that the risen Christ never appeared to anyone but his disciples? No outsider, no independent witness, ever caught a glimpse of him. The story is a party report to prove a party position and maintain a party's interests. Surely, if Christ died for *all men*, if his resurrection is the pledge of ours, and if our inability to believe it involves our perdition, *the fact* should have been established beyond all cavil. Christ should have stood before Pilate who sentenced him to be crucified; he should have confronted the Sanhedrim who compassed his death; he might even have walked about freely amongst the Jews during the forty days (more or less) during which, as the New Testament narrates, he flitted about like a hedge-row ghost. He should have made his resurrection as clear as daylight, and he left it as dark as night.

To ask what became of the body of Jesus if he did not rise, is an idle question. There is not the slightest *contemporary* evidence that his body was an object of concern. On the other hand, however, the story of the Ascension looks like a convenient refuge. To talk of a risen Christ was to invite the question "Where is he?" The story of the Ascension enabled the talkers to answer "He is gone up." It relieved them from the awkward necessity of producing him.

Space does not allow of my discussing this subject more extensively. I could swell this Easter egg into gigantic proportions, but I must leave it as it is It goes to you with my compliments, and a hope that it will do you good. If it leads any of you to "take a thought and mend," if it induces one of you to review the faith of his childhood, if it stirs a rational impulse in a single Christian mind, I shall be amply rewarded for my trouble.—Christian fellow citizens, Adieu!—I remain, Yours for Reason and Humanity.

DUELLING *

* *July 22, 1888.*

One result of the recent duel between M. Floquet and the melodramatic General Boulanger is that Bishop Freppel has moved in the Chamber of Deputies for the legal abolition of private combats. That a bishop should do this is remarkable. If Bishop Freppel possessed any sense of humor, he would leave the task to laymen. His Church did not establish duelling; on the contrary, she censured it; but it was countenanced by her principles, and her protest was unavailing. The judicial combat was an appeal to God, like the ordeal by fire or water, or the purgation by oath. The Church patronised those forms of superstition which brought men to her altars, and ministered to her profit and power, and she opposed those superstitions which were inimical to her interest. When legal proofs failed and suits were undecided; when persons were accused of crimes, of which they could neither be proved guilty nor held guiltless; or when they lay under gross suspicion of wrong, the Church proffered the ordeal. She invited the litigants, or the suspected parties, to handle hot iron, plunge their arms into boiling liquid, or be thrown into water deep enough to drown them; and if they underwent such treatment without injury, she held them innocent. Another device was the oath. The parties went to the Church altar and swore their innocence or the justice of their cause. But all these methods gave room for chicane. Kings and knights protested that the oath led to indiscriminate perjury, that if the priests' hands were tickled with money the hot iron was only painted, and that a suitable fee could render the boiling liquid innocuous to the skin of a baby. They therefore drew their swords, exclaiming, "Away with this priestly jugglery! These weapons are better than fire or water or oil, and God can decide the right in single combat as in the Churchman's ordeal."

"Is it not true," asked King Gundobald of Bishop Avitus, "that the event of national wars and private combats is directed by the judgment of God; and that his providence awards the victory to the juster cause?" The Bishop could not answer "No," for if he did he would have demolished the whole Church system of ordeals, so he yielded to the arguments of his sovereign.

Single combats, under the Gothic code, were fought according to judicial forms. They were held, Robertson says, "as solemn appeals to the omniscience and justice of the Supreme Being." Shakespeare is careful to to notice this feature. When Bolingbroke and Norfolk, in *Richard II.*, challenge each other as traitors, the king consents to their duel in the following terms:

At Coventry, upon Saint Lambert's day: There shall your swords and lances arbitrate The swelling difference of your settled hate. Since we cannot atone you, we shall see Justice design the victor's chivalry.

Modern duelling is thus a survival of the old judicial combat. The "point of honor" is the excuse for a practice which has lost its original sanction. The appeal to God is forgotten, and the duellists talk of "satisfaction." Illogical no doubt, but this is only one of many customs that survive their original meaning.

Now the Church cannot hold itself guiltless in regard to this folly. She cherished the superstition on which it rested. She taught the policy of appealing to God, and only frowned on the particular method which brought no grist to her mill. Her own methods were still more senseless. Unless the laws of nature were constantly subverted, her ordeals must have operated at random when they were not regulated by fraud. The hand of guilt might be harder than that of innocence, and more likely to bear a moment's contact with hot iron or boiling oil. Besides, as Montesquieu observes, the poltroon stood the poorest chance in the judicial combat, and the poltroon was more likely to be guilty than the man of courage. The weak, of course, were at the mercy of the strong; but in one point, at least, the combat had an obvious advantage over the other ordeals.

How amusing it must have been to a sceptic, if such then existed, to see the opposition between the nobles and the clergy. The nobles said "Fight!" and the clergy cried "That is impious." The clergy said "Swear!" and the nobles cried "That is sacrilege and leads to perjury."

No less amusing was the turn which combat took in Spain in the eleventh century. There was a struggle between the Latin and the Gothic liturgy. Aragon yielded to the papal pressure, but Castile thought the contest should be decided by the sword. Accordingly, Mosheim tells us, two champions were chosen; they fought, and the Latin liturgy was defeated. But the Romish party was not satisfied. The two liturgies were thrown into a fire, and the result of the ordeal was another triumph for the Goths. Still the divine decisions are frail when opposed to the interests of the Church. Queen Constantia, who controlled King Alphonso, sided with the pontiff of Rome, and the priest and the lady carried the day.

Though incorporated in the judicial system of Christendom, the duel is scorned by the Turks, and was unknown to the Greeks and Romans. Lord Bacon remarks this in one of his admirable law tracts:

"All memory doth consent that Greece and Rome were the most valiant and generous nations of the world; and, that which is more to be noted, they were free estates, and not under a monarchy; whereby a man would think it a great deal the more reason that particular persons should have righted themselves; and yet they had not this practice of duels, nor anything that bare show thereof." (*Charge against Duels.*)

Bacon observes that the most valorous and generous nations scorn this practice. Why then did it obtain so long in Christendom? Was it because the Northern and Western nations were cowardly and selfish? Nothing of the kind; it was because they were superstitious, and their superstition was cherished by the Church. Even at the present day the Church calls international combat an appeal to God; regimental banners are consecrated by priests, and laid up in temples when dilapidated; and Catholic and Protestant priests alike implore victory for their respective sides in time of war. And why not? Is not the Bible God "the Lord of Hosts" and "a man of war"? Did he not teach David's fingers to fight? Were not Joshua and Jehu, the two greatest tigers in history, his chosen generals? Why then should he be averse to international butchery in Europe? Should he not rejoice in the next bloody cockpit of featherless bipeds? And is it not hard to see his infinite appetite for blood reduced to content itself with an occasional duel, in which not enough of the sanguine fluid is shed to make a small black-pudding? Bishop Freppel is ill-advised. He should not rob his Deity of his last consolation.

DOWN AMONG THE DEAD MEN *

* July 2, 1893.

The ramming and sinking of the "Victoria" is the great event of the day. It is said to show the uselessness of big ironclads in naval warfare. But as the "Camperdown," which sent the "Victoria" to the bottom in a few minutes, has herself sustained very little damage, it looks as though "rams" were anything but inefficient. There has never yet been an engagement between two fleets of ironclads, and no one knows how they would behave in an actual battle. Our own impression is that both fleets would go to the bottom, and this opinion is shared by a good many practical persons at Portsmouth and Devonport. However that may be, it is a great pity that "civilised" nations are still so uncivilised as to spend their time and money on these costly engines of destruction. We are well aware that the newspapers go into hysterics over our soldiers and sailors, and no doubt many of them are very gallant fellows. But in this, we venture to think, they do not represent the masses of the people. Never have we witnessed such deep and sincere enthusiasm as was displayed by the crowd of spectators at the Agricultural Hall, while the American, Portuguese, and English firemen were going through their evolutions. The business of these fine fellows was to *save* life. They incurred the deadliest danger for human preservation, and not for human destruction. And how the people cheered them as they rode upon their engines, drawn by galloping horses! With what breathless interest they watched them climbing up ladders, sliding down ropes, and bearing men on their backs out of third-floor windows! It did one good to watch the proceedings, which showed that a new spirit was taking possession of the people, that they were beginning to be more interested in the savers than in the slayers of men.

But all this is a digression. Let us return to the "Victoria." She is now in eighty fathoms of water with her hundreds of dead. Poor fellows! theirs was a sad fate; though not more so than the fate of miners blasted or suffocated in explosive pits. We pity their dear ones—mothers, sisters, wives, and children. Hundreds, perhaps thousands, of hearts are aching on their account; mourning for the dead who will never be buried under the sweet churchyard grass, though they have the whole ocean for their tomb and the stars for its nightlamps.

On Sunday, of course, the sky-pilots, all over England, were busy at "improving the occasion." They always make profit out of death and disaster. "Prepare to meet thy God!" was the lesson which most of them derived from this catastrophe. Of course the preachers are ready *themselves*. Who can doubt it? But they are in no hurry to have it tested. They do not want to meet their God until they are obliged to. It is so much better to be a commercial traveller in God's service than to take a situation in the house.

Some of the preachers dared to talk about "Providence"—the sweet little cherub that sits up aloft, to keep watch o'er the life of poor Jack, and lets him go to the bottom or furnish a dinner for sharks. Surely that Providence is a rare old fraud. A cripple, a paralytic, a sleeper, a dead man, could have done as much for the "Victoria" as Providence managed to do. "Oh!" it is said, "but the drowned sailors are gone to Heaven; Providence looked after them in that way." Indeed! Then why do you lament over them? Still more, why do you congratulate the survivors? According to your theory, they have missed a slice of good luck.

We have frequently remarked, and we now repeat, that religion is based upon the bed-rock of *selfishness*; and nothing proves the truth of this so clearly, and so convincingly, as the talk that people indulge in about Providence. For instance, take this telegram, which is printed in the newspapers as having been sent home to a gentleman in England:—"Jack saved. Awful affair. Thank God!" This telegram was written hastily, but it was sincere; the writer had no time to drop into hypocrisy. "Jack saved" was his first thought; that is, Jack is still on earth and out of heaven. "Awful affair" was his second thought; that is, a lot of other poor devils are gone to heaven—anyhow, they are no longer on earth. "Thank God" was his third thought; that is, Jack's all right. Thus it was two for our Jack, and one for all the hundreds who perished! It may be pointed out, too, that "Thank God!" comes in the wrong place; where it stands it seems to thank God for the calamity. Yes, so it does, if we look at the mere composition; but the order of the ejaculations is all right, if we look at the sentiment, the pious sentiment, of the person who wrote the telegram. He followed the logic of his personal feelings, like everyone else who "thanks God" and talks of Providence.

Season and personal feeling often do not coincide. In this case, for instance, it requires a very slight exercise of the intellect to see that, if Providence saved "Jack," Providence drowned the rest. "No," some will reply, "Providence did not drown them, but only let them drown." Well, that is exactly the same thing. Superficially, it is the same thing; for Providence, like men, is responsible for omissions as well as commissions. If you let a blind man walk over a precipice without warning him, you are his murderer, you are guilty of his blood. Resolving not to do a thing is as much an act of will as resolving to do it. "Thou shalt" is a law as imperative as "Thou shalt not," though it does not figure in the decalogue. Profoundly also, as well as superficially, Providence, if it saved Jack, killed those who perished; for, as Jack was not visibly fished out of the water by Providence, it can only be held that Providence saved him on the ground that Providence *does everything,* which covers the whole of our contention. "I the Lord do all these things." So says the Bible, and so you must believe, if you have a God at all.

SMIRCHING A HERO

*"He who fights with priests may make up his mind to have
his poor good name torn and befouled by the most infamous
lies and the most cutting slanders."* —*Heine.*

The great poet and wit, Heinrich Heine, from whom we select a motto
for this article, was not very partial to Englishmen, and still less partial
to Scotchmen. He had no objection to their human nature, but a strong
objection to their religion, which so resembles that of the chosen people—
being, indeed, chiefly modelled on the Old Testament pattern—that he was
led to describe them as modern Jews, who only differed from the ancient
ones in eating pork. Doubtless a great improvement has taken place since
Heine penned that pungent description, but Scotland is still the home
of orthodoxy, and most inaccessible to Liberal ideas, unless they wear a
political garb. It need not astonish us, therefore, that a bitter attack on a
Freethought martyr like Giordano Bruno should emanate from the land
of John Knox; or that it should appear in the distinctly national magazine
which is called the *Scottish Review*. The writer does not disclose his name,
and this is a characteristic circumstance. He indulges his malevolence, and
airs his ignorance, under a veil of anonymity. His stabs are delivered like
those of a bravo, who hides his face as he deals his treacherous blow.

Many books and articles have been written on Giordano Bruno, but this
writer seems ignorant of them all, except a recent volume by a Romish priest
of the Society of Jesus, which he places at the top of his article, and relies
upon throughout as an infallible authority. It does not occur to him that an
account of Bruno by a Jesuit member of the Church which murdered him,
is hardly likely to be impartial; nor does he scent anything suspicious in
the fact that the documents reporting Bruno's trial were all written by the
Inquisition. He would probably sniff at a report of the trial of Jesus Christ
by the Scribes and Pharisees, yet that is precisely the kind of document on
which he relies to blast the memory of Bruno.

Some of those Inquisition records he translates, apparently fancying he
is making a revelation, though? they have long been before the scholarly
public, and were extensively cited in the English *Life of Bruno*, by I. Frith,

which saw the light more than twelve months ago. Berti reprinted the documents of Bruno's trial in Venice in 1880, so that the startling revelations of Father Previti are at least seven years behind the fair.

Before dealing, however, with the use he would make of those documents, we think it best to track this Scotch slanderer throughout his slimy course, and expose his astounding mixture of ignorance, impudence and meanness.

Let us take two instances of the last "virtue" first. He actually condescends to attempt a feeble point in regard to Bruno's name. Bruno, he sagely observes—with an air of originality only intelligible on the ground that he is conscious of writing for the veriest ignoramuses—is the same as *Brown*; and hence, if we take the baptismal name of Filippo Bruno, it simply means Philip Brown. Well, what of that? What's in a name? One great English poet rejoiced in the vulgar name of Jonson; two other English poets bore the no less vulgar name of Thomson; while at least two have descended so low as Smith. We might even remind the orthodox libeller that Joshua, the Jewish formi of Jesus, was as common as Jack is among ourselves. Perhaps the reminder will sound blasphemous in his delicate ears, but fact is fact, and if reputations are to depend on names, we may as well be impartial.

Now, for our second instance. Bruno was betrayed to the Venetian Inquisition by Count Mocenigo while he was that nobleman's guest. Mocenigo had invited him to Venice in order that he might learn what this writer calls "his peculiar system for developing and strengthening the memory," although this "peculiar" system was simply the Lullian method. What the nobleman really wanted to learn seems to have been the Black Art. He complained, and Bruno resolved to leave him; whereupon the "nobleman," who had harbored Bruno for months, forcibly detained him, and denounced him to the Inquisition as a heretic and a blasphemer. A more dastardly action is difficult to conceive, but our Scotch libeller is ready to defend it, or at least to give it a coat of whitewash. He allows that Mocenigo does not appear to have been animated "with the motive of religious zeal," and that his "conscience" never "troubled him" before the "personal difference." But he discovers a plea for this Judas in his "sworn statement" to the Inquisition that he did not suspect Bruno of being a monk until the very day of their quarrel. What miserable sophistry! Would not a man who violated the most sacred laws of friendship and hospitality be quite capable of telling a lie? Still more miserable is the remark that Bruno was not ultimately tried on Mocenigo's denunciations, but on his own published writings. Jesus Christ was not tried on the denunciations of Judas Iscariot, but on his own public utterances, yet whoever pleaded that this gave a sweeter savor to the traitor's kiss?

So much—though more might be said—for the writer's meanness. Now for his other virtues, and especially his ignorance. After dwelling on the battle at Rome over the proposal to erect a public monument to Bruno, this writer tells us that "a small literature is arising on the subject," and that the name of Bruno is "suddenly invested with an importance which it never formerly possessed." Apparently he is unaware that, so far from a small literature arising, a large Bruno literature has long existed. He has only to turn to the end of Frith's book, and he will find an alphabetical list of books, articles, and criticisms on Bruno, filling no less than ten pages of small type. He might also enlighten his ridiculous darkness by reading the fine chapter in Lewes's *History of Philosophy*, Mr. Swinburne's two noble sonnets, and Professor Tyndall's glowing eulogy of Bruno's scientific prescience in the famous Belfast address. Perhaps Hallam, Schwegler, Hegel, Bunsen and Cousin are too recondite for the Scotch libeller's perusal; but he might, at any rate, look up Lewes, Swinburne and Tyndall, who are probably accessible in his local Free Library.

What on earth, too, does he mean by Bruno's "great obscurity" when he returned to Italy and fell into the jaws of the Inquisition? Every scholar in that age was more or less obscure, for the multitude was illiterate, and sovereigns and soldiers monopolised the public attention. But as notoriety then went, Bruno was a famous figure. Proof of this will be given presently. Meanwhile we may notice the cheap sneer at Bruno as "a social and literary failure." Shelley was a literary failure in his lifetime, but he is hardly so now; and if Bruno was poor and unappreciated, Time has adjusted the balance, for after the lapse of three centuries he is loved and hated by the rival parties of progress and reaction.

Now let us disprove the Scotch libeller's statements as to "the extreme obscurity in which Giordano Bruno lived and died." Bruno was so "obscure" that he fled from Naples, and doffed his priest's raiment, at the age of twenty-eight or twenty-nine, because his superiors were proceeding against him for heresy, through an act of accusation which comprised no less than one hundred and thirty counts. He was so "obscure" that the rest of his life was a prolonged flight from persecution. He was so "obscure" that the Calvinists hunted him out of Geneva, whence he narrowly escaped with his life; the documents relating to the proceedings against him being still preserved in the Genevan archives. He was so "obscure" that he took a professorship at Toulouse, and publicly lectured there to large audiences for more than a year. He was so "obscure" that King Henry III. made him professor extraordinary at Paris, and excused him from attending Mass. He was so "obscure" that the learned doctors of the Sorbonne waxed wroth with him, and made it obvious that his continued stay in Paris would be dangerous to his health. He was so "obscure" that he lived for nearly three years as the guest of the French ambassador in London. He was so "obscure" that he was known at the court of Elizabeth. He was so "obscure" that he was a friend of Sir Philip Sidney, and an intimate associate of Dyer, Fulk Greville, and the chief wits of his age. He was so "obscure" that he was allowed, as a distinguished foreigner, to lecture at Oxford, and to hold a public disputation on the Aristotelian philosophy before the Chancellor and the university. He was so "obscure" that on his return to Paris he held another public disputation under the auspices of the King. He was so "obscure" that his orations were listened to by the senate of the university of Wittenberg. He was so "obscure" that he was publicly excommunicated by the zealot Boethius. He was so "obscure" that the Venetian Inquisition broke through its stern rule, and handed him over as a special favor to the Inquisition of Rome. He was so "obscure" that he was at last "butchered to make a Roman holiday," the cardinals having presided at his trial, and his sentence being several pages at length. Such was "the obscurity in which Giordano Bruno lived and died."

The Scotch libeller hints that Bruno was not burnt after all. He forgets, or he is ignorant of the fact, that all doubt on that point is removed by the three papers discovered in the Vatican Library. He merely repeats the insinuation of M. Desduits, which has lost its extremely small measure of plausibility since the discovery of those documents. The martyrdom of Bruno is much better attested than the Crucifixion. There always was contemporary evidence as well as unbroken tradition, and now we have proofs as complete as can be adduced for any event in history.

From the documentary evidence it is clear that Bruno fought hard for his life, and he would have been a fool or a suicide to have acted otherwise. He bent all his dialectical skill, and all his subtle intellect, to the task of proving that religion and philosophy were distinct, and that so long as a scholar conformed in practice he should be allowed the fullest liberty of speculation. The Inquisition, however, pretends that he abjured all his errors, and the Scotch libeller is pleased to say he recanted. But, in that case, why was Bruno burnt alive at the stake? According to the laws of the Inquisition, all who reconciled themselves to the Church after sentence were strangled before they were burnt. And why was Bruno allowed a week's grace before his execution, except to give him the opportunity of recanting? Despite all this Jesuitical special pleading, the fact remains that Bruno was sentenced and burnt as an incorrigible heretic; and the fact also remains that when the crucifix was held up for him to kiss as he stood amidst the flames, he rejected it, as Scioppus wrote, "with a terrible menacing countenance." Not only did he hurl scorn at his judges, telling them that they passed his sentence with more fear than he heard it; but his last words were that "he died a martyr and willingly" —*diceva che moriva martire et volontieri.*

Bruno is further charged by the Scotch libeller with servility, an accusation about as plausible as that Jesus Christ was a highwayman. A passage is cited from Bruno's high-flown panegyric on Henry III. as "a specimen of the language he was prepared to employ towards the great when there was anything to be got from them." Either this writer is ineffably ignorant, or his impudence is astounding. In the first place, that was an age of high-flown dedications. Look at Bacon's fulsome dedication of his *Advancement of Learning* to James I. Nay, look at the dedication of our English Bible to the same monarch, who is put very little below God Almighty, and compared to the sun for strength and glory. In the next place, Bruno's praise of Henry III. was far from mercenary. He never at any time had more than bread to eat. He was grateful to the King for protection, and his gratitude never abated. When Henry was in ill repute, Bruno still praised him, and these panegyrics were put into one of the counts against "the heretic" when he was arraigned at Venice.

The last libel is extorted from Bruno's comedy, *Il Candelajo.* The Scotch puritan actually scents something obscene in the very title; to which we can only reply by parodying Carlyle—"The nose smells what it brings." As for the comedy itself, it must be judged by the standard of its age. Books were then all written for men, and reticence was unknown. Yet, free as *Il Candelajo* is sometimes in its portrayal of contemporary manners, it does not approach scores of works which are found "in every gentleman's library." It certainly is not freer than Shakespeare; it is less free than the Song of Solomon; it is infinitely less free than Ezekiel. Nor was the comedy the work of Bruno's maturity; it was written in his youth, while he was a priest, before he fell under grave suspicion of heresy, and we may be sure it was relished by his brother priests in the Dominican monastery. To draw from this youthful *jeu d'e'sprit*, a theory of Bruno's attitude towards women is a grotesque absurdity. We have his fine sonnets written in England, especially the one "Inscribed to the most Virtuous and Delightful Ladies," in which he celebrates the beauty, sweetness, and chastity of our English "spouses and daughters of angelic birth." Still more striking is the eulogy in his "Canticle of the Shining Ones." Bruno, like every poet, was susceptible to love; but he was doomed to wander, and the affection of wife and babes was not for him. So he made Philosophy his mistress, and his devotion led him to the stake. Surely there was a prescience of his fate in the fine apostrophe of his *Heroic Rapture*—"O worthy love of the beautiful! O desire for the divine! lend me thy wings; bring me to the dayspring, to the clearness of the young morning; and the outrage of the rabble, the storms of Time, the slings and arrows of Fortune, shall fall upon this tender body and shall weld it to steel."

KIT MARLOWE AND JESUS CHRIST *

* *December, 1888.*

Christopher Marlowe, whose "mighty line" was celebrated by Ben Jonson, is one of the glories of English literature. He was the morning star of our drama, which gives us the highest place in modern poetry. He definitively made our blank verse, which it only remained for Shakespeare to improve with his infinite variety; and although his daring, passionate genius was extinguished at the early age of twenty-nine, it has reverent admirers among the best and greatest critics of English literature. Many meaner luminaries have had their monuments while Marlowe's claims have been neglected; but there is now a project on foot to erect something in honor of his memory, and the committee includes the names of Robert Browning and Algernon Swinburne.

This project evokes a howl from an anonymous Christian in the columns of the *Pall Mall Gazette*. He protests against the "grotesque indecency of such a scheme," and stigmatises Marlowe as "a disreputable scamp, who lived a scandalous life and died a disgraceful death." That Marlowe was "a scamp" we have on the authority of those who denounced his scepticism and held him up as a frightful warning. His fellow poets, like Chapman and Drayton, spoke of him with esteem. An anonymous eulogist called him "kynde Kit Marlowe"; and Edward Blunt, his friend and publisher, said "the impression of the man hath been dear unto us, living an after-life in our memory." Assuredly Shakespeare's "dead shepherd" was no scamp. He apparently sowed his wild oats, like hundreds of other young men who were afterwards lauded by the orthodox. He was fond of a glass of wine in an age when tea and coffee were unknown, and English ladies drank beer for breakfast. And if he perished in a sudden brawl, it was at a time when everyone wore arms, and swords and daggers were readily drawn in the commonest quarrels. Nor should it be forgotten that he belonged to a "vagabond" class, half-outlawed and denounced by the clergy; that the drama was only then in its infancy; that it was difficult to earn bread by writing even immortal plays; and that irregularity of life was natural in a career whose penury was only diversified by haphazard successes. After all is said, Marlowe was no man's enemy but his own; and it is simply preposterous to judge him by the social customs of a more fastidious and, let us add, a more hypocritical age.

Our Christian protestor is shocked at the suggestion that the Marlowe memorial should be placed in Westminster Abbey, "an edifice which I believe was originally built to the honor of Jesus Christ." "The blasphemies of Voltaire," he says, "pale into insignificance when compared with those of Marlowe;" he "deliberately accused Jesus Christ and his personal followers of crimes which are justly considered unmentionable in any civilised community," and "any monument which may be erected in honor of Christopher Marlowe will be a deliberate insult to Christ."

Now those "blasphemies" are set forth in the accusation of an informer, one Richard Bame, who was hanged at Tyburn the next year for some mortal offence. Marlowe's death prevented his arrest, and it is somewhat extravagant—not to give it a harsher epithet—to write as though the accusation had been substantiated in a legal court. One of Bame's statements about Marlowe's itch for coining is, upon the face of it, absurd, and the whole document is open to the gravest suspicion. It is highly probable however, that Marlowe, who was a notorious Freethinker, was not very guarded in his private conversation; and we have no doubt that in familiar intercourse, which a mercenary or malicious eavesdropper might overhear, he indulged in what Christians regard as "blasphemy." Like nine out of ten unbelievers, he very likely gave vent to pleasantries on the subject of Christian dogmas. There is nothing incredible in his having said that "Moses was but a juggler," that "the New Testament is filthily written" (Mr. Swinburne calls it "canine Greek"), or that "all Protestants are hypocritical asses." But whether he really did say that the women of Samaria were no better than they should be, that Jesus's leaning on John's bosom at the last supper was a questionable action, that Mary's honor was doubtful and Jesus an illegitimate child—cannot be decided before the Day of Judgment; though, in any case, we fail to see that such things make "the blasphemies of Voltaire pale into insignificance."

We candidly admit, however, that a memorial to Marlowe would be incongruous in Westminster Abbey if Darwin were not buried there; but after admitting the high-priest of Evolution it seems paltry to shriek at the admission of other unbelievers. It will not do to blink the fact of Marlowe's Atheism, as is done by the two gentlemen who took up the cudgels on his behalf in the *Pall Mall Gazette*. Setting aside the accusation of that precious informer, there is other evidence of Marlowe's heresy. Greene reproached him for his scepticism, and every editor has remarked that his plays are heathenish in spirit. Lamb not only calls attention to the fact that "Marlowe is said to have been tainted with Atheistical positions," but remarks that "Barabas the Jew, and Faustus the Conjurer, are offsprings of a mind which at least delighted to dally with interdicted subjects. They both talk a language which a believer would have been tender of putting into the mouth of a character though but in fiction." Dyce could not "resist the conviction" that Marlowe's impiety was "confirmed and daring." His extreme Freethought is also noticed by Mr. Bullen and Mr. Havelock Ellis. There is, indeed, no room for a rational doubt on this point. Marlowe was an Atheist. But a sincere Christian, like Robert Browning, is nevertheless ready to honor Marlowe's genius; quite as ready, in fact, as Algernon Swinburne, whose impiety is no less "confirmed and daring" than Marlowe's own. There is freemasonry among poets; their opinions may differ, but they are all "sealed of the tribe." And surely we may all admire genius as a natural and priceless distinction, apart from all considerations of system and creed. What Atheist fails to reverence the greatness of Milton? And why should not a Christian reverence the greatness of Marlowe? If creed stands in the way, the Christian may keep his Dante and his Milton, his Cowper and his Wordsworth; but he loses Shakespeare, Byron, and Shelley; he loses Goethe and Victor Hugo; nay, he loses Homer, AEschylus, Sophocles, Pindar, Lucretius, Virgil, Horace, and all the splendid poets of Persia whose lyres have sounded under the Mohammedan Crescent. The distinctively Christian poets, as the world goes, are in a very decided minority; and it is a piece of grotesque impudence to ban Christopher Marlowe because he declined to echo the conventional praises of Jesus Christ.

JEHOVAH THE RIPPER *

* November, 1888.

The Whitechapel monster has once more startled and horrified London, and again he has left absolutely no clue to his identity. He is the mystery of mysteries. He comes and goes like a ghost. Murder marks his appearance, but that is all we know of him. The rest is silence. The police, the vigilance societies, and the private detectives are all baffled. They can only stare at each other in blind dismay, as helpless as the poor victims of the fiend's performances. All sorts of theories are started, but they are all in the air—the wild conjectures of irresponsible imaginations. All sorts of stories are afloat, but they contradict each other. As for descriptions of the monster, it is easy enough to say that the police have advertised for nine or ten "wanted" gentlemen, of various heights, dimensions, colors, and costumes, who are all the very same person.

We have no desire to dabble in murder, nor do we aspire to turn an honest penny by the minute description of bodily mutilations. But while the Whitechapel atrocities are engaging the public attention, we are tempted to contribute our quota of speculation as to the monster's identity. We thought of doing so before, but we reflected that it was perfectly useless while such a pig-headed person as Sir Charles Warren was at the head of the police. Now, however, that he is gone, and there is a chance of common-sense suggestions being fairly considered, we venture to propound our theory, in the hope that it will at least be treated on its merits.

Well now, to the point. Our theory is that the Whitechapel murderer is——— "Whom?" the reader cries. Wait awhile. Brace up your nerves for the dread intelligence. The East-end fiend, the Whitechapel devil, the slaughterer and mutilator of women, is—Jehovah!

"Blasphemous!" is shouted from a million throats. But science is used to such shriekings. We pause till the noise subsides, and then proceed to point out that our theory fulfils the grand condition of fitting in with all the facts.

The Whitechapel murderer is shrouded in mystery. So is Jehovah. The Whitechapel murderer comes no one knows whence and goes no one knows whither. So does Jehovah. The Whitechapel murderer appears in different disguises. So does Jehovah. The Whitechapel murderer's movements baffle all vigilance. So do Jehovah's. The Whitechapel murderer comes and goes, appears and disappears, with the celerity and noiselessness of a ghost. So does Jehovah, who *is* a ghost. Thus far, then, the similarity is marvellously close, and a *prima facie* case of identity is established.

It will very likely be objected that Jehovah is incapable of such atrocities. But this is the misconception of ignorance or the politeness of hypocrisy. Jehovah has written his autobiography, and on his own confession his murderous exploits were very similar to those of the Whitechapel terror. Appealing to that incontrovertible authority, we propose to show that he has every disposition to commit these enormities.

According to his own history of himself, Jehovah is passionately fond of bloodshed. The sanguine fluid which courses in our veins is the only thing that appeases him. "Without shedding of blood," he tells us through the pen of St. Paul, "there is no remission" of any debts owing to him. He called on Abraham, his friend, to stick a knife into his own son. He slew the first-born of every family in Egypt in a single night. He accepted the blood of a young virgin offered him by Jephthah. He slew 50,070 men at Beth-Shemesh for looking into his private trunk. He ordered his "chosen" friends, a famous set of banditti, to exterminate, men, women, children, and even animals, and to "leave alive nothing that breatheth." He massacred 70,000 citizens of Palestine because their king took a census, a social experiment to which he has a rooted antipathy. He had a house especially built for him, and gave orders that it should daily be drenched with blood. According to one of his candid friends, Archdeacon Farrar, "the floor must literally have swum with blood, and under the blaze of Eastern sunlight, the burning of fat and flesh on the large blazing altar must have been carried on amid heaps of sacrificial foulness—offal and skins and thick smoke and steaming putrescence." On one occasion, when in a state of murderous frenzy, he cried out, "I will make mine arrows drunk with blood, and my sword shall devour flesh."

Jehovah's passion for bloodshed is proved out of his own mouth. Let us now see his love of mutilation. He generally did this by proxy, and enjoyed the spectacle without undergoing the trouble. Some of his friends took a gentleman named Adoni-bezek, and "cut off his thumbs and his great toes." Wishing to kill a certain Eglon, the king of Moab, he sent an adventurer called Ehud with "a present from Jehovah." The present turned out to be an eighteen-inch knife, which Ehud thrust into Eglon's belly; a part of the body on which the Whitechapel murderer is fond of experimenting. Jehovah's friend David, a man after his own heart, mutilated no less than four hundred men, and gave their foreskins to his wife as a dowry. Incurring

Jehovah's displeasure and wishing to conciliate him, he attacked certain cities, captured their inhabitants, and cut them in pieces with saws, axes, and harrows.

Jehovah is particularly savage towards females. He cursed a woman for eating an apple, and instead of killing her on the spot, he determined to torture her every time she became a mother. A friend of his—and we judge people by their friends—cut a woman up into twelve pieces, and sent them to various addresses by parcels' delivery. Another of his friends, called Menahem, made a raid on a certain territory, and "all the women therein that were with child he *ripped up.*" Jehovah himself, being angry with the people of Samaria, promised to slay them with the sword, dash their infants to pieces, and *rip up* their pregnant women. No doubt he fulfilled his promise, and he would scarcely have made it if he had not been accustomed to such atrocities. It appears to us, therefore, that he is fully entitled to the name of Jehovah the Ripper.

We have not exhausted our evidence. Far more could be adduced, but we hope this will suffice. It may, of course, be objected that Jehovah has reformed, that he is too old for midnight adventures, that he has lost his savage cunning, and that his son keeps a sharp eye on the aged assassin. But the ruling passion is never really conquered; it is even, as the proverb says, strong in death. We venture, therefore, to suggest that the Whitechapel murderer is Jehovah; and although keen eyes may detect a few superficial flaws in our theory—for what theory is perfect till it is demonstrated?— we protest that it marvellously covers the facts of the case, and is infinitely superior to any other theory that has hitherto been broached.

THE PARSONS' LIVING WAGE *

* December, 1893.

In our last week's article we criticised the attitude of the Churches towards the working classes, with especial reference to the late Conference of "representatives of Christian Churches" in the Jerusalem Chamber. It will be remembered that the Conference was a ridiculous fiasco. The upshot of it was simply and absolutely nothing. The Christian gentlemen there assembled could not bring themselves to pass a resolution in favor of "a living wage" for the workers. Mr. Hugh Price Hughes, in particular, asserted that no one could define it, and the discussion was therefore a waste of time. But suppose the question had been one of "a living wage" for the sky-pilots; would not a minimum figure have been speedily decided? Thirty shillings a week would have been laughed at. Two pounds would have been treated as an absurdity. Men of God, who have to live while they cultivate the Lord's vineyard, want a more substantial share of the good things of this world. Nothing satisfies them but the certainty of something very valuable in this life, as well as the promise of the life that is to come. No doubt is entertained in the clerical mind as to the laborer being worthy of his hire. But they give their first attention to the clerical laborer; partly because they know him most intimately, and have a deep concern for his secular welfare; and partly because charity begins at home and looking after one's self is the primary law of Christian prudence.

A burning and a shining light among the Nonconformists of the last generation was the famous Mr. Binney, a shrewd preacher who published a book on How to Make the Best of Both Worlds. We believe he combined precept and practice. At any rate, he expounded a principle which has always had the devotion of the great bulk of Christian ministers. These gentry *have* made the best of both worlds. Most of them have been comfortably assured of good positions in Kingdom-Come, and most of them have been comfortably provided for in this land of pilgrimage, this scene of tribulation, this miserable vale of tears. Come rain or shine, they have had little cause for complaint. Hard work has rarely brought them to a premature old age. Famine has never driven them into untimely graves. Even the worst paid has had a hope of better thing-. There were fine plums in the profession, which might drop into watering mouths. What if the curate had little pocket money and a small account at the tailor's, with a large account at the shoemaker's through excessive peregrinations on shanks's mare? There was a vicarage, a deanery, a bishopric in perspective. A fat purse might be dandled some day, and the well-exercised limbs repose gracefully in a carriage and pair. If the worst came to the worst, one might marry a patron's daughter, and get the reversion of the living; or even snap up the ninth daughter of a bishop, and make sure of some preferment.

Yes, the clericals, taking them altogether, have had a very good "living wage." After all these centuries, it is high time they began to think about the comfort of other classes of the community. And yet, after all, is there not something indecent in their talking about a "living wage" for the workers? Are they not parasites upon the said workers? Have they not, also, had ever so many centuries of dominance? Is it not disgraceful that, at this time of day, there should be any need to discuss a "living wage" for the workers in a *Christian* civilisation? Really, the clericals should not, in this reckless way, invite attention to their past sins and present shortcomings. If they stand up for the workers now, it shows that they have not stood up for the workers before. They have been so many hundreds of years thinking about it—or rather *not* thinking about it. It is *interest*—nothing but *interest*—which informs their new policy. They always find out what *pays*. Never did they fight a forlorn hope or die for a lost cause. As the shadow follows the sun, so priests follow the sun of prosperity. They are the friends of power, whoever wields it: of wealth, whoever owns it. When they talk about the rights of the people, it means that they feel the king-times are ending. Byron said they *would* end, nearly a hundred years ago. Blood would flow like water, he said, and tears would fall like rain, but the people would triumph in the end. Yes, and the end is near; the people *are* triumphing; and the fact is visible to the very owls and bats of theology.

But let us return to the "living wage" business. There were several Bishops at the Jerusalem Chamber meeting, and in view of their incomes their patronage of the working man is simply disgusting. Pah! An ounce of civet, good apothecary! The bishops smell to heaven. Whatever they say is an insult to the miners—because they say it. The "living wage" of the poorest bishop would keep fifty miners' families; that of the richest would keep two hundred. "Nay," the bishops say, "we are poorer than you think." Only the other day, the Archbishop of Canterbury stated that most of the bishops spent more than they received. Indeed! Then the age of miracles is *not* past. By what superhuman power do they make up the deficiency? We tell the Archbishop that *he lies*. It is not a polite answer, we admit, but it is a true one; and this is a case where good plain Saxon is most appropriate. Edward White Benson forgets that bishops die. Their wills are proved like the wills of other mortals, and the Probate Office keeps the record. Of course it is barely possible—that is, it is conceivable—that bishops' executors make false returns, and pay probate duty on fanciful estates; but the probability is that they do nothing of the kind. Now some years ago (in 1886) the Rev. Mercer Davies, formerly chaplain of Westminster Hospital, issued a pamphlet entitled *The Bishops and their Wealth,* in which he gave a table of the English and Welsh prelates deceased from 1856 to 1885, with the amount of personalty proved at their death. Of one bishop he could find no particulars. It was Samuel Hinds, of Norwich, who resigned as a disbeliever, and died poor. The thirty-nine others left behind them collectively the sum of £2,105,000; this being "exclusive of any real estate they may have possessed, and exclusive also of any sums invested in policies of Life Assurance, or otherwise settled for the benefit of their families." Divide the amount of their *mere personalty* by thirty-nine, and you have £54,000 apiece. This is how the Bishops spend more than they receive! One of these days we will go to the trouble and expense of bringing the list up to date. Meanwhile it may be noted that there is no falling off in the figures towards 1885. No less than five bishops died in that year, and they left the following personalities: —£72,000—£85,000—£29,000—£85,000—£19,000; which more than maintain the average.

So much for the poor bishops. As for the rest of the clergy, it is enough to say that the Church they belong to has a total revenue of about £10,000,000 a year. Probably twice that sum is spent on the sky-pilots of all denominations, which is more than is received in wages by all the miners in Great Britain. It is a fair calculation that the average sky-pilot is six times better paid than the average miner. Yet the latter works hard in the bowels of the earth to provide real coals for real consumers, while the former is occupied in open air and daylight in damping down the imaginary fires of an imaginary hell. It is easy to see which is the more useful functionary, just as it is easy to see which is the better paid. Let us hope that the miners, and all other workers, will lay these facts to heart, and act accordingly. There are too many drones in England, living on the common produce of labor. The number of them should be diminished, and a beginning should be made with the mystery men. Were the great Black Army disbanded, and turned into the ranks of productive industry, the evils of society would begin to disappear; for those evils are chiefly the result of too much energy and attention being devoted to the problematical next life, and too little to the real interests of our earthly existence. We should also be spared the wretched spectacle of the well-paid drones of theology maundering over the question of a "living wage" for the honest men who do the laborious work of the world.

DID BRADLAUGH BACKSLIDE? *

* November 19, 1893.

The *Freethinker* for October 22 contained a bright article by Mr. George Standring, giving an account of a Sunday service which he attended at the famous Wesley Chapel in the City-road. The preacher on that occasion was the Rev. Allen Rees, and the theme of his discourse was "The Death of the *National Reformer*" Amongst other more or less questionable remarks, there was one made by the reverend gentleman, which the reporter very justly criticised. What was said by Mr. Rees was recorded as follows by Mr. Standring:—

"Indeed, there was reason to believe that Charles Bradlaugh had himself materially modified his views before his death, that his Atheism became weaker as he grew older. Sir Isaac Holden had told him (Mr. Bees) that Mr. Bradlaugh had often spoken to him privately in the House of Commons upon religious matters, and had admitted that the conversion of his brother had profoundly impressed him. Mr. Bradlaugh had often said to Sir Isaac Holden that he often wished he were half as good a man as his brother."

To anyone at all acquainted with the relations that existed between Mr. Bradlaugh and his brother, the last clause of Mr. Rees's statement is sufficient to stamp the whole of it as false and absurd. Without going into details, it is enough to say that Mr. Bradlaugh simply *could not* speak of his brother in this manner; it is absolutely beyond the bounds of possibility; and, as Sir Isaac Holden is the authority throughout, the entire passage about Mr. Bradlaugh would have to be dismissed with contempt.

Mr. Standring sent Mr. Rees a marked copy of the *Freethinker*, and intimated that space would probably be afforded him for a correction or an explanation. Mrs. Bradlaugh Bonner was also communicated with, and she immediately wrote to Mr. Rees on the subject. The reverend gentleman replied that he had made "no positive statements" as to any change of view on the part of Mr. Bradlaugh. He had "nothing to add" and "nothing to retract." But to prevent a misunderstanding he enclosed a verbatim copy of the passage in his sermon to which she referred. It ran as follows:—

"As a rule, men who profess Atheism do not become stronger in their belief as time goes on. I think I may almost say that this was true of Mr.

Bradlaugh. Sir Isaac Holden has told me that he frequently conversed with Mr. Bradlaugh on religious subjects. The conversion of his brother deeply affected him, and on one occasion he said to him: 'I wish I were half as good as my brother.' It was the unreality of much of the Christianity with which in early life Mr. Bradlaugh was associated and the worldliness and uncharitableness of religious professors, which made an Atheist of Mr. Bradlaugh, as it has done of many others."

This is a precious sample of clerical logic, composition, and veracity. Mr. Rees must have been very ignorant of Mr Bradlaugh's writings and intellectual character, or else he was deliberately inventing or trusting to mere hearsay, when he stated that Mr. Bradlaugh was made an Atheist by the bigotry or selfishness of certain Christians. "I think I may almost say" is a strange expression. What is it to "almost say" a thing? Is it almost said when you have said it? And what a jumble of "hims" in the fourth sentence! It would really disgrace a schoolboy.

Mrs. Bradlaugh Bonner replied to Mr. Rees, hoping that his "sense of honor" would impel him to acknowledge his mistake. She told him that her father's convictions never wavered on his death-bed; that Mr. W. R. Bradlaugh was never converted, because he was always a professed Christian; that Sir Isaac Holden must be laboring under a misapprehension; and that if Mr. Rees would call upon her she would tell him the facts which made it "utterly impossible" that her father could have spoken of his brother in the way alleged. Mrs. Bonner also wrote to Sir Isaac Holden, asking him whether he "really did tell this to the Rev. Allen Rees." Sir Isaac Holden did not reply. He is a very old man, years older than Mr. Gladstone. This may be an excuse for his manners as well as the infirmity of his memory.

Mr. Rees did reply. He said that "of course" he could not tell an untruth, that he had "made no absolute statement," that he "knew he had no positive evidence," and that his remark was "a bare suggestion." Having crawled away from his clear responsibility, Mr. Rees gratuitously committed another offence. "There was," he wrote, "another remark which your father uttered at the Hall of Science." Now this *is* a "positive statement." And where is the evidence? "I can give you," Mr. Rees added, "the name of the person who heard him say it." According to Mr. Rees, therefore, it is only "a bare suggestion" when he gives the authority of Sir Isaac Holden, but an anonymous authority is a good basis for a direct, unqualified assertion. And what is the "remark" which Mr. Bradlaugh "uttered" (what etymology!)?

It is this—"A man twenty-five years old may be an iconoclast, but I cannot understand a man being one who has passed middle age."

Mrs. Bonner took leave to disbelieve (as she well might) that her father had uttered such nonsense. She told Mr. Rees that her father had lectured and written as "Iconoclast" till he was thirty-five, and only dropped the "fighting name" then because his own name was so well known. She repeated her assurance that he had never wavered in his Atheism, and begged Mr. Rees to take her father's own written words in preference to "other people's versions of his conversation." His *Doubts in Dialogue*, the final paper of which left his hands only three or four days before his last illness, would show what his last views were, and she ventured to send Mr. Rees a copy for perusal. Mr. Rees read the volume, and, instead of admitting that he had been mistaken, he had the impertinence to tell Mrs. Bonner that her father's book was full of "sophism" and the "merest puerilities," and ended by expressing his "simple contempt." It was impertinence on Mr. Rees's part, in both senses of the word, for the merit of Mr. Bradlaugh's writing was not the point in consideration.

The point was this, Did the writing—the *last* writing—of Mr. Bradlaugh show the slightest change in his Atheism? Mr. Rees could not see this point, or he would not see it; and either alternative is discreditable to a man who sets himself up as a public teacher.

Mr. Rees did one right thing, however; he sent Mrs. Bonner a letter he had received from Sir Isaac Holden, containing the following passage:—

"Your rendering of the story is a little different to what I spoke—'Mr. Bradlaugh was affected to tears when I told him that his brother James said to the Rev. Richard Allen that his brother Charles was too good a man to die an Infidel, and he believed that before his death he would become a Christian.' Tears started in his (Charles's) eyes, and he simply replied: 'My brother James is a *good fellow*,' not 'I wish I were half as good as my brother.' There was evidently a very kind feeling in each of the brothers towards each other."

What *is* clear is this—there is a very bad difference between Sir Isaac Holden and the Rev. Allen Rees. "I wish I were half as good as my brother" is a very definite expression, and not a bit like "My brother James is a good fellow." Now if Sir Isaac Holden *did* convey this expression to the Rev. Allen Rees, the old gentleman has a treacherous memory; if he *did not*, the expression must be ascribed to the reverend gentleman's invention.

Mrs. Bonner replied sharply with "mixed feelings of surprise and indignation." Her father had no brother named James. The only brother he had was most distinctly not "a good fellow," which there was "documentary evidence" to prove. There was also documentary evidence to show that the feelings of the brothers towards each other was "the reverse of kindly." Mr.

Rees had chosen to ignore all this, and, in consequence of his attitude, Mrs. Bonner intended to "give this matter publicity"—which she has done by printing the whole correspondence and sending copies to the press.

Mr. Rees wrote "surprised"—poor man! He thought it was a "private correspondence." He could not understand why he was "personally abused"—in fact, it was "vulgar personal abuse." "I entirely decline," he ended majestically, "to have any further correspondence with you."

What a sorry display of clerical temper! But it is the way of the profession when tackled. They are so used to speaking from the "coward's castle," *not* under correction, that they lose their heads when taken to task.

Mrs. Bonner appends a note to the correspondence, remarking on "the obviously loose reminiscences of Sir Isaac Holden," which Mr. Rees had "materially altered," and denying the possibility of any such conversation between Sir Isaac Holden and her father.

As to the private correspondence, surely the conversation (if it occurred) was "of a private nature," yet Mr. Rees had no scruple in retailing it from the pulpit. Mrs. Bonner adds that her demerits are beside the point, which is, "Did Mr. Bradlaugh weaken in his Atheism?" to which she answers emphatically "No." She nursed him in his last illness, and her testimony is authoritative. Respect for her father's memory justifies her in printing this correspondence, and we are glad that she has done so, for it nails down another wretched fiction to the counter of truth.

FREDERIC HARRISON ON ATHEISM *

*January 13,1889 .

Mr. Frank Harris, the editor of the *Fortnightly Review*, must be a sly humorist. In the current number of his magazine he has published two articles as opposite to each other as Balaam's blessing on Israel was opposite to the curse besought by the King of Moab. Mr. Frederic Harrison pitches into Agnosticism with his usual vigor, and holds out Positivism as the only system which can satisfy the sceptic and the religionist. Mr. W. H. Mallock, on the other hand, makes a trenchant attack on Positivism; and the readers of both articles will learn how much may be said against anything, or at least anything in the shape of a system. Mr. Herbert Spencer, in the name of the Unknowable, proffers his Agnosticism, and Mr. Harrison says "Bosh." Mr. Harrison, in the name of Positivism, proffers his Religion of Humanity, and Mr. Mallock says "Moonshine." Mr. Spencer is a man of genius, and Mr. Harrison and Mr. Mallock are men of remarkable talent. Yet, shuffle them how you will, any two of them are ready to damn what the third blesses. What does this show? Why, that systems are all arbitrary, and suited to a certain order of minds in a certain stage of development; and that system-mongers are like spiders, who spin their webs out of their own bowels.

Mr. Harrison's definition of Agnosticism shows it to be merely Atheism in disguise. Milton said that new presbyter was but old priest writ large, and we may say that the new Agnosticism is but old Atheism written larger—and more respectably. Agnosticism is the cuckoo of philosophy. It appropriates the nest of another bird, turns it out in the cold, and even adopts its progeny. All the time-honored positions of Atheism—man's finity and nature's infinity, the relativity of human knowledge, the reign of law, and so forth—are quietly monopolised by this intruder, who looks upon the object he has despoiled as the Christian looked upon the Jew after borrowing his God. Yet in England, the classic land of mental timidity and compromise, Agnosticism is almost fashionable, while poor Atheism is treated with persecution or obloquy. Elsewhere, especially in France, we find a different condition of things. A French sceptic no more hesitates to call himself an Atheist than to call himself a Republican. May it not be, therefore, that the difference between Agnosticism and Atheism is one of temperament? We might illustrate this theory by appealing to examples. Darwin was an Agnostic, Professor Clifford an Atheist. Or, if we turn to pure literature, we may instance Matthew Arnold and Algernon Swinburne. Arnold, the Agnostic, says that "most of what now passes with us for religion and philosophy will be replaced by poetry." Swinburne, the Atheist, exclaims "Thou art smitten, thou God, thou art smitten, thy death is upon thee O Lord."

This brings out the cardinal—we might say the *only* distinction between Atheism and Agnosticism. The Agnostic is a timid Atheist, and the Atheist a courageous Agnostic. John Bull is infuriated by the red cloak of Atheism, so the Agnostic dons a brown cloak with a red lining. Now and then a sudden breeze exposes a bit of the fatal red, but the garment is promptly adjusted, and Bull forgets the irritating phenomenon.

Mr. Harrison says "the Agnostic is one who protests against any dogma respecting Creation at all, and who deliberately takes his stand on ignorance." We cannot help saying that this differences him from the Atheist. Seeing that we cannot solve infinite problems, that we know nothing, and apparently *can* know nothing, of God or the supernatural, the Atheist has always regarded religious dogmas as blind guesses, which, according to the laws of chance, are in all probability wrong; and as these blind guesses have almost invariably been associated with mental tyranny and moral perversion, he has regarded theology as the foe of liberty and humanity. The Agnostic, however, usually adopts a more pleasant attitude. He does not believe in attacking theology; and "after all, you know," he sometimes says, "we can't tell what there may be behind the veil."

With his master, Comte, Mr. Harrison "entirely accepts the Agnostic position as a matter of logic," but it is only a stepping-stone, and he objects to sitting down upon it. Every religion the world has ever seen has been false, but religion itself is imperishable, and Positivism has found the true solution of the eternal problem. Parsons and Agnostics will eventually kiss each other, like righteousness and peace in the text, and the then existing High Priest of Positivism will say, "Humanity bless you, my children." But all this is for the sweet by-and-bye. Meanwhile the Churches thrust out their tongues at Positivism, the great Agnostic philosopher calls it the Ghost of Religion, Sir James Stephen declares that nobody can worship Comte's made-up Deity, and Mr. Mallock says that the love of Humanity, taking it in the concrete, is as foolish as Titania's affection for Bottom the Weaver.

Professed Atheists may watch this hubbub with serenity, if not with enjoyment. When all is said and done, Atheism remains in possession of the sceptical field. Mr. Harrison's flouts, at any rate, will do it no damage. His hatred of Atheism is born of jealousy, and like all jealous people he is somewhat inconsistent. Here he defines Atheism as a "protest against the theological doctrine of a Creator and a moral providence," there he defines it as "based on the denial of God," and again he defines it as a belief that the universe is "self-existent and purely material." Even these do not suffice, for he also adopts Comte's "profound aphorism" that "Atheism is the most irrational form of metaphysics," and proves this by a fresh definition involved in the charge that "it propounds as the solution of an insoluble enigma the hypothesis which of all others is the least capable of proof, the least simple, the least plausible, and the least useful." *Of all others* is what Cobbett would have called a beastly phrase. It shows Mr. Harrison was in a hurry or a fog. He does not specify this unprovable, complex, unplausible, and useless hypothesis. We forbear to guess his meaning, but we remind him that Atheism "propounds *no* solution of an insoluble enigma." The Atheist does not say "there is no God"; he simply says, "I know not," and ventures to think others are equally ignorant. Now, this was Comte's own position. He wished to "reorganise Society, without God or King, by the systematic cultus of Humanity," and if warning God off from human affairs is not Atheism, we should like to know what is. Mr. Harrison lustily sings the praises of religion, but he is remarkably silent about Comte's opposition to Theism, and in this he is throwing dust in the eyes of English readers.

In "militant Atheism" Mr. Harrison says that "all who have substantive beliefs of their own find nothing but mischief." But this is only Mr. Harrison's sweeping style of writing. He is always vivid, and nearly always superlative. We venture to think that his "all" merely includes his own circle. At the same time, however, we admit that militant Atheism is still, as of old, an offence to the superfine sceptics who desire to stand well with the great firm of Bumble and Grundy, as well as to the vast army of priests and preachers who have a professional interest in keeping heresy "dark," and to the ruling and privileged classes, who feel that militant Atheism is a great disturber of the peace which is founded on popular superstition and injustice.

Mr. Harrison seems to imagine that Atheists have no ideal beyond that of attacking theology, but a moment's calm reflection would show him the absurdity of this fancy. He might as well suppose that the pioneers of civilisation who hew down virgin forests have no conception of the happy homesteads they are making room for. We go farther and assert that all this talk about negative and positive work is *cant*. To call the destroyer of superstition a negationist is as senseless as to call a doctor a negationist. Both strive to expel disease, the one bodily and the other mental. Both, therefore, are working for health, and no more positive work is conceivable.

SAVE THE BIBLE! *

* March 26,1893.

Thirty-eight clergymen, a year or two ago, gave the Bible a fresh certificate of inspiration and infallibility. They signed a "round robin," if we may apply such a vulgar description to their holy document. But somehow the Bible is in as bad a position as ever. It seems, indeed, in deadly peril; and if something strong and decisive be not done for its protection, it will soon be doomed. Such, at any rate, seems the view of a large number of clergymen, who have signed a Petition, prepared by the Rev. E. S. Ffoulkes, of St. Mary's, Oxford, and addressed to "the Most Reverend the Archbishop, and the Right Reverend the Bishops, of the Church of England, in the House of the Convocation of Canterbury assembled." The petitioners call upon the Archbishops and Bishops to use "their sacred office and authority," and either to purge the Church of heresy or to "authoritatively and publicly" recommend certain "orthodox and admirable works," which are calculated to "arrest the spread" of "disastrous errors in the midst of Our Beloved Church."

In order to show the precise nature of these "disastrous errors," we print the following paragraphs from the petition:

"Whereas it is generally known that certain clergymen of the Church of England, in positions of influence and authority, are deliberately and altogether undermining, by their teachings and public writings, the faith of this Church and country in the trustworthiness of the Holy Scriptures, and are altogether repudiating the common faith of Christendom, that the said Holy Scriptures, as received by this Church of England, are the infallible and inspired Word of God.

"Also, that by what is known as the 'New Criticism,' these clergymen do attempt entirely to rob the people of God of the Holy Scriptures and altogether falsify the teachings respecting them of our Lord Jesus Christ and of his Holy Apostles-declaring some parts to be 'myths,' some 'fables,' some 'the work of dramatists,' etc."

Ah then, the enemy is within the camp! It is no-longer a question of "infidel" publications. Church professors, and doctors of divinity, are sapping the very foundations of "the faith." Orthodox clergymen cry out—in the language of this petition—for salvation from "the dangers of Rationalism and unbelief *within* the Church."

What does all this mean? It means that Free-thought is triumphing by the permeation of the Churches; that "advanced" ministers are now doing, in a sober, steady, scholarly way, the very work so brilliantly inaugurated by Voltaire and Thomas Paine; that the Bible is being subjected to rigorous criticism, in England as well as in France, Holland, and Germany; that its documents are being shifted like the pieces in a kaleidoscope, and every turn of the instrument makes them differ more and more from the orthodox pattern. At present, it is true, the process is almost confined to the Old Testament. There, however, it is nearly completed. Presently it will extend in earnest to the New Testament; and when it is completed *there*, the Bible will be something worse than Luther's "wax nose," it will be a thing of "shreds and patches."

Old Testament criticism by men like Driver, Cheyne, Ryle, and Gore, is indeed—as the petitioners assert—destroying faith in "the Holy Scriptures" as the "infallible and inspired Word o\c God." They still pretend it is *inspired*, but not infallible. "Infallible," at this time of day, is a very "large order." Professor Bruce, himself a Christian minister, is obliged to tell his orthodox brethren that "the errorless autograph for which some so zealously contend is a theological figment." "The Bible," he reminds them, "was produced piecemeal, and by the time the later portions were produced the earlier had lost their supposed immaculate-ness." And he warns the "infallible" gentlemen that their position is really "perilous" when it is considered "in what state we possess the Scriptures now." Yes, it is only country curates who can stand up now for an "infallible" Word of God; even Mr. Gladstone is obliged to admit "errors"—that is, errors in general, for he will not confess any in particular.

The reference in the petition to "myths," "fables," and "the work of dramatists," seem to be specially aimed at the Rev. Charles Gore, the Principal of Pusey House, Oxford, and editor of *Lux Mundi*. His essay in that volume on "The Holy Spirit and Inspiration" is horribly distasteful to orthodox parsons. They cannot refute him, but they say "he ought to know better," or "he shouldn't write such things"—in other words, he is guilty of the shocking crime of letting the cat out of the bag. He discards the Creation Story, just like Professor Bruce, who calls the fall of Adam a "quaint" embodiment of the theological conception of sin. He dismisses all the patriarchs before Abraham as "mythical." He admits the late origin of the Pentateuch, and only claims for Moses the probable authorship of the Decalogue. He says the Song of Solomon is "of the nature of a drama."

The Book of Job is "mainly dramatic." Deuteronomy is the publication of the law "put dramatically" into the mouth of Moses. Jonah and Daniel are "dramatic compositions." Jesus Christ, it is true, cited both as historical; but he only "accommodated" himself to the prevalent belief. He knew better, but he did not choose to say so; or, rather, the moment was inopportune; so he left us to find out the truth in this matter, as he left us to find it out in everything else.

Canon Driver is perhaps glanced at in "fables," and perhaps also Canon Cheyne. The former has publicly argued against the "reconciliations" of Genesis and Science. He has likewise written very strongly against the "historical" character of Jonah, which he treats as a story with "a moral." Canon Cheyne regards it as "an allegory." Jonah is Israel, swallowed up by Babylon; but, seeking the Lord in exile, the captive is at last disgorged uninjured.

These clerical apostles of the "New Criticism" are accused of attempting "entirely to rob the people of God of the Holy Scriptures." Poor people of God! How anxious the petitioners are for their welfare! Some persons, however, will be apt to regard the solicitude of these gentlemen as *professional*. Robbing the people of the Holy Scriptures, in *their* mouths, may simply mean rendering the clergyman's trade more difficult, or perhaps altogether impossible; and therefore the bitter cry of these "grievously beset" parsons (to use their own words) may be only a parallel to the famous old shout of "Great is Diana of the Ephesians."

Why indeed do not the petitioners refute the apostles of the "New Criticism," instead of appealing to the *authority* of Convocation? They plainly declare that the "New Criticis" rests on "utterly baseless foundations"—which is a curious pleonasm or tautology for a body of "educated" gentlemen. But if the substance of the declaration be true, apart from its logic or grammar, the orthodox parsons may scatter the heretical parsons like chaff before the wind. Principles which are "utterly baseless" may surely be refuted. To quote from Hamlet, "it is as easy as lying." Now that is a practice in which the clergy of all ages have shown great dexterity. We therefore hope the orthodox parsons will *refute* the "New Criticism." Let them try to save the Bible by argument. If they cannot it is lost, and lost for ever.

FORGIVE AND FORGET *

March 19, 1893. Written after a debate at the Hall of Science, London, between the writer and the Rev. C. Fleming Williams, on "Christian Ideas of Man and Methods of Progress." Mr. Branch, of the London County Council, presided, and there was a very large attendance.

My recent friendly discussion with the Rev. C. Fleming Williams was most enjoyable. It is so-pleasant to debate points of difference with an opponent whom you fully respect, towards whom you have not an atom of ill feeling, and to whom you disclose your own views in exchange for the confidence of his. The chairman said that he had visited the Hall of Science many years ago, and frequently heard discussions, but they were generally acrimonious, and seldom profitable. No doubt he spoke what he felt to be the truth; at the same time, however, he probably left out of sight a very important factor, namely, the tone and temper which Christian critics are apt to display on a Secular platform; the assumed superiority, which is not justified by any apparent gifts of intelligence; the implication in most of their remarks that the Freethinker is on a lower moral level than they are, though it would never be suspected by an indifferent observer; the arrogance which is often the undercurrent of their speech, and sometimes bursts forth into sheer, undisguised insolence. Christian critics of this species have, perhaps, stung Freethought lecturers into hot resentment, when it would have been far preferable to keep cool, and continue using the rapier instead of seizing the bludgeon. It is always a mistake to lose one's temper, but it becomes excusable (although not justifiable) under intense provocation. On the whole, it is safe to say that Christians have received more courtesy than they have shown in their controversies with Freethinkers.

So much for the debate itself. What I want to deal with in this article is the plea of the chairman, and also of Mr. Williams, for a more charitable understanding. Christians have abused, ill-treated, and even butchered Freethinkers in the past, but the best Christians are ashamed of it now. Let us then, it is urged, bury the past; let us forgive and forget.

So far as it concerns *men* only I am not insensible to the appeal. Far be it from me to blame Mr. Williams for the follies and malignancies of his Christian predecessors. On a question of character, of merit or demerit, every man stands or falls alone. Imputed wickedness is just as irrational as imputed righteousness. I no more wish to make Mr. Williams responsible for the butcheries of a Torquemada or an Alva than I wish to be saved by the sufferings of Jesus Christ. So far as Mr. Williams is concerned, I have no past to bury. I am not aware that he has ever desired anything but absolute justice for all forms of opinion; and I know that he denounced my imprisonment for the artificial crime of "blasphemy." Evidently, then, Mr. Williams' plea is more than personal. It is really a request that I should judge Christianity, as a great, ancient, historic system, not by what it has in the main taught and done, but by what a select body of its professors say and do in the present generation.

Now this is a plea which I must reject. In the first place, while I admit it is unfair to judge Christianity by its *worst* specimens, I regard it as no less unfair to judge it by its *best*. This is not justice and impartiality. The Chief Constable of Hull* is probably as sincere a Christian as Mr. Williams. I have to meet them both, and I must take them as I find them. The one pays me a compliment, and the other threatens me with a prosecution; one shakes me cordially by the hand, the other tries to prevent me from lecturing. The difference between them is flagrant. But how am I to put Mr. Williams to the credit of Christianity, and Captain Gurney to the credit of something else? What *is* the something else? They both speak to me as Christians; is it for me to say that the one is a Christian and the other is not? Is not that a domestic question for the Christians to settle among themselves? And am I not just and reasonable in declining to take the decision out of their hands?

** This gentleman was trying to prevent me from delivering
Sunday lectures at Hull under the usual condition of a
charge for admission.*

In the next place, since Christianity is, as I have said, not only a great, but an ancient and historic system, its past *cannot* be buried, and should not be if it could. History is philosophy teaching us by example. Without it the present is meaningless, and the future an obscurity. Now history shows us that Christianity has been steady and relentless in the persecution of heresy. We have therefore to inquire the reason. It will not do to say that persecution is natural to human pride in face of opposition; for Buddhism, which is older than Christianity, has not been guilty of a single act of persecution in the course of twenty-four centuries. Another explanation is necessary. And what is it? When we look into the matter we find that persecution has always been justified, nay inculcated, by appealing to Christian doctrines and the very language of Scripture. Unbelief was treason against God, and the rejection of Christ was rebellion. They were more than operations of the intellect; they were movements of the will—not mistaken, but satanic. And as faith was essential to salvation, and heresy led straight to hell, the elimination of the heretic was in the interest of the people he might divert from the road to paradise. It was simply an act of social sanitation.

I am aware that this conception is not paraded by "advanced" Christians, though they seldom renounce it in decisive language. But these "advanced" Christians are the children of a later age, full of intellectual and moral influences which are foreign to, or at least independent of, Christianity. Their attitude is the resultant of several forces. But suppose a time of reaction came, and the influences I have referred to should diminish for a season; is it not probable, nay certain, that the old forces of Christian exclusiveness and infallibility, based upon a divine revelation, would once more produce the effects-which cursed and degraded Europe for over a thousand years? Such, at any rate, is my belief; it is also, I think, the belief of most Freethinkers; and this is the reason why we cannot forgive and forget. The serpent is scotched, not slain; and we must beware of its fangs.

THE STAR OF BETHLEHEM

Matthew, or whoever was the author of the first Gospel, had a rare eye (or nose) for portents and prodigies. He seems also to have had exclusive sources of information. Several of the wonderful things he relates were quite unknown to the other evangelists. They were ignorant of the wholesale resurrection of saints at the crucifixion, and also of the watch at the sepulchre, with all the pretty circumstantial story depending upon it. At the other end of Christ's career they never heard of the visit of the wise men of the east to his cradle, or of Herod's massacre of the innocents, or of the star which guided those wise men to the birthplace of the little king of the Jews. That star is the sole property of Matthew, and the other evangelists took care not to infringe his copyright. Indeed, it is surprising how well they did with the remnants he left them.

Matthew was not a Jules Verne. He had no knowledge of astronomy. Consequently he did not make the most of that travelling star. It was seen by wise men "in the east." This is not very exact, but it is precise enough for a fairy tale. Those wise men happened to be "in the east" at the same time. They were really "Magi"—as may be seen in the Revised Version; that is, priests of the religion of Persia; and it requires a lot of faith to see what concern they could possibly have with the bantling of Bethlehem. However, they saw "his star," and they appear to have followed it. They must have slept by day and journeyed by night, when the star was visible. At the end of their expedition this star "stood over" the house where little Jesus was lying. Truly, it was a very accommodating star. Of course it was specially provided for the occasion. Real stars, rolling afar in the infinite ether, are too distant to "stand over" a particular spot on this planet This was an ideal star. It travelled through the earth's atmosphere, and moved according to the requirements of the gospel Munchausen. What became of it afterwards we are not informed. Probably it was born and died in Matthew's imagination. He blew it out when he had done with it, and thus it has escaped the attention of Sir Robert Ball.

Those star-gazing magi went into "the house," which, according to Luke, was an inn; Jesus Christ having been born in the stable, because the "pub" was full, and no gentleman would go outside to oblige a lady: They opened their Gladstone bags, and displayed the presents they had brought for the little king of the Jews. These were gold, frankincense, and myrrh. No doubt the perfumes were very welcome—in a stable; and very likely Joseph took care of the gold till Jesus was old enough to spend it on his own account, by which time it appears to have vanished, perhaps owing to the expenses of bringing up the numerous progeny of the Virgin Mother. Then the Mahatmas—we beg pardon, the Magi—went home. Perhaps they are there still. But no matter. We leave that to the Christian Evidence Society, or the Theosophists.

Candid students will see at a glance that the whole of this story is mythological. Like other distinguished persons, the Prophet of Nazareth had to make a fuss, not only in the world, but in the universe; and his biographers (especially Matthew) duly provided him with extraordinary incidents. Not only was he born, like so many other "saviors," without the assistance of a human father, but his birth was heralded by a celestial marvel. There was a star of his nativity. The wise men from the east called it "his star." This puts him in the category of heroes, and bars the idea of his being a god. It also shows that the Christians, amongst whom this story originated, were devotees of astrology. Fortune-tellers still decide your "nativity" before they cast your "horoscope." We are aware that many commentators have discussed the star of Christ's birth from various points of view. Some have thought it a real star; others have had enough astronomy to see that this was impossible, and have argued that it was a big will-o'-the-wisp, created and directed by supernatural power, like the pillar of day-cloud and night-fire that led the Jews in the wilderness; while still others have favored the idea of a supernatural illusion, which was confined to the wise men—and thus it was that the "star" was not seen or mentioned by any of their contemporaries. But all this is the usual mixture of Bible commentators. There is really no need to waste time in that fashion. The Star of Bethlehem belongs to the realm of poetry, as much as the Star of Caesar, to which the mighty Julius ascended in his apotheosis.

Thousands of sermons have been preached on that Star of Bethlehem, and these also have been works of imagination. We have been told, for instance, that it was the morning star of a new day for humanity. But this is a falsehood, which the clergy palmed off on ignorant congregations. The world was happier under the government of the great Pagan emperors than it has ever been under the dominion of Christianity. For a thousand years the triumph of the Cross was the annihilation of everything that makes life pleasant and dignified. The Star of Bethlehem shone in a sky of utter blackness. All the constellations of science, art, philosophy, and literature were in disastrous eclipse. Cruelty and hypocrisy abounded on earth, toil and misery were the lot of the people, and bloodshed was as common as rain.

Religions, said Schopenhauer, are like glow-worms; they require darkness to shine in. This was quite true of Christianity. It was splendid when it had no competitor. To be visible—above all, to be worshipped—it needed the sky to itself.

One by one, during the past three hundred years, the stars of civilisation have emerged from their long eclipse, and now the sky of humanity is full of countless hosts of throbbing glories. The Star of Bethlehem is no longer even a star of the first magnitude. It pales and dwindles every year. In another century it will be a very minor light. Meanwhile it is drawn big on the maps of faith. But that little trick is being seen through. Once it was the Star of Bethlehem first, and the rest nowhere; now it takes millions of money, and endless special pleading, to keep its name on the list.

Christ himself is coming more and more to be regarded as a fanciful figure; not God, not even a man, but a construction of early Christian imagination. "Why," asked a Unitarian of a Positivist, "why is not Christ in your Positivist calendar?" "Because," was the reply, "the calendar is for men, not for gods."

THE GREAT GHOSTS *

* *March, 1889.*

Long before there were any kings there were chiefs, Even in the early Feudal days the king was only the chief of the barons, and many centuries elapsed before the supremacy of the monarch was unquestioned and he became really the *sovereign*. It was a process of natural selection. A mob of chiefs could not rule a mob of people. There was a fierce struggle, with plenty of fighting and intrigue, and the fittest survived. Gradually, as the nation became unified, the government was centralised, and out of the chaos of competing nobles emerged the relatively cosmic authority of the Crown.

Similarly in the world of religion. All gods were originally ghosts. But as polytheism declined a supreme god emerged from the crowd of deities, as the king emerged from the crowd of nobles, and ruled from a definite centre. It was Zeus in Greece, Jupiter in Rome, Brahma in India, Thor in Scandinavia, and Yahveh in Israel. "I, the Lord thy God, am a jealous God," was an exclamation that sprang from Yahveh's lips (through his priests) when his godship was still in the thick of the competitive struggle.

The ghosts become gods, and the gods become supreme deities, looked after the interests of their worshippers; gave them long life, good harvests, and prosperity in warfare, if they were true to them, and plagued them like the very devil if they slighted them or nodded to their rivals. According to the Old Testament, when everything went well with the Jews their God was pleased, and when things went wrong with them he was angry. This state of mind survives into our advanced civilisation, where people still talk of "judgments," still pray for good things, and still implore their God for victory when they have a scrimmage with their neighbors.

But this infantile conception is dying out of educated minds. Prayer is seen to be futile. The laws of nature do not vary. Providence is on the side of the big battalions. God helps those who help themselves — and no one else.

Long ago, in ancient Greece and Rome, the acutest thinkers had come to the same conclusion. Lucretius, for instance, did not deny the existence of the gods; he merely asserted that they no longer concerned themselves with human affairs, which he was heartily glad of, as they were mostly bad characters. He observed "the reign of law" as clearly as our modern scientists, and relegated the deities to their Olympian repose, so beautifully versed by Tennyson.

> *The Gods, who haunt*
>
> *The lucid interspace of world and world,*
>
> *Where never creeps a cloud, or moves a wind,*
>
> *Nor ever falls the least white star of snow,*
>
> *Nor ever lowest roll of thunder moans,*
>
> *Nor sound of human sorrow mounts to mar*
>
> *Their savored everlasting calm.*

Even the savage, in times of prolonged peace and prosperity, begins to speculate on the possibility of his god's having retired from business; for religion is born of fear, not of love, and the savage is reminded of his god by calamity rather than good fortune. This idea has been caught by Robert Browning in his marvellous *Caliban upon Setebos*, a poem developed out of a casual germ in Shakespeare's *Tempest*.

> *Hoping the while, since evils sometimes mend,*
>
> *Warts rub away and sores are cured with slime,*
>
> *That some strange day, will either the Quiet catch*
>
> *And conquer Setebos, or likelier He*
>
> *Decrepit may doze, doze, as good as die.*

But presently poor Caliban is frightened out of his speculation by a thunderstorm, which makes him lie low and slaver his god, offering any mortification as the price of his escape.

There is a good deal of Caliban in our modern multitudes, but the educated are working free from his theology. Science and miracle cannot live together, and miracle and providence are the same thing. How far from us is the good old God of the best parts of the Bible, who held out one ear for the prayers of his good children, and one hand, well rodded, for the backs of the naughty ones. The seed of the righteous never begged for bread, and the villain always came to a bad end. It was the childish philosophy of the "gods" in a modern theatre. The more critical want something truer and more natural, something more accordant with the stern realities of life. Renan has some excellent remarks on this in the Preface to his second volume of the *Histoire du Peuple d' Israel.*

"The work of the genius of Israel was not really affected until the eighteenth century after Jesus Christ, when it became very doubtful to spirits a little cultivated that the affairs of this world are regulated by a God of justice. The exaggerated idea of a special Providence, the basis of Judaism and Islam, and which Christianity has only corrected through the fund of liberalism inherent in our races, has been definitively vanquished by modern philosophy, the fruit not of abstract speculation, but of constant experience. It has never been observed, in effect, that a superior being occupies himself, for a moral or an immoral purpose, with the affairs of nature or the affairs of humanity."

Kenan has elsewhere said that the negation of the supernatural is a dogma with every cultivated intelligence. God, in short, has faded into a metaphysical abstraction. The little ghosts vanished long ago, and now the Great Ghost is melting into thin air. Thousands of people have lost all belief in his existence. They use his name, and take it in vain; for when questioned, they merely stand up for "a sort of a something." The fear of God, so to speak, has survived his personality; just as Madame de Stael said she did not believe in ghosts, but she was afraid of them. Mrs. Browning gives voice to this sentiment in one of her poems:

> *And hearts say, God be pitiful,*
> *That ne'er said, God be blest.*

The fear of the Lord is, indeed, the beginning and the end of theology.

When the Great Ghost was a reality—we mean to his worshippers—he was constantly spoken of. His name was invoked in the courts of law, it figured in nearly every oath outside them, and it was to be seen on nearly every page of every book that was published. But all that is changed. To speak or print the name of God is reckoned "bad form." The word is almost tabooed in decent society. You hear it in the streets, however, when the irascible carman calls on God to damn your eyes for getting in his way. There is such a conspiracy of silence about the Great Ghost, except in churches and chapels, that the mention of his name in polite circles sounds like swearing. Eyebrows are lifted, and the speaker is looked upon as vulgar, and perhaps dangerous.

Thus theology gives way to the pressure of science, and religion to the pressure of civilisation. The more use we make of this life the less we look for another; the loftier man grows the less he bows to ghosts and gods. Heaven and hell both disappear, and things are neither so bad nor good as was expected. Man finds himself in a universe of necessity. He hears no response to his prayers but the echo of his own voice. He therefore bids the gods adieu, and sets himself to the task of making the best of life for himself and his fellows. Without false hopes, or bare fears, he steers his course over the ocean of life, and says with the poet, "I am the captain of my soul."

ATHEISM AND THE FRENCH REVOLUTION *

* July, 1889 .

Sunday, July 14, is the hundredth anniversary of the fall of the Bastille, and the occasion will be splendidly celebrated at Paris. In itself the capture of this prison-fortress by the people was not a wonderful achievement; it was ill-defended, and its governor might, had he chosen, have exploded the powder magazine and blown it sky-high. But the event was the parting of the ways. It showed that the multitude had got the bit between its teeth, and needed a more potent master than the poor king at Versailles. And the event itself was a striking one. Men are led by imagination, and the Bastille was the symbol of centuries of oppression. Within its gloomy dungeons hundreds of innocent men had perished in solitary misery, without indictment or trial, consigned to death-in-life by the arbitrary order of irresponsible power. Men of the most eminent intellect and character had suffered within its precincts for the crime of teaching new truth or exposing old superstitions. Voltaire himself had twice tasted imprisonment there. What wonder, then, that the people fixed their gaze upon it on that ominous fourteenth of July, and attacked it as the very citadel of tyranny? The Bastille fell, and the sound re-echoed through Europe. It was the signal of a new era and a new hope. The Revolution had begun—that mighty movement which, in its meaning and consequences, dwarfs every other cataclysm in history.

But revolutions do not happen miraculously. Their advent is prepared. They are as much *caused* as the fall of a ripe apple from the tree, or the regular bursting of the buds in spring. The authors of the Revolution were in their graves. Its leaders, or its instruments, appeared upon the scene in '89. After life's fitful fever Voltaire was sleeping well. Rousseau's tortured heart was at rest. Diderot's colossal labors were ended; his epitaph was written, and the great Encyclopaedia remained as his living monument. D'Holbach had just joined his friends in their eternal repose. A host of smaller men, also, but admirable soldiers of progress in their degree, had passed away. The gallant host had done its work. The ground was ploughed, the seed was sown, and the harvest was sure. Famished as they were, and well-nigh desperate at times, the men of the Revolution nursed the crop as a sacred legacy, shedding their blood like water to fructify the soil in which it grew.

Superficial readers are ignorant of the mental ferment which went on in France before the Revolution. Voltaire's policy of sapping the dogmas by which all tyranny was supported had been carried out unflinchingly. Not only had Christianity been attacked in every conceivable way, with science, scholarship, argument, and wit; but the very foundations of all religion—the belief in soul and God—had not been spared. The Heresiarch of Ferney lived to see the war with superstition carried farther than he contemplated or desired; but it was impossible for him to say to the tide of Freethought, "Thus far shalt thou go and no farther, and here shall thy proud waves be stayed." The tide poured on over everything sacred. Altars, thrones, and coronets met with a common fate. True, they were afterwards fished out of the deluge; but their glory was for ever quenched, their power for ever gone.

Among the great Atheists who prepared the Revolution we single out two—Diderot and D'Holbach. The sagacious mind of Comte perceived that Diderot was the greatest *thinker* of the band. The fecundity of his mind was extraordinary, and even more so his scientific prescience. Anyone who looks through the twenty volumes of his collected works will be astonished at the way in which, by intuitive insight, he anticipated so many of the best ideas of Evolution. His labors on the Encyclopaedia would have tired out the energies of twenty smaller men, but he persevered to the end, despite printers, priests, and governments, and a countless host of other obstructions. Out of date as the work is now, it was the artillery of the movement of progress then. As Mr. Morley says, it "rallied all that was best in France round the standard of light and social hope."

Less original, but nearly as bold and industrious, D'Holbach placed his fortune and abilities at the service of Freethought. Mr. Morley calls the *System of Nature* "a thunderous engine of revolt." It was Atheistic in religion, and revolutionary in politics. It challenged every enemy of freedom in the name of reason and humanity. Here and there its somewhat diffuse rhetoric was lit up with the splendidly concise eloquence of Diderot, who touched the work with a master-hand. Nor did this powerful book represent a tithe of D'Holbach's labors for the "good old cause." His active pen produced a score of other works, under various names and disguises, all addressed to the same object—the destruction of superstition and the emancipation of the human mind. They were extensively circulated, and must have created a powerful impression on the reading public.

Leaving its authors and precursors, and coming to the Revolution itself, we find that its most distinguished figures were Atheists. Mirabeau, the first

Titan of the struggle, was a godless statesman. In him the multitude found a master, who ruled it by his genius and eloquence, and his embodiment of its aspirations. The crowned king of France was pottering in his palace, but the real king reigned in the National Assembly.

The Girondists were nearly all Atheists, from Condorcet and Madame Roland down to the obscurest victims of the Terror who went gaily to their doom with the hymn of freedom upon their proud lips. Danton also, the second Titan of the Revolution, was an Atheist. He fell in trying to stop the bloodshed, which Robespierre, the Deist, continued until it drowned him. With Danton there went to the guillotine another Atheist, bright, witty Camille Desmoulins, whose exquisite pen had served the cause well, and whose warm poet's blood was destined to gush out under the fatal knife. Other names crowd upon us, too numerous to recite. To give them all would be to write a catalogue of the revolutionary leaders.

Atheism was the very spirit of the Revolution. This has been admitted by Christian writers, who have sought revenge by libelling the movement. Their slanders are manifold, but we select two which are found most impressive at orthodox meetings.

It is stated that the Revolutionists organised a worship of the Goddess of Reason, that they went in procession to Notre Dame, where a naked woman acted the part of the goddess, while Chenier's *Ode* was chanted by the Convention. Now there is a good deal of smoke in this story and very little flame. The naked female is a pious invention, and that being gone, the calumny is robbed of its sting. Demoiselle Candeille, an actress, was selected for her beauty; but she was not a "harlot," and she was not undressed. Whoever turns to such an accessible account as Carlyle's will see that the apologists of Christianity have utterly misrepresented the scene.

Secondly, it is asserted that the Revolution was a tornado of murder; cruelty was let loose, and the Atheists waded in blood. Never was greater nonsense paraded with a serious face. During the Terror itself the total number of victims, as proved by the official records, was less than three thousand; not a tenth part of the number who fell in the single massacre of St. Bartholomew!

But who caused the Terror? The Christian monarchies that declared war on Freethinkers and regicides. Theirs was the guilt, and they are responsible for the bloodshed. France trembled for a moment. She aimed at the traitors within her borders, and struck down many a gallant friend in error. But she recovered from the panic. Then her sons, half-starved, ragged, shoeless, ill-armed, marched to the frontier, hurled back her enemies, and swept the trained armies of Europe into flight. They *would* be free, and who should say them nay? They were not to be terrified or deluded by "the blood on the hands of the king or the lie at the lips of the priest." And if the struggle developed until the French armies, exchanging defence for conquest, thundered over Europe, from the Baltic to the Mediterranean, from the orange-groves of Spain to the frozen snows of Russia—the whole blame rests with the pious scoundrels who would not let France establish a Republic in peace.

PIGOTTISM *

* March, 1889.

*"Is there any thing whereof it may be said, See, this is
new? it hath been already of old times, which was before
us."—Ecclesiastes i. 10.*

Everybody is talking about the flight of Pigott. The flight into Egypt
never caused half such a sensation. Pigott has gone off into the infinite. He
was shadowed, but he has performed the feat of running away from his
own shadow. Where he will turn up next, or if he will turn up anywhere,
God only knows. But wherever he re-appears—in the South Pacific as a
missionary, in America as a revivalist, or in India as an avatar—it will be
the same old Pigott, lying, shuffling, forging and blackmailing, with an air
of virtue and benevolence.

The edifice of calumny on Mr. Parnell and his closest colleagues rested
on the foundation of Pigott, and Pigott is exploded. He has entirely vanished.
Not a hair of him is visible. He is gone like last winter's snow or last summer's
roses. He is in the big list of things Wanted. But advertisements will not
bring him back, and considering who is in power, it is very problematical if
the officers of justice will be any more successful.

We have no wish to be disrespectful to the Commission, and it is far
from our intention to pronounce judgment on a case which is *sub judice*,
though who can help sundry exclamations when the chief witness on one
side bolts, leaving no trace but a few more lies and counter lies? Our object,
indeed, is not political but religious. We desire to make the noble Pigott
point a moral and adorn a tale. He and his achievements in connection with
the *Times* splendidly illustrate the process by which Christianity was built
up. Pigottism was at work for centuries, forging documents, manufacturing
evidence, and telling the grossest lies with an air of truth. What is still
worse, Pigottism was so lucky as to get into the seat of despotic power, and
to crush out all criticism of its frauds; so that, at length, everyone believed
what no one heard questioned. It was Pigottism in excelsis. The liar gave
evidence in the witness box, stifled or murdered the counsel for the opposite
side, then mounted the bench to give judgment in his own favor, and finally

pronounced a decree of death against all who refused to own him the pink of veracity.

Just look for a moment at these Parnell letters. They were printed in facsimile in the *Times*, published in *Parnellism and Crime*, circulated among millions of people, and accepted as genuine by half the population of England. And on what ground? Solely on the ground that Parnellism was heterodox and the *Times* was a respectable journal. That was enough. The laws of evidence were treated with contempt. Investigation was thought unnecessary. Thousands of people fatuously said, "Oh, the letters are in print." And all this in an age of Board schools, printing presses, daily papers, and unlimited discussion; nay, in despite of the solemn declaration of Mr. Parnell and his colleagues, backed up by a demand for investigation, that the letters were absolute concoctions.

Now if such things can happen in an age like this, how easily could they happen in ages like those in which Christianity produced its scriptures. Credulity was boundless, fraud was audacious, and lying for the profit of the Church was regarded as a virtue. There was no printing press, no free inquiry, no keen investigation, no vivid conception of the laws of evidence; and the few brilliant critics, like Celsus and Porphyry, who kept alive in their breasts the nobler spirit of Grecian scepticism, were answered by the destruction of their writings, a process which was carried out with the cunning scent of a sleuth-hound and the remorseless cruelty of a tiger.

The Church produced, quite as mysteriously as the *Times*, certain documents which it said were written by Matthew, Mark, Luke, John, Peter, Paul, and James. Others were written by Pagans like Pilate, and one at least by Jesus Christ himself. No commission sat to examine and investigate, no Sir Charles Russell cross-examined the witnesses. The Pigotts, the Houstons, and the Macdonalds kept quietly in the background, and were never dragged forth into the light of day. The Mr. Walters took the full responsibility, which was very trifling; and as Englishmen relied on the respectability of the *Times*, so the illiterate and fanatical Christians relied on the respectability of the Mother Church.

Some of those documents, so mysteriously produced, were as mysteriously dropped when they had served their turn. Hence the so-called Apocryphal New Testament, a collection of writings as ancient, and once as accepted, as those found in the Canon. Hence also the relics, either in name or in fragments, of a host of gospels, epistles, and revelations, which primitive Pigottism manufactured for the behoof of Christianity, Every single scrap no doubt subserved a useful end. But whatever was no longer required was discarded like the scaffolding of a house. The real, permanent work, all the while, was going on inside; and when the Church faced the world with its completed edifice, it thought itself provided with something that would stand all winds and weathers. It was found, however, in the course of time, that Pigottism was still necessary. Hence the Apostolic Constitutions, the Decretals, the Apostles' and the Athanasian Creeds, and all the profitable relics of saints and martyrs.

About two hundred years ago an informal Commission began to sit on these Christian documents. The precious letter of Jesus Christ to Abgarus soon flew off with the Veronica handkerchief, and many other products of Christian Pigottism shared the same fate. The witnesses were examined and cross-examined, and the longer the process lasted the sorrier was the spectacle they presented. Paul's epistles have been shockingly handled. The Commission has positively declared that all but four of them are forgeries, and is still investigating the claim of the remnant under reprieve. Nor is the judgment on the gospels less decisive. The Court has decided that they were not written by Matthew, Mark, Luke, and John. Who wrote them, when they were written, or where, is left to the Day of Judgment.

Unfortunately the press has given little attention to the proceedings in this Court of Commission. Its reports are published in expensive volumes for scholars and gentlemen of means and leisure. Some of the results, indeed, are given in a few journals written for the people; but these journals are boycotted as vulgar, unless they go too far, when they are prosecuted for blasphemy. Yet the truth is gradually leaking out. People shake their heads ominously, especially when there is anything in them; and parsons are looked upon with a growing suspicion. They look bland, they assume the most virtuous airs, and sometimes they affect a preternatural goodness. But in all this they are excelled by the noble Pigott, whose bald head, venerable beard, and benevolent appearance, qualified him to sit for a portrait of God the Father. Gentlemen, it won't do. You will have to bolt or confess. The documents you have palmed off on the world are the products of unadulterated Pigottism. You know it, we know it, and by and bye everyone will know it.

JESUS AT THE DERBY *

*June, 1890.

This is the age of advertisement. Look at the street-hoardings, look at the newspapers, look at our actor-managers, look at Barnum. Scream from the housetops or you stand no chance. If you cannot attract attention in any other way, stand on your head. Get talked about somehow. The only hell is obscurity, and notoriety is the seventh heaven. If you cannot make a fortune, spend one. Run through a quarter of a million in three years, be the fool of every knave, and though you are as commonplace as a wet day in London, you shall find a host of envious admirers.

Should the worst come to the worst, you can defy obscurity by committing a judiciously villainous murder. Perhaps Jack the Ripper had a passion for publicity, and liked to see his name in the papers; until he grew *blase* and retired upon his laurels.

Yes, it is an advertising age, and an advertising age is a sensational age. Religion itself—the staid, the demure—shares in the general tendency. She preaches in the style of the auction room, she beats drums and shakes tambourines in the streets, she affects criminals and dotes on vice, she bustles about the reformation of confirmed topers. By-and-bye she will get up a mission to lunatics and idiots. She is now a very "forward" person. Forward movements are the rage in all the churches. But Methodism bears the palm, though Presbyterianism threatens to run it hard in the person of John McNeill. Hugh Price Hughes is a very smart showman. When truth is stale he is ready with a bouncing lie, and has "face" enough to keep it up in five chapters. But the West-End Mission is getting rather tame. The dukes and duchesses are not yet converted. Money is spent like water and the aristocracy still go to Hades. A new move is tried. The "forward" Methodists organise a Mission to Epsom, Jesus Christ goes to the Derby; that is, he goes by proxy, in the person of Mr. Nix. A van, a tent, and a big stock of pious literature, with mackintoshes and umbrellas, form his equipment. He is accompanied by a band of workers. Their rules are to be up for prayer-meeting at seven in the morning, and "never to look at any race, or jockey, or horse." This is a precaution against the Old Adam. It saves the Mission from going over to the enemy on the field of battle.

Mr. Nix gives an account of his performance in the *Methodist Times*. He converted a lot of people. So has Hugh Price Hughes. "At one time," he says, "there were three Church of England clergymen and their wives and some distinguished members of the aristocracy in the tent"—probably out of the wet. Of course *they* were not converted. But what a pity! A "converted clergyman" would have been a glorious catch, worth five thousand pounds at St. James's Hall. And fancy bagging a duke! It was enough to make Mr. Nix's mouth water. He must have felt some of the agony of Tantalus. He was up to the neck, so to speak, in lords and parsons, and could not grasp one. Dissenting ministers and their wives did not show up. Naturally. They would not go to such a naughty place—except in a mission van. Mr. Nix has a keen eye for the Methodist business. He has open and sly digs at the Church clergy. One of the tipsters said his father was a clergyman, but "his religion was no good to him." He would give anything for the religion of "the little chap that stood on the stool." That was Mr. Nix.

We suspect the Epsom races will outlast Mr. Nix. There is more boast than performance about Missions. Christianity is always converting drunkards, profligates, prostitutes, and thieves; but somehow our social evils do not disappear. Even the drink bill runs up, despite all the Gospel pledges. *Nix* is the practical result of the efforts of gentlemen like Mr. Nix. They are on the wrong tack. They are sweeping back the tide with mops. The real reformatory agency is the spread of education and refinement.

Yet the mission will go on. It is a good advertisement. Mr. Hughes gives it a special leading article. He cries up the Epsom mob as the "most representative gathering of Englishmen," and "therefore a fair specimen of the mental and moral condition of the English people." This is stuff and nonsense, but it serves its purpose. Mr. Hughes wants to show that Missions are needed. He finds that "the great majority of the people are outside the Christian Church," that "this is still a heathen country." Perhaps so. But what a confession after all these centuries of gospel-grinding and Church predominance! There are fifty or sixty thousand churches and chapels, and as many sky-pilots. Six million children go to Sunday-school. The Bible is forced into the public day-schools. Copies are circulated by the million. Twenty millions a year, at the least, is spent in inculcating Christianity. Yet England is still "a heathen country." Well, if this be the case, what is the use of Mr. Nix? What is the use of Mr. Hughes? Greater preachers have gone before them and have failed. Is it not high time for Jesus to run the job himself? "Come, Lord Jesus," as John says. Let him descend from the Father's right hand and take Mr. Nix's place at the next Derby. He might even convert the "clergymen and their wives" and the "distinguished members of the aristocracy." Anyhow he should try. He will not be crucified again.

The worst that could happen is a charge of obstruction, and perhaps a fine of forty shillings. But surely he will not lay himself open to such indignities. He should triumphantly assert his deity. A few big miracles would strike Englishmen more than the Jews, who were sated with the supernatural. He might stop the horses in mid career, fix the jockeys in their saddles, root the Epsom mob where they stood, and address them from the top of the grand stand. That would settle them. They would all go to church next Sunday. Yes, Jesus must come himself, or the case is hopeless. Missions to the people of this "heathen country" are like fleas on an elephant. What the ministers should pray for is the second coming of Christ. But we guess it will be a long time before they sing "Lo, he comes, in clouds descending." Besides, it would be a bad job for *them*. Their occupation would be gone. A wholesale conversion would cut up the retail traders. On the whole, we have no doubt the men of God prefer the good old plan. If Jesus came he would take the bread out of their mouths. That would be shabby-after they had devoted themselves to the business. The very publicans demand compensation, and could the sky-pilots do less? But perhaps Jesus would send them all *home*. We should like to see them go. It would give the world a chance.

ATHEIST MURDERERS *

* *January, 1894.*

An Open Letter to the Bishop of Winchester.

Bishop,—You are a high and well-paid dignitary of the Church of England. You are therefore a State official, as much as a soldier or a policeman; and, as such, you are amenable to public criticism. It is possible that you never heard of me before, but I am a member of the English public, and as a citizen I help (very unwillingly) to support the Church, and therefore to support *you*. My right to address you is thus indisputable. I make no apology or excuse for doing so; and, as for my reason, it will appear in the course of this letter.

I notice in the daily and weekly newspapers a paragraph which concerns you—*and me*. The paragraph is exactly the same in all the papers I have seen; it must therefore have emanated from, and been circulated by, one hand; and that hand I suspect is yours, particularly as it insinuates the necessity of supporting Christian Missions in England—that is, of subscribing to Church agencies over and above the nine or ten millions a year which your Establishment spends (or devours) in ministering to what you call "the spiritual needs" of the English people.

The paragraph I refer to states that you have converted and confirmed an Atheist, and that this Atheist has been hung for the crime of murder; and it plainly hints that his crime was the natural result of his irreligious opinions.

As you make so much of this case, I presume that this murderer—who was not good enough to live on earth, and whom you have sent to live for ever in heaven—is the only Atheist you have ever converted; so that in every way the case is one of exceptional interest.

And now, before I go any farther, let me tell you why the case concerns me as well as you. I am an Atheist, and a teacher of Atheism. I am the President of the National Secular Society, which is the only open organisation of Freethinkers in England. My immediate predecessor in this office was Charles Bradlaugh, of whom you *must* have heard. Not to know him would argue yourself unknown. My personality is not so famous as his, but my office is the same, and you will now understand why I address you on the subject of your converted murderer.

The newspaper paragraph to which I have referred is brief and inadequate, but fuller particulars are given in your *Diocesan Chronicle*, for a copy of which I am indebted to the kindness of a gentleman who is technically a member of your flock. He is a Freethinker, but I do not believe you will convert him, and still less that you will ever "assist" at his execution.

The murderer for whom you made the gallows the gateway to heaven was called George Mason. He was nineteen years of age. Serving in the militia, he was liable to severe discipline. His sergeant had him imprisoned for three days, and in revenge he shot the officer dead while at rifle practice. It is an obvious moral, which I wonder your lordship does not perceive, that it is dangerous to put deadly weapons in the hands of passionate boys. Your lordship's interest in the case seems to be entirely *professional*.

While this lad was simply a militiaman your lordship would not have regarded him as an object of solicitude. As a convicted murderer, he became profoundly interesting. No less than three clergymen took him in hand: the Rev. J. L. Ladbrooke, the Rev. James Baker, and yourself. Three to one are long odds, and it is no marvel that you conquered the boy. Still, it is unfortunate that we have only *your* account of the conflict, for your profession is not famous for what I will politely call *accuracy*. Herder remarked that "Christian veracity" deserved to rank with "Punic faith." How many falsehoods has your Church circulated about *great* Freethinkers! Why should it hesitate, then, to tell untruths about *little* ones? A Wesleyan minister, the Rev. Hugh Price Hughes, has published a long circumstantial story of a converted Atheist shoemaker, which is proved to be false in all its main features. It is far from certain, therefore, that your lordship's account of the conversion of George Mason is true. You and your two clerical colleagues can say what you please; your evidence cannot be tested; and *such* evidence, especially when given by persons who are confederates in a common cause, is always open to suspicion.

Nevertheless I need not doubt that George Mason made an edifying end. It is the way of murderers. What I venture to doubt is your statement as to his life. You write as follows:—

"His early life was lived in the east of London, his trade being that of a costermonger, and he was brought up by his father, a professed atheist, who was in the habit of reading the Bible with this boy and a company of other freethinkers, verse by verse, and deliberately turning it into ridicule, by way of commentary. It is hard to imagine a more deliberate training for the gallows than what his father gave him."

Later on, you say the boy was "insignificant, almost stunted to look at," and you add that "his only opportunity was to learn how to be a child of the Devil."

Now I wish to observe, in the first place, that you have not said *enough*. You do not say whether George Mason's father is still living. I have not been able to hear of him myself. If he be still living, have you taken the trouble to obtain *his* version of the matter? And if not, do you think it kind or just to speak of him in this manner? Nor do you say what religion George Mason professed in the Militia, whether he attended "divine service," and what was its influence upon him. You were in too great a hurry to capture your Atheist, and insult all who do not believe the dogmas of your Church.

You regard it as "deliberate training for the gallows" to let a boy laugh at the Bible. Has it ever occurred to you to inquire how it is that the Bible is so easy to ridicule? Have you ever reflected that what is laughed at is generally ridiculous? Are you not aware that the most risible imp could hardly laugh at *all* the contents of the Bible? Who laughs at the saying, "Blessed are the peacemakers"? Who laughs at the horrid massacres of the Old Testament? But who does *not* laugh at cock-and-bull stories like that of Jonah and the whale? Your lordship does not discriminate. Very little thought would show you that some parts of the Bible *cannot* be laughed at, that where it *can* be laughed at it is probably absurd, and that to laugh at an absurdity is certainly no "training for the gallows."

Your lordship evidently wishes to convey the idea that Atheists are very likely to become murderers, or *more* likely than their Christian fellow citizens. This I deny, and I ask for your evidence. All you adduce is the case of this "insignificant" and "stunted" boy. Let us suppose for a moment that your statement about him is entirely accurate. What does it prove? Simply this, that it is not impossible for an Atheist to commit a murder. But who ever said it was? Who asserts that Atheists are absolutely free from the passions and frailties of human nature? Has your lordship never heard of a Christian murderer? Is it not a fact that Jesus Christ himself could not select his apostles without including a villain? "Twelve of you have I chosen," he said, "and one of you is a murderer." Is not one in twelve a large percentage? Why, then, is the world to be alarmed, and invited to subscribe to Christian Missions, because one Atheist out of all the thousands in England commits a murder —and that one an "insignificant" and "stunted" boy, apparently bred in poverty and hardship?

Mind you, I am not admitting that George Mason *was* an Atheist, or the *son* of an Atheist. I say that has to be proved. I am taking your lordship's account of the matter as true merely for the sake of argument.

Let me draw your attention to some *facts*. So many of the clergy in your own Church "went wrong" that you were compelled to obtain a special Act of Parliament to enable you to get rid of them. Is it not true, also, that the greatest swindlers of this age have been extremely pious? What do you make of Messrs Hobbs and Wright? What do you think of Jabez Balfour? Are not such scoundrels a thousand times worse than a passionate boy like George Mason? Were not the "Liberator" victims fleeced and ruined by professed Christians? What have you to say about Mr. Hastings, Captain Verney, and Mr. De Cobain, who were all convicted of bad crimes and expelled from Parliament? Have you ever heard of the text, "Physician heal thyself"?

Here is another fact. A few months ago an Irish clergyman, the Rev. George Griffiths, deliberately shot his own mother for the sake of what cash he could find in her desk. He was tried, found guilty, and sentenced to be hung. Would you think me justified in saying that the Rev. George Griffiths committed a murder because he was a Christian? Why, then, do you pretend that George Mason committed a murder because he or his father was an Atheist?

Lay your hand upon your heart, and answer this question honestly. Do you really believe that an Atheist has a special proclivity to murder? What is there in Atheism to make men hate each other? When a man holds the hand of the woman he loves, or feels about his neck the little arms of his child, do you suppose he is likely to injure either of them because he is unable to accept your dogma about the mystery of this illimitable universe? Shall I hate my own boy because I disbelieve that Jesus Christ was born without a father? Shall I keep him without food and clothes because I see no proof of a special providence? Will Shakespeare's *Hamlet* poison my mind because I think it finer than the gospels? If I treat the Creation Story and the Deluge as legend and mythology, and smile at the feats of Samson, shall I therefore commit a burglary? If I think that my neighbor's life in this world is *his all*, that death ends his possibilities, do you really think I shall be the more likely to rob him of what I can never restore?

I am at a loss to understand your lordship, and I invite you to explain yourself. At present I can only see in your account of George Mason, a very common exhibition of Christian logic, and Christian temper. Your lordship's is not the charity that "thinketh no evil." You ascribe wickedness to those who differ from you in opinion. I conceive it possible for men to differ from you in religion, and yet to equal you in morality. I conceive it even possible that some of them might surpass you without a miracle.

A RELIGION FOR EUNUCHS *

* June, 1890.

This is a strong title, and it requires a justification. We have to plead that nothing else would serve our purpose. But is our purpose a sound one? That will appear in the course of this article. Let the reader finish what we have to say before he forms a judgment.

We purpose to criticise the view of Christianity recently put forth by the greatest writer in Russia. Count Leo Tolstoi enjoys an European fame. He is one of the classics of modern fiction. His work in imaginative literature, as well as his work in religion, said the late Matthew Arnold, is "more than sufficient to signalise him as one of the most marking, interesting, and sympathy-inspiring men of our time." Whatever such a man writes deserves the closest attention. Not, indeed, that this needs to be bespoken for him. He has the qualities that compel it. There is the stamp of power on all his productions. We pause at them involuntarily, as we turn to look at a physical king of men who passes us in the street.

For some years Count Tolstoi discontinued his work as a novelist. His mind became occupied with social and religious problems. He ceased to be a man of the world and became a Christian; and his being a most sincere nature, endowed with a certain large simplicity which is characteristic of the Russian mind, he did not rest in ecclesiastical Christianity. He embraced the religion of Christ, and began working it out to legitimate issues. To him the Sermon on the Mount is divine teaching, not in a metaphorical sense, but in its literal significance. Accordingly he tells the Christian world, in such volumes as *My Religion* and *My Confession*, that it is all astray from the religion of Christ. He points to what its Savior said, takes his words in their honest meaning, and brands as un-Christian the whole framework of Christian society, with its armies, its police, its law courts, its wealth, and its institution of property. The Bishop of Peterborough and Count Tolstoi are at one in believing that if the Sermon on the Mount were carried out the State would go to ruin; only the Bishop of Peterborough shrinks from this, and jesuitically narrows the scope of Christ's teaching, while Count Tolstoi accepts it loyally and calls on Christians to square their practice with their profession.

Mirabeau said of Robespierre, "He is in earnest, he will go far." This is what we felt with respect to Count Tolstoi. Sooner or later he was certain to follow Jesus to the bitter end. After property comes the institution of marriage, upon which the teaching of Jesus may be found in the gospels. Count Tolstoi now insists on this teaching being practised. He has written a novel, *The Kreutzer Sonata*, to show the evils, not only of marriage, but of all sexual relations. Since then he has written a sober article to justify the sentiments of the hero, or the protagonist, of that terrible story. It is no longer possible to say that Pozdnischeff's ideas are those of a person in a drama. Count Tolstoi accepts the full responsibility of them, and presses them still further. He is now the un-blenching apostle of real Christianity—not the Christianity of the Churches, but the Christianity of Christ; and his new evangel will alarm the growing army of "advanced Christians," who are always canting, in their sentimental way, the very phrase which he develops in all its terrific meaning. To be a Christian, he tells them, is to crucify the body, to kill the animal passions, to live the pure life of the spirit, and, in short, to practise every austerity of asceticism.

Tolstoi did not jump to this conclusion. Writing on his novels, Mr. W. E. Henley called him "the great optimist." The *Kreutzer Sonata* is the work of a profound pessimist. Concluding *What To Do*, Tolstoi wrote a noble passage on the sacredness of motherhood. Now all that is changed. Motherhood must go too. It will take time, for the old Adam is strong in us. But go it must, and when we have all brought our bodies under, no more children will be born. The race will expire, having perfected its imitation of Christ, and the animals that remain will hold the world in undisputed possession; unless, indeed, they catch the contagion, and wind up the whole terrestrial business.

Before we treat Tolstoi's evangel in detail we must remark that he does not explain the "primeval command" of Jehovah to Adam and Eve—"Be ye fruitful and multiply and replenish the earth." This is very inconsistent with the gospel of absolute chastity. Jehovah says, "Get as many children as you can." Christ says, "Get none at all." If it was the same God who gave both orders he changed his mind completely, and having changed it once he may change it again. In that case the Koran will succeed the New Testament, and the *Imitation of Christ* give place to the *Arabian Nights*.

Revenons a nos moutons. The *Kreutzer Sonata* is a terrible story, but like all novels with a purpose, it is inartistic. Othello kills Desdemona without moralising on the sinfulness of marriage, and Pozdnischeff stabs his wife from sheer jealousy. All the preaching is by the way. It might be cut out without affecting the work, and that is its condemnation. When the preacher steps forward the artist retires. And as we are dealing with Tolstoi the preacher we shall go straight to his article in the *Universal Review*.

Tolstoi admits that what he now teaches is incompatible with what he taught before. When writing the *Kreutzer Sonata*, he says: "I had not the faintest presentiment that the train of thought I had started would lead me whither it did. I was terrified by my own conclusion, and was at first disposed to reject it; but it was impossible not to hearken to the voice of my reason and my conscience." This is the language of earnest sincerity.

The conclusion is this—"Even to contract marriage is, from a Christian point of view, not a progress but a fall. Love and all the states that accompany and follow it, however we may try in prose and verse to prove the contrary, never do and never can facilitate the attainment of an aim worthy of men, but always make it more difficult."

This is sufficiently dogmatic. Chapman thought otherwise.

Without love
All beauties bred in women are in vain,
All virtues born in men lie buried;
For love informs them as the sun doth colors:
And as the sun, reflecting his warm beams
Against the earth, begets all fruits and flowers,
So love, fair shining in the inward man,
Brings forth in him the honorable fruits
Of valor, wit, virtue, and haughty thoughts,
Brave resolution and divine discourse.

Thus the great Elizabethan. Now for the laureate of the Victorian age.

For indeed I knew Of no more subtle master under heaven
Than is the maiden passion for a maid,
Not only to keep down the base in man,
But teach high thought, and amiable words
And courtliness, and the desire of fame,
And love of truth, and all that makes a man.

Chapman's strain is higher than Tennyson's, but they harmonise. Tolstoi's is a harsher note. He vilifies the flesh to exalt the spirit, as though the two never mingled. He would abolish the springs of life to purify its stream! He bids us see in our passions "foes to be conquered rather than friends to be encouraged." Why not try to establish a just harmony between them? Is there no medium? Must the passions be kings or slaves, in prison or on the throne? "It is thought an injury to reason," wrote Diderot, "to say a word in favor of her rivals; yet it is only the passions, and strong passions, that can lift the soul to great things; without them there is nothing sublime, whether in conduct or in productions—art becomes childish and virtue trivial."

But let us hear Tolstoi simply as a follower of Christ. We cannot do better than reproduce some of his sentences *in extenso*.

"Christ not only never instituted marriage, but, if we search for formal precept on the subject, we find that he rather disapproved it than otherwise. ('And every one that hath forsaken houses, or brethren, or sisters, or father, or mother, or wife, or children, or lands for my name's sake, shall receive an hundredfold, and shall inherit everlasting life.' Matthew xix. 29, Mark z. 29, 30, Luke xviii. 29,30). He only impressed upon married and unmarried alike the necessity of striving after perfection, which includes chastity in marriage and out of it."

"There is not and cannot be such an institution as Christian marriage.... This is what was always taught and believed by true Christians of the first and following centuries.... In the eyes of a Christian, sexual relations in marriage not only do not constitute a lawful, right, and happy state, as our society and our churches maintain, but, on the contrary, are always a fall, a weakness, a sin."

"Such a thing as Christian marriage never was and never could be. Christ did not marry, nor did he establish marriage; neither did his disciples marry."

"A Christian, I say, cannot view sexual intercourse otherwise than as a deviation from the doctrine of Christ—as a sin. This is clearly laid down in Matt. v. 28, and the ceremony called Christian marriage does not alter its character one jot. A Christian will never, therefore, desire marriage, but will always avoid it."

"In the Gospel it is laid down so clearly as to make it impossible to explain it away, that he who is already married when he discovers and accepts the truth, must abide with her with whom he has been living, i.e., must not change his wife, and must live more chastely than before (Matt. v. 32, xix. 8-12), that he who is single should remain unmarried and continue to live chastely (Matt. xix. 10, 12), and that both the one and the other, in their yearning and striving after perfect chastity, are guilty of sin if they look on a woman as an object of pleasure (Matt. v. 28, 29)."

Pozdnischeff, at the close of the *Kreutzer Sonata*, clinches all this by saying—"People should understand the true significance of the words of St. Matthew as to looking upon a woman with the eye of desire; for the words apply to woman in her sisterly character—not only to another man's wife, but also, and above all, to one's own."

If this view of marriage prevailed, and perfect chastity obtained, the human race would come to an end. Tolstoi says he cannot help that. Carnal love perpetuates the race, and spiritual love will extinguish it. But what if it does? It is a familiar religious dogma that the world will have an end, and science tells us that the sun is losing its heat, the result of which must in time be the extinction of the human race.

The great Russian does not shrink from the logic of Christ's teaching. He follows Christ as St Paul did; as St. Peter did, who forsook his wife; as the Fathers did in crying up virginity and running down marriage; as the monks and nuns did who severed themselves from the world and the flesh, though they often fell into the hands of the Devil. Still there is another step for Count Tolstoi to take. He has not pressed one important saying of Christ, and it is this—

"For there are some eunuchs, which were born so from their mother's womb: and there are some eunuchs, which were made eunuchs of men: and there be eunuchs, which have made themselves eunuchs for the kingdom of heaven's sake. He that is able to receive it, let him receive it" (Matt. xix. 12).

The great Origen followed this advice and emasculated himself. Nor was he alone in the practice. All the disciples of his contemporary, Valens of Barathis, made themselves eunuchs. Mantegazza considers them the spiritual fathers of the Skopskis, a Russian sect dating from the eleventh century. They have been persecuted, but they number nearly six thousand, and regard themselves as the real Christians, the only true followers of Christ. They castrate themselves, and sometimes amputate the genitals entirely; the women even mutilate their breasts as a mark of their sex.

Will Count Tolstoi take the final step? It seems logically necessary even without the text on eunuchs, for the only certain way to avoid sexual intercourse is to make it impossible. In any case we are very much obliged to him for holding up the *real* Christianity, as far as he sees it, to the purblind and hypocritical mob of professed Christians. It will fortify Freethinkers in their scepticism, and warn the healthy manhood and womanhood of Europe against this oriental asceticism which pretends to be a divine message to the robust Occident. When Tolstoi goes the one step farther, and embraces the teaching of Jesus in its entirety, he will be the most powerful enemy of Christianity in the world. By demonstrating it to be a religion for eunuchs he will array against it the deepest instincts of mankind.

ROSE-WATER RELIGION *

* April, 1894.

Most of our readers will recollect the controversy that was carried on, more than twelve months ago, in the columns of the *Daily Chronicle*. Mr. Robert Buchanan had published his new poem, "The Wandering Jew," in which Jesus Christ was depicted as a forlorn vagrant, sick of the evil and infamy wrought in his name, and for which he was historically though not intentionally responsible. This poem was reviewed by Mr. Richard Le Gallienne, a younger poet, who is also a professional critic in the *Star*, where his weekly *causerie* on books and their writers is printed over the signature of "Logroller." Mr. Le Gallienne took Mr. Buchanan to task for his hostility to "the Christianity of Christ," the nature of which was not defined nor even made intelligible. Mr. Buchanan replied with his usual impetuosity, declining to have anything to do with Christianity except in the way of opposition, and laughing at the sentimental dilution which his young friend was attempting to pass off as the original, unadulterated article. Mr. Le Gallienne retorted with youthful self-confidence that Mr. Buchanan did not understand Christianity. Other writers then joined in the fray, and the result was the famous "Is Christianity Played Out?" discussion in the *Chronicle*. It was kept going for a week or two, until parliament met and Jesus Christ had to make way for William Ewart Gladstone.

Mr. Le Gallienne hinted that he was preparing a kind of manifesto on the subject of Christianity. The world was to be informed at length as to the "essential" nature of that religion. Divines and Freethinkers had alike misunderstood and misrepresented it. After a lapse of nearly two thousand years the "straight tip," if we may so express it, was to come from "Logroller." He would soon speak and set the weary world at rest with the triumphant proclamation of the real, imperishable religion of Jesus Christ. Presently it was announced, in judicious puffs, that the manifesto was growing under Mr. Le Gallienne's hands. It would take the form of a book, to be entitled *The Religion of a Literary Man*. The title had little relation to the Galilean carpenter or his fishing disciples. Nor was it in any sense happy. It smacked too much of the "shop." Sir Thomas Browne, it is true, wrote a "Religio Medici," and gave a physician's view of religion; but he was a man of rare genius as well as quaintness, and allowance was to be made for his idiosyncrasy. Besides, there is a certain speciality in a doctor's way of looking at religion, if he compares his knowledge with his faith. But what is the speciality of a literary man on this particular subject? Other trades and professions might as well follow suit, and give us "The Religion of a Porkbutcher," or "The Faith of a Farmer," or "The Creed of a Constable." Even the "Belief of a Barman" is not beyond the scope of a rational probability.

Mr. Le Gallienne's long-promised evangel "burst upon the town" a month ago. The "Religio Scriptoris"—which a puzzler at Latin might render as "The Religion of a Scribbler"—made a dainty appearance. The title-page was in two colors, with a pretty arabesque border. The type throughout was neatly leaded, with a column for summaries in the old fashion, and a wide margin of imitation hand-made paper. The book was pretty, like the writing, and opposite the title-page was a pretty verse:—

'The old gods pass'—the cry goes round,

'Lo! how their temples strew the ground';

Nor mark we where, on new-fledged wings,

Faith, like the phoenix, soars and sings.

Yes, it is *all* pretty. There is an air of dilettanteism about the whole production. It will probably be grateful to the sentimentalists who, despite their scepticism, still cling to the name of Christian; but we imagine it will rather irritate than satisfy other readers of more strenuous and scrupulous intelligence.

The book is dedicated to "A. E. Fletcher, Esq.," editor of the *Daily Chronicle*, who may well be proud (not of this dedication, but) of the high position to which he has raised that organ of Radical principles. Mr. Le Gallienne refers to the old controversy in the *Chronicle* as "raising an important question—to me the most important of questions—as to whether Christianity was really so obsolete to-day as its opponents glibly assume." "I could not stand by," he continues, "and see the sublime figure of Christ vulgarised to make an Adelphi holiday." For this reason, he modestly says, he "ventured to play David to Mr. Buchanan's Philistine." Mr. Fletcher allowed him a battlefield and "thence sprung [he means *sprang*] the following pages." Thus much for the origin of the work, and now for its character. "I have condensed in its pages," the writer says, "much religious experience, and long and ardent thought on spiritual matters." No doubt he believes this statement, but is it true? Is not the writer too young to have had "much experience"? and where are the traces of the "long and ardent thought"? Mr. Le Gallienne might reply that his thought *has* been long and ardent, whatever the value of the result; but, in that case, he is not cut out for a thinker; and, indeed, he seems aware of the fact, for he often prints "thinker" in inverted commas to show his disdain of the article. His "one cure" for "modern doubt" is to "think less and feel more," and some may be tempted to remark that he has certainly followed the first part of the prescription.

Mr. Le Gallienne is a long time in coming to "the sublime figure of Christ." He has a considerable ground to cover before he undertakes the cleaning and painting of the old idol. First of all, he has to establish his native superiority over the common herd. He divides the world into "natural spiritualists and materialists." The first have a Spiritual Sense (capitals, please), while the second have not; and "it is obvious that the large majority of mankind belong to the latter class." Mr. Le Gallienne, of course, belongs to the former. He is a member of Nature's (or God's) aristocracy. It is for them that he writes, although on his own supposition the task is superfluous. The common herd of materialists are warned against wasting their time in reading him—which also is somewhat superfluous. The fault of materialists—or rather their misfortune, for they are born that way—is that they are such sticklers for facts, and have "no conception of aught they cannot touch and handle, eat, or see through a microscope." Not, indeed, that Mr. Le Gallienne objects to eating, for instance; he speaks of it with wet lips, and looks down upon the Vegetarian as a person whose "spiritual insight" is not "mercifully intermittent," especially at meal times. But barring meal times, and other fleshly occasions when the spiritualists join the materialists, the former habitually see facts as "transitory symbols" of "transfiguring mysteries," so that the whole world (and perhaps the moon) is "palpitating with occult significance."

For instance. A materialist eats rook-pie, and cares for nothing else but a sound digestion. The spiritualist also eats rook-pie, but after the repast he will sentimentalise over dead rooks, without losing his belief in an all-merciful Providence. He will assure you, indeed, and try to convince you, that the shooting of rooks and the pulling off their heads to prevent the rook-pie from tasting bitter, is simply one of the "terrible and beautiful mysteries" which make the world so interesting—especially to gentlemen of comprehensive natures, who combine a taste for rook-pie with a taste for optimistic theology.

When we come to test Mr. Le Gallienne's conception of mystery, we find it to be nothing but muddle. The whole mystery of life, he says, may be found in a curve: as thus, Why isn't it straight?

"Color in itself is a mystery, and are there not trance-like moments when suddenly we ask ourselves, why a *colored* world, why a *blue* sky, and *green* grass, why not *vice versa*, or why any color at all?"

Mr. Le Gallienne is evidently prepared to stand aghast at the fact that twice two make four. Why *always* four? Why not three to-day and seven to-morrow? Yea, and echo answers, Why?

Here is another illustration of "mystery" —

"Science can tell us that oxygen and hydrogen will unite under certain conditions to produce water, but it cannot tell us why they do so; the mystery of their affinity is as dark as ever."

Mr. Le Gallienne has a whole chapter on the Relative Spirit, yet his "long and ardent thought" does not enable him to see that he is himself a slave of metaphysics. All this "mystery" is nothing but the "meat-roasting power of the meat-jack." He question of *why* oxygen and hydrogen form water is a prompting of anthropomorphism. Intellectually, it is simply childish. It could only be put by one who has *not* grasped the great doctrine of the Relativity of Knowledge. Man can no more get beyond his own knowledge — which is and ever must be finite — than he can get outside himself, or run away from his own shadow.

"The sacred mystery of motherhood," of which Mr. Le Gallienne speaks, is a pretty expression. It may pass in the realm of poetry, with the "everlasting hills" and the "eternal sea," which are but transient phenomena in the infinite existence of the universe. The "mystery" of human motherhood is no greater than the "mystery" of any other form of reproduction, while its "sacredness" depends on circumstances; the term, in short, being a compendium of a great variety of personal and social feelings, which may or may not be present in any particular case. What becomes of the "sacred mystery of motherhood" when a poor servant girl brings her child into the world unaided, and casts it into the Thames? What becomes of it when violation takes the place of seduction, and a woman bears a child to a man she loathes and hates?

"Mystery," like other words we inherit from the theological and metaphysical stages, is only fit for use in poetry; it is out of place in science or philosophy; and we advise Mr. Le Gallienne to get a comprehension of this truth before he takes fresh excursions in the "realm of long and ardent thought." The subjective ideas of poetry cease to be admirable and stimulating when they are projected into the external world, and become our masters instead of our servants.

Mr. Le Gallienne follows the beaten track of theology in talking about "mysteries," which are only subterfuges to cover the retreat of a nonplussed debater, or a warren for the fugitive game of the hounds of reason. He also follows the beaten track in arguing—or rather assuming—that the elect spiritualists have a "sense" which is lacking in the reprobate materialists. There is nothing like a good lumping assumption for begging the question at issue. It settles the discussion before it opens, and saves a world of trouble. But even an assumption may be looked in the face; nay, it is best looked in the face when you suspect it of being an imposture.

According to Mr. Le Gallienne, the religious sense—or, as he also writes it, the SPIRITUAL SENSE, with capital letters—is not after all a special faculty, but a special compound, or interaction, of common faculties. He does, indeed, treat these common faculties as "tribautaries" of the Spiritual Sense; but it is very evident that the tributaries make the stream, which is merely a name without them. First, there is the Sense of Wonder, which is nothing but the positive side of ignorance; second, the Sense of Beauty, which "is not necessarily a religious sense," but may be pressed into its service; third, the Sense of Pity, which really originates, as we conceive, in parental affection, and has even been noticed in rats as well as in religionists; fourth, the Sense of Humor, which is a peculiarly "candid" friend of religion, so that Mr. Le Gallienne is obliged to give its devotees an impressive warning against running into Ill-nature and Sacrilege; fifth, the Sense of Gratitude, which in religion, so far as we can see, appears to consist in a lively sense of favors to come, through the medium of prayer, to which thanksgiving is only a judicious preliminary, like the compliments and flatteries that are addressed to an oriental despot by his humble but calculating petitioners.

Now all these senses are perfectly natural. Every one of them is found in the lower animals as well as in man. How then can there be anything supernatural, supersensible, or "spiritual,", in their combination? Is it not evident that Religion works, like everything else, upon common materials? Chiefly, indeed, upon the unchastened imagination of credulous ignorance. We may prove this from Mr. Le Gallienne's own testimony.

"Are there not impressions borne in upon the soul of man as he stands a spectator of the universe which religion alone attempts to formulate? Certain impressions are expressed by the sciences and the arts. 'How wonderful!'—exclaims man, and that is the dawn of science; 'How beautiful!'—and that is the dawn of art. But there is a still higher, a more solemn, impression borne in upon him, and, falling upon his knees, he cries, 'How holy!' That is the dawn of religion."

Mr. Le Gallienne does not see that this is all imagination. "The heavens declare the glory of God," exclaims the Psalmist. On the other hand, a great French Atheist exclaimed, "The heavens declare the glory of Copernicus, Kepler, and Newton."

Mr. Le Gallienne does not see, either, that man did not exclaim, "How holy!" when he first fell upon his knees. His feeling was rather, "How terrible!" The sense of holiness is a social product—a high sublimation of morality. Man had to possess it himself, and see it highly exemplified in picked specimens of his kind, before he bestowed it upon his gods. Deities do not anticipate, they follow, the course of human evolution.

Mr. Le Gallienne is an Optimist. He is young and prosperous, and, judging from his poetry, happily married. He is therefore satisfied that all is for the best—if properly understood; just as when an alderman has dined, all the world is happy.

There are such people, however, as Pessimists, and Mr. Le Gallienne hates them. Schopenhauer, for instance, he rails at as a "small philosopher," whose ideas were only the "formulation of his own special disease, the expression of his own ineffably petty and uncomfortable disposition." At which one can only stare, as at a mannikin attacking a colossus. Spinoza too can be treated jauntily if he does not fall into line with Mr. Le Gallienne. George Meredith is treated with abundant respect, but he is wronged by being enrolled as a facile optimist, and "the strongest of the apostles of faith." He is certainly nothing of the kind, in Mr. Le Gallienne's sense of the words. He has faith in reason and humanity, but this is a very different thing from faith in the idols—even the greatest idol—of the Pantheon.

"There is too much pain in the world," said Charles Darwin, who knew what he was talking about, and always expressed himself with moderation. In the moral world, pain becomes evil; and the problem of evil has ever been the crux of Theism. It cannot be solved on Theistic grounds, and accordingly it has to be explained away. Pain, we are told, is the great agent in our development; in the ethical sphere, it is the "purifying fire," which purges the gold in us from its dross. All of which sounds very pretty in a lecture, and looks very pretty in a book; but is apt to excite disgust when a man is suffering from incurable cancer, or utter destitution in the midst of plenty; or when a mother stands over the corpse of her child, mangled in some terrible accident, or burnt to a cinder in a fatal fire.

Certainly, pain subserves a partial purpose. It is sometimes a warning, though the warning is often too late. But its function is immensely overrated by Mr. Le Gallienne and other religionists. It is all very well to talk about the "crucible," but half the people who go into it are reduced to ashes. Mr. Le

Gallienne will not accept Spinoza's view that "pain is an unmistakable evil; joy the vitalising, fructifying power." But the great mystic, William Blake, said the same thing in, "Joys impregnate, sorrows bring forth." George Meredith has expressed the same view in saying that "Adversity tests, it does not nourish us." Even the struggle for existence does not add any strength to the survivors. It sometimes cripples them. By eliminating the unfit—that is, the weak—it raises the average capacity. But what a method for Infinite Wisdom and Infinite Goodness! There was more sense, and less cruelty, in the ancient method of infanticide.

Mr. Le Gallienne seems to feel that his theory of pain is too fantastic, so he falls back on "mystery." "We can form no possible conception," he says, "of the processes of God." Why then does he talk about them so consumedly? Ignorance is a good reason for silence, but none for garrulity.

We must be "humble," says Mr. Le Gallienne, and recognise that we only exist "to the praise and glory of God." We are his servants and soldiers, and the pay is life!—"Had he willed it, this glorious gift had never been ours. We might have still slept on unsentient, unorganised, in the trodden dust." Very likely; but who could lose what he never possessed? It is a small misfortune that can never be realised.

Mr. Le Gallienne leaps the final difficulty by exclaiming that "Man has no rights in regard to God." He shakes hands with St. Paul, who asserts the potter's power over the clay. Yes, but man is not clay. He lives and feels. He has rights, even against God. The parent is responsible for his child, the creator for his creature. The opposite doctrine is fit for cowards and slaves. It comes down to us from the old days, when fathers had the power of life and death over their children; it dies out as we learn that the first claim is the child's, and the first duty the parent's.

Mr. Le Gallienne's god is the old celestial despot of theology in a new costume. On the question of a future life, however, we are pleased to find a vein of heterodoxy and common sense. Mr. Le Gallienne asks, with respect to the "hereafter," whether we "really care about it so much as we imagine." We talk about meeting our old friends in heaven, for instance, but do we not "meet them again already on earth—in the new ones"! It is said that if fine, cultivated personalities do not survive death, they are wasted, and have existed in vain. Mr. Le Gallienne's reply to this objection is clear, sufficient, and well expressed:—

"But how so? Have they not been in full operation for a lifetime? 'Tis a pity truly that the old fiddle should be broken at last; but then for how many years has it not been discoursing most excellent music? We naturally lament when an old piece of china is some sure day dashed to pieces; but then for how long a time has it been delighting and refining those, maybe long dead, who have looked upon it. — If there were no possibility of more such fiddles, more such china, their loss would be an infinitely more serious matter; but on this the sad-glad old Persian admonishes us: —

> .... *fear not lest Existence, closing your*
>
> *Account and mine, should know the like no more;*
>
> *The Eternal Saki from the bowl has pour'd*
>
> *Millions of Bubbles like us, and shall pour.*

Nature ruthlessly tears up her replicas age after age, but she is slow to destroy the plates. Her lovely forms are all safely housed in her memory, and beauty and goodness sleep secure in her heart, in spite of all the arrows of death."

Without saving what they are, or which of them he considers at all convincing, Mr. Le Gallienne observes that the arguments as to a future life are "probably stronger on the side of belief" — which is rather a curious expression. But, whichever theory be true, it "does not really much matter." Very likely. But how does this fit in with the teaching of Christ? If he and his apostles did not believe in the "hereafter," what *did* they believe in? "Great is your reward in heaven," and similar sentences, lose all meaning without the doctrine of a future life, about which the early Christians were intensely enthusiastic. It was not in *this* world, as Gibbon remarks, that they wished to be happy or useful.

Mr. Le Gallienne argues that Christ taught in parables. He promised heaven, and threatened hell, but he spoke in a Pickwickian sense. However he used such phrases, it is "certain" that the evangelists "have distorted their importance out of all proportion to the rest of his teaching." By "certain" we are not to assume that Mr. Le Gallienne has access to occult sources of information. We are only to infer that he deals with the gospels arbitrarily; accepting them, or rejecting them, as they accord or disagree with his preconceptions. Indeed, this is what "essential Christianity" must always be. What each picker and chooser likes is "essential." What he does not like is unessential, if not a positive misrepresentation.

Short and easy is Mr. Le Gallienne's criterion for deciding when Christ is literal and when parabolical. "It is only Christ's moral precepts that are to be taken literally" — "all the rest is parable." What a pity it is that the Prophet of Nazareth did not give us a clear hint to this effect! The theory is one of admirable simplicity. Yet, for all that demure look of his, Mr. Le Gallienne is not so admirably simple as to work it out in practice. Accepting the moral precepts of Christ literally, a Christian should hate his father and mother, take no thought tor the morrow, live in poverty to obtain the kingdom of heaven, and turn his left cheek to everyone who takes the liberty of striking him on the right. Mr. Le Gallienne does not ask us to do these things; he does not say he performs them himself, He would probably say, if pressed, that allowance should be made for oriental ways of speaking. But, in that case, what becomes of the "literal" method of reading the "moral precepts" of Christ?

Mr. Le Gallienne, who despises "thinkers," is all at sea in his chapter on Essential Christianity. He does not know his own mind. He declares that Christ "combined" in his own person and teaching "the intense spirituality of the Hebrew, the impassioned self-annihilation of the Hindoo, the joyous naturalism of the Greek." Yet he also remarks that there is something beautiful in "such presences as Pan, Aphrodite, and Apollo," which we do not find in Christianity; though he is careful to add that there is not "actually any strife between them and the sadder figure of the Galilean." "All the gods of all the creeds," he says, "supplement or corroborate each other." Perhaps so; but what becomes of that "masterful synthesis," in which Christ gathered up the "joyous naturalism of the Greek," no less than other ancient characteristics? It is well to have a good memory (at least) when you are setting the world to rights.

Christianity has been historically a failure. Mr. Le Gallienne more than admits the fact; he emphasises it, and tries to explain it. In the first place, he says the priests have been too many for Christ; they got hold of Christianity, and turned it into the channel of their interests. In the next place, the world was not ready for "essential" Christianity; an argument in flat contradiction to the doctrine of "preparation," which has placed so important a part in Christian apologetics ever since the time of Eusebius. In the third place, "essential" Christianity is an idealism, and "a throng of idealists is an impossibility." The horde of earthly-minded people have simply trodden upon the precious pearls of Christ's teaching. It is not true that the world has tried the Gospel of Christ and found it wanting; the world has never tried it at all, and "in this nineteenth century of the so-called Christian era, it has yet to begin."

Supposing all this to be true, what does it prove? On the theory that Christ was God, or sent by God, it proves either that Providence interfered too soon, or that it is incapable of making any real impression upon the stubborn inhabitants of this planet; either alternative being a reflection on the wisdom or the power of the deity. On the theory that Christ was only a man, it proves that he taught an impossible gospel. After all these centuries it is still contested and still to be explained. Would it not, after all, be better to put aside this source of confusion and quarreling, and to rely upon reason and the common sentiments of humanity? Mr. Le Gallienne admits that in some respects "such a book as Whitman's *Leaves of Grass* is more helpful than *The New Testament*—for it includes more." Why then all this chatter about Christ? Can we ever be united on a question of personality? Is it not absurd, and worse than absurd, to thrust this object of contention into the arena where the forces of light should be fighting, like one man, the strong and disciplined forces of darkness?

All this talk about "the sublime figure of Christ" is a reminiscence of his faded deity. We do not indulge in heated discussions as to the personality of any other *man*. We speak of other "sublime" figures, but the expression is one of individual reverence. We do not say that those who do not share our opinion of Buddha, Socrates, Mohammed, Bruno, Cromwell, Danton, or even Plato or Shakespeare, are grovelling materialists and candidates for perdition. No, the chatter about Christ is only explicable on the ground that he was, and still is by millions, worshipped as a god. The glamor of the deity lingers round the form of the man.

It is impossible for persons of any logical trenchancy to remain in this stage. Francis Newman gave up orthodox Christianity, and also the equivocations of Unitarianism, but he clung to "the moral perfection of Christ." In the course of time, however, the scales fell from his eyes. He had been blinded by a false sentiment. Letting his mind play freely upon the "sublime figure" of the Prophet of Nazareth, he at length perceived that it had its defects. No mortal is endowed with perfection. Such monsters do not exist. Indeed, the teaching of Christ is as defective as his personality, Its perfection and sufficiency can only be maintained by those who never mean to incur the perils of reducing it to practice. Who really tries to carry out the Christianity of Christ? Only one man in Europe that we know of, and his name is Count Tolstoi; but he is saved from the worst consequences of his "idealism" by the more practical wisdom of his wife, who will not see him, any more than herself and her children, reduced to godly beggary.

Mr. Le Gallienne seems to us to belong to the sentimentalists, though we hope he will grow out of their category. He appears to dread accurate thinking, and to imagine that knowledge destroys the charm of nature. "Which," he asks, "comes nearest to the truth about love—poor Lombroso's talk about pistil and stamen, or one of Shakespeare's sonnets?" The root, he says, is no explanation of the flower.

This may be fine, but it is fine nonsense. Lombroso and Shakespeare are both right. The physician does not contradict the poet. And if the root is no explanation of the flower, what will happen if you are careless about the root and the soil in which it is planted? Does a gardener act in that way? Is it not the horticulture of Fleet-street sentimentalists?

Mr. Le Gallienne is great on what he calls the "root" fallacy. Wishing to keep the "irreligious instinct" in mystery, or at least obscurity, he objects to anthropological "explanations." He cannot tolerate talk about ancestor-worship, and other such "rude beginnings of religion," although it comes from the lips of his intellectual superiors, such as Tylor, Lubbock, and Spencer. Even if they are right, he falls back upon his old exclamation, "What does it matter?" If the flower began as a root, he says, that is no argument against "the reality of the flower." But this is a shifting of ground. The reality of the flower, the reality of the "religious instinct," is not in dispute. The question is, What is its explanation? No one denies that man idealises and reveres. The question is, How did he come to let these faculties play upon ghosts and gods? And the explanation is to be found in his past. It cannot possibly be found in his present, unless we take him as a savage, in which case he is an embodiment of the past of our own ancestors, from whom we derive every vestige of what we call our "religion."

Man's nature, like his destiny, is involved in his origin. However he may be developed, he will never be more than "the paragon of animals." And it is the recognition of this unchangeable truth which makes all the difference between the evolutionist, who labors for rational progress, and the sentimentalist, who fritters away his energies in cherishing the delusions of faith.